WICKED ALLURE

The Immortal Reign
Book 4

ARIEL MARIE

RNB PUBLISHING

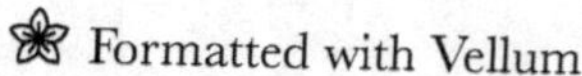 Formatted with Vellum

Prologue

"Kane, I'm going after her!" Dru snarled.

She pulled her sword from the dead lycan who lay on the ground at her feet. The stench of lycan blood filled the air. Dru spun around to seek out Captain Kane Thaddeus in the melee. Her gaze landed on the elder vampire in the midst of a heated battle of his own.

They had invaded a lycan den deep underground in the sewers that ran underneath Crystal Cove. This was a mission of the utmost importance. The lycan alpha was here, and Lethia, the commander, had disappeared after her.

Dru Moldark had led the manhunt to help find the woman who'd threatened not only her princess but the entire royal family. The alpha had been hard to track down, and she was on a mission to take out the vampire nation.

That was something Dru refused to allow to happen. While there was air left in her lungs, she'd defend her kind. Dru whipped her sword around and slid it into the sheath on her back. She rushed forward in the direction Lethia had gone. The underground lycan den was in complete chaos. The vampires had surprised them, and they had never expected an ambush to occur on their own territory.

Dru arrived at a metal ladder attached to the wall and hauled herself up to a ledge. She stalked along a narrow walkway and glanced down a dark tunnel. The hairs on the back of her neck rose. Dru reached for the weapon on her waist and aimed it true. She flipped the safety off and went down the hall. She was sure this was the way Lethia had gone. She released a curse and picked up her speed.

Her longtime friend may be the only one here who could take down an alpha, but there was no way Dru was going to let her do it alone. For all

Dru knew, Lethia could have been running into an ambush.

Dru arrived at an opening and paused. She glanced through the doorway and found a large room with television monitors along the walls, a table in the center, a cot in the corner, and a few scattered boxes stacked up against the wall. Other than that, the room was empty.

An opposite door had been left open, and Dru's senses told her that Lethia had certainly come this way.

Dru pushed forward and raced across the room to the door. It led her to another darkened hallway. She exhaled and quickened her steps. She had to get to Lethia. Dru didn't trust the lycans, and an urgency swept through her. A metal door stood ahead. Dru slammed her shoulder into it and forced it open.

The cool night air greeted her. There was no sight of Lethia. Dru raised her fingertips to the comm in her ear.

"Your Highness, where are you?" Dru stalked forward while listening intently for any sounds of a fight or scuffle.

A pain-filled cry sliced through air. It sent a ripple of fear through Dru's spine.

Lethia!

"Where is the princess?" a voice growled behind her.

Some of her men must have followed her out. Dru motioned for them to go with her. She took off in the direction of the sound and rounded a corner. Ice froze her veins at the sight that greeted her.

Lethia was pinned to a thick tree with the alpha's claws buried in her side. Dru instantly raised her weapon and fired several rounds of argentite bullets. The alpha's body jerked. More gunfire rattled through the air. Azura snarled and turned away from Lethia then raced off into the woods. Lethia slid down the tree and hit the ground as Dru and her vampires advanced. Dru arrived at her side while most of the warriors went after Azura.

"Your Highness!" Dru fell to the ground in front of her. Panic filled her at the sight of all of the blood. "Fuck. Are you okay?"

Lethia's hand pressed against her wound that bled profusely. She grimaced and inhaled sharply.

"I'll be good as new in a second," Lethia gasped.

"Let me see." Dru pulled her hand away and glanced down at the sizable gash on Lethia's abdomen. She cursed and raised a hand to her comm. "We need help. The princess is down."

"I'm fine," Lethia growled. She pushed up to stand, but she fell back down.

Dru reached out a hand to rest it on her stubborn friend's shoulder. "Rest, my princess. We'll get someone to help you."

More vampires poured out of the door, flooding the area. A stubborn glint appeared in Lethia's eyes. Dru was extremely familiar with the look.

"I've got to get up."

Dru sighed and jerked her head in a nod. Dru stood by with her gaze locked on the princess. Lethia pushed up and leaned back against the tree before she stood straight on her own two feet. Her golden hair was braided away from her face in an intricate design, but a few wisps had escaped. She held her head high, but there was something different in her eyes. Dru's body was tense. She'd fought by Lethia's side for decades and knew her as well as she knew the back of her hand. The color drained from Lethia's face as she blinked.

"Report." She blinked again and tilted to the side.

She stumbled slightly, and Dru flew to her.

She brushed Dru's hand away. "I'm fine."

Lethia's eyes rolled back, and her knees gave way.

"Shit!" Dru caught the princess before she hit the ground. She was completely dead weight. Now that the princess was out of commission, Dru was in charge. She bent down and scooped Lethia up into her arms and glanced around.

"We have the van prepared for the princess." Talbot stopped in front of her. A few of his blades were missing. The experienced vampire waited for her.

"Good. Secure the area," Dru shouted.

The men around her would comply. She didn't see any sign of Kane yet. He must still be down in the den dealing with the lycans. He'd be able to hold his own. She had to get the princess to healers. Lethia's head rolled to the side. The blood wasn't stopping. She might bleed to death.

"We need to hurry."

"Come this way. It's not too far from us now." Talbot motioned for her to follow.

Dru carried her the commander through the throng of men. Once she'd secured Lethia, she'd try to stop the flow of blood.

Dru thought of one thing she knew Lethia always stressed to her about their warriors.

"One other thing." Dru bit back a smirk with what she was about to say. "None of you saw me carrying the commander."

* * *

THERE WAS SO much blood on her from holding pressure to Lethia's abdomen. Dru sat back in the van, satisfied that the flow of blood from the wound had slowed down. Talbot sat in the front with the driver who drove fast. Lethia had been out cold for minutes. Dru was starting to get worried.

"Fuck. What happened?" Lethia groaned.

Her eyes flew open, and she tried to sit up, but Dru gently pushed her back down. A growl escaped Lethia, but she settled back once she saw Dru sitting next to her.

"Don't move, Your Highness. Otherwise, you'll completely bleed out," Dru said.

Relief filled her at the sight of Lethia's blue eyes. This had been a close one. They had both been gravely injured before in battle, and it never got easier. Her friend would need blood to heal. It would help the wound close within minutes if she were able to consume it.

"Report," Lethia snarled.

Dru held back her eye roll but submitted to her princess. She shared with her that the den was taken care of and a few lycans had escaped with the alpha. Lethia nodded at the information. Even a hairsbreadth away from death and the commander was still trying to fight. Dru had always had high respect for the king's daughter.

That was why she'd remained loyal to Lethia and the Riskel name.

They arrived at the castle quickly to a group waiting for them, thanks to the warrior's skilled driving. The truck halted, and the door was practically torn off the frame by Lane, Lethia's personal guard. Concern filled his eyes as he reached for Lethia.

"I'll walk into my home," Lethia growled.

Lane took a step back from the vehicle and gave her a nod.

"I wouldn't dream of trying to carry you." Lane waved his hand for her to step out of the vehicle.

"I've already had to carry her, and let me tell you, she's not as light as she appears." Dru smirked.

Lethia's blue eyes cut to her, and if looks could kill, Dru would have perished from the glare alone.

"Tell anyone else you had to carry me, and I'll kill you," Lethia threatened.

Dru chuckled and exited the truck from the door closer to her. She ambled around the back of the vehicle and took in all of those waiting for them. Dru had called ahead to Aubrey to notify her that the princess had been gravely injured. She wasn't happy with the news and assured Dru the house would be on standby to receive Lethia.

Only thing was, Aubrey did not share that the queen would be waiting as well.

"When did she get here?" Lethia muttered. She stood to her full height with her hand pressed against her stomach. Her gaze was locked on her mother, Queen Mira Riskel. She walked toward her, leaving Dru with Talbot and the other warriors.

"Has there been word from Captain Thaddeus?" Dru turned to Talbot. She had cut off her communicator while trying to staunch the flow of blood from Lethia.

"Yes. They're currently burning the bodies of the lycans who were killed," he replied.

Dru gave a nod. "You warriors did well today. Rest up. I'm sure we'll be called back for duty soon." She stalked toward the castle. Her job was far from over. With the amount of lycans they had found, she was sure it was only a matter of time before they'd be at war. Azura had promised one, and Dru's gut screamed that it was coming.

While Lethia was being taken care of in the infirmary, Dru would continue to devise a plan. Hopefully her friend would find a way to consume blood so she could heal properly. It was easy to see that Lethia hadn't fed from her mate yet. There was no way Azura should have gotten the drop on her. Now that the queen was here, maybe she'd be able to talk some sense into the commander.

Dru entered the building and headed to her quarters. She pushed aside the thought of Lethia and her mate. Now that they were home, her friend would be fine, she was sure of it. The queen would not allow her daughter to perish.

Dru devised a quick plan. First wash the stench of lycan from her body and put on a clean uniform. Then she'd call for a donor. After a battle like that, she'd need nourishment. Infiltrating that den had given her much knowledge. Now she was going to have to do what she did best, and that was to prepare for war.

CHAPTER ONE

"You don't have to do this. I'll figure something out until you can find another job," her brother announced from the doorway of her bedroom, his voice gruff.

Tomesha Clay stared at the few items of clothing hanging in her closet. A sad smile ghosted her lips. Tarek, her elder brother, was protective of her. He'd always been that way since they were children.

The big brother shielding the little sister from the harshness of reality.

If only he could have kept her from truly seeing

how cruel people really were, but that wasn't the case. The world they'd grown up in was different than when their parents or grandparents were the same age. Tomesha and Tarek had listened to the tales of their grandmother who loved sharing the way of things when she was a young woman.

The twentieth century had been much different. Times had been rocky according to Delonda Clay. The world had always had to face certain changes. From the civil rights movement, hippies, rock and roll, and a war on drugs. The great accomplishment of man making it to the moon, wars between countries to man making leaps and bounds in the development of technology with the creation of computers and the internet. It was amazing to think her grandmother had been a witness to it all. It was fascinating to hear how humans had lived in the past.

Humans did as they pleased.

Wait—it was never a thing to say 'humans' before.

It had always been taken for granted there was only one race. What their grandmother did experience was being treated differently because of the color of her skin. Throughout time, one thing hadn't changed for Black American people.

Racism.

The stories Tomesha had heard about how Black people were treated made her heart hurt.

The war had changed all of that.

At the turn of the millennia, when vampires presented themselves, humans had banded together for once to fight this new race who wanted to take over the world. The color of one's skin no longer mattered. The war had commenced, and with all of the advances in military weapons, the humans were no match for the vampires.

No one had known vampires had truly existed. They had always been considered a myth or legends. Tomesha had watched all of the old movies from the twentieth century that were based around vampires. Some of the lore and customs shown were outrageously off about vampires. There was no sparkly vampire skin, nor did they turn into bats.

These vampires were strong and overtook the world by storm. The human government rolled over and allowed the seven vampire kings to rule their lands they had apparently overseen, and humans were ignorant to it.

Tomesha and Tarek were born during the war. Their father, Maynard, was a Marine Veteran who'd fought. He'd come home a changed man according to their grandmother. Tomesha and Tarek only knew their father as the quiet, stoic man who liked to sit on the porch and drink his whiskey.

Fighting in the war hadn't made him a hero.

There was no special treatment for those who'd risked their lives in going off to fight for those who were unable. Not that many had choices. Men and women were both drafted. A weapon was placed in their hands, and they were sent off to fight. Their mother, Maggie, had been saved from being drafted. She hadn't passed the health physical test and was deemed unfit to serve. Maggie had done her best while their father was gone.

Unfortunately, their beautiful mother passed away due to complications of a gall bladder removal surgery. Something that should have been an easy hospitalization and discharge turned into a nightmare with Tomesha losing her mother at the age of thirteen.

Not wanting to fall into a puddle of sadness thinking of her parents, Tomesha pushed aside the clothing she was staring at and took out a dress she'd made herself at her old job. She loved to sew. It had been something she'd been taught when she was younger, and she'd always had an eye for fashion. If she could have, she'd have attended one of the fashion schools that still existed. Not many were left, and it was extremely hard to be accepted. Tomesha had chosen not to even apply. Even if she got in, how would she pay for tuition? Her family could barely afford to keep a roof over their head and food on the table.

So Tomesha had taken jobs wherever she could. Her most recent was as a seamstress for five years. It hadn't paid the best but provided her an income where she could contribute to the family housing needs and still do something she loved.

Two weeks ago, she'd been let go. Mrs. Davenport could no longer afford to keep her on.

"We need the money, and I have to contribute someway." Tomesha sniffed. She took the black dress out and ran her hand along the detailed stitching. She'd imagined herself using this to attend a fancy party when she'd created it. The dress was her most prized possession, and it always made her feel confident and beautiful.

"It's only been two weeks, Tomesha. There are other places you can apply," her brother snapped.

She held her dress up to her chest and turned to face him. He stood with his hands braced on his hips and a scowl on his face.

"I've applied for ten jobs and have received ten

rejections, Tarek. This may be my only chance. Plus, it's not even guaranteed that I'll be hired." She shrugged. It was true. There were so many women and men applying to work at the establishment.

Madam Rice's was an exclusive club for vampires. Tomesha had done her research after hearing the rumors of the type of place it was. Her cheeks warmed at what she'd learned. It was a place that was considered safe grounds for vampires and humans. It was a lounge that catered to vampires. The humans were paid well to service the vampires. Humans were known to be willing donors of their blood, allowing the vampires to drink from them. Her breath caught in her throat at the thought of someone piercing her neck with their fangs.

But what really had her cheeks burning was the tidbit about humans being allowed to offer more than their blood for money.

From what she'd learned, that allowed the humans to be paid even more. No expense had been spared when the building had been constructed. Working for the madam was a way for her to get her family out of poverty.

Tomesha had heard the bite of a vampire during sex was an out-of-this-world experience and was the reason why many humans lined up to apply for the open positions.

Who would have thought they'd put such an establishment in their small town of Butterbush, North Carolina.

But then again, the vampire presence in their town had been strong ever since the war ended. Butterbush was a vampire outpost run by their military.

"Then apply for ten more!" Tarek stalked into her small bedroom and stopped before her. Concern was evident on his face along with the frustration in his voice.

Tomesha's heart all but lurched into her throat. He was really against her having to sell her body. They hadn't talked about it, but she was sure he knew exactly what type of establishment the madam's was.

Tomesha stared up at him. Her lip quaked as emotions raced through her. Tears blurred her vision. She blinked, a warm trail of tears burning down her skin. She never wanted to disappoint anyone, much less her brother. They had grown up close, and she always tried to make him and their grandmother proud. Would he think of her differently if she were to allow vampires to drink from her?

She had to admit the thought was thrilling.

And the money alone was something they needed.

Tarek's finger rested on her chin and nudged her head up to meet his gaze. He sighed, his features softening as he wiped her cheeks.

"I can do this. Don't worry about me." Tomesha tightened her grip on the dress. It was her body, and she could do with it as she wanted. She inhaled sharply and stood to her full height. "It's my decision and I'm sticking to it."

Tarek's deep-brown eyes were the same as hers. They shared many of the same features they had inherited from their father. Their warm brown skin, dark hair, and slim build. His temper he got from their father, while Tomesha was like their mother, calm and loving.

He closed his eyes and bent down to rest his forehead on hers. More tears flowed as she sensed the pain and frustration radiating from him.

"I wish there was more I can do," he said. "Maybe I'll go down to the blood bank and donate—"

"Tarek. This is my decision," she repeated.

She blinked and stepped back away from him. Tarek had to understand that she was an adult and this decision was hers to make. She couldn't stand by and watch him work himself to death to try to provide for her and their grandmother. She wiped furiously at her cheeks, now angry that her emotions had got the best of her.

"Now if you'll excuse me, I need to dress for my interview."

Tarek stared at her for a brief moment before jerking his head in a nod.

"If you're sure about this then I guess there is no persuading you otherwise." He ran a shaky hand over his face. His gaze dropped to the dress in her arms. "Working somewhere around the vampires could be a good way to make connections to where you may not have to work there long. Maybe you can—"

"Tarek." She nudged him toward the door. It was good he was coming to terms with her applying for the club. "I cannot be late."

He tried to get another word in, but she successfully pushed him out and shut the door. She turned around and leaned back against it. Out of all the applications she'd submitted, this was the first one she'd actually gained an interview for. Hundreds of people had applied for the club, and Tomesha was one of the lucky ones to be called for an interview and tour.

She pushed off the door, determination filling her.

She would get this job.

She would be the best damn human blood donor or prostitute they had ever seen.

She cringed at the term prostitute, but to be honest, that was what she was applying for. She was no virgin and enjoyed sex. It had been a while since her last relationship with a woman had ended. Chanel had been someone she'd a light sexual relationship with where there were no promises of a future. It was just what they'd needed. A way to release built-up sexual tension, but then Chanel had moved to Oklahoma, and they'd decided to end what they had between them.

Tomesha held up the dress again so she could take one last glance at it. A small smile played on her lips. Dressed in this, she was bound to get the job.

TOMESHA'S NERVES got the better of her. She blew out a deep breath and continued down the sidewalk toward Madam Rice's. When she'd left home, Tarek had made himself scarce. Her grandmother had sat on the porch and gushed over her dress.

"Where you going dressed so pretty?" Delonda asked.

Her grandmother smiled up at Tomesha from her rocking chair. Delonda spent a lot of time on the porch watching the neighborhood each day. Some days she was confused and delirious. Other days the matriarch of their family was sharp as a tack. Today was a day Delonda had the spaced-out vacancy in her eyes that alluded today was a day she wasn't all there.

"Off for a job interview," Tomesha replied. She smoothed a hand along the short black skirt of her dress. She hoped she looked good enough to fit in with the other humans who were already working at the club. She'd ensured her hair was washed, dried, and straightened. It hung past her shoulders in dark waves. She'd bartered with a woman a few months ago for some makeup at a swap meet. She didn't know where she'd be wearing it at the time. She'd traded a pretty blouse she'd found and mended to obtain the makeup set. Tomesha just had a feeling that one day she'd need it.

"You're going to get the job, my dear." The wrinkles in the corners of Delonda's eyes deepened with her smile.

Tomesha moved closer to her and bent down to press a kiss to her cheek. Her grandmother may not know where exactly Tomesha was going to get a job, but it felt good to know she had confidence in her.

Tomesha eyed the neighborhood of the club and took in the prosperity the community certainly held. It was much different than hers. The homes where she lived may not scream wealth, but they at least showed some kind of pride. The humans were hard workers. Many jobs had become available as of late. For some strange reason, Tomesha just couldn't snag one. That was why her brother wanted her to continue to apply for more, but she couldn't wait. She wasn't one to sit around and let someone take care of her. She had to contribute to their household.

If they didn't pay their bills, they were at risk of the collectors coming to pillage anything of value from their home to make up the payments missed, or if rent wasn't paid…become homeless.

Tomesha didn't want to put that type of pressure on her brother. If she landed it—no, *when* she landed it—the money she'd bring in would do much for them. Her lips curved up into a smile at the thought of having extra money. She didn't know what that felt like. They'd always been poor and barely making it.

The vampires were now helping humans in ways they'd never seen before, and it had to be because of their new mates—human mates. Everyone had heard that Princess Lethia, who was the warden, had mated with a beautiful human, Alima.

Rumors had it that Alima had been a member of the human group, the Rebels. It had been an organization that was supposed to be for human rights and assisting humans who wanted to escape the mating draft.

But that appeared to not be the case.

It had been all over the news that the Rebels' leader had betrayed those he'd been helping. Humans had been disappearing at record numbers, and it seemed he was at the center of it. Now it was he who was missing, and speculations were that the princess had dealt with him.

Tomesha swallowed hard at the thought.

Had the princess tortured him? Drained him dry? No one knew or at least was talking about it.

Anyone who tried to go against the royal vampire family would be an idiot. The princesses, Velika, Lethia, and Hegna, were all known as vicious vampire warriors. Vampires were just now fighting the lycans, and they had so far defeated them. These wolf shifters were enemies of the vampires and desired to wipe them out.

But so far they'd failed in their attempt.

How had the humans thought they'd win against a race as strong as the vampires? Tomesha snorted. Humans were arrogant in thinking they were the stronger race. The number of vampires existing on the planet along with humans was staggering.

And now they had to worry about the wolf shifters. Who knew how many different races were truly out there. Who would be next to come out? Earth was a large planet, and it would be ignorant to assume there wasn't anyone else calling it home.

Princess Lethia and Alima were very up front on how they'd rule together. Tomesha didn't miss a broadcast when the two were on television. She was infatuated with the couple. She'd ensure she was at the local diner where she could catch them onscreen. The women were absolutely breathtaking. Anyone with eyes could see they were in love with each other. The heat in Lethia's eyes when her gaze landed on Alima was enough for Tomesha to fan herself. She loved a good romance story. She was sure there was a hot one between the princess and her mate. Two women from different sides of a coin had fallen in love. It hadn't mattered that they'd been matched in the draft.

They were made for each other.

Tomesha sighed.

Is there anyone out there for me?

Someone like Princess Lethia? A badass woman who wanted to protect her and provide for her? Not that she needed anyone to provide for her; Tomesha would do what she must to ensure she had what she needed, but it would feel damn good to have a partner she could go through life with.

Tomesha came to a stop. She stood on the corner of the street and took in the fancy structure. It was located in the center of town near the business district. It was made of black slate, with big glass windows outlined in what appeared to be pure gold. The awnings were even black and hung over the windows. Two large doors dripped in gold paint and stood out against the dark colors of the building. There were no markings; it didn't need any signage.

A guard stood well over six feet tall, muscular in a dark suit and sunglasses. It was hard to tell if he were human or vampire. Tomesha glanced up.

There wasn't any sun out today. Clouds filled the sky, keeping any rays from reaching through. It may be dreary, but the temperature was nice in the low seventies. Thankfully, it wasn't too hot, otherwise she'd worry about sweating and trying to stay fresh for her appointment.

"Now or never," Tomesha muttered. She stood to her full height and pulled out a welcoming smile. The butterflies in her stomach began to freak out and flutter hard. She waited for the few cars to pass before walking across the street. With her head held high, she approached the building.

A few people strode along the sidewalk going about their business. She arrived in front of the guard and widened her smile. She had to tilt her head back to look him in the face. His dark glasses hid his eyes from her.

"Hello, sir. I'm here for—"

"Go around to the back," he interjected.

"I'm here for an interview," she announced, confused. Maybe he thought she was someone else.

"The human interviewees need to enter through the back. This door is for paying customers." He leveled her with his gaze.

She could feel his eyes on her through the dark

shades. She jerked her head in a nod and pointed down the street. "Around that corner?"

"Take a left, and then you'll see an alleyway. That's the door." He turned his attention from her, apparently done with their conversation.

"Thank you." She smiled even wider, not letting his rude attitude ruin her day. She was still a little early.

He snorted and folded his hands in front of him. She spun on her heels and headed down the street.

Nope, Mister Grumpy wasn't going to ruin her mood. She was going to stay upbeat and positive. She was going to get this job. If her grandmother was confident she would, then she'd believe it, too.

Tomesha arrived at the alleyway and paused. In the daylight, the area was suspect. She'd hate to see what it looked like at night.

"Oh boy," she murmured. The scent of human or animal waste filled her nostrils. She grimaced and walked toward the back of the building. Scattered trash lined the pavement. She picked up her pace, stepping around a dead animal carcass.

Well, she certainly wasn't a paying customer. She'd be considered the help. She arrived at the end of the alley and peeked around the corner, unsure what to expect. She breathed in fresh air and saw a cleaner area where a line of people waited at a red door. Men and women dressed in all kinds of fashions. Some were in business casual while others were in skimpy outfits with body parts hanging out.

Tomesha hadn't expected this. She'd received a time for an interview and assumed she'd be the only one at that time. The hope inside her dimmed.

You're going to get this job, she reminded herself.

Tomesha held her head high again and joined the line. She needed this job and she'd best all of these people. With a jolt of confidence, she looked around, taking in her competition. The guy in front of her was young with bright-blue eyes and thick brown hair. He'd opted for ripped jeans, and a clean turquoise shirt highlighted his eyes.

"Your first time applying?" His gaze did a quick sweep of her before returning to meet her eyes.

His softened in the corners, and she immediately felt comfortable with him. She really didn't have any friends.

"Yeah, it is." Tomesha nodded.

She peeked around him and eyed the line again. A large man in a suit opened the door and waved a couple of women in. She sent up a prayer that she'd be invited in.

She turned her attention back to the guy in front of her. "Is this yours?"

"Yeah, but I have some experience." He held out his hand to her. His face softened completely, and he appeared younger than her thirty-four years.

She smiled and slid her hand into his for a firm shake.

"My name is Conner."

"Tomesha," she replied softly. She cleared her throat and took her hand back from his. It would appear that her gut was right.

"Well, Tomesha, I can tell you that I think you're a shoo-in," he said.

Tomesha's eyes widened at his confident comment. She glanced around and took in the beautiful women and handsome men, all different nationalities present.

"Thank you, but why would you think that?" she asked nervously. Tomesha reached up and tucked her hair behind her ear. She hoped what he'd said would come to fruition. She needed this job.

"You're a knockout. You have smooth flawless skin, big pretty eyes, a toned figure, and a smile that is captivating," Conner said.

Tomesha was speechless. She'd never had

anyone describe her in such a way. If someone asked her, she'd have just said dark-brown skin, plain brown eyes, and a body that needed some work.

"I don't know what to say." She swallowed hard, a smile forming. Tomesha stood to her full height. If he, a stranger, was confident she'd be able to get the job, then she had to believe the same. "Thank you. You sure know how to make a girl feel good about herself."

"I just call them like I see them." He chuckled.

They faced the door. A woman stepped out of the building. The bodyguard in the suit followed her. She had extremely pale skin, oval-shaped blue eyes, and chin-length dark hair. Her black dress hugged her figure and stopped just below her knees. Her heels were staggering, adding about four or five inches to her height.

A vampire.

She had to be. There was no other explanation for how pale her skin was. This wasn't Tomesha's first time meeting a vampire. They were all over, but it was the first time she'd be judged by one. The air fell silent. The woman strolled down the line observing the men and women. She pointed to a woman in a pink barely there dress with almost white hair.

"You," the pale woman said.

The lady in pink stepped forward. The vampire continued down the line and chose a tall muscular male with dark hair. He went to stand by the lady in pink.

Tomesha held her breath. The woman came toward her and Connor. Tomesha's heart raced. Was this how they were chosen? She stood straight. The woman stopped in front of Connor, her gaze sweeping over him.

"You," she said, pointing to him.

Tomesha celebrated on the inside for him. Her newfound friend was moving on to the next step in the process.

The woman's eyes cut to Tomesha who froze in place. She met the bright-blue eyes. The woman assessed her, and by the time her attention reached Tomesha eyes again, she thought she'd have passed out from lack of oxygen.

"And you," the woman said.

Tomesha exhaled and stared at the finger aimed at her. She blinked as the woman spun on her heel and marched back toward the building. Tomesha scurried behind the others, beside Connor.

"I told you so," Connor whispered.

Tomesha grinned at him and took note of the groans and shouts of complaints that followed them. Additional security appeared and took control of the crowd growing rowdy.

They arrived at the door, and Tomesha paused. Connor stopped ahead of her with curiosity in his eyes. She looked at the unruly people who were upset they hadn't been chosen. Tomesha breathed a sigh of relief and turned around, entering the building.

At that moment, her life would be forever changed.

CHAPTER TWO

"My name is Romana Beatrix, and you may call me Mistress," the vampire announced. She stood tall as she paced in front of the line of humans she'd handpicked. She stopped in front of the lady in pink and eyed the entire line. "I run this establishment under Madam Rice. You will answer to me."

Tomesha's heart had yet to slow down. She was still in shock that Mistress had chosen her out of the lineup of humans vying to get in. Now that she'd made it this far, what was next? Was she automatically hired?

"Consider yourselves very lucky. As you saw,

competition for new positions is very stiff," Mistress continued.

They had been escorted into a fancy receiving room. With the decor, Tomesha felt as if they had been thrust back in time: a large fireplace, high-backed chairs, thick drapes covering the windows, and even sconces on the wall burning bright with fire.

The four of them were lined up before the fireplace. A guard stood at the door, and Mistress spoke with them. Tomesha took a quick glance down the row. The others appeared to be in the same state of shock she was in.

"Madam Rice's is an establishment that began hundreds of years ago. I'm sure you're surprised to hear this, but humans have been donors for vampires since the beginning of time. We've lived amongst each other in harmony. Humans providing vampires something they need to survive while being compensated handsomely." Mistress paced in front of the group again with her hands collapsed behind her back, an air of superiority to her.

She held power.

Tomesha had seen it immediately the way she'd exited the building to make her choices. Mistress held Tomesha's new career choice in her hand. To secure a financial future for herself and her family, she'd have to do as this woman said.

"This is not the type of establishment that forces a human to do anything they don't want to do or are not comfortable with." Mistress stopped in front of the woman in pink again. She eyed her for a moment before gazing down the row.

Her focus landed on Tomesha whose breath caught in her throat.

Yes, the vampire held power.

"We're not savages. You'll be highly paid for your services. In order to prepare you for your new career, you'll be paired with an experienced associate who will train you well."

At that moment, two men and two women entered. They were all beautiful and dressed in a provocative manner. Black sheer dresses draped along the females' bodies and did nothing to hide their figures. The men were dressed in similar fashion with black pants that rested low on their waists. They stood behind Mistress without saying a word.

"Have no worries. Each of these men and women have worked for me for some time, and I trust their insight on whether you'll make it here or not."

Tomesha blinked.

She hadn't thought that she'd get the job but then not succeed at it. How could one not succeed at being a donor? Vampires needed blood. She had blood. Where in this process could she fail?

Tomesha swallowed hard. She couldn't afford to lose this opportunity. Her family needed this money. There was no way she'd be released from another employment. Determination settled inside her.

She'd do what she must to secure this job.

"Ah, I see it has dawned on some of you that this isn't a guaranteed employment." Mistress moved down the line and stood in front of Tomesha.

She met the vampire's bright-blue eyes. Tomesha tried to not tremble as she came under the eye of the powerful woman.

"But I'm sure you'll prosper. This job is not easy and will demand a lot from you physically and mentally. My one piece of advice to you is not to get attached to any of your clients. They're just that—paying clients. They provide your salary. They provide the food you'll purchase with your monies earned here. Make them returning clients and you'll be successful."

There was an icy note in her words. Tomesha

didn't plan to get involved with the vampires. She understood what Mistress had said. Tomesha nodded gently to confirm she'd got the message.

The vampires were her ticket out of poverty.

"Yes, ma'am," Tomesha murmured.

There was an approving glint in Mistress's eyes. Tomesha breathed a sigh of relief. The others followed, expressing the same sentiment. A smirk appeared on the vampire's lips.

"Good." She spun around and moved over to the men and women who'd entered. "Mortan, you'll be paired with him." She pointed to the male who Tomesha hadn't caught the name of.

Mortan walked over to the taller guy who stood next to Connor. She matched each person up before she turned and pointed to Tomesha.

"Starla, I want you with her."

"Yes, Mistress." The woman was a tall leggy blonde with makeup as flawless as her body. Starla walked over to Tomesha with a welcoming smile on her lips.

Tomesha began to feel uncertain. She didn't look anything like this woman. Yes, she'd tried to keep herself together and worked out when she could, but this woman was a knockout.

Starla stopped next to Tomesha and faced Mistress along with everyone else.

"Each person you're paired with will be the ones responsible for your training. It is not their responsibility to make sure you succeed. That is on you." Mistress clasped her hands in front of her and nodded. "You're all dismissed."

Tomesha's heart skipped a beat. It was time for her to learn what she needed. She glanced over at Starla who smiled.

"Hello. I'm Tomesha." She reached out her hand to the woman.

Starla took it in a light shake.

"That is a beautiful name. Unique. I love it," Starla replied in a husky voice. She motioned for Tomesha to follow the others leaving the room.

"You two wait. I want a word with the both of you," Mistress said.

Tomesha panicked and watched Connor leave with the others. He glanced over his shoulder with a worried look in his eyes. Once the security guard closed the door, it left Tomesha alone with Mistress and Starla.

"Have I done something wrong?" Tomesha asked warily. Whatever it was, she'd apologize profusely for it. She clutched her hands together and waited as Mistress approached her.

"Not at all, my dear." She stopped in front of Starla and Tomesha. Her gaze perused Tomesha again before meeting her eyes. "You, my dear, I feel are a special one. You will not be a donor until I say so."

"I don't get it. I thought that was the real reason I was hired." Tomesha swallowed hard. She hoped she wasn't going to get kicked out already for defending her position. Being a donor paid well, and she needed that money.

"Don't worry. You'll still be paid handsomely." Mistress reached out a finger and caressed the side of Tomesha's face. "You, my dear, I can scent that your blood is special. Many will want to taste it, but we'll reserve it for only special guests. The first bite of someone like you should be reserved."

Tomesha relaxed but still didn't understand. How could Mistress scent her blood? She didn't have any cuts on her. What was special about her blood?

"Okay," Tomesha replied shakily. "Then what will I be trained to do?"

"You'll work the blood bar and be a server. You may also indulge in any sexual acts you desire and be rewarded for them. What the vampires pay you, you keep aside for a small tax that we impose to provide for you."

"This is an amazing offer, Tomesha." Starla turned to Tomesha and took her hand. "You'll get used to being paid for your sexual favors. Having a stipulation that vamps can't drink from you will make you even more desirable to them. They'll pay more just because you're something that they can't have fully."

"She's correct." Mistress raised an eyebrow. "Believe me. I know what I am doing. Work the bar, turn your tricks, and you'll be a wealthy woman soon. When the time is right, I'll allow you to become a donor. The vampires will be practically fighting to have you. Starla here started the same as you."

Starla nodded, tightening her grip on Tomesha's hand.

"I trust that you would know best," Tomesha murmured.

A pleasing glint passed through Mistress's eyes. Tomesha was a fish out of water. She had no choice but to do as Mistress had suggested. If she felt that this would lead to Tomesha being wealthy, then she'd do what she must. She was tired of living in poverty, living a life fearful of being put out on the street or going without necessities.

So she'd work the blood bar, serve, sell her body...she'd expected all of that. But to hear that she was special, this was a first for her.

"You honor me with your trust. Starla, show Tomesha around and get her outfitted." Mistress paused and ran a hand along Tomesha's shoulder, caressing the material of her dress. "Who made this dress?"

"I did." Tomesha fought hard to keep from glancing down at her outfit.

"Hmmm...talented. I'll keep this in mind." Mistress stepped away and jerked her head toward the door.

"Yes, Mistress." Starla smiled at Tomesha and led her from the room. She released Tomesha's hand and walked beside her. She guided them down a long hallway and through a door that led them to a lower level. "Come. Let's get you measured for your uniform."

TOMESHA STARED at herself in the mirror and had to keep her jaw from touching the floor.

Uniform was a loose term for the sheer material draped over her body. The way it caressed her skin sent a shiver down her spine. The white dress had a single tie on the side. One tug and the outfit would fall to the floor. Her tawny skin appeared soft and supple, her dark areolas visible through the fabric.

This person staring back at her was beautiful.

Sexy.

A siren.

Starla had done her makeup and promised to teach her how to do it herself.

"Now this is a human the vampires will be begging to bite." Starla chuckled. She stood behind Tomesha and rested her hands on her shoulders. Her smile disappeared. "It may be hard at first, you know. Getting paid for sex, but once you have paid your bills and put food in your pantry, it gets easier."

Tomesha met Starla's gaze in the mirror. They had gone to Starla's private quarters at the club. Soon, Tomesha would have her own room where she could entertain clients. She swallowed hard again, but determination filled her. Just thinking of being able to provide for her family gave her the will to do this job.

"Who was your first bite?" Tomesha would

worry about the sex part later. What worried her was who Mistress deemed as worthy to be the first vampire to drink from her.

"It was a wealthy councilman. He was traveling from afar and had visited the club for nourishment. Mistress was honored he chose our establishment to feed." Starla took a step back from her and went over to snag a pair of sandals. She brought them over to Tomesha. "Try these on. I think they're your size."

"And?" Tomesha slid them on. They were the perfect fit. She hadn't worn anything new in a long while. She returned her gaze to the mirror, still in awe of her appearance. "How was it?"

Tomesha had heard stories of humans becoming addicted to the bite of a vampire. There was something in their saliva that activated something inside humans that left them craving more from vampires.

"I can't really describe it. I mean, after the initial bite, the pain disappears almost immediately and you get this euphoric state. I remember feeling as if I were floating on clouds and didn't want to come down from it. I know this sounds weird, but it's very pleasurable."

"Did you have sex with him?" Tomesha was

asking too much, but this was the first time she'd actually spoken with a donor.

"I did." Starla smiled and shrugged. "He comes around once a year for business to see me."

Tomesha canted her head and studied Starla. She didn't appear to be some addict or a human strung out on vampire bites. She seemed healthy and strong. Her small suite was decorated with the finest that money could buy. If she could start out like Tomesha and have become one of Mistress's top donors, then one day maybe Tomesha would be like her.

"Now enough about me. Important question for you. Do you have a preference between men or women?" Starla folded her arms in front of her.

"I've been with both in the past, but I do prefer women," Tomesha responded honestly. She'd had her share of lovers and had always preferred females. Her last few lovers had been women, and she hadn't really looked at another man since.

"That's the good thing about working for Madam Rice. We have the power to determine which clients we'll take. Any other type of establishment, you may not have a choice on who you service." Starla picked up a box from a table in the corner and walked back to Tomesha. It was pink with a black lace bow on top. She held it out to her. "And this is the last part of your uniform. Go ahead. Put them on."

Curious, Tomesha took the box from her. It was almost too pretty to tear open. She slipped her nail underneath the edge to keep from tearing the box. She lifted the lid and found three black leather straps inside. Each of them carried the large initial M.

"What are these?" Tomesha picked up the largest one. It looked like a collar with a button to collapse it closed. Two smaller ones nestled inside the tissue paper.

"This is to remind the vampires they're not to bite you. As long as you wear this around your neck and those around your wrists, you won't be bitten."

Starla took the leather collar and helped Tomesha put it on. They quickly put on the bracelets as well. They were not uncomfortable at all.

"And what if this doesn't deter a vampire from biting me?" Tomesha glanced at herself in the mirror after the finished touches of her uniform were now on.

"That vampire will pay well, and believe me when I say, no one wants to get on Madam Rice's bad side." Starla snorted. She waved to Tomesha. "Come, it's time for your first lesson."

"Should I be afraid of this?" Tomesha chuckled nervously.

She followed Starla out of the room. They walked down the hallway that Tomesha remembered would lead into the club. The leggy blonde glanced back at her over her shoulder with a smirk on her lips. They arrived at the doorway that opened out to the main area of the establishment. A large vampire guard stood watch to protect the women who stayed in this section.

"It's time for a quick crash course in serving our clients, and I'm not talking taking them a goblet of blood." She tossed Tomesha a wink and took her hand.

The guard sensed them behind the door and opened it for them. The sounds of the club filtered through the air.

Tomesha inhaled sharply and nodded.

There was no turning back now.

CHAPTER THREE

"Their heat signatures have still spread," Dru murmured. She stared at the digital map of the North American continent highlighted on the wall of her office. The royal military had top-notch technology that was recently developed to track the lycans. She stepped forward with her hands behind her back. A growl threatened to erupt at the sight of so much of the enemy.

For centuries, they had believed they had hunted the lycans down to abysmal numbers. To see they had been wrong and the mangy animals had not only brought their numbers back but had organized and had an alpha who was set on conquering the world astounded Dru. Never before had the lycans showed such organization. In the past, they had been overcome by their beasts. Even when they were under vampire ruling, they were difficult to control.

Dru had truly believed, as everyone else had, that the lycans were almost extinct. She'd been on many of the missions where they had wiped out entire dens. She scowled at the thought of their current numbers.

Next time, they'd obliterate the lycans. There would be no coming back.

"How are their numbers still increasing?" Ishmael murmured.

Dru had called in her most trusted warriors who fought under her. These vampires had assisted with her mission to hunt down the lycans. Gale and Ciro stood behind her as they, too, took in the high-lighted areas on the map.

There was only one answer to the question they all were thinking.

"They have a new alpha," Dru murmured.

Pure-born lycans' numbers wouldn't explode in this way. It would take decades, if not centuries, to increase in the way they had from new births. This was a result of lycans turning humans. Not many humans could survive a lycan bite. There was no telling how many had died in the process.

Dru ran a hand along her face and blew out a deep breath.

"Azura's sister?" Gale moved closer to the map and studied it.

Dru eyed her and gave a slow nod. It would only make sense that the twin of the alpha who was killed would take over and lead.

"I need proof." Dru turned to face her warriors.

They all stood to their full height. She'd need to put as many ears to the ground as she possibly could. Azura may have been a powerful alpha who'd led the lycans on their attempt to dominate and overthrow the vampire rule, but little was still known about this twin, Rayna Vaughn. For all they knew, another lycan could have overthrown the prior alpha's twin.

"We need hard evidence of who's now in charge."

Azura had made her intentions known publicly. Not only had she boldly contacted the royal family to threaten them, but the deranged female had boasted on national television what she'd planned to do.

But this new alpha—they were moving in silence.

And that made them all the more dangerous.

"What would you have us do?" Ciro had helped develop the technology in which they were able to track the lycan dens. He was a younger vampire who'd caught Dru's attention with his intelligence and willingness to enhance technologies to assist vampires in staying ahead of the lycans.

"We're going to target the larger dens. Recently turned lycans may not be as loyal. We know from experience that any who may have human families may talk," Dru said.

Gale came back to stand next to her fellow warriors. Lycans had been turning humans against their will. Thousands of humans had gone missing, and most had been blamed on the lycans. Those who may not be lost to the beasts may be willing to rat out the whereabouts of the new alpha for a price.

"I have an algorithm put together to determine the fastest-growing dens," Ciro announced.

Dru folded her arms. She nodded to have him continue. This just proved her gut feeling about the vampire was going to pay off. She'd mention this to

Lethia so they may reward him well for his contributions in the fight against the lycans.

"Many of the newly turned lycans have gone feral and are unable to change back to human forms, but there are those who are not. I already have information that can help us determine which dens to infiltrate first."

"Well done. I want a few teams to go out and hunt down the most vulnerable targets who may talk. Ciro, I want you on Azura's sister. Princess Hegna has a computer hacker who would be the perfect person to connect with. Her name is June. Reach out to her," Dru said.

June had played a key role in the vampires overrunning the human government.

"I'll connect with her immediately." Ciro bowed his head. He sat at the table where his computer awaited him.

Dru respected those who were technologically savvy. She was a vampire not born of this century and didn't depend on much of the new ways, but she appreciated those who were able to.

A knock sounded at the door. She was not to be disturbed during this meeting unless it was urgent, and if there was an urgent matter—she'd know about it.

"Enter!" Dru moved back to her desk and glanced down at her meticulous plans she'd drawn up before the meeting. So far, they had covered everything she'd wanted.

"Captain Moldark."

Dru glanced up in surprise at the sight of the castle's butler, Sterling, standing at the doorway. He had a hand in all of the workings of the castle. He'd been employed by Lethia for decades and was well revered.

"Sterling. What can I do for you?" Dru folded her hands behind her back. Why would he personally come and see her? If there was something he needed, he could have sent a servant.

"You're being summoned to the throne room, Captain." He bowed his head slightly.

The room fell silent. Dru frowned. Summoned to the throne room?

"By whom?" She hadn't heard word of the king or queen arriving in Crystal Cove.

She moved to stand in front of her desk. Lethia never used the room for her own purposes, and if she chose to, Dru would be informed. As Lethia's right hand, there wasn't much that went on about the castle or in the territory that Dru wasn't aware of.

"Princess Lethia has requested that you come immediately," he said.

"The princess?" Her eyebrows jerked up high. She blinked then stood to her full height. She turned to the warriors who all had their attention on her. "Gale and Ishmael, I want you to put together small teams. Each of you take a top den to target using Ciro's algorithm. Find me the information I need."

"Yes, Captain," Gale and Ishmael echoed simultaneously.

They thumped their fists against their chests. She nodded to Ciro then stalked to the door. Her warriors had their orders, now she needed to find out why she was being summoned. Sterling stepped to the side to allow her to pass.

She paused outside the office at the sight of Lethia's guards awaiting her. Enoch and Izora. They stood in their formal uniforms.

"Captain," Enoch's deep voice echoed through the hallway.

"Captain." Izora rested a fist above her heart.

"What is the meaning of this?" Dru demanded. The hairs on the back of her neck rose. Curiosity burned in her chest. Had she done something wrong?

"We're to escort you to the princess. She's instructed us to ensure you come straight to her," Enoch said.

Dru jerked her head in a nod and walked down the hall. The two guards flanked her on both sides. Her mind raced, and she couldn't think of one damn thing she could have done to piss off the princess. She quickened her pace. Lethia was going to give her answers.

* * *

ENOCH STEPPED in front of her and pushed open the double doors that bore the insignia of the royal house. Dru relaxed her hands from balled fists. She didn't want to appear anxious when she came before the princess. Her heart thundered as she followed Enoch inside. It had been a long time since she'd been in this room. Lethia rarely used it, and the last time they'd utilized it was for the king and queen.

The throne room with its stone walls and vaulted ceiling was breathtaking. Massive pillars lined the chamber, their shadows stretching across the dark marble floor. The air was heavy with silence other than the sound of her footsteps. Paintings of past battles were draped along the walls while gold-and-diamond chandeliers provided lighting. The windows were hidden behind the steel coverings that blocked out the sun.

Dru strode forward. She didn't know what the hell was going on, but she refused to appear anything else but strong. The room was filled with vampires, and all eyes were on her. She recognized members of the local coven and council along with other notable warriors who fought underneath Lethia.

Dru zeroed in on Lethia Riskel who looked every ounce a royal princess. She sat on the throne, her long blonde hair flowing over her shoulders. Her expensive blue gown highlighted her eyes. Out of the three Riskel sisters, it was Lethia who enjoyed the luxury and wealth of her family.

She may be dressed in a formal gown with her makeup done, but one shouldn't be deceived by her looks. Lethia was a deadly vampire who Dru had fought beside during many battles and wars in their lifetime. Dru flicked her gaze to the figure who stood beside Lethia—her mate, Alima.

Dru came to stop at the bottom of the stairs. The room remained silent as she bent down to one knee and lowered her gaze. Whatever was the meaning of this, it was official royal business, and Dru would show the utmost respect.

"Your Highnesses." Dru kept her eyes to the floor. Her heart rate increased. She inhaled to try to will the pounding muscle to slow down. She'd at first thought she'd be demanding the meaning of this, but seeing how there was an audience, she bit her tongue. She may be the right hand of the commander, but that didn't mean she was above anyone else who served Lethia.

"Captain Moldark." Lethia's strong voice carried through the room. "Rise."

Dru pushed off the floor and stood. She folded her hands behind her and held Lethia's gaze. Dru couldn't get a read on her.

"Your Highness. Have I done something to——"

"How long have you served me?" Lethia's face was devoid of all emotions. Her sharp, crystal-blue eyes bored into Dru.

Taken back by the question, Dru blinked at first. Lethia knew the answer to this question. Why would she ask such a thing?

"Decades, Your Highness. About forty-five years, I think," Dru answered.

When Dru had first joined Lethia's army she'd started out as a basic warrior. She'd been a late bloomer when it came to warrior training. The younger Dru never would have dreamed that she'd be fighting for the royal family or hold a rank in the Royal Army.

Dru came from a family of healers. Her father was a master healer while her mother was a botanist. At the age of twenty, she'd trained under her father. Her younger sister, Zada, had joined her. She'd grown up in a peaceful village in the Grampian Mountains. Dru was dedicated to preserving life and mending wounds. She'd believed in compassion and mercy.

It wasn't until the lycans arrived at her village that she'd been forced to watch the destruction of her people. Lycans slaughtered vampires—their former oppressors. Vampires had been at war with the lycans for centuries. Her family had survived and relocated to North America. It was then she'd answered a call to the Riskel family. They'd offered her something no one else could.

Power to protect those she loved most. Vengeance for all of those who'd perished under the lycan attacks, and a new purpose. As a healer, her job had been to patch up those who were injured.

As a warrior, she could end threats before they began.

Dru had easily transitioned to the warrior life. She had no regrets. She'd tucked her family away in a small town in Canada while she went off to serve her new king. She'd worked her way up through the ranks until she'd earned the position of captain and the right hand of the commander, Princess Lethia Riskel.

"Would you say you have been a loyal servant to vampires in the current position you hold?" Lethia dipped her head to the side and continued to study Dru.

"Yes, Your Highness," Dru answered without hesitation. She lifted her chin in a silent challenge to Lethia. She dared her to try to make an argument of any time Dru had not put their people first.

"And would you say that you're loyal to me and the Riskel family?" Lethia asked.

"Yes, Your Highness." Dru's voice rang out strong and clear. She pounded a fist above her heart to show her fealty. The Riskels were one of the most powerful vampire families in the world. It was an honor to serve under them.

Lethia rose to her feet. She sauntered down the

stairs and came to stand in front of Dru. The air was taut with tension. Dru's gaze didn't waver from her commander. Lethia smirked.

"On your knees again, Captain," Lethia ordered.

The sounds of quick inhales circulated around the room. Dru immediately followed the order. She knelt and cast her gaze to the floor. If she'd done something to warrant the wrath of the princess then she hoped she'd know what it was before her punishment.

Dru remained still. Her ears picked up the sound of Lethia's blade sliding out of its sheath. Her muscles tensed the moment the blade rested on her shoulder. Dru closed her eyes, prepared to meet death. She wasn't a vampire who was afraid of transitioning to the afterlife. She'd led a good life that one would be proud of. Her breath caught in her throat as the weapon lifted from her shoulder.

"Now rise, General Moldark," Lethia commanded.

Dru's eyes flew open. Had she heard the princess correctly? She blinked and glanced up at her longtime friend. Lethia's smirk turned into a fully fledged grin. Thunderous applause spread through room. Dru stared at Lethia, unable to believe what she'd just heard.

General?

She was being promoted to general?

Dru inhaled sharply and pushed off the floor. She shook her head. "Are you serious?"

Lethia stepped forward and rested her hand on Dru's shoulder.

"I should have done this years ago." Lethia's smile vanished, and a seriousness overtook her. "There is no other person more worthy of the title of general to lead my army. General Dru Moldark has been an integral member of our armies. She's led many warriors to battle and has even taken the new recruits under her wing to ensure we vampires continue to be protected. Her fierce nature, cunning skills with her weapons, and intelligent nature to lead have been valuable assets. And I can't forget to mention that she's saved my ass a time or two."

A few chuckles rippled through the air. Dru's chest filled with pride. She bowed her head to Lethia in acceptance of her new position. Lethia faced the room, the dagger still in her hand.

"Will there be any objections?" Lethia called out. Her grip on the weapon sent a silent message.

Dru turned and took in the council members at the front of the audience as well as plenty of familiar faces. A hush fell over the room.

There would be no objections.

CHAPTER FOUR

"General, congratulations." A firm hand came to rest on Dru's shoulder.

She turned, met by the council member, Caedmon Wells.

"Thank you, Councilman Wells." Dru nodded.

In royal fashion, Lethia had garnered a celebration in secrecy. There wasn't much that went undetected under Dru's nose at the castle, but somehow Lethia had planned to promote her and then throw a party in her honor.

"I've always known you were special. I

remember the day you made captain." Wells chuckled.

Dru's name was called out again. She bowed to him and made excuses. She didn't have the energy to fall into a long discussion with the elder vampire. She remembered that day completely differently. There had been objections to her being made a captain.

Dressed in her formal uniform, she made her way through the throng of vampires. Her people loved a good party. The entire coven had to be here tonight. The ballroom had been transformed. The high vaulted ceilings reflected the flickering of candlelight in black iron chandeliers. Each flicker gave a soft appearance to the room where the shadows hid secret feedings from human donors.

Musicians played from a raised alcove, their stringed instruments weaving a magical sense of danger and elegance. Cerulean banners decorated the walls with the royal crest threaded in gold.

Dru continued on taking in the room decked out in her honor. She'd never had such an event thrown for her. Lethia had certainly outdone herself tonight.

Her gaze landed on the dais at the far end. Twin throne chairs draped in gold velvet sat empty.

The music ceased, and the crowd fell quiet, the focus on the double doors opening. A royal guard stepped forward with a gold sash resting across his chest. He clicked his heels together.

"You have been graced with the presence of the royal couple. It is my great honor to introduce His Royal Majesty, ruler of North America, King Niall Riskel and her radiant Majesty, Queen Mira Riskel. All hail the royal house." His voice carried through the air. He stepped to the side and bowed low.

The royal couple appeared in the doorway. King Niall, with his dark hair, was a dashing older vampire who was fit and still wielded his sword. Queen Mira was a beauty with long blonde hair styled into a high bun. Both had dressed in lavish luxury, as expected of a royal couple. The two made a beautiful couple, and both were deadly vampires.

Dru joined everyone in the customary bow to the royal couple. They made their way to the dais where they were seated on their thrones. Conversations resumed as well as the music.

"Why is the honorary guest hiding off in the corner?" Lethia appeared at Dru's side.

Dru held back an eye roll and turned to her. Alima was at her side, their arms entwined.

"Your Highnesses." Dru nodded to both of them.

Alima smiled at her and leaned into Lethia.

Dru blew out a deep breath. "I'm not hiding. I'm just taking it all in."

"Whatever. You're hiding, and don't think you're going to disappear from your party to go plotting on the enemy." Lethia's blue eyes twinkled with laughter. The commander apparently knew Dru only too well.

"You know, for a princess, you sure can be an ass," Dru muttered. She shook her head. What else was she supposed to be doing? As the general of the eastern armies, it was her job now more than ever to ensure their warriors were ready.

"You may want to watch what you say to your commander." Lethia tossed her a wink. "I've cut out tongues for lesser offenses."

"Aye, that I know. I was right there beside you." Dru folded her hands behind her back and turned to Lethia. "You just couldn't give me a warning that you were going to promote me?"

Lethia threw back her head and laughed. "Why? So I can miss the look on your face? You didn't have a clue what you were in for. I could see the gears in your brain turning." She snickered.

"A heads-up would have been nice," Dru muttered.

"Would it have made a difference? Would you have thought about it? Would you have declined the position? Which, I might add, you were not going to get the choice to do anyway." Lethia eyed Dru and shrugged. "As I said, I should have done it long ago."

A few attendees walked past them and offered their congratulations to Dru. She gave a curt nod to them and focused back on Lethia.

"I have been in the midst of——"

"I don't want to hear anything about the lycans, plans, attack battles, or anything that has to do with war at the moment. Save that for the morning." Lethia rested a hand on Dru's shoulder. "You're to mingle. Take the night off. Find a donor to drink from, or better yet, go find a donor to fuck. It looks like it's been a while since you've experienced the pleasure of a donor's company." She grinned.

"I beg your royal pardon?" Dru sputtered. Her private business need not be the concern of the princess. Lethia may be right that it had been a long while since she'd experienced the company of a lover, but she'd been knee-deep in her work.

"I am ordering you to go feed and fuck, General," Lethia deadpanned.

"Your Highness. There is much to do——"

"I just gave you an order. If you only want to feed, then so be it, but please…release some of that pent-up tension you carry." Someone signaled to Lethia, drawing her attention away.

"Don't listen to her. Do what you want." Alima chuckled.

"Thank you, my lady." Dru smirked.

"Don't listen to my mate. I am the commander." Lethia flashed a fang. She motioned to her parents. "Come. The honored guest is being summoned to the king and queen."

Dru followed Lethia and Alima through the thick crowd. She continued to acknowledge everyone who attempted to gain her attention. She was thankful she could use the excuse of the king and queen requesting her. The celebration was ramping up, and she was itching to disappear and leave. Vampires loved a good party and to enjoy their immortality.

Dru, on the other hand, preferred solace and being left to plan her battle strategies. Large crowds bothered her. Maybe it was the warrior in her, but her gaze swept the area looking for any signs of danger. Her hand rested on the small dagger she kept on her waist. She didn't quite trust everyone in this damn room, but she knew at the moment there couldn't be a safer place to be with the royal couple being in attendance. There were plenty of guards and warriors around the castle at a time like this with the addition of the vampire dignitaries present. She didn't need to have her full array of weapons on her person, but she did feel vulnerable without them.

The king and queen sat regal in their twin thrones. Two royal guards stood near them. The couple always had a detail assigned to them. Enemies could present themselves any time. They'd be fools to try anything as the royal couple were both fierce warriors.

Lethia and Alima stopped at the base of the stairs that led up to where the Riskels sat.

"Mother. Father."

Lethia and Alima bowed deeply to her parents. They moved to the side so Dru could come forward. She ignored the stares as the room turned its attention to her and the royal couple. Her new ranking of general put her in a higher status underneath the king and queen in the collective army that served them. Dru stepped forward and met the steady gaze of the king then the queen.

"Your Majesties." Dru knelt before them in a show of utmost respect. She'd grown up listening to stories of the king and his father. It was the Riskels who'd saved the North American continent vampires. She didn't care what stories that lycan alpha had tried to weave on national television. It had been a string of lies. All vampires knew the truth.

"You may rise, General," the king's deep voice boomed.

Dru lifted her gaze and met the king's cunning stare. She stood. It was always an honor to hold an audience with the royal couple.

"My daughter has made a fine choice in choosing her general," Queen Mira noted.

Pride filled Dru again. It was one thing to have recognition from Lethia, but to hear it come from the queen's own lips gave Dru even more confidence of her abilities to lead Lethia's army.

"Your reputation proceeds you. We need more vampires warriors like you, General Moldark."

"I will not let the crown down," Dru announced with a clear, steady voice. She caught Lethia's nod at her announcement. Her hard work and dedication had paid off as she'd always known it would. Dru was a vampire who was always determined to succeed at whatever she put her mind to. Had she remained a healer, she was sure she'd have been one of the best. Her sister, Zada, was well known for her healing abilities. It was in their genes. The Moldark name carried weight.

"I am sure that you will not. You have done much for the vampire nation. I trust that each warrior will continue to follow your lead." The king leaned forward and rested his elbow on his knee. "You remind me of myself when I was younger. Hungry. Intelligent. A true warrior who has taken an interest in the next generation of warriors. General, you'll go far in life."

Dru bit back a few tears that threatened to appear. She wasn't one who got emotional. Even when she'd made the decision to leave the life of a healer and choose the harsh warrior life, she'd been sensible and headstrong.

But there was something about hearing the king acknowledge her that opened up something in her.

"Come, General. Walk with me. I need some fresh air and want to view the gardens." The queen pushed up from her chair and motioned for Dru to go with her.

"Yes, Your Highness." Dru flicked her gaze to Lethia who shrugged.

Apparently, the princess didn't know what this private conversation was about. The queen floated down the stairs with one of the guards following her. Dru strode next to the queen as they headed in the direction of the double doors that led outside. They exited the ballroom and arrived on the veranda that overlooked the gardens.

The moon was high and helped provide light. Stars twinkled in the dark canvas. Dru followed the queen down the staircase. Once they were on the stone path, the guard blended into the shadows. Her curiosity was piqued. Why had the queen wanted her to accompany her outside?

"It's a beautiful night, isn't it?" the queen asked.

They strolled along the walkway of the lush gardens. Dru inhaled and took in the floral aroma that surrounded them. Lethia's gardeners took great pride in ensuring the beauty of nature was only a few steps away from the castle doors.

"It is," Dru murmured.

They slowly continued until the music had faded somewhat off in the distance. The queen held her head high, her hands folded before her. The woman was intriguing and an older version of Lethia.

"I'm sure you're wondering why I've taken you away from your celebration." The queen chuckled.

"It's quite all right. Parties in my honor are not my thing," Dru admitted.

"Either way, I will not hold you long." The queen paused and turned to Dru.

Her eyes hardened slightly. The air around them grew tense. Dru immediately sensed there was a serious reason why the queen had brought them away from the castle and the coven. Why else would she guide them away from potential prying eyes and eavesdroppers?

"I wanted privacy for what I need to discuss with you. Out here, there is no one but us and my guards. What I am about to say is not to be shared with anyone else. Not even my daughters know what I am about to ask of you."

Dru held back her surprise. This certainly confirmed that Lethia was in the dark about this meeting. Dru swallowed hard and faced the queen.

"Your Majesty, you have my solemn swear of fealty and confidence of my silence." Dru pounded a fist above her heart. It made her feel damn good to be trusted.

"Something has arisen that I need someone to take care of. I feel you would be the best person for this job. I know you're now a general, but this job is something I will not trust with just anyone," Mira said.

"Whatever it may be, I'll take care of it," Dru automatically said. She was honor bound to the woman before her. She may serve under Lethia, but ultimately she served the vampire crown. Determination filled her. If the queen determined she was the best for this assignment or task, then so be it.

"There was a time where my mate had a vampire whom he trusted solely. The right hand of the king. He betrayed not only my mate but the crown and all vampires," Mira snapped. Her fangs flashed as she spoke. A scowl that was unfit for a queen spread across her face.

Hearing this information shocked Dru. She hadn't heard of any tales of betrayal of someone close to the king. She had a love of history and had studied the Riskel rise to power. Niall wasn't the first Riskel to sit on the throne.

"We've suppressed this information because my mate killed the vampire," the queen continued. "He did not deserve the honor to have his name scribed into the history books."

Dru nodded in satisfaction that the king had handled the traitor. She folded her arms. If he was dead, then what did the queen need from her?

"Or at least, we thought him to be dead," Mira announced.

Dru froze. Her interest was definitely piqued.

Mira took a few steps away and stared at the moon. She exhaled before glancing over her shoulder at Dru. "I want you to confirm whether or not this vampire lives."

"Do you have proof or —"

"There have been rumors of things going around that only he'd know. What caught my attention was what that lycan alpha had said. She knew things that weren't made public. Conversations that were private. There were only three people privy to them, and two of them are present now at your celebration."

Hearing this brought about a fierceness in Dru. That would be similar to her, Lethia, and Alima. Dru would never betray the princess or her mate, and certainly not the crown. Her loyalty knew no boundaries. What could have caused the vampire to cross the king? And the right hand of the king at that? Her hand balled into a fist at the thought of the deception.

"What is this vampire's name?" Dru said. To think that someone close to the king would betray him, their people, had a dark nature rising in Dru. That vampire didn't deserve to breathe air or have the pleasure to drink blood. She thought of all of the tales she'd heard of the centuries past, and not once had she known of a vampire betraying the king. Even if he was erased from the history archives, there must be some information on him. She'd dig until she found what she was looking for.

If he was truly alive and hiding, she'd find him.

"He went by the name of Solomon Winterborne centuries ago. If he's alive today, there is no telling what name he uses. But I want him found and brought to me," the queen demanded. She stalked to Dru and stopped inches from her. Her fierce glare met Dru's. "I trust you'll complete this mission, General."

"You have my word, Your Majesty. And if there is resistance?" Dru asked.

"Then you have my permission to bring me his head."

CHAPTER FIVE

Tomesha glanced down at the gold coins resting in her drawer. It had been two weeks since she'd started working at Madam's. She was still in training, but so far, Starla had said she'd been a quick study.

Maybe it had something to do with being close to eviction or needing food on the table that drove Tomesha. She blinked. She hadn't seen this much money at one time—ever. Even with her years as a seamstress, she'd never brought in this amount in such a short time. It would take years for her to earn this, and here she'd done it in a matter of two weeks.

She bit back a smile.

She'd been praised for being a fast learner. Tomesha was determined to succeed; she didn't have a choice. Learning the bar wasn't hard. The process of preparing the blood was new for her. Warming it for consumption wasn't something a human did. She compared it to preparing an alcoholic drink for humans. Some drinks had to be made certain ways for it to taste good. Some vampires had certain preferences for blood types, warmed or chilled.

Servicing her first customer had been a little challenging. From the moment she'd hit the club, offers were being tossed to her left and right. Mistress had been correct. Apparently, there was something sweet about her blood that drew the vampires to her, and the fact that she wasn't to be bitten made the allure of her all the more enticing for them.

She'd at first thought having sex with a random stranger would be hard, but again, with everything hanging over her head, Tomesha was able to perform well enough, and the vampire tipped her generously. She fingered a few of the coins and sighed. Each one became easier than the next. Thankfully, she hadn't had any difficult patrons.

Leaving to come to work today hadn't been easy. Tarek was still upset at her choice in employment. He hadn't said a word when she'd left. He'd sat on the front steps of their house as she'd bid goodbye to their grandmother. She loved her brother dearly and prayed he'd eventually come to terms with what she did for a living. This was her decision, and she was going to stick by it.

Tomesha closed the drawer and went over to her closet. It was almost time for her shift. As promised, she'd been given her own private room. It was a standard suite with the basics. She hadn't had a chance to think of how she wanted to personalize it. At the moment, she left it as it was presented to her. Spending money for lavish decorations wasn't at the top of her priority list. It was nice and cozy as it was. The bed was large enough to fit four grown people in it. The artwork was tasteful, and they'd even provided a drawer of toys for her to utilize for her customers.

The only request she'd made was for a sewing machine and plenty of fabrics. She wanted to make her own uniforms. Mistress had approved the request but stated she had to stick with the sheer material that was standard for all donors and servers.

Tomesha slid the door back to reveal the standard uniforms she'd been given, but then her gaze landed on her latest design. She smiled and reached for the dress. Mistress had seen the other two outfits she'd concocted and had even mentioned she liked them.

She moved over to the bed and placed the dress down. She had a towel wrapped around her and wanted to do her makeup first before getting dressed. She'd waited until she'd arrived at the club to take a shower. She wanted to ensure she was fresh and clean for work.

Tomesha eyed the vanity that held more makeup then she knew what to do with it. She flicked on the bright lights and stared at herself. Her dark eyes were large while her long dark hair was still contained in her shower cap. Starla had taught her how to do her makeup. She wanted to keep everything light and natural-looking. Some of the donors were always dolled up with a face full of makeup, but Tomesha didn't feel that was for her.

Her thoughts turned to tonight as she moisturized herself. She was to work the bar. It was a weekend, and she was sure it would be busy. Even in their small town, there were plenty of vampires arriving, since Butterbush was a vampirian outpost. Ever since the vampires had taken over, they had instilled their outposts throughout the country. It had been built as a defensive post during the war. It proved to be a strategic location that allowed the vampires to exert their presence and control.

The town of Butterbush once only held less than ten thousand occupants. Once the outpost was set up, it brought more humans. Vampires in the area should have equaled more job opportunities, but with the amount of humans who'd flocked to the town, demands outweighed the opportunities. Some businesses struggled while other certain areas flourished.

One good factor about living in a town with a vampire outpost run by their military was the protection from rogue vampires. Butterbush was a safe haven for humans. The royal vampire military had been battling the rogue vampires, those who did not abide by the vampire laws. Even humans would rather be protected by the vampire Royal Army than take their chances with lawless vampires.

It didn't take Tomesha long to finish getting ready for her shift. She stood back from her floor-length mirror and almost didn't recognize the person standing before her. She looked healthier. Her color was radiant. One thing Mistress wasn't going to go for was a starving server. Plenty of food was provided for the humans. They'd need their full strength to be able to service the vampires.

Her white sheer dress stopped just above her knees, showcasing her legs. She'd received many compliments about them. She'd never really paid them any mind before, but if potential clients liked them, then she'd ensure they were on display. If she wanted to bring in top money then she'd have to appeal to the sensual nature of vampires. She'd pulled her hair up into a top bun. Even though she had to wear the collar and wristlets, it hadn't kept vampires from sniffing her neck.

"You can do this," she murmured.

A nervousness always settled upon her as she was about to go out into the club. Would today be the day Mistress allowed a worthy vampire to sink their fangs into her flesh? A shiver rippled down her spine at the thought. She gave herself another look over before spinning on her heels and heading out of her room.

She made her way down the private corridor. The music playing in the club was muffled, but she could hear the steady beat of the base. Moans of pleasure echoed from some doors—some people were already busy with work. She arrived at the end of the hall and jogged up the few stairs that led to the guarded door.

"Good evening." The security guard, Boris, opened the door for her. He nodded to her as she passed by. He was tall and broad-shouldered, his dark hair slicked back from his face, his fangs noticeable when he spoke.

"Evening, Boris." She exhaled slowly.

The men and women who provided protection for the club were vital. In her two weeks there, she'd seen a couple of vampires who had to be removed for being unruly. The security team acted swiftly, and business was back to usual within minutes.

"I hope you have a smooth night," she said.

"Same to you, Tomesha."

She smiled at him and continued on.

The madam's establishment was a sanctuary of indulgence, where elegance and temptation were entwined. Candlelight glowed from golden sconces, and crystal chandeliers bathed the room in a soft light. Tapestries of silk and velvet were draped on the walls, giving the place the look of luxury. Plush lounges, private alcoves, and sweeping curtains offered intimacy if guests wanted to be hidden away or to become spectacles if they chose to be on display.

Tomesha paused in the doorway and inhaled. She was met with the scent of sandalwood, rose, and the faint, metallic hint of blood. Humans and vampires filled the room. Tomesha was no longer in shock at the show of open feedings. It was a necessity for the vampires. Something that she thought would be barbaric could actually be tender and intimate. She took in the writhing bodies in a corner and a human reclining, willingly offering themselves for a vampire to drink from them.

A grand bar gleamed at the heart of the establishment with its polished mahogany base and marble countertops. That was where she'd be working tonight. Crystal decanters held rich wines and the precious blood for vampires.

Tomesha would have never guessed there were so many ways a vampire could consume prepared blood. One of the first things she'd been taught was providing and preparing the blood for the vampires. She'd just assumed it would be in a container and she'd pour.

Oh no.

Serving blood was similar to serving the finest

of wines with a presentation that was stylish and almost ceremonial. Tomesha was blown away by what she'd learned and all that was available for the vampires.

"You're a little early today. Ready to make that money?" Ada, one of the vampire bartenders, winked.

"Well, I figured I better hurry so I can help. It looks busy out there." Tomesha slid behind the counter and took in the crowd around the bar.

Vampires gathered there, some sipping from goblets while humans lingered nearby. The hum of the music threaded through the club, weaving a rhythm that matched the thrum of desire in the air.

Tomesha had learned quickly this was a place free of judgment and fear. This world in the club was different than what awaited them on the outside.

"I appreciate it. Jacob and Viessa are already running drinks to a few tables. I have some other orders that I need you to take," the experienced bartender said.

"No problem." Tomesha grabbed a serving tray. She'd gotten a lot of practice walking through the club while balancing heavy bottles and goblets of blood. She turned and placed the tray on the counter and picked up napkins to add.

"It's table four I need you to go over to. I'm telling you now, this table holds some heavy-weights." Ada set down a crystal decanter filled to the brim with crimson liquid.

The aroma of copper hit Tomesha.

"Heavy hitters?" Tomesha glanced in the direction of the table.

Three females who could only be vampires. Curiosity filled her. Their pale skin was noticeable in the low light. One in particular caught her attention. With her long dark hair, pouty red lips, and almond-shaped eyes, she was quite beautiful. She was slightly taller than the other two and was noticeably more muscular. Her spaghetti strap dress left little to the imagination.

This vampire was looking for more than a simple drink from the bar.

As if sensing Tomesha's attention, she met her gaze. Her lips curled up in the corner. She nodded then turned back to the conversation at the table.

"That, my dear, is a very prominent vampire." Ada added three goblets to the tray for Tomesha. She leaned in close and kept her voice low. She must have identified who Tomesha was locked in on. "Her name is Valentina Feng. She's the daughter of Lord Feng. She's been here awhile visiting."

"For what?" Tomesha tore her eyes from Valentina.

Ada shrugged and leaned against the bar. "Who knows. Something secretive, I'm sure."

"Who are we discussing?" Viessa arrived with her empty tray. She was a friendly person who'd been working at the club for a while.

"Lady Feng." Ada chuckled. She nudged Tomesha and grinned. "If you play your cards right, you can make some good money tonight."

"But she won't be allowed to bite me," Tomesha automatically responded.

That hadn't been a problem with any of the other vampires she'd serviced so far. They all wanted a taste of what she'd had to offer for now with the promise to return once they could drink from her.

"It won't matter, and if she makes an offer for you, I'd take it. Hell, if you want, I'll go serve her table," Viessa said.

"No, I'm sending Tomesha." Ada motioned to Viessa. "I have another table for you to serve. Give me a second and I'll get the order ready."

"What's so special about Valentina?" Tomesha asked Viessa once Ada was out of earshot. Tomesha wanted to know what she was getting herself into if there would be a problem going over to the table.

"All I'm going to say is that Valentina is working with some equipment that most of us females are not born with." She wagged her eyebrows and giggled.

"Come again?" Tomesha frowned. What was Viessa talking about?

"Oh, you know. She was born with some equipment down there that we don't naturally have."

She motioned to her groin area, and then it dawned on Tomesha. She glanced over at Valentina again. She had large breasts and gave off a beautiful feminine appearance. She turned back to Viessa. Her curiosity was definitely piqued.

"Are you saying she has...um...a dick?" Tomesha whispered.

Viessa threw her head back and laughed. She rested a hand on Tomesha's arm and nodded. Tomesha's heart rate increased. She grew a little nervous at the fact and inhaled sharply. This was part of her job. She was to provide a service for the vampires and she wanted to be the best. This, she was sure, would not be the first time coming across someone who was slightly different from her.

And different was never a bad thing. She always loved to embrace what made each person unique.

"It's the best of both worlds, hun. That's why I said if you don't want to go serve her, then I most definitely will. She tips very well."

"I said I have another table for you, Viessa. Leave Tomesha alone." Ada came back to where they were. She jerked her head to the club floor. "Tomesha, you best hurry before the blood chills. They like for it to be warm, and I have it at the perfect temperature."

"Yes, ma'am." Tomesha lifted her tray and positioned it on her forearm so she wouldn't spill it. She glanced over at Viessa who winked. Tomesha smiled and shook her head. She began to make her way through the tables. She held her head high as Starla had encouraged her to do. She needed to exude confidence, sensuality, and the vampires would vie for her attention. She added a little sway to her hips.

She sensed eyes on her. She ignored the vampires and humans engaged in the open feedings and sexual acts. She kept her gaze on the table that was her target. According to Starla, the vampires would appreciate her undivided attention. It did something to their egos if they were her sole focus. Starla had taught her much since she'd been working for Madam. Everything she'd taught her had worked.

Tomesha kept in mind why she was doing this. The money she was bringing in was already going to help. Their house note would be caught up, she'd be able to help purchase her grandmother's medications, put food in the pantry, and her brother wouldn't have to work himself into the ground.

The three vampires turned their eyes to her as she arrived at the table.

"Hello there," Tomesha said. She gave them all a nod in a show of respect. If Valentina held a title, then it would be expected. "My name is Tomesha, and I'll be your server tonight."

"Tomesha? What a unique name. It's beautiful," the brunette vampire said. She offered Tomesha a fangy smile. Her gaze slipped over Tomesha before coming back to her face.

"Thank you." Tomesha smiled. She meticulously set down napkins in front of the three women, before placing their goblets on them. "The bartender has sent the best for you tonight."

"Ada always takes care of us." The third

vampire with a short blonde pixie cut chuckled. Her fangs were on display as well. "My name is Emerald. This is Renee and Valentina."

"It's so nice to meet you," Tomesha said.

Valentina had yet to take her eyes off Tomesha. Butterflies fluttered in Tomesha's stomach. She couldn't read her expression at the moment. Did the vampire find her appealing? She hoped so. She really needed the money. If Viessa was right and the vampire chose her, then she'd do her best to please her.

"You have never been bitten before?" Valentina asked. Her voice was soft and melodic. She leaned forward to study Tomesha.

Her hand paused on the crystal decanter. Her gaze flicked to Valentina. She shook her head.

"No. Not yet. I'm new, and Mistress is not allowing any vampires to drink from me yet," Tomesha replied.

It was the honest truth. It wasn't the first time someone had asked. A few had even been so bold as to demand to speak with Mistress to bargain to be the first to sip from Tomesha. Tomesha cleared her throat and lifted the decanter. She started with Emerald, since she was next to her, and filled her goblet.

"You know Romana has rules." Emerald snickered.

Tomesha moved to Renee next and filled hers. When she stopped, the vampire motioned for her to add a little more to the goblet. She did as was requested before moving over to Valentina's side.

"She's always particular about her humans." Renee tucked a few strands of hair behind her ear. "She wants top dollar for the first bite on certain humans."

Valentina remained silent as she watched Tomesha fill her goblet. Once it was full, Tomesha set the almost empty container in the center of the table. A hand ghosted the back of Tomesha's thigh. She glanced over and found Valentina's attention on her ass.

Well, that answered her question on whether or not the vampire was interested in her. Valentina's hand slipped down her smooth skin and came to cup her ass cheek.

"How much does she want?" Valentina asked. Her large hand gripped Tomesha's round globe then slid back down to her thigh.

"I'm not sure. She hadn't shared that information with me. She's only said she'd let me know when she's chosen," Tomesha said.

Valentina's hand lingered.

"You're going to ask, aren't you?" Emerald chuckled.

"You know she is. Look how she's staring at poor Tomesha." Renee laughed. She reached for her goblet and motioned to the other vampires. "Come. Let's toast to a well-deserved night out at the club."

Emerald lifted her goblet, as did Valentina.

"I shall leave you to your—"

"No. Stay. Or do you have to go service someone else?" Valentina asked. Her hand took Tomesha's and tugged her to her.

Tomesha slipped down onto Valentina's lap. Another server walked past and held out her hand. Tomesha slipped the empty tray into it. It was common thing that servers did. They all looked out for each other.

She smiled at the vampire. Starla's teachings echoed in her mind.

Even if you aren't feeling the vampire completely, find something about them that is pleasing.

Tomesha's attention dropped down to Valentina's large breasts. She did have a thing for a woman's ample bosom. She shifted on the woman's lap, and it was then she felt the bulge beneath her hip.

"Does that bother you?" Valentina asked.

"No," Tomesha answered truthfully. She offered her another smile of assurance.

"To a night we all deserve. May we all find pleasure." Valentina lifted her goblet.

She wrapped a strong arm around Tomesha's waist as she leaned forward to touch her goblet to the other women's. She leaned back and took a healthy sip of the blood. Once she placed the cup down on the table, a hint of the liquid rested on her top lip. Tomesha reached out and scooped up a napkin and used it to blot the excess blood off her face.

"Thank you."

"You're welcome."

"Well, since you appear to have found your entertainment for the night, it would look as if we're going to be on our own," Renee said.

"You know she's always quick to find tasty pussy when we come here," Emerald said.

Tomesha's face warmed at the comment. Crude words were always thrown around in the club. She'd certainly heard worse.

Tomesha leaned into Valentina, determined to

serve the vampire well tonight. Her lips brushed Valentina's ear.

"Is that what you're looking for? A tasty pussy?" Tomesha whispered. Would this have been something she'd have asked anyone else before working at the feeding club?

Hell no.

But when it came to offering herself up for money, she was going to do her best to ensure her clients were satisfied. So far, those she'd serviced were satisfied and had tipped her well.

"I know I have found it. I can scent it." Valentina nuzzled her face into the crook of Tomesha's neck. The leather collar blocked her from Tomesha's main arteries. The woman's hand made its way down Tomesha's thighs. She spun Tomesha around so her back was to her chest. "Well, my friends. You two are slow to the choosing, and you know I don't like to share."

"We know." Emerald rolled her eyes. She knocked back the rest of her drink and reached for the decanter and refilled her goblet. She turned and glanced around the club. A slow grin spread across her face. "I'll be back around."

She stood and sauntered away from the table with the goblet in her hand. Renee chuckled and leaned back in her chair and sipped on her blood. Her gaze remained on Tomesha and Valentina.

"Maybe I'll just sit here and be jealous," Renee said.

Valentina chuckled low. Her hands slipped between Tomesha's legs. She automatically widened them to allow the vampire to have access. Her fingers arrived at Tomesha's core. Her breath hitched in her throat. She felt herself becoming aroused. She smile seductively and leaned back against Valentina.

Valentina's fingers parted her slit and connected with Tomesha's clit. When she'd first taken this job, she'd thought the main focus would be on the vampires, but she'd soon learned that vampires had a thing for ensuring their partners were pleased as well. Valentina's fingers dipped farther down and pushed into Tomesha. She was met with Tomesha's slickness. She pulled her finger out and brought it to her lips. She licked it clean with her chest rumbling a low growl.

"Just as I suspected. Sweet as I'm sure your blood will be," Valentina murmured.

She lifted Tomesha and turned her around so she could straddle her lap. Tomesha smiled coyly, playing into the part as she'd been taught. Her hand drifted down to the ties of her sheer dress and undid them. She bit her lip and allowed the material to fall off her shoulders. Valentina's gaze swept over her before landing on her breasts. Tomesha ignored those around them who may be watching. She concentrated on the vampire in front of her and inhaled sharply. She rotated her hips, her core rubbing Valentina's hard member, which earned a low moan from her new client.

This was the job she'd signed up for.

The job that would allow her to support her family.

That's all this was.

A job.

She'd never have thought her pleasure would be a priority for vampires. She thought she was to just serve and nothing else. It was no wonder the sex workers enjoyed their jobs immensely. She'd focus on the positive sides of this new life she was embracing.

CHAPTER SIX

"We shouldn't be wasting money on going out for dinner." Tarek stood in the living room and rested his hands on his waist, his infamous scowl embedded.

She remembered the days when he used to smile. He was quite handsome and reminded her of their late father. It had been so long ago since he'd laughed and smiled freely that it made her sad to think of the man he'd become.

"This is the first time we've gone out in..." Tomesha had to pause. When was the last time they had eaten at a restaurant or diner? She racked her brain. "Well, now that I think of it, I can't even remember when we have. One time isn't going to hurt." She ambled over to him and smiled.

He sighed and folded his arms. "I just don't like this," he grumbled.

"Eating or the fact that I'm paying?" She tried not to let it hurt her feelings.

It had been a little over two months since she'd started working at the feeding club. The cash flowing in had been a great help for her family. They were caught up on their rent. They had food in the pantry and fridge. She'd even been able to purchase new clothing for all of them.

"Well, I guess I'm ready," Delonda announced, strolling into the room.

Tomesha turned and grinned at the sight of their grandmother in a pretty dress and her new shoes. Her eyes were bright, and at the moment, it would appear she was in her right state of mind.

"Look at you!" Tomesha rushed over to Delonda and took hold of her hands. She pressed a kiss to each of her cheeks. "You're so beautiful, Gran."

"Oh, girl, please. Something must be wrong with your eyes." Delonda chuckled. She eyed Tarek and gave an approving nod. "You're looking quite dashing over there, Tarek. Just like your father when he was younger."

Tomesha entwined her fingers with her grandmother's and walked alongside her. Delonda stopped in front of Tarek and brushed the backs of her fingers on his cheek. He visibly relaxed at her touch.

"You shouldn't be so angry all of the time, grandson," Delonda whispered.

"I'm not." Tarek sniffed and glanced away.

Tomesha bit her lip to keep her eyes from filling with tears. She released her grandmother's hand and waved hers in front of her eyes. This wasn't supposed to be an emotional moment. They were meant to be enjoying each other's company while she spoiled them a bit with dinner out on the town.

"You are. I can sense it. Life has a way of beating us all down, and we're strong enough to survive anything. Together." Delonda's hand slid down to his chest and patted him above his heart. She motioned for him to lower his head.

He bent down, and she pressed a kiss to his cheek. He lifted his head, and a ghost of a smile appeared.

"Now, let's go out for dinner and enjoy each other's company. Yes?"

"Yes, ma'am," he replied.

His gaze flicked to hers for a moment. He motioned for them to head to the door. They stepped outside while he locked up the house. Tomesha offered her grandmother her arm and assisted her down the few steps of the porch. The small diner they were going to wasn't located far from their home. They lived in a residential area populated with people like them. Hard-working humans who were just trying to make it.

Tarek stayed close behind them while they walked arm in arm.

"It's such a beautiful day, isn't it?" Tomesha gazed at the sky. It was a mixture of blues with a little darkness to it. The clouds were scattered about, and the sun was nowhere to be seen. She inhaled and could almost tell there was going to be rain later. They were going to dine early so they'd make it home before darkness settled in and the rainstorm arrived. Tomesha glanced over at her grandmother who had a small smile on her face.

"It is. I remember a day when your father was younger. I had extra money and wanted to see his face light up. I took him into town so we could purchase him a toy." Delonda patted her on the arm as she went into the tale of their father's childhood.

Tomesha loved hearing about the past. Her grandmother was a wealth of knowledge. Even when she slipped away from them and was in her delirium, a part of her still stayed around.

"I remember Dad talking about his favorite car you had purchased him," Tarek spoke up. "He always talked about how much he loved that damn thing. He'd wanted to get me one like it, but he could never find one."

Tomesha remained quiet. Maynard Clay had been a man of few words when he'd returned from war. His bottle of whiskey had been all he'd wanted. Occasionally, he'd spoken of the past. Tomesha believed that it hurt for him to be in the present with their mother not there. He'd lost a part of himself in the war, and then when his wife died, that had taken the rest of him. He'd been a shell of his former self and never recovered.

Then he'd gone missing. They never knew exactly what had happened to him. His disappearance had been blamed on the lycans. She shuddered to think of the attacks just over two years ago. Lycans had targeted their town, but thankfully, the vampire army successfully defended it, but not without the cost of human casualties.

"I miss him and Mom," Tomesha murmured.

It wasn't often they spoke of her parents. Maynard and Maggie had been a handsome couple, but unfortunately, fate had other plans for them. She hoped one day she'd find someone who loved her as much as her father had loved her mother. Maggie had been the apple of Maynard's eye.

"We all do, but just know they'll forever live in our hearts. No grief allowed today," Delonda said. Her voice was strong, and her eyes were just as clear.

"Gran, what would we do without you?" Tomesha said.

"Oh, I'm sure you would figure it out. You two are Clays, and there is a strength inside the both you that gives you the will to survive."

Tomesha glanced over her shoulder at her brother. He walked with his hands in his pockets. He had a relaxed look to him. Maybe this was what they all needed. Just one day to escape the reality of what they faced. Their eyes met, and he had the nerve to wink at her. She gasped and smiled at him.

Yes, this was what they needed.

She turned back around and continued on their trek. Delonda spoke of what she planned to cook the next day. Excitement bubbled out of her as she gushed about all the baking she had planned. They arrived at the center of town and were only a block away from the diner.

There were plenty of pedestrians out for the day. It looked as if everyone was taking advantage of the decent weather before the storm. They stopped at a corner and waited for the light to change. Cars made their way along the street.

"We're almost there." Tomesha pointed to the diner's sign just up ahead.

"Oh, thank God. This walk has certainly made me hungry," Delonda said.

"Me, too." Tomesha couldn't wait to see what the diner had to offer. She'd heard good things about it from a few of the servers at the club. Her small purse that rested against her hip had enough money to ensure they each could order what they wanted.

"Hey!" someone called out.

Tomesha swiveled toward the voice. Two men stood against the brick building nearest them. She stiffened at the sight of them. Their sinister grins caused her to go on guard. They were dressed as if they had just come from working in the local factory.

"Ignore them," Tarek muttered behind them. He moved closer to her and folded his arms. He glared over at them while they waited to cross the street.

"I'm talking to you, girl. Don't hide behind him. We just want to talk with you for a second," one of the men called out.

"Leave her be," Tarek snapped.

Tomesha reached out a hand and rested it on his forearm. His muscles were tensed as he continued to glare at the men.

"You ignore them," she said softly.

He wasn't even following his own advice. She gave a tight squeeze. The men were probably drunk and being assholes. She eyed them and had never seen them before.

"Come. The light has turned."

The others who were waiting for the light began walking across the street.

"How you get time with the whore? We want a piece of her, too. Don't be a cock-blocker," the taller of the two said.

"What the fuck did you say?" Tarek growled.

Tomesha pulled Delonda back from the street. Tarek spun and stalked toward them. Tomesha released her grandmother and tried to tug her brother back from the men.

"Oh, did we touch a nerve? He must have feelings for her." The second one laughed.

"She's my sister and she's not a whore," Tarek shouted.

Trying to hold him back was like stopping a charging bull. Her feet slid on the stone sidewalk.

"Tarek. Let it go. It's all right," she cried out. She didn't want her brother to get hurt at the expense of two drunken men shouting barbs at her. She'd admit it hurt, but she'd live with it. What she couldn't live with was if her brother got hurt defending her, or even killed.

"What are you going to do? Defend her honor?" the taller of the two snapped.

"What honor? She's a whore. She sells her body for the vampires. She's too good to take a human cock?" The shorter one grabbed his junk and sent a wink her way.

"Get off me. Go back to Gran." Tarek shook her hands off him.

"No. Come back. Ignore them!" she shouted.

Delonda arrived at her side as she dove for Tarek again.

"Stay back, my dear," Delonda said.

"But Gran," Tomesha cried.

Tears filled her eyes, and she watched her brother size up with both men. The second one moved behind him. Tears began to flow, and she wiped her face. She glanced around. Most of the pedestrians ignored the commotion.

"Someone, help!"

"What kind of man lets his sister whore herself out to the vampires?" The taller one was about the same height as Tarek. He poked his fingers into Tarek's chest and pushed.

"Watch what you fucking say about my sister." Tarek shoved the first man away from him.

Two black SUVs came to a screeching halt in the street near the curb. The back doors flew open, and men dressed in royal vampire uniforms stepped out. Tomesha recognized the uniforms immediately. The dark clothing, weapons, and the crest imprinted in blue on their chests spoke of the house of the middle vampire princess.

Lethia Riskel.

Was the princess in town? She was sure the entire town would have heard if the warden of their territory was present. Tomesha watched the vampire guards stalk toward her brother and the other two men.

"What is the meaning of this?" the first of the vampires demanded. His dark hair was swept back from his face in intricate braids. His glare was hard and threatening.

Tomesha sensed this situation was about to go farther south.

"Nothing you should worry about. This is human business," the shorter of the two men said.

Tomesha's eyes widened at the boldness of the idiot. Did he not realize who he was speaking to?

"It doesn't look like nothing," another vampire guard with blond hair replied. He folded his arms. His bicep muscles bulged as he glared at the men.

Four guards stood around, each of them outfitted with enough weapons for a small militia.

"Please. Don't hurt my brother. He was defending me from them." Tomesha stepped forward. She'd be damned if the vampires thought her brother was like those thugs. That's what they were. They were starting stuff for no reason.

"Stay out of this, Tomesha," Tarek said over his shoulder.

"Is that so?" the first guard said. He moved over to her.

She swallowed hard at the size difference between the two of them. She tilted her head back and nodded.

"Yes. My brother, grandmother, and I were on the way to dinner when these two men started shouting insults about me," she said.

The blond guard stepped between Tarek and the men and motioned for him to come to her and Delonda.

"Why would they do that?" the guard asked. He softened his facial features.

Tomesha looked away. A crowd stood around, observing. None of them had been willing to help Tarek, but they had no problem being nosey. Tomesha's gaze landed on the second black truck. A shiver rippled down her spine. There was someone else in the back of it that she couldn't see, but she sensed their eyes on her.

Who was it?

She tried to see, but the vampire before her moved to cut her view of the truck. She blinked and focused back on him.

"I work for the madam," she said quietly. From her experience working at the club, she was sure he'd heard of her. She just didn't want the humans standing around to hear what she'd said.

He nodded. "We'll take care of these two, ma'am. Would you like an escort to your destination?"

Tomesha blinked and peered over at her brother then her grandmother. This wasn't what she'd expected. The vampire hadn't even batted an eye at her announcement.

"No. We should be fine. We're just going to the diner right over there." She tilted her head in that direction.

"Very well then. Please go on and enjoy your dinner. We'll take care of these two. They won't bother you again," the vampire guard assured her.

Tomesha glanced over and found the two men pressed against the building with their hands resting on it. Some satisfaction filled her to see the vampire guards searching them. She hoped they'd learn their lesson.

But how did they know she worked at the feeding club? She'd never seen them before. At least, she didn't think she had. She made a mental note to pay closer attention to her surroundings when she went to work.

"Thank you." Tomesha offered her arm to her

grandmother who entwined hers with Tomesha's. She gave the vampires a smile and ushered Delonda across the street with a very visibly pissed-off Tarek alongside them.

They walked in silence for a moment before Tomesha reached out and slid her hand into her brother's. He turned to her with a surprised look in his eyes. He didn't say a word but squeezed her hand. No words needed to be said between them. Tarek had always been her defender. Even when they were young children. It was who he was.

"I hope you two still have your appetite," Tomesha said as they arrived at the diner's entrance. She checked behind them, and her gaze landed on the black SUV. Again, she felt as if whoever sat back there watched her. She didn't know how, but she was sure they were. If only she could see through the dark tint on the windows. She turned back to her brother and grandmother. She dug deep for a genuine smile. "Let's not have that spoil our family dinner."

Tarek opened the door for them. She allowed Delonda to enter first. With one last look at the vehicle, she entered the building after her grand-mother. Tarek followed them. This was much needed for her family, and she refused to have two random men spoil it for them.

No matter what they called her, she knew who Tomesha Clay was.

She walked over to the hostess. "A table for three, please."

CHAPTER SEVEN

"The human police will charge them with public intoxication." Talbot slid back into the SUV next to Dru.

The human police had placed the two men in the back of their squad car. She glanced back down the street where the human and her family had disappeared. She and her men had just arrived in the small town of Butterbush, North Carolina.

After much research into Solomon Winterborne, there had finally been a lead, and it was in this town. She'd utilized her most resourceful vampires and human contacts to track it down.

They were to report directly to the central post where she had a meeting set up with the postmaster of Butterbush. They had sent word the post was coming under inspection with her assuming the new title of general. She didn't want anyone to suspect anything else. This reason for arriving in town would not be suspicious. As the general of Lethia's army, she had every right to come and inspect each vampire army post throughout their territory to ensure they were all functioning to the highest capacity. Their military posts were vital. They were to provide a military presence to deter the enemy as well acting as a training facility for their warriors.

She'd been reading the file on Postmaster Eldon Alexander when their driver, Orenda, released a curse. There was about to be a violent altercation between three men. Dru had given the word to intervene. The woman's scream for help had reached her, but she hadn't known where the scream had originated from.

The entire time Talbot and Niles were defusing the situation, Dru couldn't take her eyes off the beautiful young woman who'd been in tears. Dru had to resist stepping from the vehicle to see to her. She had her orders, and comforting a female wasn't amongst them. This mission was extremely important, and Dru refused to fail her queen.

But it hadn't kept her from memorizing the woman's features. Her large brown eyes, her long dark hair, her smooth brown skin, and her shapely form that wasn't hidden by her dress. Dru cleared her throat and acted as nonchalantly as she could.

"Are the females okay?" she asked.

The police cruiser pulled off. The crowd was now gone. Everything appeared back to normal. She settled in her seat as Orenda put the vehicle in drive and continued. She halted at the red light where the human and her family had crossed. Dru glanced in the direction they had gone, but there were no signs of them. She wasn't sure why her curiosity was piqued about this woman.

"They seemed to be. The male with them was defending her," Talbot said.

"Good," Dru murmured. At least the woman had someone willing to defend her. Dru tried to push her face from her mind. She needed to be prepared for this meeting.

She picked up her tablet and read through the files on the postmaster again. It would appear that Postmaster Alexander had been in charge of Butterbush for a little over twenty-five years. He'd been promoted when the last postmaster had retired. She scanned the file and found him to be a warrior who'd received multiple awards and recognitions throughout his career.

They drove through the town which appeared to have grown since the last time Dru had been there. She'd accompanied Lethia there about ten years ago, but she'd been assigned to other duties at the time and had not met with the postmaster. She set the device down on her lap and watched the scenery flow past.

She wondered where the woman lived—

Dru blinked.

She had to get her out of her head. She highly doubted they'd cross paths while she was here to hunt down a fugitive.

Orenda guided the vehicle onto a dirt road. The SUV ahead of them held the other vampires who'd accompanied them. They were to appear as if they were on official royal business representing Lethia's house. The post was due for inspections anyway. It had been several years since a member from Lethia's house had paid them a visit.

They drove down the long winding road until they arrived at the first of several buildings on the military base, which was old, and some of the buildings had been constructed underground. For centuries, these posts had existed in secrecy. It wasn't until the war and the vampires had taken over that many of the bases had been renovated to include buildings aboveground. There was no need to hide any longer.

Vampires were the superior race and in charge.

There was a training field within sight. Dru made a mental note to assess their training to ensure it was up to her standard. She wasn't sure how long she'd be here in Butterbush, but she'd ensure this post was thoroughly inspected before she left.

Hopefully with the vampire traitor in chains— or with his head in a bag.

She refused to return to the queen empty-handed.

"We're here, General." Orenda brought the vehicle to a halt in front of the main building.

Dru eyed the tall structure and the men who exited. They came out in formation and lined the stairs. She took notice of Postmaster Alexander being one of them. He stood in his full formal uniform, front and center.

Talbot and the others left the vehicle. Her door was opened. Dru nodded to the vampire and stepped out. Her long auburn hair was pulled back from her face in a top bun. She, too, had on her formal warrior uniform. One thing that was new was her insignia stating her position of general. She stalked toward the postmaster with Talbot, Orenda, and her other warriors behind her.

"General Moldark. Welcome to Butterbush," Postmaster Alexander stated.

He and the other warriors with him stood to full attention. She stopped in front of him and met his gaze before sweeping hers to the others. She gave a nod.

"Postmaster Alexander."

The warriors pounded their fists above their hearts. She returned the motion.

She met the postmaster's gaze. "At ease, Postmaster. Thank you for the warm welcome."

"I was ecstatic to learn you would be making it a priority to inspect the posts. You'll find Butterbush to be a top-notch," he said.

"We'll see about that," she muttered. She nodded to the building. "Shall we?"

"But of course. Please follow me." He nodded, too, spun on his heel, and headed up the stairs.

She followed him. Once their meetings were

done for the day, it would give her time to start on the real reason why she was in this town.

* * *

"I AM IMPRESSED." Dru sat back at the head of the conference table.

Since they had entered the room, she'd received presentation after presentation on the workings of the post. Alexander was very thorough and appeared to be the correct choice in succeeding the previous postmaster. Talbot was positioned by the wall behind her while the other warriors were outside the room securing the area. She leaned forward and remembered mention of something in Alexander's file.

"Now, tell me about the lycan attacks that occurred recently."

The postmaster stood tall and met her gaze. A snarl appeared on his face.

"Those mangy animals thought they'd come into my town and try to overrun our hold," he stated.

When Azura was causing her ruckus, lycans all over the country were going on the attack. Not only had the lycans invaded towns that had little to no vampire involvement, but some had grown bold and infiltrated towns with strong vampire military holds.

He went into an elaborate description of the events that had taken place. He discussed utilizing not only the active vampire warriors but those who were in training. They had succeeded in protecting the townspeople of Butterbush.

"How many vampire casualties were there?" she asked.

"More than we would have liked. We lost seven good vampires during that time. Humans, we're not quite sure. Some bodies were never found and have been marked as missing." The postmaster stood next to the wall where the holograms had been projected for his presentation.

"Do we know how many of the humans were changed?" she asked.

"That we do not know. We're assuming the humans' bodies that we did not recover are now lycans, General."

Dru gave a short jerk of her head. This wasn't surprising news to her. That was why the lycans were going on the attack. They were trying to change as many humans as they could to increase their numbers. They didn't care if the humans objected to the change. They couldn't care less if the humans did not survive the change. All Azura cared about was making more lycans.

Dru pushed back from the table and stood. It had been a long day, but she wasn't done with her first day at the base.

"Take me to the training grounds. I want to see the new warriors in action," she stated.

"Yes, General." He strode over to the door and opened it for her.

Talbot fell in line behind her as she exited the boardroom. She'd been cooped up entirely too long. Dru wasn't used to being in boardrooms and meetings. She was a warrior who stayed on the move. Even when she had to work in her office, she normally stood while she hashed out her plans.

Their footsteps echoed through the halls as the postmaster guided them outside. Darkness was upon them, but the grounds were very much alive. The sounds of metal clashing with metal filled the air. Dru had a love for the art of fighting. She'd trained in the deadliest of combat. She desired to the be fiercest fighter for the crown.

"Our warriors take great pride in their skills they're developing. We've studied many of the skills that you have established yourself," Alexander said.

"Is that so?" she murmured.

They strolled along a dirt path and headed toward the first area where warriors were being schooled in hand-to-hand combat. This was extremely important for foot soldiers. Dru scanned the area and remained silent. She didn't want to distract the young warriors from their lesson, but that didn't go to plan. Whispers must have gone around about her arrival. She could practically palpate the excitement among the warriors.

"Gather round," Alexander called out.

Talbot and Orenda were behind her. The warriors fell into a formation and stood to attention. Seeing how they recognized her status from the moment their attention landed on her gave her the sense that the trainers here were doing their jobs well.

The postmaster motioned to Dru and beamed with pride. "Warriors. We have an honored guest visiting our post. Please welcome the esteemed General Moldark, the right hand of your commander, Princess Lethia Riskel."

Wide eyes watched her. She remembered being in their shoes so many years before. She, too, had been a young warrior trying to learn all that she could, and having an important member of the royal court visiting had been a big deal. The need to want to impress and be chosen for an important role had blossomed in her chest. She still remembered the pledge she'd made to herself.

Be the best that you can be.

"Thank you for such a warm welcome. Butterbush appears to be in very good hands under the guidance of Postmaster Alexander." Dru walked up to the front line of the warriors and slowly made her way through their lineup. "You have taken a pledge that is important. Not only have you pledged your life to defend the crown, but you're here to defend vampires everywhere."

Dru spoke from the heart.

"Our kind has been under threat for centuries, and recently it has increased. Our enemies are constantly trying to overthrow us." Just the mention of lycans had the air thick with tension. "I have heard praise of how well this post defended the town. You should be proud. That is why posts like this are so important. You're our first line of defense against the enemy."

She'd made her way through the entire group and stalked back to the front. She turned to them and folded her hands behind her back.

"General, your words will not be forgotten."

Alexander came to stand next to her. "I'm sure each warrior before you will hold them near and dear to their hearts."

"I hope so. I was once in their shoes," she stated.

"We all were. This goes to show that hard work pays off and you'll be rewarded well for it." He motioned to the group. "How about a demonstration of the skills they have learned."

"That would be perfect," Dru murmured.

Talbot came to her side and leaned down close to her. "General, while we've been here, I took the liberty to send Niles on. He'll start scouting the town for the fugitive." He kept his voice low.

She nodded to confirm she'd heard him. Niles was the one vampire who could probably pass for a human. She trusted that he could probably get information out of humans before she or Talbot could.

"Good thinking," she replied.

The warriors created a half circle, and two males were chosen for the first demonstration. Talbot stepped back from her as the warriors faced her then pounded their fists over their hearts.

"Hank and Roman have been quick studies," Alexander noted as he came to stand beside her.

The two males circled each other. She could already sense they both had skills.

Oh, to be a new warrior again. She held back a smile at the other's reaction when Hank tossed Roman over his shoulder to the ground. The fight grew fiercer, and this reminded her of why she loved what she did when it came to training warriors.

The hunger in their eyes. The desire to impress their general. She saw herself in both of the males. When the bout was over, Hank was deemed the winner. The other warriors cheered and went over to the two warriors.

The air fell quiet as Dru walked over to the two vampires. She held out her hand for Roman who was once again on the ground. He stared at her hand in shock. Dru was never too good to help a warrior who fought for her. He took her hand and allowed her to help him stand.

"That was some fine fighting. Now tell me, how did he best you twice?" she asked.

The teacher in her was never far away. Other warriors called out their answers and suggestions. She had the two replay the move and guided them on how to evade such a thing the next time. All eyes were on her as she went through evasive maneuvers.

After her short lesson, she went back to Talbot and Alexander.

"You have done a fine job," Dru said to Alexander.

He beamed liked a proud papa of his children. This class of warriors were patient, open to listening and receiving suggestions.

"Thank you, General. They still have much to learn—"

"And I'm sure you'll continue to ensure the warriors here will be thoroughly trained to fight for their king and queen," she said.

"Every vampire here will lay down their life for the crown," Alexander said fiercely.

"Good. Now let's walk around. I want to see the other training facilities," she demanded.

"Please, General. Follow me."

CHAPTER EIGHT

"General, please allow us to escort you out tonight," Alexander said.

Dru had received tours of all of the training facilities which she was impressed by. They had all of the latest technology which she'd expect.

"It is not necessary," she said.

They entered through the back doors of the main building. Talbot and Orenda trailed behind them. She was anxious to leave so they could find out if Niles had discovered anything yet.

The post itself was a solid facility, but for some strange reason something was off with the town.

Why would lycans attack a town that was known to have a strong vampire military post? That would be suicide, but then again, Azura hadn't been a sound alpha. The woman had been deranged, and she'd sent more than one group of lycans to their deaths on purpose.

Had that attack been a test for the vampire military? Or was there some other reason the lycans had chosen Butterbush? So many questions continued to come to Dru. Another main one was why had the lycans stopped? They were not known to be entirely too sensible. Was there something here in this town they wanted besides the humans? Or was it someone here who'd stopped them besides the vampires defending the town?

"But you must feed. Do you not require nourishment?" Alexander came to stand in front of her.

She came to complete stop, sighed, and met his gaze. She was sure her men would appreciate a good healthy feeding. Her last meal had to have been yesterday. The last few days before leaving for this mission were all a blur.

"We do, Postmaster. What do you have in mind?" Dru immediately regretted the question by the smile that appeared on his face.

"Why, Butterbush has the best club in all of

North America. Madam Rice has spared no expense here in our quaint little town to ensure that all of our warriors are well taken care of," Alexander boasted.

Dru didn't have time to spend at a feeding club. This important mission required that she remained focused. Alexander must have read the hesitation in her expression.

"Please. Allow me to escort you there for at least one night. You and your men have traveled long and hard to get here. I'm sure you're going to be inspecting more than just the base. Why not enjoy one night at Madam's?" Alexander folded his arms and arched an eyebrow.

She sensed the eyes of her men on her. She expected a lot from them while here in North Carolina. She guessed she could give them one night to enjoy before they jumped feetfirst into work.

"Fine. We'll go because you have been such a gracious host to us," she murmured.

"Very well. We've also made accommodations for you and your warriors at the local inn. They'll be expecting you as well." The postmaster bowed his head.

"Postmaster Alexander!" someone called out.

Dru peered over his shoulder. A slender woman rushed down the hall in a frugal blouse, slacks, and with her hair up in a tight bun on top of her head. She carried a tablet in front of her as she made her way to them.

"Yes, Silvanna?" Alexander turned toward her.

She arrived at his side with the most flustered expression. "I was trying to catch you, sir."

"Where are my manners? Allow me to do introductions first. General Moldark, this here is my assistant, Silvanna Webb. Silvanna, this is General Moldark." Alexander motioned between the two of them.

"It's nice to meet you, General," Silvanna said. A blush spread across her cheeks. She reached out a hand to Dru.

"Likewise." Dru shook the woman's hand before stepping back.

"Well, what is the matter, Silvanna?" Alexander asked her.

"I have confirmed with the feeding club your and our esteemed guests' attendance this evening," Silvanna announced.

Alexander flicked his gaze to Dru who arched her eyebrow. Apparently, the postmaster had been sure he was going to convince her to attend tonight.

"I just wanted to ensure the club would be able to take a large crowd. You know we're a small town, and sometimes with all the warriors, the club could be overextended," Alexander explained. He tugged at the collar of his shirt.

"I see." Dru released a sigh. One visit wouldn't hurt. She wouldn't want to insult the postmaster who was trying to lay down the red carpet for her and her warriors. "It's fine. No worries. We shall attend Madam's and enjoy ourselves."

"Fantastic." He straightened and turned back to Silvanna. "Ready the transportation for us."

Silvanna continued with a few other issues with him.

Dru moved over to stand near Talbot to give them a moment to finish their conversation. Dru leaned toward Talbot and dropped the level of her voice so that the postmaster and his assistant wouldn't overhear her.

"We'll stay an appropriate amount of time so that our host will not be insulted," Dru murmured.

"Yes, General."

"And I want on-the-hour updates from Niles." She should be out there with the vampire seeking out the traitor, but for now, she had to play the part of the general inspecting one of the military posts.

This secret mission had to be kept under wraps. If this Solomon truly lived, she did not want him to know she was on his trail.

"He's aware. He's currently infiltrating a human bar, not too far from the center of town," Talbot replied.

"General. Our transportation is ready," the postmaster said.

Dru spun on her heel and smiled. "Lead the way, Postmaster."

They stalked through the building and exited through the front doors. Awaiting them were a few dark military vehicles. A warrior opened the door to the one in the center for her. She entered and took her seat. Talbot and the postmaster joined her. Their door shut behind them, sealing them inside.

"These are a new sunproof armored vehicle," Alexander said.

Dru took in the sleek appearance of the interior and nodded. The latest technology was rolling out on vehicles to allow the vampires to travel during the brightest of days.

"These are nice. I remember seeing the specs on the first few test vehicles," Dru noted.

"Less than one percent of UV rays pass through this glass," Alexander said.

The vehicle rocked as the driver began following the one in the front.

The ride to town didn't take long. Dru tried to keep her features from displaying her boredom. Alexander had moved on to speak about the town of Butterbush. Dru's patience was wearing thin, but she kept a small smile while he shared some history of the town.

"It would appear we're here," Alexander said.

With the multitude of businesses in the area, Dru assumed they were at the center of town. The club stood like a dark jewel in the heart of the city's business district. Its sleek structure was crafted from black slate, the surface gleaming beneath the moon's rays. Tall panes of glass framed in gold reflected the world outside, while deep-onyx awnings hung over the windows, casting shadows that hinted at what awaited them within. The entrance, two massive doors, lavishly painted in gold, gleamed bright against the stark darkness of the building.

Dru's fangs pushed at her gums. She inhaled sharply, a little disturbed that she couldn't control her body's reactions. She eyed the tall muscular vampire guard who made his way to the vehicles.

"Greetings," his deep baritone voice greeted them. His dark shades hid his eyes from her.

She took his extended hand and allowed him to assist her from the vehicle.

"Good evening," she murmured.

Postmaster Alexander and Talbot exited. She took in the street and the few figures ambling around. The businesses in the area were still open, alluding to the notation that they either catered to vampires or they were owned by vampires. From listening to tales from Alima, Dru knew that most humans avoided walking around at night.

Dru frowned at the thought. Vampires should be able to control themselves, but she knew Alima spoke of the rogue vampires who'd been a thorn in her side for years. Rogues did not align with the laws set for vampires. They felt they were above the laws and could do what they wished. Before the lycans began attacking, it had been the rogue vampires they had been dealing with. Not that the rogues had gone away and become law-abiding citizens. Dru and the others had to deal with both rogues and lycans. Dru had come up with special teams of warriors to focus just policing the rogues while the lycans became top priority.

"Welcome to Madam Rice's, General." The

security guard gave a bow. He spun on his heel and walked over to the doorway. He opened one of the massive doors and bowed his head again. "My name is Dommick. If I can be of service, please don't hesitate to call on me. Enjoy everything Madam has to offer you tonight."

"Thank you, Dommick," Dru murmured. A thrill zipped through her. She pushed down the excitement. She wouldn't drink from a live donor. She knew where that would lead while being in Madam's. She needed a clear mind tonight, and the extracurricular activities that would be available with a live feeding would be distracting.

They entered the building. The moment the door closed behind them, the outside world ceased to exist. The faint thrum of music carried through the air which mingled with the sweet floral scent of roses and the delicious hint of copper—blood. The low pulse of the beat caused Dru's heart to skip a beat as anticipation filled her.

The dark marble walls were painted with gold veins which shimmered in the soft light of the crystal sconces. White marble floors carried the echo of their footsteps as they strode deeper into the building. Velvet crimson benches lined the space, creating a seating area near the entrance for patrons who either needed to wait their turn to enter the lower domain, or for those who needed to wait for their transportation.

At the center of the foyer, a winding staircase would carry them to the lower level, the heart of the club. The iron banister continued the decor of obsidian and gold. Something urged Dru to hurry and descend the alluring staircase. She inhaled again, and that sense of urgency grew.

When was the last time she'd fed?

Was that why she was feeling this way?

They went down the winding staircase and arrived at a welcoming area just before the club's entrance where a small female with extremely long blonde hair and bright-blue eyes waited for them. Her tight leather dress stopped mid-calf, and heels added about six inches to her height.

"General. Postmaster. Welcome to Madam Rice's," she said. Her fangs peeked from underneath her ruby-red lips. She offered them a warm smile. "My name is Callidora. I am tonight's hostess. Come. I already have your tables ready for you."

"You shall enjoy tonight, General. Even if it's just a drink from prepared blood. This establishment has the most unique of blood types." The postmaster chuckled and followed Callidora.

Dru stayed behind and motioned to the club to Talbot and Orenda. "Enjoy yourselves. I do not plan to stay long."

"When you leave, we leave," Talbot said.

Orenda gave him a sharp look. Dru bit back a chuckle at her warriors. She respected Talbot's loyalty to the mission, but tonight he could relax a little.

"I'm serious. Enjoy yourselves tonight. Tomorrow, we hunt the traitor."

CHAPTER NINE

A knock sounded at her door. Tomesha turned from her floor-length mirror in her suite at the club. Today she had a good feeling about her upcoming shift. A light fluttering commenced in her stomach. Earlier, her family had enjoyed dinner together, and she couldn't have been happier. Tarek had even relaxed a bit and cracked a couple of jokes. It had almost felt as if things were normal again in their family.

She'd designed another dress that she was going to wear for the first time. She'd taken the sheer material and wrapped it around herself in a fashion that put her cleavage on display and showed off her soft brown thighs. Her outfits had been the talk of the other donors. A few had asked if she could make their outfits and offered to pay her for her time.

"Who could this be?" Tomesha murmured. She wasn't late or expecting any clients that she was aware of. She opened the door and found Mistress's trusted assistant standing in the hallway.

"Aisling." Tomesha blinked.

It wasn't often the assistant presented herself. She usually existed in the background while assisting with all of the workings of the club. Mistress was very hands-on when it came to the human donors.

"Tomesha. You are well?" Aisling asked.

"I am. How are you?" Tomesha grew a little nervous. If Aisling was coming to see her, some-thing must be wrong. Had she had a complaint? Tomesha would have known if any of her clients were not happy. She tried her best to ensure they all enjoyed themselves with her. Each of her clients were unique, and their time with her was very different. She chewed on her bottom lip as the worry grew.

"I am well. Thank you for asking. You're being

summoned to Mistress. Please walk with me." Aisling motioned for her to step out of her quarters.

She was being summoned. Oh, crap. She must have done something wrong. She nodded and pulled the door to her suite closed behind her.

"Of course." She smiled and attempted to appear calm.

They walked in silence. Tomesha tried to think of the last few days she'd worked and couldn't think of any issues that had come up. She was sure her clients would have shared with her any disappointments.

But none had ever left her unsatisfied—at least not sexually.

They were all disappointed that she was still required to wear the collar and wristbands. It had been a while since she'd started, and Mistress still wasn't allowing any vampire to feed from her. Tomesha's clientele had grown, but she'd a few customers who visited her quite often and paid her handsomely for her time.

"Have I done something wrong?" Tomesha asked. In the past few weeks, her confidence had grown by leaps and bounds, but now that she was being summoned to Mistress, she was having doubts about herself. She was no longer under Starla's watch. Her mentor had praised her and was always close by if she needed anything.

They descended a stairwell that took them farther underground. The club extended beneath the earth's surface. Since working here, she'd learned a lot about the vampire underground tunnels that extended across town. It was a wonder to see how vampires used to travel during the daylight centuries ago.

"You shall soon learn. Mistress would like to speak with you." Aisling guided her through the back hallways of the administration side.

Tomesha held back rolling her eyes. She wished Aisling would give her a little more to go on so she could be prepared for this impromptu meeting.

Well, whatever it is I did wrong, I'm sure Mistress will tell me.

Tomesha sent up a prayer that she wasn't about to be fired. She inhaled sharply at the thought. She couldn't afford to not have this job. The money she was making was mind-boggling, and once she was allowed to become a fully fledged donor, it would only increase. Her family needed this.

They arrived at their destination, and Tomesha's breath caught in her throat. A set of massive double doors awaited her—glossy black lacquer etched with golden thorns. Aisling rapped on a door with two quick taps.

"Come in." Mistress's muffled voice came through.

Aisling nodded to Tomesha as she stood back.

Tomesha smiled and reached for the handles. She pushed them open to reveal a chamber steeped in power. Tomesha had never stepped foot inside Mistress's office until now. She'd heard rumors of it but never had the pleasure of being summoned to her before. Any time Mistress met with her and the other donors, it was upstairs in one of the lounges.

Tomesha's curiosity got the best of her. Her gaze quickly swept the room, taking in the walls draped in blood-red silk, their folds heavy and consuming, while the marble floor beneath gleamed like dark glass. The sound of the doors closing behind her caused her heart to skip a beat. She was now alone with Mistress in her domain.

Her steps echoed too loudly in the quiet. Gilded mirrors hung at angles that caught every move-ment, reflecting the room like a watchful set of eyes. Nothing would go unnoticed here. This office was a mixture of luxury, beauty, and power. Tomesha's stomach twisted in knots.

In the heart of the room, Romana's desk stood

—a colossal black wood monolith intricately carved with serpents and roses engaged in an eternal struggle. Behind the desk sat Mistress in her oversized plush chair. She was a portrait of grace wrapped in feminine elegance. Her dark gown clung to her, the fabric shimmering faintly whenever she moved. She silently watched Tomesha's every step.

"Mistress." Tomesha stopped in front of the desk. Her hands trembled. She balled them into fists to keep from revealing her nervousness. She reached deep inside and pulled up all of her confidence. If she were to be disciplined for something, then she'd take it like a woman.

"Tomesha, you look ravishing in your uniform. A new design?" Romana leaned back and eyed Tomesha.

Her heart fluttered. Tomesha glanced down at herself, and pride overtook her. She always worked hard to ensure she looked her best. She'd gained the weight back she'd lost from rationing her meals. No longer did she have a sunken face; there was a little extra meat on her bones now that she was proud of.

"Thank you, Mistress. Yes, it's a new design of mine." She smiled and folded her hands in front of her. Maybe she wasn't here because of a complaint or issue.

"I'm sure you're wondering why I have summoned you." Mistress stood and strolled around her massive desk. Her dress trailed behind her with a soft rustling on the floor. She sat on the edge of the desk.

"Yes, Mistress. Have I done something wrong?" Tomesha boldly asked.

Romana smirked and cocked her head. "You're not here for any wrongdoings. Quite the opposite. I've called you down here because we're going to have a very distinguished guest that I would like you to entertain tonight."

Tomesha's eyebrows rose at this announcement. Excitement filled her. This was completely opposite of what she thought she was being summoned for.

She was being chosen for an honored guest. That was a compliment from Mistress.

"Thank you, Mistress." Tomesha stood taller and continued to listen.

"There is no need to thank me. I have been monitoring you, and you have quite the following. I can't tell you how many requests I have received from vampires clamoring to be the first to drink from you." She pushed off the desk and came to stand in front of Tomesha. She tilted Tomesha's chin back and stared down into her eyes. "But no amount of money was good enough. I was saving the first taste of your blood for a high-profile guest, and she should be arriving any minute now."

Tomesha blinked. Today would be the day she'd have her first bite. Her heart pounded against her chest wall. The rapid succession caused her to have to take a deep breath. Romana stepped away from her and reached for the crystal decanter and goblet that sat upon her desk. She poured herself a drink. The familiar copper scent reached Tomesha. She turned and took a small sip and eyed Tomesha.

"May I ask who this esteemed guest is?" Tomesha breathed.

"But of course you may." Ramona smiled, revealing her fangs. "Tonight, my dear, you'll be entertaining a general. She's the right hand of our warden and commander, Princess Lethia Riskel. General Dru Moldark should be arriving any minute. You're not to take any customers tonight. You'll be the general's for as long as she wants you."

"Yes, Mistress."

A general? The second hand to the princess? Tomesha blinked, unable to believe what she was hearing. She took a step back. She'd never even been in the presence of royalty or someone that close to the royal family.

"Now run along so you can be ready to greet our guest. We want to ensure that she enjoys her time while here in Butterbush." Mistress downed the rest of her blood and set the empty goblet on the desk.

"Yes, Mistress. I promise she won't be disappointed." Tomesha bowed her head and backed away from Romana. She spun on her heels and rushed toward the double doors.

"I have confidence she won't be able to get enough of you."

"WHERE HAVE YOU BEEN? Started entertaining early tonight?" Ada asked.

Tomesha stepped behind the counter and moved over to her. She wasn't sure what to think after her meeting with Mistress. She bit her lip and glanced around the club. It looked like any other normal night. It was full of vampires coming for whatever they may desire.

Feeding or fucking.

Hell, some may even be here to just socialize. Have a goblet or two of their favorite blood while holding conversations as if the table next to them didn't have a pair or a throuple participating in sexual acts.

Yes, just a normal night.

But tonight was the night she'd have her first bite. Her heart rate spiked at the thought. How would she react? Would it be pleasurable? Painful? She shook her head. From what some of the other donors had shared with her, they had climaxed harder than they ever had before. She was curious by nature and had asked others about it. They were open with her since everyone knew Mistress was saving her for a special person.

"I was with Mistress," Tomesha whispered.

Ada leaned closer to her with wide eyes. "You in trouble or something? Whose ass do I have to kick?" She spun around, seeking out an imaginary threat.

Tomesha grabbed her arm and brought her back around. Ada may be the blood bartender, but she looked out for the human servers. She also ensured security was called when she sensed something wasn't right.

"No, I'm not in any trouble." Tomesha chuckled.

Ada had a bloodthirsty look to her, and it wasn't for the need to drink blood but spill it. She relaxed a little.

"Then why did you have to go see her?"

"Tonight's the night," Tomesha breathed.

Ada's eyes widened. There was no need to explain what she meant.

"Oh, shit. For real? It must be someone really important. She's been holding you back for a while." Ada dragged Tomesha over to the corner near the kitchen door. "You've been taking your kenaf weed like you're supposed to, right?"

Tomesha nodded at the mention of the herb all human donors took. It was a necessity to ensure their blood stores remained intact. It helped with blood production to ensure the humans would be able to make more blood after being a donor.

"Of course. It's required." Tomesha had never known when this day would come so she had to make sure she was ready at a moment's notice.

"Good. Did she say who?" Ada asked.

"Hey, are you two going to be whispering over there all night? Or are you going to be serving?" a rough voice called out.

Ada's head snapped around to the vampire. A scowl slipped onto her face.

"Hold your horses, Harold. You aren't going to fucking wither away if you have to wait another damn minute," Ada growled. She turned back to

Tomesha with her face softening. "Well, whoever it is must be special. Now try to relax. You look as nervous as a hooker in a church."

"Well, I'm sort of—"

"You know what I mean." Ada rolled her eyes.

Tomesha laughed at the vampire using a human phrase. She nodded and blew out a deep breath.

"If you need to, take a shot of whiskey or vodka to calm your nerves."

"You know I don't drink when I'm working." Tomesha shook her head. That was one rule she stuck to. Some of the donors were known to have a drink or two to help them work, but she stayed away from liquor. She needed a clear head to be able to focus and ensure her vampires felt as if they were her top priority.

"Well, then go mingle. See if anyone needs a drink. I'm sure you're not allowed to service while waiting for your VIP."

"I'll do that. I'm just too nervous right now to concentrate on anything else," Tomesha admitted. She went over to snag a small tray along with a few empty glasses. She grabbed a crystal decanter that held a warmed blood type O. It was a common blood type that most vampires didn't mind consuming. She collected a couple of napkins and made her way around the club.

The butterflies in her stomach were in overdrive. She went around to tables in an attempt to keep her mind busy. She didn't want to think about the general until she had to. She focused on refilling goblets and mugs to bypass the time.

"Tomesha, darling. Come here," a familiar voice called out to her.

She turned and took in Valentina making her way to a chaise. The tall vampire was dressed in a skintight, one-piece leather outfit that highlighted all of her voluptuous curves and the large bulge between her legs. The beautiful woman offered Tomesha a sensual smile and bid her to come to her.

Tomesha smiled and strolled over. She already knew Valentina would be wanting her. The nights she'd serviced her were always pleasurable.

Tomesha was one of the only humans that Valentina allowed to service her. She paid top dollar for Tomesha's time. Valentina's gaze roamed her as she made her way to her. The heat in her gaze wasn't missed.

Only Tomesha was going to have to let her down easy tonight.

The general was to be the only person whom she serviced. Which meant Valentina was going to have to find someone else if she had an itch to be scratched.

"Hello, Valentina," Tomesha greeted her. She stopped near her but kept a little distance between them.

Valentina immediately frowned and patted the cushion next to her. "Come sit, darling. I want you next to me." Her eyes lit up, her smile spreading to a sexy grin.

Her fire-engine nail color caught Tomesha's eyes.

"I can't right now." Tomesha didn't know what to say. She'd dismissed plenty of suitors when she was already occupied with Valentina or another. Valentina, she'd never declined before.

"Why?" Her smile immediately disappeared.

"I'm reserved," Tomesha whispered. It sounded so cold and as if she were a product being sold in a store. She blew out a deep breath and stepped forward. "How much longer will you be in town?"

"Reserved? By whom?" Valentina stood abruptly. She moved to Tomesha and took her by the arm. Anger filled her eyes.

Tomesha stepped back. Her muscles grew tense.

She'd never seen Valentina upset, and it scared her. As if recognizing Tomesha's reaction, Valentina loosened her hold on her arm.

"I'm sorry, my darling. It's just that I've been waiting to see you." She reached up and caressed Tomesha's face. A smile appeared again on her lips. She studied Tomesha. "Maybe I can offer up more money for an inconvenience fee to Mistress and she can find another human for them."

"I'm not sure how that would work," Tomesha said.

"Excuse me, Lady Feng, but as Tomesha has been so kind to share with you, she's reserved. You'll have to excuse her." Callidora, the club hostess, appeared at Tomesha's side. The hostess bowed her head to Valentina then turned her attention to Tomesha. "Your very important guest has arrived. Please follow me."

"Now wait a fucking minute. What do you mean 'very important guest.' Am I not an important guest? I want Tomesha tonight," Valentina demanded.

"I am sorry, Lady Feng. Give me a moment, and we'll present you with other choice donors who would be of great service to you," Callidora said.

"How much do I have to pay? I'll pay extra."

Valentina's gaze flicked to Tomesha then returned to Callidora.

"I'm sorry, Lady Feng. We're following the direction of the mistress. Now please. Have a seat, and I'll send someone to you." Callidora didn't wait for a response. She spun on her heel and motioned for Tomesha to follow her.

Tomesha tried to smooth it over and smiled at Valentina, scurrying away after Callidora.

Valentina was pissed.

CHAPTER TEN

Dru attempted to relax as best as she could. There was no reason for her to be in the madam's club and scowling. She understood the postmaster was trying to make a good impression on her. She was quite impressed with the fort.

Dru's gaze swept Madam Rice's club. This establishment wasn't merely a place to sate hunger —it was a haven where desire and temptation met in equal measure. Every touch, every offering, was consensual. Blood from a willing donor was always better than a human filled with fear. Here, predator and willing prey could come together, free of judgment, free of fear. If she wasn't here in town for a purpose, she'd probably enjoy the club for what it was worth.

Callidora had offered her seating with the postmaster, but Dru declined. The hostess had escorted her to a single alcove that gave her a full view of the place while also shielding her and providing privacy should she desire. She settled into her comfortable chair with a small round table in front of her. From her viewpoint, she took in Talbot across the room speaking with a human female, while Orenda had disappeared with her donor.

Dru had opted to be served from the club's prepared blood. She picked up the menu and scanned the title and description.

The Crimson Cellar — A curated selection of rare and exquisite offerings, harvested with reverence and consent. Each pour celebrates the union of taste, experience, and intimacy.

The menu presented house vintages, specialty reserves, and more. One of the selections caught her eye.

The Dionysian — From donors who indulge in red wine before offering, imparting lush berry undertones and a heady warmth.

She reviewed the rest of the menu and decided she'd go with the Dionysian. She scanned the room to track down a server and caught sight of Callidora headed back her way. Dru froze in place as the human trailing behind the hostess came into view.

It was the human from the street.

Only she wasn't in regular clothing.

Tonight, she was dressed as a donor for Madam. Her dark hair was left flowing around her shoulders, and her makeup was flawless, allowing her smooth brown skin to glow. Her dark eyes, almond in shape, had a smokiness to them. Her figure was curvy, and the white sheer dress did nothing but highlight all of the assets the woman had been born with. Dru pushed up from where she was seated inside the alcove and strode forward.

Her gums burned and stretched, then her fangs slipped through. Dru inhaled sharply as the female drew closer to her. She stepped outside of the intimate area to wait. Where was the hostess taking the female? Surely not to the postmaster? Or any other vampire in the room.

"General," Callidora murmured. A teasing glint entered her eyes. She stopped in front of Dru and bowed her head. "Is something wrong?"

"No, nothing's wrong." Dru stared at the human who had yet to look at her.

The woman glanced over her shoulder before

finally turning to face Dru. Her beauty hit Dru straight in the chest. The air in her lungs escaped.

"It was brought to our attention that you had requested to dine off the menu tonight, but Mistress Beatrix refuses to allow such an esteemed guest to dine off the menu when she'd reserved such an exquisite treat for you." Callidora moved to the side and held out a hand to the woman.

She slipped hers inside Callidora's and allowed her to guide her forward. The woman stopped in front of Dru and tipped her head back to meet her gaze. Dru's lungs burned; they screamed for air. She finally inhaled, and in doing so, she breathed a scent that she attributed to the female before her.

It was captivating. She carried the aroma of soft fruit and golden honey. A sweetness clung to her skin like perfume. Dru's composure faltered. She, a tough warrior, a general, was almost willing to beg the woman for her name. Her fangs throbbed, while her hunger sharpened to an intensity that shook Dru to her core. Her gaze fell to the leather collar around the woman's neck.

She was a virgin to the bite of a vampire.

An almost primal need rose in Dru—to be the first to sink her fangs into the woman's artery and drink her life-giving ambrosia. She blinked, unsure of why she was having this reaction to the human. She'd never cared about being the first to drink from a donor.

"General, may I present to you, Tomesha," Callidora continued.

"Tomesha," Dru breathed.

She took the woman's hand from Callidora and brought it to her lips. She pressed a soft kiss to the back of her hand. Her skin felt as soft as Dru imagined it to be. Her gaze skated down and lingered on her dark areolas pressing against her sheer dress. She ran her tongue across her fangs. The need to sink them into Tomesha grew. Instead of acting on her savage nature that flared to life, she smiled. "A beautiful name, for a beautiful woman."

"Why thank you." Tomesha's eyes lowered.

Dru ached to bring her closer, but she didn't want to scare the human off. The last thing she wanted to do was make this woman afraid of her.

"Tomesha shall be your *sanguina* for the night," Callidora murmured. "Curtesy of Mistress and Madam."

"Tell your bosses that I am pleased by their offer," Dru said.

"Whatever it is you may desire tonight, it shall

be yours." Tomesha's brown eyes lifted to meet Dru's.

"Yes, anything." Callidora stepped toward Tomesha who released Dru's hand.

Immediately, she wanted to take it back. Something inside her didn't like to see another so close to her human, *her sanguina.* Callidora reached up and fiddled with the collar around Tomesha's neck. She removed it in a dramatic fashion before also doing the same to Tomesha's wristbands.

The hunger to drink from Tomesha grew even more.

"I demand to speak with Mistress!" a sharp voice called out.

Dru tensed and reached for her dagger on her waist. A woman with dark hair hanging around her shoulders who was dressed in a leather one-piece outfit strode forward. Her eyes were narrowed on Tomesha, and immediately, Dru went into protector mode. She pushed Tomesha behind her as the woman arrived to them.

"Lady Feng, this is not how we conduct ourselves." Callidora spun toward the new arrival.

"I don't care how you do business. Mistress should be accommodating her loyal customers above anyone else. Even if they're a general," Lady Feng sneered.

She stood the same height as Dru. After a quick perusal of her and her muscular physique, Dru dismissed the female—she wasn't a true threat. The clubs security began to make their way over to them. Dru kept one hand behind her and felt Tomesha's smaller frame pressed against her. Dru's gaze connected with Talbot. She gave a quick shake of her head at his unspoken question. She wouldn't need him. She could handle this situation—or the security could. She doubted they'd want her to truly handle this angry interloper.

"What Mistress chooses to do here at the club is her business, and you'll respect that." Callidora's voice was firm. She rested her hands on her waist.

The large vampires in dark suits arrived and stood behind Lady Feng. Dru slipped her dagger back in its sheath. It looked as if the hostess and her security would be handling this with no issues.

"Now either respect our facility or be banned. Your choice."

"You don't have the power to ban me," Feng sneered.

"Once I share your conduct, I'm sure Mistress

won't have any issues coming here to remove you herself," Callidora said.

"I'll speak with her. Have no worries about that!" Feng spun on her heels and pushed her way through the security guards.

They gave the hostess a nod before dispersing. Dru relaxed now that the interrupting woman was gone. Callidora turned back to Dru and smiled.

They had gained the attention of those nearest them, but seeing how there was no fighting or bloodshed, the vampires all returned to minding their own businesses. Dru glanced around the room and pulled Tomesha from behind her. The need to protect her was strong. Tomesha hesitated to move at first, then came around to stand next to her. She brushed a few strands of her dark hair behind her ear.

"My apologies, General. You will not have any more interruptions. As I was saying before, Tomesha will be your *sanguina* tonight. If you need anything else, please don't hesitate to call for me." Callidora gave a bow of her head.

"I appreciate you handling everything so quickly." Dru was a little pissed at the scent of fear that hovered in the air from Tomesha. She didn't want her to ever be afraid while she was near her. The human would always be protected while Dru was around.

"But of course." She flicked her gaze to Tomesha and nodded. "Tomesha."

"Callidora." Tomesha smiled.

Callidora headed off, leaving them alone. Tomesha widened her smile at Dru. The human closed the gap between them. She slipped her daintier hand into Dru's and pressed her warm body to her.

"Would you like to feed here, or would you like somewhere more private? Just the two of us?"

The fear was now gone from Tomesha's eyes. Her wide brown irises touched something deep inside Dru. Did she want to feed from her in front of others? No. She wanted the human's first bite to be experienced by her alone. Something possessive snuck its way inside her. The pulse at the base of Tomesha's neck raced.

"Let's go somewhere we can be alone," Dru replied.

Tomesha's eyes darkened. She spun on her heel and led Dru through the establishment. Eyes were on them as they navigated through the club. The presentation of Tomesha to her was for everyone to see. Tomesha was deemed special. Mistress purposely did not allow anyone to feed from Tomesha.

Tonight, Tomesha was being offered as a gift to Dru.

It was a move to gain a favor from Dru—or her house. Dru held back the smirk. She'd be interested in hearing what it was Mistress would request. Her gaze settled on the material brushing Tomesha's ass as she walked. The sway of her hips had Dru mesmerized within seconds. Thoughts of Mistress disappeared from her mind. Tomesha glanced over her shoulder with a shy smile. It was then Dru knew she'd follow this human anywhere.

"MAKE YOURSELF COMFORTABLE." Tomesha closed the door to her private suite.

Dru strode forward and took in the room. It was simply decorated while the air held the scent of Tomesha. Furniture was scattered around, but what caught Dru's attention was the large bed that was the focus. She turned to find Tomesha standing with her back to the door. Her beauty was breathtaking and left Dru struggling to breathe.

"Would you like some help with your uniform, General?"

Dru was never one to be at a loss of words. She gave a quick jerk of her head. She pushed off the door and ambled over to Dru. Tomesha reached for Dru's jacket and slid it off her shoulders. A smile lingered on her lips while she worked.

"Dru," Dru announced.

Tomesha paused, confusion lining her face.

"My name is Dru. You don't need to call me by my title."

"Oh, are you sure?" Tomesha gathered the jacket to her chest. She glanced down at it before looking back to Dru.

"Positive." Considering what Dru wanted to do to this female, titles were not needed. She wanted to hear her name on the human's tongue.

"I'm sure you've had a long day." Tomesha walked over to hang the jacket on a hook near the door. She came back to Dru and hesitated when her gaze dropped to the daggers on her waist.

"I'll get those." Dru cleared her throat. She unhooked her belt and pulled it off. The daggers remained in their coverings.

Tomesha placed them on the nightstand by the

bed. Dru appreciated it. She was always a warrior who needed to keep her weapons near her.

"Call me crazy, but I feel as if I know you somehow, General—Dru," Tomesha said sheepishly. She laughed and shook her head. "Weird, huh? I'm sure we've never even been in the same room before—"

"You're the woman from the street. You were with that male and older woman," Dru admitted.

Tomesha froze in place. Her eyes grew wider as she stared at Dru.

"It was my warriors who intervened with that altercation."

"You were in that black truck." Tomesha slowly came to stand before Dru. She studied her. "I could feel someone watching me, but I couldn't see in the truck to work out who it was."

"I'm sorry. I should have gotten out to check and ensure you were okay." Dru silently cursed. Was that male her lover? Had he been defending her honor from the other men? Even though the woman worked for the madam, it didn't mean she couldn't be married. Plenty of women did what they had to, to survive.

"That's okay. Thank you for sending your men to help. Those men were going to try to hurt my brother," Tomesha said.

Dru wasn't sure why, but relief filled her at hearing the male was her relative and not a lover or mate. She reached out and brought Tomesha to her. Her plump lips parted. The hint of a spicy aroma gently rose. Dru inhaled deeply and breathed it in. This little human was becoming aroused. Dru leaned down and didn't wait for permission. Her mouth crashed down on Tomesha's lips, hard and claiming, the kiss seared with hunger that was barely contained.

This wasn't going to be just a simple feeding. The sensual touch of their lips brought out a possessive nature. Dru wanted to consume this woman in her arms. Tomesha inched closer to her. Her lips parted, allowing Dru's tongue to slip inside.

Dru gripped Tomesha's hip and held her still while the other hand tangled in her hair, pulling her closer until there was no space left between them. She sensed the frantic pounding of the human's heart. Every instinct screamed for her to bite her, drink her nourishing blood—mark her.

It had been a while since Dru had fed from a live donor, and this one in her arms was so damn tantalizing.

Tomesha trembled, but instead of shrinking away from Dru, she surged forward and pressed into her. Her fingers clutched Dru's shoulders, her nails digging deep. The slight pain fueled the fire burning inside Dru. A guttural sound escaped her when their tongues danced together.

She tore her lips from Tomesha's and stared down at her. With each breath she took, Dru felt the possessiveness inside her grow.

Mine.

The hunger that coiled deep in her belly had nothing to do with blood. She ignored the word that echoed in her head. There was no way this woman belonged to her. Just for the night, she'd been gifted to Dru. Dru focused on that. Not on how beautiful Tomesha was or how sweet her kiss was. Dru lifted her hand to Tomesha's jaw, and she grazed the soft curve of her cheek with her thumb. Tomesha's breath came ragged, her pupils wide, and she slowly rubbed her breasts against Dru's.

The white sheer dress needed to go. She reached down and tried to find how she could remove it. She was moments from ripping the damn thing off Tomesha until her hands brushed Dru's away.

"Here," Tomesha whispered. She stepped back and opened the dress to reveal her shapely form.

The material was forgotten as it slipped down her arms and fluttered to the floor.

Dru's hands trembled as she took in the very naked Tomesha.

She didn't know this human, but suddenly she needed to know everything there was about her. Who was she? Where did she come from? How many vampires had the pleasure to taste what was between her brown thighs, and who was she going to have to kill for touching this woman?

Dru dragged air into her lungs and stepped forward.

"Please. Let me help you remove your clothing." Tomesha came back to her and reached for the top button of Dru's shirt.

She quickly opened it and pushed it down Dru's arms. The human was fast. Each weapon was removed and carefully placed on the nightstand until Dru was now just as naked as she was. Tomesha smiled and guided Dru backward until the bed met the backs of her legs.

"I'm here to please you."

Dru snagged her arm and tugged her forward.

"And who pleases you?" Dru asked. She wasn't sure if she truly wanted to know the answer. The woman was a paid whore. It didn't take much to realize how she'd be making her money if she wasn't allowed to be a donor.

A confused look appeared momentarily in the human's eyes then disappeared.

"Don't worry about me." Tomesha smiled and ran her hands up Dru's arms. Her brown-eyed gaze traveled over Dru's toned body. She lifted her gaze back to Dru. "I'm here for you—"

Dru cut off whatever Tomesha was about to say. She captured her lips with hers in another deep kiss. This one harder and hungrier. She spun them around until Tomesha was against the bed. They tumbled down on the mattress with Dru landing on top. She stared down into her eyes.

"Then allow me to please you," Dru said.

Tomesha's lips parted, but Dru placed a single finger to them to silence her. It didn't matter to Dru what this woman did for a living. She'd never judge someone for trying to survive. All that Dru knew was she wanted to see Tomesha's face as she took her pleasure, as she reached her climax. The burning need to know she could please this human grew in her chest.

Tomesha hesitated for a moment before nodding.

"Good, *miere.* Now lie back and let me explore all there is to you."

CHAPTER ELEVEN

Tomesha didn't know what it was about this vampire, from the way her icy-blue eyes had watched her when Callidora had presented her, to the way the woman had put herself in front of her when Valentina had stormed over.

The general lowered her head and took her lips hungrily. Their mouths fused together in a slow, deep kiss that left Tomesha trembling. She wrapped her arms around Dru and gave in to her. She'd never had this reaction before. She enjoyed the company of all of her clients, but there was something different about the general—Dru.

Strong hands slipped over her skin and cupped her breasts. Dru lifted her head; her bright-blue eyes appeared to see into Tomesha's soul.

"Your skin is so soft," Dru whispered.

She bathed one of Tomesha's nipples with her tongue. Tomesha groaned at the feel of it sliding over her. The general trailed her tongue up the full mound, coming back to suckle the taut bud into her mouth. Tomesha threaded her fingers into the deep auburn hair, displacing the bun from the top of her head. She arched her back as the woman tugged on her. She gasped and held on tight. Dru nipped her with her sharp fangs.

Tomesha's core clenched from the hint of pain. Would it hurt when Dru sank those same fangs into her flesh? Would she go for Tomesha's neck first? Or her wrist? Or her inner thigh? Tomesha's heart rate increased with the thought of Dru drinking from her.

Her blood was needed.

She'd be this woman's nourishment tonight.

What she had to offer was lifesaving. Something the woman needed to survive. Tomesha gasped when Dru released her breast. Her warm breath skated over her skin; she moved to Tomesha's other breast. She repeated her actions with her tongue, suckling this nipple deep within her mouth. Dru's hand traveled down her torso and came to rest on her thighs.

Tomesha parted her legs. She wanted to feel her fingers dive between her slick folds. Dru took the invitation and guided her hand between Tomesha's thighs. Her strong hands pushed Tomesha's thighs even farther apart.

"The scent of you is addicting," Dru murmured.

Her lips brushed Tomesha's sensitive skin. She trailed hot kisses down her abdomen. Tomesha kept her eyes on the powerful vampire who came eye level with her center. A growl rippled from Dru. The sound did something to Tomesha. Her core clenched, and her juices slipped from her. It wasn't the first time she'd heard a vampire growl during their intimate moments, but there was something about the way it vibrated Dru's body that sent an electric current through Tomesha. Dru buried her face between Tomesha's legs. Her nose ghosted over Tomesha's swollen bundle of nerves while she breathed in her scent.

It was one of the most erotic sights Tomesha had ever seen. Dru's eyes flicked to hers and held her gaze.

"Your pussy is slick and ready. Does the little human want my tongue here?" Her finger brushed Tomesha's clit.

Tomesha jerked her head in a quick nod. Her breaths were coming fast, rendering her almost speechless. She whimpered at the feeling of Dru's fingers trailing softly from her clit to her opening.

"Look at how it's pouring out of you."

Her finger surged into Tomesha's cunt which contracted around her. Dru thrust it fully in, then withdrew it from her. She flashed her fangs at Tomesha, inserting two fingers deep into her. Tomesha moaned at the feeling of her pussy being stretched by the vampire.

"Oh!" Tomesha blew out a deep breath and tried to bring Dru's head down to her core. She wanted to feel her mouth on her. She pushed down everything that Starla had taught her about appealing to the vampire's ego.

This one wanted Tomesha's pleasure. She was going to throw caution to the wind and allow this vampire to do what she wanted.

"Ah, my little human is showing me what she wants. Is this what you desire?" She toyed with Tomesha's clit using her tongue. She sucked the swollen flesh between her lips.

"Yes," Tomesha hissed.

She closed her eyes and allowed her head to fall back onto the mattress. There was something about hearing this vampire claim her as her human. Tomesha gave in to the pleasure flowing through her. Dru feasted on her while fucking her hard and slow with her fingers. Her moans and gasps filled the air. The woman was clearly an expert at what she was doing.

Tomesha gripped her hair again and flexed her hips, riding rode Dru's tongue. Her body trembled, and she gave in to the sensations coursing through her. Dru latched on to her bud and brought Tomesha to the brink of her climax. Tomesha cried out her frustration when Dru paused.

"Please," Tomesha gasped.

Dru's chuckle was the only response she received. Dru's head lowered again. She arched upward and rode the waves once again. Dru consumed her. This time, she didn't hold back. She continued her delicious assault on Tomesha's clit while her fingers continued to plunder Tomesha's pussy. Dru twisted her fingers around and thrust them upward and hit a certain spot that sent Tomesha off to the stars. A scream erupted from Tomesha.

Her body shook and trembled from the force of her orgasm. She couldn't breathe while she basked in the glow of the most powerful climax she'd ever had. She fell back onto the bed and lay spent, her muscles like liquid. She closed her eyes and focused on breathing while Dru continued to slowly lick her pussy.

"Come here," Dru growled.

She dragged Tomesha to the edge of the bed. Tomesha's eyes fluttered open. She eyed the strong vampire whose body looked as if she'd seen plenty. Her pale skin was filled with healed scars, but her muscles were well defined. She was the epitome of strength and a badass warrior. Her auburn hair fell in waves around her shoulders, while her bright-blue eyes were locked in on Tomesha.

Dru brought Tomesha to her feet. Her legs barely held her weight. She leaned into Dru who wrapped her arms around Tomesha's waist. Tomesha tilted her head to offer what she knew Dru needed. She caught sight of Dru's sharp fangs peeking underneath her lip. Her legs trembled with the fear of what was to come.

"There is no need to fear me, *miere*," Dru murmured. She tipped Tomesha's chin to where she could look her in the eyes.

Tomesha was captivated by the beautiful vampire. She wasn't scared of her. It was just the unknown of what would happen once she drank from her. How would she react to being bitten?

"I'm not afraid," Tomesha whispered, her voice hoarse but steady.

She fought to stand upright on her own but didn't want to pull herself away from Dru's toned body. Hers still hummed from her release, every nerve tender and sensitive. She lowered her gaze. Her jugular artery would be large enough so Dru could take what she needed. That was why she'd been gifted to the vampire. For food and pleasure.

"You need to feed. Take from me."

Dru's chest vibrated again with a deep growl. She leaned forward and trailed her tongue up Tomesha's neck. A chill rippled down Tomesha's spine. Her body stiffened, and she waited. Would it be painful? Would she remember? She bit her lip in hopes that she didn't scream.

"No harm will ever come to you while I'm around." Dru's lips moved up Tomesha's neck. She licked the delicate column of again. "You will be protected."

"Why?" The word fell from Tomesha's lips

before she'd even thought about it. Her eyes widened. She didn't want to anger the vampire with her questioning.

Dru paused. Her breath skated over Tomesha's skin. She lifted a hand and threaded it into Tomesha's hair. She moved Tomesha's head farther to the side to expose more of her neck.

"I don't know," Dru said.

She sank her teeth into Tomesha's flesh. Pain exploded in her neck, but it quickly disappeared, followed by an intense pleasure that stole Tomesha's breath away. Heat rippled through her. Every pull of her blood was answered by a deeper throbbing between her thighs. It was as if she were experiencing pure ecstasy. She came undone with Dru's fangs deep in her neck.

Tomesha held on to Dru's shoulders. Her moans flowed from her while a guttural groan spilled from Dru as she drank from her. The tugging on her neck was intoxicating. Tomesha had only felt that brief pinpoint of pain, then nothing but pleasure filled her. She'd never felt more alive or connected with another being until now. It was as if she were binding herself to Dru.

She knew that wasn't the case. Humans fed

vampires all the time, and that didn't mean anything. But this with Dru felt somehow different. It was if the world had paused around them the second her blood flowed from her into Dru.

Tomesha closed her eyes and rode the waves that weaved through her. It was as if she were floating amongst the clouds. A smile came to her lips, and she basked in the overwhelming feeling of pleasure. She barely felt Dru lift her head from her, or the faint sensation of her tongue sealing the holes on her neck. Her body flushed with a warmth that had her writhing in Dru's arms.

She wanted more.

She wanted Dru to bite her again.

DRU STARED down at the human on the bed bedside her. Tomesha rested in the crook of Dru's arms. Tomesha had reacted as most humans did when they were first bitten. She'd gone into a euphoric state of pleasure, no pain. Dru reached up and brushed Tomesha's dark hair from her face.

What was it about this human?

Besides the fact that she was gorgeous. Or that

her cunt tasted sweet and divine. Her blood was like an ambrosia, addictive and delicious.

Dru had tucked them into the bed underneath the covers to allow Tomesha time to recover. With it being her first bite, Dru didn't want to overdo it with her. She trailed her fingers down the soft skin, and for the time she'd spent with Tomesha, not once had she thought of her mission and why she was even in Butterbush.

That was a problem.

She'd been sent here for a job, and daydreaming about this woman in her arms didn't fit into her plans. As she'd told her warriors, they'd indulge tonight, but then tomorrow, it was time to hunt down the traitor.

"Why did you let me sleep?" Tomesha's husky voice broke the silence. She blinked and pushed up from where she lay. The blanket fell away, revealing her tantalizing body.

"How do you feel?" Dru ignored her question. She zeroed in on the area where she'd bitten her. The skin was darkening. Dru released a curse. She reached out and gently caressed the area. There would be a bruise by morning. She'd tried to be as gentle as possible, but the moment her blood had touched Dru's tongue, she'd almost turned savage. She'd had to reel in the emotions that had whipped through her and regain control of herself.

Not once in all of her years had she ever lost control when drinking from a human.

"My neck is a little sore, but I'm told that is normal," Tomesha said. A visible shudder went through her as Dru touched her skin. She licked her lips and smiled. "You aren't what I expected."

"Oh?" Dru arched an eyebrow. She was curious as to what Tomesha told her. "How so?"

"I don't know. When they told me I would be given to a general, I imagined someone older, harsher, not as beautiful—" She paused, those brown eyes of hers wide.

Dru chuckled and reached for her. Even though she'd only known her for a few hours, she already didn't want to stop touching her. She ignored the little voice in the back of her head.

This wasn't uncommon. Two individuals could have chemistry between them. It didn't mean they were destined to be together or anything.

Dru swallowed hard.

Tomesha wasn't her mate.

She was just a human who was here to service her. She was being paid to be here with Dru. Any other time Dru wouldn't have cared, but now it had her wondering.

Had Tomesha been faking?

She did work for the madam and had probably received training. She frowned as she thought of Tomesha's body writhing on the bed while she'd feasted on her delicious pussy. Or how her muscles tightened around her fingers when she'd reached her climax, or how the juices had flowed from her.

No, Tomesha couldn't be acting. No amount of training would portray the pleasure she'd experienced or the shouts, cries, and the way her body had responded to Dru.

Dru glanced back at her and found those beautiful eyes staring at her. She was obviously waiting on Dru to respond to something she'd said.

"What did you say?"

"I said, you took such good care of me that I need to return the favor," Tomesha said. She pushed the blanket away from Dru and lifted her leg over to straddle her.

Dru straightened herself and rested back against the pillows. "Believe me, I got much pleasure watching you reach your climax."

"See, that is what I'm talking about. I figured you would be a hardened vampire who'd just want to use me." Tomesha brushed Dru's hair away from her face.

"Is that what you're used to?" Dru asked softly.

Tomesha's expression shut down. She blinked and looked away for a moment. Dru immediately recognized the signs that it was time to change the subject. She didn't want their time together to be awkward. She was enjoying the company of her little human.

"Well, *miere*, you aren't too far off. I'm very old. I'm sure compared to you, I'm ancient."

Tomesha turned back to her, the hint of her smile flickering. She studied Dru.

"What are you, forty?" Tomesha asked.

Dru barked a laugh. Vampires lived very long lives compared to humans. She rested her hands on Tomesha's waist. It was hard to concentrate on the conversation at hand when a beautiful woman was sitting naked on top of her.

"I just celebrated my two hundred and twenty-fifth birthday," Dru admitted.

Tomesha's mouth dropped open at the announcement. A couple of weeks ago, Dru had celebrated the anniversary of her birth. She'd received a letter from her parents wishing her well. She smiled at the thought of her parents still holding on to the older days. They refused to assimilate to the technology of today. She agreed some of the old ways were better, but with the state of the world right now, she had to embrace technology in order to protect her people.

"What? I mean…damn…um, happy birthday?" Tomesha sputtered. She reached up and tucked her hair behind her ears. She grinned wide and leaned forward to where her lips hovered above Dru's. "Then allow me to give you a birthday gift."

Dru gripped the back of Tomesha's neck. Their kiss was soft and sensual. Tomesha scooted forward, placing her center against Dru's stomach. The scent of her filled the room. Dru growled softly, wanting to taste her again.

Tomesha lifted her head and left a trail of kisses on Dru's face and neck. She moved down and stopped at Dru's breasts. Tomesha took her time suckling and licking both of Dru's mounds. It would appear her human wanted to return the favor. She wasn't going to argue with her.

Tomesha explored her body which left Dru in a painfully aroused state. Her core dripped with her honey by the time Tomesha had arrived there. Her body trembled, and she parted her legs for Tomesha. The human took her time exploring her cunt just as she did exploring her body. Her fingers, tongue, and lips all teased her.

Dru should never have let this much time pass between her sexual encounters. She had to keep reminding herself that Tomesha was a human and she couldn't be as rough with her as she would her vampire lovers. Just the memory of the bruise forming on Tomesha's neck was proof.

"Fuck," Dru uttered.

Her breath escaped her; Tomesha's lips closed around her clit. Her legs fell open completely to give Tomesha access to every inch of her center. She threw her head back while Tomesha's tongue pushed against her slick opening. Her small fingers drew circles on her clit while her tongue slid through her folds.

"*Miere*, put those fingers in me."

Dru threaded her fingers back into Tomesha thick hair. Tomesha covered her clit with her mouth and suckled it. She was just as unforgiving as Dru had been to her. Dru's body writhed on the bed while Tomesha worked her. Tomesha's fingers sank deep in her while she focused on Dru's clit.

She hummed and tugged on Dru's sensitive flesh until she had Dru screaming through her own climax. Dru blinked, unable to believe she'd reached her peak that fast. Her body tingled and shook as she lay back. She lifted her head and met her little human's gaze.

"Come here, *miere*," Dru growled. She reached down and practically dragged Tomesha over her. She flipped them over to where she rested on top of Tomesha. She took Tomesha's lips in a brutal kiss.

Mine.

The word was whispered again in the back of her mind, but she ignored it.

This human was hers—for the night. Whatever she wanted, Tomesha would provide for her. The scent of sweat, sex, and sweetness clung to Tomesha's skin. It overwhelmed Dru's senses, but it didn't hide the intoxicating thrum of Tomesha's blood that called to Dru. It was the sweetest invitation that she couldn't resist.

Tomesha tilted her head in a silent offer. That gesture caused something to snap inside Dru. She gripped Tomesha's hair to hold her in place, then she bent down and sank her fangs deep into Tomesha' neck. The rush of blood hit her tongue and filled her mouth. She drank deeply and moaned as if she hadn't eaten in decades.

She swallowed, the blood sliding down her throat, providing the nourishment and power she needed. She immediately felt stronger, invincible, and faster. Tomesha gyrated underneath her, while her fingers dug into Dru's skin. The hint of pain from Tomesha's nails went ignored.

Tomesha's moans and cries filled the air. Her hips undulated against Dru as if seeking her. Dru slipped a hand between them, met with Tomesha's slickness. Her finger connected with Tomesha's clit. It was swollen, and with a few strokes, Tomesha screamed through her next climax. Her heart raced, sending her blood flowing into Dru's mouth in abundance. She drank deeply and almost lost herself in that moment. Dru lifted her head and stared down at the second wound she'd left. She couldn't continue or she'd bleed Tomesha dry. Blood slowly seeped from the small holes. She quickly licked the skin; the enzymes in her saliva would seal the holes. Tomesha shuddered and fell back against the mattress, spent.

Dru stared down at Tomesha who was flushed, radiant, and beautiful. Dru closed her eyes and inhaled sharply. What was this between them? Two hundred and twenty-five years she'd walked this earth, and never had she reacted this way to a human. She swallowed hard, still tasting Tomesha's sweet blood on her tongue.

This woman was dangerous. She'd be a distraction, and Dru couldn't afford to fail at her mission.

She shook her head and knew what she had to do.

She must leave.

CHAPTER TWELVE

She winced as she turned over. Tomesha inhaled sharply and moaned. She opened her eyes and blinked. The lights in her suite were low. Someone had turned off the main ones and only left on the bathroom. Without checking, Tomesha already knew Dru was gone. The room was too silent. She reached out a hand behind her and confirmed what she already knew. When had she left? The sheets were cool, so it must have been a while.

Her gaze fell on her nightstand, where the general's weapons had sat, and found them gone. In their place sat a stack of gold coins. Tomesha's eyes widened at the amount of money left for her. She pushed up slowly. The skin on her neck was raw and ached. She carefully reached out and picked up the gold to count them.

Ten royal gold coins.

Tomesha stared at them in disbelief. Her hands shook. Tomesha had never received this amount of a tip from a client before. This was enough money to pay her rent and bills for a full year and more. The most she'd ever received before as a tip was one, maybe two gold coins. It didn't include what she received from the club.

But the coins were never royal.

The only reason she knew they were the royal gold coins, worth more than the standard coins, was because of the imprint of the vampire king's profile on them.

She leaned back against the headboard and pillows in disbelief. Why would the general—Dru —leave her this much money? It was entirely too much. She pushed the blankets off her and swung her legs over the side of the bed. The cool air caressed her naked skin. She winced from the tightness of the skin around her neck and the area between her thighs where Dru had fed as well. She paused and drew in a deep breath. Her heart pounded. She frowned, unsure why.

She held the coins in one hand while she prodded the area between her legs. There was going to be a bruise. There were two small pinpoint holes on her inner thigh where Dru's fangs had sunk. Tomesha closed her eyes as the memories of the night surfaced. Her time with Dru had been something she couldn't explain. There had been something between the two of them. A chemistry, so to speak. But Tomesha shook her head. She was probably reading too much into it. Dru had come to the club for a reason.

Feed and to fuck. She gotten both last night, hence the reason she was gone.

Tomesha stood, a weakness in her bones. She carefully padded over to her dresser where she stored her tips. She slid the money in the drawer with the rest. She made a mental note to take it home with her when she left. She dragged in a deep breath again while holding on to the dresser. The room spun slightly.

Once it stopped moving, she headed into the bathroom to relieve her bladder. It was screaming that she hadn't emptied it in a while. She hurried as best she could to the toilet and handled her business before she stopped at the sink to wash her hands. She turned the water on and placed her hands underneath it and looked up at the mirror.

Tomesha froze at the sight that greeted her. The skin at the base of her neck was darkened on both sides. There was a trail of dried blood on the left side. She blinked, and her hands shook. She switched the water off and stared at the markings on her. Reality set in for her.

This was what she'd signed up for.

To offer her life's blood to a vampire for money. She shouldn't be surprised that it came with consequences.

Her knees shook. She gripped the edge of the counter and breathed in deeply. She felt lightheaded again, and the room tilted. Fear settled in, and she tried to hold herself up to keep herself from falling. She turned around and stumbled to the door. She leaned against it for a moment and reached for her robe that hung on a hook on the wall. It took what little strength she had to slide the material on. Her breathing was rapid and shallow.

"This isn't normal," she whimpered. Tomesha closed her eyes; she had to get over to her bed before she fell onto the floor. She moved with slow, easy steps. She celebrated the moment her hand touched the mattress. She sat on it and groaned. The pillows appeared to be a long distance away. "I can make it."

Panic set in. Was she supposed to feel this way after a feeding? How did the others do this on a regular basis? She crawled the few inches to where her pillows were and fell onto them. She stared at the ceiling while attempting to focus on breathing. A knock sounded at the door. Tomesha's eyes fluttered closed. She barely had the strength to answer.

"Come in." Her voice was weakened, but apparently whoever was on the other side of the door had heard her.

The door opened, and footsteps made their way to her.

"Tomesha?" a familiar voice called out. Starla.

Tomesha groaned in response. She couldn't lift her head from the pillow. Warm hands rested on Tomesha's face. They turned her head from side to side.

"Shit. Call for the healer!"

Starla released Tomesha, her footsteps fading. Tomesha felt as if she were floating in an abyss. She relaxed back and exhaled. She was exhausted. She just wanted to rest. There was nothing wrong with her wanting to sleep a little. Her trek to the bathroom had taken all of her strength from her. She didn't know why Starla was screaming for help. She'd just take a nap, then she'd be fine.

"I said call for a healer!" Starla hollered. The bed dipped down near Tomesha, and hands took her chin in their grasp. "Tomesha. Open your eyes. Don't go to sleep."

"But I'm so tired," Tomesha murmured. She tried to shake Starla's hands from her face. Why was she making such a big deal?

"No, honey. I need you to stay with me. Don't go to sleep." Starla's voice held a bit of a panic in it.

Tomesha frowned and tried to roll away from her, but her body wasn't cooperating.

"Tomesha, open your eyes."

Tomesha complied, but only one opened. She took in Starla's frantic expression before it fluttered closed again.

"I'm fine," she grumbled.

"You are not. I think that general took too much blood from you," Starla said.

Another voice, one Tomesha didn't recognize, joined her and began speaking with Starla. Tomesha couldn't hear what they were saying. They spoke in low voices.

The bed dipped down again as Starla moved. "The healer is here. Let her check you out."

"Tomesha. My name is Lamaya. I'm the healer. How are you feeling?"

"Tired," Tomesha murmured.

Gentle hands took her head and moved it from side to side. Her robe was disrupted, but Tomesha couldn't care less. She just wanted to go get some sleep.

"She was bitten here as well." Lamaya prodded Tomesha's leg. "Each bite has been sealed. I believe more was drained than her body could handle."

"Will she be okay?" Starla asked.

"She needs to drink ifalla tea. It will give her strength and help replenish what she lost much faster than the kenaf weed will."

The room fell silent.

Good. Now Tomesha could rest. They were worried for no reason. This was nothing a little sleep couldn't fix. She burrowed down on the bed and felt herself drift off into a slumber. It didn't last long before they were forcing her to awaken again.

"Leave me be," Tomesha groaned.

"Sorry, my dear. You must drink this. Wake up," Lamaya said.

Tomesha was brought to a sitting position. She

opened her eyes to find an older woman with kind eyes and dark hair that appeared to be purple when she turned away from Tomesha. She brought back a small porcelain mug with steam rising from it. "You need to drink this."

Tomesha frowned and took the mug from her. She brought it to her face and bent over it to sniff. She wrinkled her nose at the strong scent of herbs.

"I don't think I can—"

"You must. That vampire drank too much from you. This must be drunk right away for it to work." Lamaya gave her a stern look.

Tomesha glanced away from her to find Starla leaning against the wall with an expression of concern.

"You can do it," Starla encouraged. She smiled, came over, and sat on the edge of the bed. "I'm glad I came to check on you when I did. The general has been gone for a while now, and we didn't see you come out of your room. I figured you'd be cleaning up, but then another hour or two went by and I didn't see you and I got concerned."

Tomesha sipped some of the brew. It was definitely an acquired taste. It wasn't anything she'd choose on her own. She shook her head and tried to hand it back to the healer, who gently pushed it back to her.

"More. You need to drink all of it," Lamaya said.

Tomesha swallowed another sip then turned to Starla.

"Thank you for checking on me. I felt weak and shaky when I first awakened. But by the time I went into the bathroom, it felt as if all of my energy just left me." She had another sip of the dreadful drink. This time she did a bigger gulp to try to hurry and get this over with. Even after a couple of sips, she already sensed her strength coming back. But then something Starla said caught her attention. "Wait, how long has Dru—the general—been gone?"

Just because Dru said she could use her given name, didn't mean the others would be granted permission to do so. Starla and Lamaya glanced at each other for a brief moment. Tomesha grew concerned. How much time had passed?

"Don't worry. After you finish the tea, we'll get you home. I notified Mistress about what has happened, and she's ordered you to go home to rest."

"Go home?" Tomesha sat up and almost spilled

her tea. She didn't want to appear as if were weak and couldn't handle being a donor. She'd go and speak with Mistress if need be.

Starla must have recognized the panic in her expression. She placed a hand on Tomesha's knee.

"Don't worry. Your rest is needed since this was your first time allowing a vampire to feed from you. Believe me when I say that this happens quite often." Starla patted her on the knee. Her expression was open and honest.

Tomesha relaxed. She was still tired and would like nothing better than to go home to her own bed and get some sleep. Tomesha took a few more sips of the tea.

"Good. Now finish working on the tea. I'll return shortly." The healer nodded again, striding to the door. She glanced at Tomesha once more, disappearing through the door.

"Please finish or you'll make Lamaya upset, and you don't want to get on her shit list." Starla smiled. She stood and went over to Tomesha's closet. "When you're done, I'll help you get cleaned up and dressed. By tomorrow you'll feel like a million bucks."

Tomesha sighed and sipped the tea. She was

almost done. She rested back against the headboard and blew out a deep breath. Now she was able to be a donor, she'd need to pay attention to how much the vampires took from her. She knocked back the rest of the drink and shuddered.

"There. Done." She flipped the cup upside down to show Starla it was empty. She hoped they were right. She couldn't show up at her home weak as a babe. Tarek would lose his mind. "Thanks again, Starla."

Her friend turned around with a pair of leggings and long tunic in her hand. Starla smiled at her.

"Of course. What are friends for?"

* * *

"WHAT HAPPENED?" Tarek stormed out of the front door. It slammed behind him. He paused on the porch then made his way toward her.

Tomesha grimaced as she'd hoped to avoid him this morning. She felt a little better but was still weak. All she wanted to do was crawl into her bed and sleep. She'd hoped she'd have had a chance to recover before he came home from work.

Boris had been assigned to drive her home to ensure she made it safely. She held on to the security guard's arm as they made their way up the path. Tarek stopped in front of her. He glared at Boris, in full protector mode.

"What happened to my sister?" Tarek barked again.

Boris's glasses hid his eyes, but the way his muscles tensed set off alarms inside her.

"Hello, I'm right here." She waved a hand at him. She offered an apologetic smile to Boris. Apparently, she hadn't arrived late enough to avoid a confrontation. She sighed and figured she might as well get this over with. "Thanks for bringing me home, Boris. I'll see you tonight?"

"Tomorrow. Don't forget Mistress would like for you to take tonight off," his deep voice rumbled.

There would be no arguing with him. She was sure Mistress had given him explicit instructions before he'd taken her home to remind her. He placed her hand on Tarek's waiting one. He eyed her brother, nodding to her. The large vampire turned and headed back to his vehicle.

"You didn't have to be so rude to him." She shifted her small cross-body tote to rest on her hip.

Tarek helped her up the few steps to the house. According to Lamaya, she needed a full day's rest, then she'd feel like herself again.

"Are you going to answer me?" Tarek snapped.

Her eyes cut to him and held his gaze. His expression softened. He guided her to the door and opened it.

"I will, but why are you like this? It's too early in the morning to be causing all of this ruckus," she muttered.

They entered the house which smelled of lemons and cleaning solutions. She smiled, knowing their grandmother must have been up late cleaning again.

"What do you mean? I look out the window and see a man almost carry you out of the car—"

"He did not carry me." She released Tarek's arm and headed to her bedroom.

Her brother followed her. She sighed and opened the door to her bedroom.

"Why are you moving like you're ninety?" Tarek leaned against the doorjamb and eyed her.

She switched on the light on her nightstand. She turned to face him, and he grew still. His focus immediately dropped to her neck. The only way she'd have been able to hide the markings and bruises was if she'd worn a turtleneck or a scarf.

"What. The. Fuck." He pushed off and slowly walked to her.

She swallowed, unsure how she could truly explain to him what had happened. She remained where she was. He came to her and lifted her chin as he examined her neck. A string of curses flew from his mouth.

"You're not going back there." He released her and shook his head. "They practically mangled you."

"It's not as bad as it looks," she said.

He ran a hand over his face, a stubborn glint in his eyes.

She opened her bag and went over to her bed to pour the coins she'd earned for the week. "See what I brought in? The mistress decided last night that it was time to allow the vampires to feed from me."

"Vampires? As in more than one?" He didn't even pay any mind to the bed.

She tucked her dark hair behind her ear.

"No, just one." It was her turn to shake her head. She immediately regretted it. The skin of her neck was still tight. She blew out a deep breath and took her bag off. She tossed it onto the bed and walked back over to him. "I promise I'm fine. The bruising will go away. The vampire was actually nice, and she tipped me with royal coins."

"All money isn't good money, Tomesha. We can figure out a way." He flicked his gaze over to the pile of coins sitting on her bed. His scowl deepened. "There are a few places I hear that are hiring."

"And none of them are going to pay me what I'm getting at Madam's." She folded her arms in front of her. Tarek was going to have to understand that she made the decisions for her. She loved her brother dearly, but he was going to have to let her live her life. "I promise I'm safe. Boris, who you were rude to, is one of the guards who keep the humans safe at the club. Nothing gets past them. He's actually nice."

"I'm sure he is." Tarek glanced down at his watch and cursed. "Shit. I gotta go. Gran is back in bed. She got up around two and started cleaning."

"I can smell it." A smile came to her lips. She followed him out of her room and down the hall to the living room.

He grabbed his jacket and bag from the floor then headed to the door. He pulled it open and stepped out onto the porch. She followed him and held the door open.

"I love you, big brother."

"Yeah, I love you, too." He jogged down the stairs and threw up a wave.

She shut the door and leaned back against it.

"That could have been worse," she murmured.

If Tarek didn't have to go to work, she was sure they'd still be in their heated discussion about her job that they had at least once a week. She ensured the locks were engaged before going to their grandmother's room.

She gently opened the door and peeked inside. Gran's soft snores filled the air. Tomesha backed away and closed the door. She slowly ambled to her room. She left her door ajar so she'd hear when Gran came out of her room. She changed into her jammies and climbed into bed.

She reached over and set her alarm clock. She didn't want to sleep the entire day away, but she'd catch a quick nap. Lamaya had given her instructions to increase the amount of kenaf weed she took to ensure her stores would be high.

Tomesha rolled over onto her back. She tugged the blanket up higher, and the exhaustion returned. She closed her eyes, and the image of Dru came to mind.

Her bright-blue eyes.

Her auburn hair.

Her sharp fangs that had peeked out from underneath her lips and the way her fangs and tongue had taken her to the stars. A smile graced Tomesha's lips as she succumbed to sleep.

Would she see the vampire general again?

CHAPTER THIRTEEN

"Have I ever said that I hate sewers?" Dru muttered.

"I believe I've heard this before." Talbot chuckled. The vampire warrior pried a steel covering off the opening to the sewers that ran beneath Butterbush.

Dru rolled her eyes in the most un-general-like manner. One would think that in the year they were living in, no vampires would still be underground. It wasn't uncommon, but Dru really hated the sewers.

"They're hot, dark, and always stink." Dru stepped forward decked out in her fighting leathers.

She drew in a deep breath and pulled a dagger out of its sheath. She glanced down and shook her head. "Here we go."

She jumped down and landed on her feet in a defensive crouch, her grip on her weapon tight. Not sensing any threats, she motioned for Talbot and the others to follow suit. She took a few steps forward and eyed their surroundings. They all landed without making a sound. They were after information, and the vampire who supposedly had it was located in the underground community. The scent that greeted her had her scrunching her nose.

As the general, she could have easily sent her men to obtain the information, but that wasn't the way Dru operated. She was going to be hands-on with this particular mission. The queen trusted her, and Dru wasn't going to fail.

She sighed. Just hours ago, she'd been between the thighs of one of the most beautiful women she'd ever seen. Her scent had been something Dru wanted to drown in. Something that she'd want to smell every day. Tomesha's blood had been so damn addicting. Dru had to fight the savage nature to drink more than she had. The memory of Tomesha lying in the bed when she'd left came to the forefront of her mind.

Her curvy frame had barely been covered by the blankets. Dru had a hard time walking away, but it was for the best. She couldn't afford to have a distraction while here in Butterbush.

But she had to admit Tomesha's blood had given her such strength. She felt as if she could face ten full-blooded lycans at the moment. Her gums ached and stretched as her fangs threatened to fall.

She had to stop thinking of Tomesha. Not focusing on the mission at hand could get her or her warriors killed. She blinked and tried to push the tempting memory of Tomesha reaching her climax on her tongue from her head.

Fuck.

"According to the instructions, we need to go this way." Talbot brushed passed Dru.

She blinked and looked around at her warriors. None of them seemed to notice their general had been lost in memories. They were securing the area and ensuring they were alone in this part of the sewers.

"Very well. Lead the way." Dru marched behind Talbot.

Niles, who'd been sent ahead to scope out the town, had located this contact for them. She just hoped that the human wasn't sending them into a trap. She'd go and personally visit them if so.

She wasn't one to cross.

They continued through the maze of sewers. They had stopped carrying water long ago. What flowed through the sewers now was life of a different kind—vampires clinging to the old way of existing. The tunnels stretched endlessly beneath the town, a labyrinth of collapsed archways and broken pipes that groaned like dying beasts when the earth shifted.

The air was damp and rank. The stench of mildew mixed with smoke from the fire pits where some squatters burned scraps of wood and trash. Dru scowled. She hated to see her people like this. Why they refused to come to the surface, she never understood. People moved like shadows through the tunnels. Violence lingered in the air. Dru could almost taste it. These vampires governed themselves and rarely came to the surface.

Even the rogue vampires didn't venture down here.

It wasn't a place to live. This was a place to survive. And down here was someone who had information on the whereabouts of Solomon Winterborne.

The hairs on the back of Dru's neck rose. They were being watched. She was sure it wasn't often they saw royal warriors in their little world. Dru tightened her hold on her dagger.

"There." Talbot jerked his chin.

Dru followed his gaze and saw where they needed to travel. The market sat in one of the widest chambers of the old sewer system.

"Let's hurry so we can get the fuck out of here," Dru murmured.

The warriors behind her echoed the same sentiment. They navigated their way through the packed area. The floors were slick with grime, uneven from collapsed stone and broken tiles.

Rickety stalls leaned together, cobbled from scavenged crates and rusted pipes and raggedy material as awnings. Vendors called out their wares, their gazes watchful as the crowd grew thick. Dru's careful gaze moved along each of the vendors, trying to identify the person they were here to meet. A figure came to stroll next to her.

Niles.

"Do you see him?" she asked.

"I do, General. Second to last stall over on the right," he said.

Talbot, in the front, heard him and gave a confirming nod.

"Everyone else spread out. Talbot and Niles, you're with me," she instructed.

They headed over to where Niles mentioned. The older-looking male glanced up and took notice of them. He whispered to the young male who was working the table with him before he turned and walked away. They picked up speed and followed him away from the central area of the market.

Their contact slipped through a narrow gap in the wall, a crack half hidden by a decaying pillar. Dru pushed past Talbot. She'd be the first to go after the contact. The air was thicker in this area, heavy with the sour reek of stagnant water and waste. They were led into a rectangular room, the low ceiling dripping with condensation into dark puddles on the floor. The walls were brick, blackened by mold and decades of dirt.

In the center stood a battered table, its legs uneven. A lantern burned low upon it, the flames weak but providing enough light. Dru's eyes adjusted. Chairs were placed around the table. The male stood off on the other side of the table and met her gaze. Talbot and Niles paused behind her.

"Do you know who I am?" Dru asked.

"Aye. I do. Even word reaches the likes of us down here. You're General Dru Moldark and you're here for information," the male replied. He eyed the dagger in her hand, then flicked his gaze to Niles and Talbot. "Those weapons are not needed. I am a very old vampire, and believe me when I say that I have never wielded a sword in me life."

Dru slid her dagger into her sheath. He'd be a fool to try anything with the three of them. She nodded.

"And your name?" She arched an eyebrow at him and folded her arms. It was wise that he knew who she was. Hopefully it gave him less of a reason to try to cross her.

"Roderick. Please have a seat. It's not much, but mine nevertheless." He motioned to the table.

"We would prefer to stand. We won't be here long, depending on the information you provide," Dru said.

He nodded slowly. She strode across the room and stopped at the table. Scattered parchment papers lined it with a few gold coins.

"I figured as much," he replied.

Talbot and Niles shifted behind her. She didn't need to look to know that they were covering the door.

Dru reached into her leather vest and pulled out a small velvet bag that held a hefty amount of gold coins. She took one out and placed it on the table. She pushed it to the middle of the wooden structure.

"I trust that this conversation between us will be discreet," she murmured.

Roderick's gaze fell on the gold coin. His eyes widened at the sight of it.

"I've never seen you a day in me life," he muttered.

She lifted her hand from the coin, satisfied by his response. He practically dove across the table and snatched up the money. He eyed it before slipping it into his pants pocket.

"I am looking for a vampire male. Someone who's supposed to be dead. He was once known by the name of Solomon Winterborne," she accounted quietly.

She gripped the bag in her hand and kept it in Roderick's eyesight. He eyed the pouch and nodded.

"Is that so?" Roderick met her gaze. "What did this Solomon do? Why would a general for the crown be looking for him? Especially if he's dead?"

"That's my business," Dru replied dryly. She

pulled out another coin from the bag and held it between two fingers where he could see it. "Now are you someone who has information that I need, or are you wasting my time? I assure you, you don't want to be wasting my time."

Dru flashed her fangs. Roderick's audible gulp was the only sound aside from the water dripping from the ceiling.

"I may have information." He combed his fingers through his dark hair and nodded. His gaze was now locked in on the coin she held. "What did this vampire do?"

She put it down on the table but this time kept it near her.

"He's a traitor," she growled. "And anyone helping this traitor will become an enemy of the crown—and me."

Roderick took a step back from the table. He glanced around at her warriors, then returned his gaze to her.

"I know someone. He's aboveground. He lived here for years, then about ten years ago he went to the surface. He comes back here once in a while. He may be who you're looking for." He eyed the prize on the table.

She smirked. It was funny how a few gold pieces could get a person to talk.

"And if this person is who I'm seeking, why are you willing to give him up?" she asked.

"I don't want to become a target of the crown. It's just me and my boy. I don't want any trouble with the royal family." He rested his hands on the table and met her gaze head-on. "If I tell you where he stays, will me and my son be safe?"

Dru slid the coin across the table to him. She had a weakness for a father who wanted to protect his child. He snatched the coin up and slipped it into his pocket with the other one.

"I have never seen you before a day in me life," she repeated what he'd said.

He nodded again. "I'm serious. This man is a danger to vampires. He's not a good man. He's ruthless and don't care about our kind."

Dru paused. This sounded just like the individual they were hunting. She eyed the vampire across from her. He was telling the truth. She had a good sense about detecting those who lied to her, and this vampire was being completely honest.

"You don't say. How is he a danger to vampires?" she asked.

"That lycan attack that happened years ago? Its

rumored that he's in cahoots with them." He ran a trembling hand across his face. Fear filled his expression and eyes now. He leaned forward. "I need your word that at least my boy will be safe."

"You have my word, Roderick." Her word as a general for the crown was solid. It held much weight. If she said the kid would be safe, then he'd never have to fear anything.

Ever.

"Very well then. If this is who you're seeking, he goes by the name Sol Winters. From what I know he lives out in the woods in a cottage. Deep in the woods. There's a ravine near his home. If you get to the ravine, you've passed it."

Dru held back her smirk. The son of a bitch was cocky. He could have at least changed his name more. He probably figured after all of these years he could keep a similar one. She reached in her bag and took two more coins out and tossed them to Roderick. He fumbled but caught them before they hit the floor.

"If he's the vampire who I'm seeking, you'll be well rewarded."

"I FIND it funny that I promote you, then you leave on a mission for my mother." Lethia's holographic form stood in the center of Dru's private quarters at the inn she and her men were staying at.

"What was I supposed to do? Refuse Her Royal Majesty's request?" Dru arched an eyebrow at her friend. She removed her daggers from her waist and placed them on the nightstand. She paused, remembering how Tomesha had taken great care in ensuring her weapons were near her. She blinked, unsure why she couldn't get the human out of her head. She straightened and turned to face Lethia. The moment she'd walked into her suite, the holograph had started ringing.

"I guess if you did, my mother would have been within her rights to take your head." Lethia shrugged.

"I like my head exactly where it is," Dru muttered. She sat on the edge of the bed and reached for the ties of her boots. She eyed her friend. "Is there a reason you have called, Your Highness?"

"Don't get all formal with me." Lethia blew out a deep breath. She paused and stared at Dru. "Oh, my goodness. You've fed, and if I didn't know any better, you've had sex recently."

"What?" Dru sputtered. She dropped her foot on the floor and stared at Lethia. Did she have a warrior amongst her spying for Lethia? She pulled the boot from her foot and reached for the other one.

"You have. It's about fucking time." Lethia clapped and barked a laugh. "Did you call for a donor?"

"The postmaster escorted us to the local madam's," Dru admitted. She removed her other boot and set them both at the foot of the bed. She never knew when she had to leave in a hurry. She wanted to be able to reach them at a moment's notice.

"Good for you. You needed a good fucking. You were too uptight." Lethia snickered.

"I was not. I have been fine. Drinking prepared blood is almost as nutritious as drinking directly from a source."

"Key word is *almost*." Lethia chuckled. Her smile disappeared. "I'm happy you finally released some of that tension you carried. Go back a few more times before you come home."

"Is there a real reason you're calling, or did you just want to make sure I fucked someone?" Dru asked, exasperated.

"The post. It's been a while since it has been inspected. What are your thoughts on the faculty and the postmaster?"

Now this was what Dru could tolerate. She stood and went over her findings of the vampire military base. She paced back and forth as she spoke. This helped her keep her mind off the beautiful soft brown skin she'd licked and kissed. Or the deep bedroom eyes that had held her gaze as she'd reached her climax.

Dru paused and drew in a shaky breath. Maybe Lethia was right. Maybe she should go back to Madam's once more before she returned home. Maybe she couldn't get Tomesha out of her head because it had been so long since she'd been with a woman.

That was it.

It had to be.

She didn't want to think how good Tomesha's skin felt against hers. Or how the taste of her blood had exploded on her tongue. How delicious it was. How sweet and fulfilling it was to drink from her.

"What is it?" Lethia's voice cut into her thoughts.

Dru blinked. "Um." Shit. She couldn't remember what the hell she'd been saying. She turned and glanced over at Lethia who had a smirk on her lips. "What was the last thing I said?"

"Who is she?" Lethia asked softly.

Dru rolled her eyes. *There she goes again.* Just because she was mated, didn't mean that everyone had to find someone. Dru was currently on a very important mission and could not afford to mess this up. It wasn't often the queen asked for personal favors.

"Don't worry about it. I'll write up my official report once I return to Crystal Cove." Dru reached up and pulled her hair out of the tight bun. Her thick hair fell in waves around her shoulders.

"Oh, I'll get to the bottom of this." Lethia smirked.

"Whoever is spying on me for you will pay heavily," Dru threatened.

"Spying on you for me? How is it spying when the commander demands information about a mission her general and warriors are on? You all report to me." Lethia's figure came to stop in front of Dru. There was a teasing glint in her eyes.

"Call it what you want, but you're spying." Dru glared at her longtime friend. If she was home right now, she'd challenge Lethia to sparring.

"Well, whoever she is, I hope she's your mate."

"This conversation is over." Dru went over to the hologram box and hit the disconnect button.

Lethia's figure disappeared, but not before her laughter reached Dru's ear. She stripped off her clothing and headed into the connecting bathroom. She needed to take a shower to get the stench of the sewers off her.

It felt as if the scent and aromas down there had invaded her pores. She turned the water to the hottest setting. She reached for the soap and cloth and washed herself.

Sol Winters.

That was who she needed to focus on. The vampire had been accused of horrific crimes that if he was alive, she'd be only too happy to drag his ass back to face the king and queen.

CHAPTER FOURTEEN

"General, welcome back to Madam Rice's." The same hostess who'd greeted her yesterday smiled and bowed her head. "My name is Callidora, and I shall be your hostess again."

"Thank you." Dru took in the club. Music throbbed, low and primal, each note a seduction. Dru's gums stretched to accommodate her fangs descending. She didn't know why she was here—she knew but didn't know why so soon. She'd just fed the day before, and it had been fulfilling. She'd left very satisfied. Tomesha had sated the hunger that had burned inside her.

So why was she back already?

She should have been fine for another day or two.

"Would you like a private alcove or open seating?" Callidora asked.

"Alcove." Dru had left the inn with the promise to return soon. She hadn't told anyone where she was going. She'd taken one of the vehicles and had driven herself to the club. She inhaled deeply and caught the scents of the humans, tempting and all available for a price.

Her gaze roamed the room, seeking out a certain brown-skinned beauty. Was she entertaining another? A growl rippled through her at the thought of another touching Tomesha. Drinking from her. Tasting what was between her thighs.

"Follow me." Callidora smiled and turned on her heel.

Dru cleared her throat and hoped the hostess didn't hear her growl. She followed Callidora in the direction she'd been seated yesterday. They arrived at another alcove that was nestled in the corner.

"Please have a seat. Would you like to review the menu or would you like to be presented live donors?"

Dru, dressed in her fighting leathers, sat on the

cushioned bench. She scanned the room and ignored the vampires who leaned over their chosen partners in plain view or the gasps of ecstasy that carried over the music. Others were sprawled on lounges participating in the sins of the flesh. A male vampire rested back on a chair while a female rode him. Her cries reached Dru from across the room.

"Is Tomesha working?" Dru zeroed in on the hostess. She tried to appear calm and collected.

"I'm sorry. She's not."

There was a hint of something in her eyes that Dru couldn't read. Immediately, alarms went off in Dru's mind. She recovered quickly with a wide smile.

"If you desire a human donor, I'll arrange—"

"Give me the menu," Dru interjected.

The moment the hostess had mentioned another live donor, Dru's stomach quivered. She was unsure why she suddenly felt sick to her stomach at the thought of drinking from a donor. She'd done it countless times in her two hundred and twenty-five years on this earth. Why all of sudden would she feel ill to her stomach at the thought of feeding from a random human?

"Certainly. Give me a moment to grab one." Callidora bowed her head and disappeared.

Dru blew out a deep breath. Was it Tomesha's scheduled day off? Or was she home recovering? It had been the first time she'd been fed from. Dru had ensured she'd tipped Tomesha well. The woman had left an impression on her.

Clearly.

Which would explain why she was trying to see her again after she'd said she needed to focus on her mission—not the human.

"Here you are, General." Callidora reappeared and slid the menu onto the table to Dru. "Would you like me to recommend—"

"No," Dru snapped. She cleared her throat and reached for the menu. She softened her tone. "Let me look it over first. If I have any questions, I'll ask."

"Of course." She tipped her head to Dru before leaving.

Dru picked up the menu. She glanced at it but could barely read the words. She should leave. If Tomesha wasn't here, then maybe she could come back on another day when she worked. Her breaths came faster at the thought of seeing the human again. Maybe she could just ask when Tomesha worked. Then she could come back for a direct feeding and more. Her breath caught in her throat at what *more* entailed.

Since she was here, she might as well have one glass. That wouldn't hurt. She eyed the menu again. She read the selection she'd almost ordered last time.

The Dionysian – From donors who indulged in red wine before offering, imparting lush berry undertones and a heady warmth.

She might as well get it this time. It at least sounded more appealing than feeding from another female. Dru looked up and caught the eye of a server. She flagged her down. The woman navigated her way over to Dru.

"Hello. I'm Viessa. Can I get you something?"

Her husky voice grated on Dru's nerves. She held back a wince and pointed to the selection she'd chosen.

"A glass of the Dionysian." Dru eyed the human who smiled widely. Her sheer uniform revealed all that she had to offer. Her thin frame and high, small breasts would certainly attract anyone's attention.

"You sure you want prepared? I'd be willing to sate your hunger," Viessa murmured. She leaned her hip against the table. Her gaze raked over Dru. The interest burned bright in her eyes.

Dru gave her the once-over again and didn't feel anything.

"Thank you for the generous offer, but the Dionysian, please," Dru replied.

"Okay." Viessa pouted. She spun on her heel and disappeared in the crowd.

Dru leaned back, and her gaze landed on an alluring figure making their way to her. A woman with pale skin, high cheekbones, lips the color of fresh blood, and large, oval-shaped eyes. Her chin-length dark hair brushed her cheeks. Power clung to this woman as tight as the leather dress that was draped over her body. This had to be the mistress who oversaw this location.

Dru waited for her to arrive.

"General. Welcome to Madam's. I'm thrilled that you chose to come back so soon. I do apologize I wasn't here to greet you last time you were here." Her crimson lips spread into smile.

"You must be Mistress." Dru stood and waved her to sit on the other side of the bench.

Mistress made her way to the edge of the booth and took a seat. Dru sat back on the bench and eyed the woman.

"I am Romana Beatrix and I am the mistress of this house." Romana settled back and met Dru's gaze. This was a woman who may oversee vampires and humans in a feeding establishment, but there was a glint in her eyes hinting there was more to her than what she presented.

"What can I do for you?" Dru asked.

"Oh, but it is I who shall be asking what I can do for you?" Her smile widened. She studied Dru. "I hear that you were asking for Tomesha again."

"I did."

"I'd have to say when I saw you had sent a payment, even though she was to be a gift to you, that left me a little perplexed."

"I'm not a woman who likes to owe anyone anything," Dru said matter-of-factly. By accepting the gift, that left her open to one day needing to hear a request of the woman before her. She knew the game, and Dru for one, wasn't one who liked to indulge in little games.

"But you're an honored guest. The right hand of our warden—"

"What do you want, Romana?" Dru stared at her.

The woman wanted something. Dru was actually surprised she didn't just come out and say what it was. Mistress barked a sharp laugh and shook her head.

"There is nothing that I want at the moment. All that I want to ensure is that you're well taken care of while you're here in Butterbush. It's not often we have a direct representative from the royal family here in our little town."

"Well, it may happen more. I am here on business," Dru reminded her.

"But yet you're here in my club a second day in a row." She leaned forward and paused just as Viessa returned.

The human set a goblet down on the table in front of Dru and one for Ramona. She smiled at them.

"Thank you." Dru reached into her pocket and held a small coin out.

Viessa snatched it up and tossed her a wink.

"The offer still stands if you change your mind," she said.

"I won't," Dru replied.

The human shrugged and walked off, heading to another alcove. Dru picked up her glass and inhaled. She scented the undertone of sweet berries mixed in with the metallic hint of copper. The thick liquid had been warmed.

Ramona lifted her glass and tipped it to Dru.

"To the crown," Ramona murmured before taking a healthy sip from her chalice.

"The crown," Dru echoed. She took a small sip then placed hers back down on the table. She swallowed and bit back a grimace. The blood smelled delicious, but for some strange reason the taste was off. It almost tasted as if it were sour. Were the berries they used to infuse with it not ripe enough?

"Is that not to your satisfaction?" Ramona's perfectly sculpted eyebrow arched. The woman didn't miss a thing.

Dru smiled tightly.

"It's fine." she lied.

"As I was about to say, we do need to speak about Tomesha," Ramona continued. Her fake smile disappeared, and a seriousness came over her.

Dru tensed. What was it about Tomesha that had the woman glaring at her?

"What about her? I thought she wasn't here tonight?" Dru's gaze roamed the establishment again, hoping to catch a glimpse of her. Her heart rate increased at the thought of seeing the beautiful woman.

"I gave her the night off because of an issue," Ramona stated curtly.

"What issue?" Dru snapped. She reached for

the goblet to have something to do with her hands. She sipped and held back a shudder. She kept her face devoid of all expression. Would the woman get straight to the point? Why was she tiptoeing around whatever she wanted to stay?

"You almost bled her dry."

Dru froze, a chilling sensation coursing through her body. Her heart skipped a beat as she flicked her gaze to Ramona. There was no way. She'd been careful when she'd fed. The urge had been strong. More so than she'd ever experienced, but there was no way Dru had taken that much from her.

"What?"

"I don't need to repeat myself. She was found in her bed barely conscious and weakened. I'm just glad one of the other donors found her when she had," Ramona said.

"Is she okay? Don't your humans take kenaf weed?" The former healer in Dru came to the forefront. It may be a life that she'd left behind, but it didn't mean she'd forgotten all of her training. Now she wished she'd woken Tomesha to assess her before she'd left. It was common knowledge that humans who donated for the first time may have some side effects. Either the euphoria was too great, which some could get addicted to, or their stores weren't high enough beforehand and the donors could become anemic afterward—hence the importance of the kenaf weed.

Dru had thought the woman was sleeping soundly after the night of passion they'd shared. Her breathing had been even, her heartbeat had been slow and steady. Dru had been determined to leave, and maybe she'd misjudged Tomesha's condition.

Now hearing what had happened, it was apparent she had.

"Of course they do. Don't start questioning how my humans are prepared and ignore the fact that you drained her more than you should have. If you'd required additional—"

"I did not. Tomesha was perfect," Dru growled. She didn't even want to consider another human. The only one she wanted was Tomesha. Dru blinked at the thought. She lifted the goblet and took a small sip.

Why were these feelings so damn strong for Tomesha? It wasn't like she was Dru's mate.

Dru froze in place.

There was no way.

Dru hadn't entered the draft yet and didn't know if she had a match out there. Was Tomesha her fated mate? Was she the one for Dru? Was this why the blood in this damn goblet tasted sour? She'd remembered how Lethia was unable to feed from another human once she'd met Alima. Even when she was mortally injured, the commander refused to take blood from a donor.

"Tomesha is something special. That's why she'd been reserved for an honored guest. Now that she's been fed from, I can offer her out. There are other vampires who will pay me handsomely for the opportunity to feed from her."

"How much do I have to pay to render her services completely to me?" Dru asked.

Ramona's eyebrows shot up high again. Dru knew what she was asking. She didn't want anyone else to feed from Tomesha. Even thinking of it had her wanting to reach for her dagger.

"While I'm here in town."

"Well, that is a hefty cost. Tomesha is one of my prized humans. I'll have some disappointed clients," Ramona said.

"Send them to me, and I'll fix them." Dru couldn't care less if someone would be disappointed that they couldn't feed from her human. She ignored the fact that she'd just claimed Tomesha as her human, but instead glared at the mistress.

Tomesha was for her, and she'd be damned if another vampire's fangs pierced her soft, delicate flesh.

The memory of the vampire female who'd tried to take Tomesha away when she'd been presented to Dru came to mind. She snarled at the thought of that woman touching Tomesha. Apparently, she was already familiar with Tomesha and wanted first claim of feeding from her. If she voiced her disapproval again while Dru was present, Dru wasn't going to hesitate to take action.

Tomesha was hers.

"I don't need to do that. I can handle my clients. What I want to ensure from you is that you will not kill my donor. We have a reputation here. I don't know how the vampires are in Maine—"

"It won't happen again. I thought I had controlled my urges, but apparently I was wrong." The thought of causing Tomesha harm sent a wave of pain through Dru. "Increase her kenaf weed dosage."

"Again, don't tell me how to prepare my humans." Ramona lifted her chalice and finished off her blood. She set the empty cup down on the table. A devious smirk came to her lips. "Now about these services you're requesting. They come with a pretty price."

"Money is not an issue," Dru replied dryly.

Did the mistress seriously think money would be a problem for Dru? She was a general. A high-ranking member of their warden's house. She didn't care how much it would cost to have Tomesha—she'd pay.

"I didn't think it was. Please, let's go to my office. We can hash out the details and payment there."

* * *

"GENERAL, I didn't think you'd be returning so soon." The warrior who stood guard at the inn's entrance greeted her. He pounded his fist above his heart.

"I didn't know I had to answer to anyone here." It did irk her that she was returning to the inn, not having fed. The small sips of blood that she'd purchased had lacked in every way. What she needed was blood from a live source.

Tomesha's blood.

She marched past him and entered the building. It was a private mansion that she and her warriors had commissioned to stay in while in Butterbush. There was a human working on a computer behind the desk. She eyed a few of her men sitting around a table playing a game of cards. She strode over to them, in a foul mood.

She'd signed a contract with the mistress to have exclusive rights over Tomesha while in their town. Tomesha would be available for Dru at her beck and call. The amount of money the mistress elicited from her should have been a crime, but Tomesha was worth every penny. Finding out she'd almost brought harm to the human didn't sit right with Dru. She needed to see Tomesha for herself to confirm she was truly okay as the mistress had assured.

"Is this what we do while on a direct mission from the queen? Play games?" Dru paused by the table and eyed each of the men.

They flew from the table and stood at attention.

"General. It was only a friendly game to occupy our time," one of the warriors said.

She eyed him and came to stand in front of him. She couldn't remember his name. He'd been chosen by Talbot to accompany them, so he must be a trusted vampire. She'd asked him to pick his best men.

"Where is Talbot?" she asked.

"He's out in the back. Just returned. He told us to rest for a few hours," another one said.

Dru sniffed. She didn't know why she was being hard on them. She nodded, motioning back to the table.

"Carry on, but be prepared for orders," Dru said.

"Yes, General."

The four of them pounded their fists above their hearts. She spun on her heel and stalked off down the hallway that led to the back entrance of the inn. Talbot had better have an update for her.

Since their informant had given them the possible location of the traitor, she'd wanted a group of warriors to scout out the area mentioned. If the informant had crossed her, he'd regret it dearly. She quickened her pace, wanting to speak with Talbot for his report.

She pushed through the door and found Talbot, Niles, and Orenda standing near a truck with a map spread across the hood of it. The small parking lot provided by the inn only held the vehicles of her party. While here on business, they had commissioned the entire inn. The owners were paid well to accommodate the royal warriors. Dru strode down the stairs and headed toward the group.

It was still early in the night. Dru had hoped by now she and Tomesha would have been entangled together in the sheets of her bed. She ran her tongue over her fangs which had yet to return into her gums. The taste of Tomesha's sweet yet nourishing blood still lingered on her tongue, as did the taste of her creamy nectar as it flowed from her slick cunt. Dru bit back a growl. She'd have to wait another day before Tomesha was checked out by the club's healer again.

Dru wasn't known too much for her patience when it came to some things, but for Tomesha, she'd wait. She wanted her human to be healthy when she fed from her again. Ramona's words came to mind.

She was found in her bed barely conscious and weakened.

Dru winced. She'd apologize to Tomesha. She never wanted to cause harm to her. Thankfully, someone had found her before it was too late. To think if she'd caused her to—

Dru cut that thought from her mind. Tomesha was fine. She'd received care and rest. She had half a mind to call her sister. Dru was sure the madam employed the best healers, but there was no one better than Zada.

"General."

The three of them stood to attention as she arrived near them. She gave them all a nod.

"At ease. Report. What have you found?" she asked, immediately getting to business.

They relaxed. Talbot motioned to the maps they had strewn on top of the vehicle. She stood next to him and folded her arms.

If she wasn't able to be with Tomesha on this night, she'd do the next best thing on the agenda.

Hunt a traitor.

"We've gained access to the most recent map and even older ones to compare. We've located a cottage deep in the woods where Roderick suggested." Talbot tapped on an area of a map.

It was far from the town. Roderick had been right. If this was Sol—Solomon—he'd removed himself from the townspeople.

But why would he continue to stay in an area where a military post was? She'd have thought that if one was hiding from the king and queen, they'd remain far from military. Dru narrowed her eyes on the map.

There was a reason he was staying close by.

Dru's suspicion was growing for the vampire. If Roderick was right and the vampire was working with the lycans, it would make perfect sense for him to take the risk to remain near the military post.

"We drove out there, but the best way for us to get close to the house would be by foot," Niles said. The warrior glanced over at Dru. "From what I hear, not many of the locals go out to that part of the woods anymore."

"Why?" Dru asked.

"Apparently it's filled with traps. The owner of that cottage doesn't want anyone to get close to his property," Niles replied.

"And the last time the lycans attacked, guess what direction they came from?" Orenda asked. A devious glint appeared in her gaze.

"Let me guess," Dru murmured sarcastically. She moved forward and studied the map. It didn't look impenetrable, but if the old vampire warrior had outfitted it with traps, it was going to be damn dangerous. He was a vampire who'd fought by the king's side at one time. That made this challenge harder and more dangerous. "The lycans came from this area."

"Bingo." Orenda scowled.

It was no wonder Roderick was insistent that

they provided protection for his boy if it was discovered that he'd ratted out the old hand of the king. The former hand had been accused of ordering the murders of the lycan king's children. Just babes. Thirteen, eight, and three years old. Only a monster would kill innocent children. A male like that wouldn't hesitate to harm a vampire kid. Especially as a payback for the sins of the father.

Well, the kid would remain safe, and Dru was going to keep a promise to the queen. Either she took Solomon alive to face them, or she'd deliver his head to the royal couple.

"Well, it looks like we need to drop in for a visit, now don't we?"

CHAPTER FIFTEEN

Tomesha entered through the employee entrance of Madam's. She inhaled sharply and could admit she felt much better. Rest and relaxation were what she'd needed. She'd need to prepare for tonight's shift, but before she did, she had to make a stop at the healer's office for an exam. If Lamaya felt she wasn't ready to work, there would be a problem. If she wasn't working, she wouldn't get paid.

She hefted her bag up on her shoulder and jogged down the stairs to the lower level. She anxiously made her way through the winding hallway to Lamaya's office. She arrived at the open door and peered inside. It carried the same elegance as the club above. Velvet curtains draped between each bed, offering privacy, lessening the feeling of being in a hospital, and the bedding itself was soft silk but still clinical white. Golden sconces held candles that burned with a warm glow, making the room inviting.

The scent of herbs carefully masked the faint undertone of antiseptic. Tomesha stepped inside the doorway and paused.

"Hello?" she called out.

At the back of the infirmary stood a large, partially open oak door. It swung fully open with Lamaya walking through it.

"You certainly look much better," the healer said.

"I feel like myself." Tomesha chuckled. She couldn't believe how weak she'd become after Dru had fed from her. Today, she was able to walk to work as she normally did.

"Well, let me take a look at you. Mistress will want to ensure you're back to normal." Lamaya waved her over to one of the cots.

"I'm sorry if I scared everyone." Tomesha placed her bag on the chair next to the bed before hopping onto it.

"You humans are a delicate lot. Allowing a vampire to feed from you can be taxing on your body. That is why we have to prepare you beforehand." Lamaya went through the motions of examining Tomesha. She was very thorough and even took a small sample of blood. "I'll be right back. I want to test this to see how high your blood levels are. This will ultimately decide if you can donate again."

Lamaya slid open the curtain and stepped away with Tomesha's blood sample. Tomesha settled back on the comfortable cot and tried not to be nervous. What would happen if she was unable to donate? Now that she'd no longer be on reserve, it would be expected for her to donate as she performed her services. But if she was deemed unable to work by the healer…

She'd been saving so if she needed to take off a few days to recover, she'd be fine, but she didn't want this to jeopardize her job. She wasn't sure if Mistress would keep her on as a server only if she couldn't donate. The health of the humans was very important, which Tomesha understood.

Movement outside her curtain caught her attention. She leaned over and took in who'd come into the infirmary. Concerned filled her when she saw who it was.

"Conner?" She jumped down and padded over to the curtain.

He was escorted over to the other private areas by a security guard. He glanced over at her and winked. She followed him so she could find out why he had to see Lamaya. They had spoken plenty of times during downtime in the club. She'd even consider him a friend. He'd shared everything he'd learned. They had started together, but he was made a donor much faster than she was.

"Fancy seeing you here." He held his arm to his chest. It looked bruised. He grimaced as he sat on the cot.

She paused by his curtains.

He nodded to the large guard. "Thanks, man."

"No worries. Let me know if you have any other problems." The guard brushed past her and disappeared through the doors.

She turned back to Connor who looked paler than normal.

"What happened?" she asked softly.

"This is nothing. Just a client who got a little rough with me. I was with another client, and he just didn't want to take no for an answer." Connor blew out a deep breath. He leaned back against the pillows and smiled, but the stress around his eyes revealed there was more to the story.

"It's not broken, is it?" She moved to the foot of the bed.

Connor was much younger than her, and he'd lived a life that was far beyond his years.

"I don't think so. Just bruised, and it hurts like crazy, but nothing I haven't been through before." He combed his hair with his uninjured hand.

Life as a human in this world was hard. They were accomplishing so much since the war, but it was still a challenge. She thought of when she was his age and how lucky she'd been to have Tarek shielding her as best he could. She was able to help with odd jobs here and there until she'd gotten her seamstress job. She hadn't even thought of becoming a donor or working for the madam until times had gotten desperate for them.

But Connor was only twenty-four, still a kid, who was on his own. He was surviving, but at what cost? He never mentioned a family, and she knew not to bring it up.

"I'm sorry." Her heart went out to him.

Life as a donor wasn't as glamorous. She was lucky she hadn't had any issues with her clients.

She'd been worried that some would want to take advantage of her. That was a fear that always sat at the back of her mind. The vampires were much stronger than them, and if they wanted to take something—they could.

The madam had strict rules, and many vampires who frequented her establishment didn't want to cross her. That was one thing Tomesha had learned since working for her. She'd never met Madam Bethany Rice who was once a prostitute then turned businesswoman. She'd opened her first feeding house centuries ago. She was known as shrewd and had royal connections, hence why many vampires didn't want to get on her bad side.

"What are you apologizing for? It's a hazard of the job. We all signed up for this when we applied to work as a donor." His smile vanished, and he suddenly appeared older than his young age. He grimaced and adjusted his injured arm higher on his chest. "I'll be okay. It will heal, and I'll soon back at work."

Tomesha reached up and tucked her hair behind her ear. He was right. This was a dangerous job. Yes, the vampires may have consequences to their actions, but if a human was mortally injured and died, there was nothing that could be done to bring them back. She shuddered to think if something like this were to happen to her. The memory of Valentina's reaction to not being the first vampire to bite her surfaced.

Would she be angry with Tomesha the next time she requested her?

"Tomesha," Lamaya's voice sliced through the air.

"I'm over here." Tomesha moved to the edge of the curtains where Lamaya could see her.

The healer ambled over to her and waved to Connor. "I'll be with you in just a minute." Her gaze swept over him in a silent assessment.

"I'm not going anywhere." Connor's smile returned. He gave Tomesha a nod. "I'll see you later."

"You take care of yourself. Don't rush to come back to work." Tomesha slipped over to the side of his bed and took his good hand in hers. She gave it a squeeze. He was like the little brother she never had. She hoped the vampire who'd done this to him was held accountable for their actions.

"Same for you. I heard you were worse off than a bruised arm. You make sure you're ready to come back," he said softly, returning the squeeze.

She wasn't surprised that news had traveled throughout the club amongst the humans.

"I feel much better. Lamaya has been taking great care of me." She squeezed him again then released him. She turned and followed Lamaya over to her area. Worry was still heavy in her chest. This could happen to any of them. Even though as humans they obeyed all of the rules and suggestions of the club, that didn't mean the vampires would.

She hopped back on her cot. Lamaya pulled the curtain closed to give them a sense of privacy. Butterflies in Tomesha's stomach fluttered to life. What did the test reveal?

"So am I good?" Tomesha asked.

"You are. I want you to continue taking the increased dose of the kenaf weed. After feedings, I want you to also do the ifalla tea each night. Only one donor per shift also. I know some humans may allow multiple feedings, but I don't think you can be one of them."

Lamaya handed Tomesha a piece of paper. It held the results of the blood test that she'd performed, but Tomesha didn't understand any of it.

"But my blood stores are good? Is this what this means?" She looked up from the paper.

"Yes. We want to keep humans who are constant donors with a slightly elevated hemoglobin to account for the loss when you donate. You're a little below what I would like to see, but I believe with the kenaf weed and teas, you'll get there and be fine. I have sent my recommendation to Mistress," Lamaya said.

"Perfect." Relief filled Tomesha. She trusted Lamaya to know what would be best when it came to humans and donation. She hopped down from the cot and reached for her bag. She needed to get prepared for tonight's shift. She already had an outfit in mind—

"Mistress did reply to my message. She'd like to see you," Lamaya announced.

Tomesha straightened. "Now?"

"Yes. Also, I'll have the ifalla tea leaves delivered to your suite with instructions. It's very simple to make. If you need any assistance, just call on me."

"I'm sure I'll be fine. Thank you for everything." Tomesha draped the strap of her bag on her shoulder. She wasn't sure why Mistress would be sending for her, but she'd go and find out. It wasn't like she could ignore the request.

"You're most welcome." Lamaya bowed her

head then opened the curtain. "Again, call if you need anything."

Tomesha smiled and brushed past the healer. She stuffed the paperwork into her bag and waved to Connor before heading toward the exit. She'd quickly go to see Mistress. If all was well with her, what could she want now?

* * *

"WHAT?" Tomesha blinked and stared at Romana who sat behind her great desk as though it was an altar built solely for her.

Mistress's sharp gaze didn't waver from Tomesha after she'd dropped the bomb of an announcement. Crimson nails tapped against the polished wood as Mistress remained calm even though Tomesha's heart was going into overdrive.

"Would this be a problem?" Mistress asked. Her perfectly arched eyebrow rose. She studied Tomesha.

"I mean no. I guess not. I just didn't think…" Tomesha paused and blinked.

Dru was requesting Tomesha be her private donor while she was in town. Her breath caught in her throat at the thought of seeing the strong vampire again. Even though Dru had taken too much blood from her, she didn't hold any ill will toward her.

If anything, she grew excited.

"It is a great honor, my dear. General Moldark is the right hand of the warden, Princess Lethia Riskel—"

"I know. I'm just shocked. I guess I was thinking that with what happened, you would want another donor for her. Someone with more experience. You know, someone who doesn't almost die after her first donation." Tomesha tried her hand at a small joke, but it fell flat. She glanced down at her hands as she sat in the chair across from Mistress's desk. She'd heard of donors doing private jobs or making house calls. She glanced back up at Romana. "So what does that mean exactly?"

She'd been too shocked when Mistress had announced Dru's request that she hadn't heard anything else.

All she'd heard was Dru wanted only her.

A shiver rippled through her body at the thought of seeing Dru again. Her kisses hadn't been far from her mind. Or the orgasms the woman had pulled from her. She straightened in her seat to pay attention to what Mistress was saying.

"It means that you'll be at the beck and call of the general. She's paying a big fee to be the only vampire who will feed from you. No other services are to be provided to another while she's here," Ramona said. Mistress spoke as if she were speaking of a business deal for goods, not that of providing a human being to a vampire. "You'll be paid well along with whatever tips or gifts the general will bestow upon you. It will be up to the general if you provide services here or at her local place of residence while in Butterbush."

Tomesha nodded as she continued to listen to the other details. This agreement included stipulations that Tomesha didn't even have sex with any other client. She could work as a server only when not entertaining the general. No sexual favors, no feeding. Be on call for the general. Whatever the general wanted, Tomesha had to provide.

"What if I'm working as a server and someone gets upset that I tell them I can't service them?" she asked.

Valentina's reaction surfaced again. She had other clients who she was sure would be upset if they saw her working and had to decline their invitation for a private or not-so-private dalliance.

"You leave that to me. If you have any issues,

you notify security immediately. Your safety is top priority here at Madam Rice's," Romana said matter-of-factly.

There was coldness that settled in her eyes that made Tomesha grateful she was on the vampire's good side. She actually did like and respect Romana. She was strict but a fair employer.

"Yes, Mistress," Tomesha said. She felt confident that she was going to be safe with this private duty assignment.

She didn't want to end up back in the infirmary. Connor was right. They all knew what they were signing up for when they'd become donors. They were lucky to work for the madam. There were some illegal feeding houses she'd heard whispers of that didn't protect their humans the way the madam did.

Madam Rice's was known as a safe haven for humans and vampires. It was a place where vampires could be their true nature. They needed blood to survive. Tomesha equated the feeding houses to a restaurant that humans attended. Only their meals weren't live, breathing beings.

"She's requesting your presence tonight at the inn. We'll have a driver take you. Notify Boris when you're ready. She's asking for you to be there by midnight."

Tomesha stood from her chair and lifted her bag from the floor. Now that she knew she wasn't going to be working the floor tonight, she was going to have to figure out what she'd wear to go and see the general.

"If you need clothing, alert Aisling, and she'll provide something appropriate," Mistress said.

Tomesha blinked. How did Romana know what she was thinking? Was the woman a mind reader?

A smile appeared on Romana's red lips. "No, I'm not a mind reader. I could just tell by your expression what you were thinking. I'm sure you wouldn't want to wear your uniform out in public."

"Yes, I was just thinking that I had clothing at home, but I only keep my uniforms here," she said.

"Then I'll have Aisling bring you a few outfits to pick between." Romana pressed a button on her desk.

"Thank you." Tomesha turned and headed out of the office. She closed the large door behind her and paused. She breathed a heavy sigh. Nervousness filled her at the thought of seeing Dru again. It was one thing to service her here at the club.

Leaving the safety of the club heightened her senses of how dangerous this job could be.

She began making her way through the halls to her suite. She shook her head. What was she worried about?

Dru wouldn't hurt her. Not on purpose, at least. She hadn't known that she'd taken too much from Tomesha the last time they'd been together. She even doubted the vampire knew what had happened to Tomesha after she'd left. There was no reason for Tomesha to share that little information with the vampire. She was under the care of the healer, and they had a plan to keep it from happening again.

Dru wanted her.

She hadn't asked for another donor. There were plenty to choose from. Plenty who were more experienced than her. Dru had known that no other vampire had fed from Tomesha. But apparently that didn't matter. A smile formed on Tomesha's lips.

She was being requested to be the private *sanguina* for the general.

It was an honor she'd hold close to her heart.

Tomesha arrived at her suite and tossed her bag on the chair and beelined it for the bathroom. She'd grab a quick shower and ensure she looked perfect tonight. She switched on the shower then glanced at herself in the mirror. Her eyes widened at the sight of a smile on her lips.

Dru was drawing up emotions in her that she needed to push down. This was a business deal. Apparently, Tomesha had satisfied her client so much that she wanted her again. It didn't mean anything. Dru was a vampire who needed to feed. Tomesha was a human who had blood. Dru had sexual urges and needs. Tomesha was a sex worker. She wrinkled her nose at the term.

Maybe they needed another way to label what they did for a living.

She reached for her brush and dragged it through her long dark hair. She'd would wrap it up for now so she could shower then style it afterwards. She had a few hours before she was to report to her vampire—

She paused.

When did Dru become her vampire?

"She's not my vampire. She's *a* vampire," Tomesha muttered. She wrapped her hair, stripped her clothes off, and threw on a shower cap before entering the shower. The warm water flowed over her skin. She turned her back to the stream.

But if Dru wasn't her vampire, then why did she have these butterflies in her stomach? How long would Dru want her? How long was she planning to stay in Butterbush? And what would happen once she left the town? Would Tomesha ever see her again?

Worry set in.

"What are you doing?"

These were crazy thoughts. Dru was her client, not a lover who had feelings for her. Tomesha was going to have to learn to keep developing feelings for the vampire at bay.

Yes, she was going to have to learn to put up a wall around her heart to keep her from getting hurt.

CHAPTER SIXTEEN

Dru's private quarters at the inn had a desk and chair in the corner. She was deep in writing up her reports on the military post. She had plenty to recommend for the postmaster and was sure he'd be open to her suggestions. Not that he truly had a choice. Reviewing this post had her interested in visiting other ones throughout their territory. She glanced at her tablet and pulled up the former reports that had been submitted on them.

A message came through. Ciro requesting a video chat. She hit the accept button. Within seconds a call came through on the screen. She tapped the second accept button. Ciro's face came into view.

"General." The vampire warrior bowed his head to her.

Dru set the tablet on the desk where it could stand up. "I take it you have news for me if you're video calling me."

"That I do. I won't keep you long."

He panned out the video to show a female warrior sitting next to him. They were in a darkened room with plenty of monitors and computers. She recognized the female, June Kline.

"Hello, General." June offered a tight smile.

"June. I hope the two of you have found some information that will be useful," Dru said.

From the looks of it, Ciro had traveled to Princess Hegna's in order to work with June. These two vampires were extremely smart and talented with technology. If anyone could find the new alpha of the lycans, it would be them.

"We have. It's not much, but it's definitely more than we had. I've stayed in contact with Gale and Ishmael who have infiltrated the two dens," Ciro announced.

This piqued Dru's interest. She hadn't expected to hear from Gale and Ishmael so soon, but if the two had already found something out, then it proved her team was phenomenal.

"What do we have?" Dru asked.

"Gale is in Oklahoma right now, and Ishmael is in Oregon. They have gained one piece of information that is identical," Ciro said. The sound of fingers flying on a keyboard clattered in the background. He shifted to the side and got a little closer to the screen.

"And that is?" Dru arched an eyebrow at him. She glanced at the time in the corner of her tablet and saw that Tomesha should be arriving at any moment.

"Both of the lycans they interrogated claimed there is a female in charge. A pure-born who's extremely intelligent," he said.

"We need more than that. It's likely they're speaking of Rayna. They need to keep hitting the lycans harder until they find one who's desperate." She tapped her nails on the desk. Maybe this was why the two warriors hadn't reached out to her. Anyone could have thrown out that kind of thing. She needed confirmation of the damn lycan alpha and the whereabouts of said alpha.

"The only problem they're running into is that the newly turned lycans aren't being told anything.

Of course they tried to get the name of the alpha, but even with extreme measures, they failed. I truly don't think they know," Ciro said.

Dru froze at this.

If the lycans wanted to protect certain data, it would make sense to not have critical plans be known by all. Dru bit back a growl. That would have been a move she'd have suggested.

"Then it looks like they need to expand the targets. Someone is going to talk. I don't care what or who they have to kill to get the information, we need to know if this is Rayna and where her location is," Dru snapped.

"Yes, General. I do have some news as well. June here is a genius—"

"I don't know about that," June muttered from off the screen.

"Anyway, we've been combing the dark web—"

"The who?" This time it was Dru who interrupted Ciro. What the hell was the dark web? She knew what the internet or what websites were, but the dark web? He was losing her quickly.

"It's part of the internet that is sort of off the books, so to speak. Its's a non-indexed part of the internet with hidden sites that cover up illegal activities," Ciro explained nonchalantly.

"And anyone can access it?" Dru ran a hand down her face.

"Not really. It would request certain software and configurations." Ciro paused. He must have seen Dru's blank expression. "People like me and June are able to access it. What I was alluding to is there are a few forums where it's been discussed about an appearance of the alpha."

"Really?" Now this was information that Dru needed to know. This alpha had been eluding them since Azura was killed. If they could find her, then they could end this war before it began. "And this is confirmed?"

"Nothing is ever confirmed online, General," Ciro said.

"But we're going to keep looking into this. There are too many inconsistencies with what we're finding, but this lets us know that some of the lycans are chatting amongst each other." The view turned to June who glanced away from her screen to face Dru. "We all know what happens when people get comfortable in certain spaces."

"They'll unknowingly give us what we want," Dru murmured.

"Bingo." June gave a harsh chuckle. "Don't

worry, General. We're not going to let them slip away. I've created a false persona and will see how many of these forums I can gain access to. We have an advantage over most of the lycans who are on the web."

"Yeah? What is that?" Dru asked.

"Me." June stared into the camera without blinking.

"Good job, you two. Keep me up to date and contact me immediately if you confirm anything."

"Yes, General."

The screen went blank. She sighed. Her gaze went back to the papers before her. This was what she trusted. Her works on parchment that no one could hack. Too many people relied on their computers, and nothing was ever safe. People like Ciro and June could have access to anything within minutes.

A knock sounded on the door. Dru's heart picked up its pace. It would appear that her guest was a few minutes early.

"Come in." Dru sat up straighter and eyed the door. She hoped it was Tomesha and not someone else needing something from her.

"General." Orenda appeared in the doorway. She gave a bow of her head. She stepped to the side and waved someone in the room. "Your guest, Miss Tomesha Clay, has arrived."

Dru pushed back from the desk and stood. Her gaze locked on the breathtaking beauty who sauntered through the door in a simple off-the-shoulder blouse with a flowing skirt that went down to her ankles. Her hair was left down in waves around her shoulders. Her eyes, those big brown orbs... She curiously looked around the suite until her gaze landed on Dru.

"Thank you, Orenda." Dru cleared her throat to remove the huskiness.

Her attention was fully on Tomesha. Orenda took her leave, the door shutting quietly. Dru's tongue stuck to the roof of her mouth as she watched Tomesha take a few more steps into the room.

"Good evening, General—"

"It's Dru," she rasped.

Tomesha stepped around the desk and paused. She reached down and tugged the blouse over her head and dropped it to the floor. What little air was left in Dru's body escaped. The woman was bold and wore nothing beneath the material. Her perfect brown mounds with their pebbled nipples were now in view.

A smile appeared on Tomesha's lips along with a teasing glint.

"Dru," she said, her voice laced with seduction. Her hands slipped to her waist and pushed down the skirt. It fell into a pile on the floor. She stepped out of it, leaving her completely naked. She kicked off her sandals and made her way to Dru. "I hear that you personally requested me."

"I did." Dru's voice dropped low.

She was unable to look away from such perfection. Tomesha glided toward her and stopped mere inches from her. The scent of Tomesha filled Dru's nostrils. She breathed in the light floral aroma and the hint of musk. Unable to resist touching her, Dru reached out and palmed Tomesha's face.

Even though lust filled her and her heart thundered, Dru still heard Mistress's words.

You almost bled her dry.

Dru froze in place. Tomesha leaned into her touch. Trust and desire burned bright in her eyes.

"I must apologize," Dru blurted out. She couldn't stand the thought that she'd caused this woman harm. She vowed to never go so long in between feedings again. She'd be careful from now on when she fed from Tomesha. In the future, she—

She paused.

What future? Once her business was concluded here she'd be leaving. Tomesha would remain. She'd continue to work for the madam. Once Dru was gone, she'd be free to service vampires again. Allow them to have access to this delectable body, taste what was between her legs, feed from her, take from her—

A growl ripped from Dru's throat. Tomesha stiffened at the scent of fear hitting the air. Dru blinked and stared down into Tomesha's eyes. She trailed her hand down to Tomesha's waist and held her close. There would never be a reason for this woman to fear her. Dru would do what she must to protect her at all times.

This was her woman.

No other will ever touch her again.

"I see someone told you. It's quite all right. I'm fine. The healers were able to help me." Tomesha smiled. She backed away from Dru and spun around slowly.

Dru greedily took in her wide hips, ample ass, and soft thighs.

"I promise if I wasn't, Mistress would not have allowed me to come tonight."

"I didn't mean to take so much. I'll try to

restrain myself next time." If she needed more, then she'd try another prepared type. Maybe she'd contact the local blood bank and have them send some over just in case. She wasn't sure why a vampire like herself could not control her thirst. She wasn't a newly turned vampire, she was a full-blooded born vampire.

"I trust you," Tomesha murmured, stepping back into Dru's arms.

She reached up and entwined her arms around Dru's neck. The move placed her heavy mounds directly against Dru's. The warmth of her body, the softness of her skin underneath Dru's touch, sent a ripple of savagery through her again.

What was it about this human?

"That you'll always be able to do," Dru snarled, and she meant it.

Tomesha should trust her. Somehow they'd have a future together. Dru leaned down and tipped Tomesha's chin upward and claimed her lips. It was a kiss with a promise. Tomesha's body molded to hers. It was astounding how well their bodies fit together.

Dru tilted her head to the side as the kiss deepened. Tomesha wasn't shy at all. Her tongue boldly met Dru's and entwined with hers in a tantalizing dance. Dru skated her hand down Tomesha's back to her ass. She gripped the ample meat in a firm hold.

As much as the lust and desire burned in her, she again couldn't shake the fact that she'd almost harmed this woman. She tore her lips from Tomesha's and stared down into her bedroom eyes.

"Will you allow me to do something?" Dru murmured.

"Of course." Tomesha smirked.

Dru stepped away from her and gathered her clothing and held it out.

Confusion lined Tomesha's face as she took it. "Um, you want me to put my clothing back on?"

"Yes. There's someone I want you to speak with." Dru spun away and moved behind her desk to reach for her holographic box.

Tomesha quickly redressed, questions hidden in her eyes. Dru placed the box on her desk and stepped back over to Tomesha. She took her hand in hers and smiled.

She programmed the hologram to call the only person she trusted to truly tell her that Tomesha was okay and safe to feed from again.

"Hell must have frozen over," a familiar voice and figure came into view.

"Hello to you, too, sister," Dru said dryly.

Her sister rolled her eyes and pushed a few wayward strands of hair out of her face.

"And I wouldn't know if Hell has frozen over. I haven't been sent there yet."

"It's been a while, sister, and it must be serious if you're calling me. I am busy, you know. I may not be an important woman like yourself, but I am needed here." There wasn't an ounce of animosity in Zada's expression. This was the one who loved to laugh and tease while Dru was more stoic and focused. Zada's attention fell to Tomesha. Her expression brightened immediately. "And who is this we have?"

Tomesha's head turned slowly as she took in Dru and Zada.

"You're twins?" Tomesha gasped.

Dru bit back a sigh. She knew what was coming from Zada.

"So my elder sister hasn't mentioned me? The one who shared a womb with her? The only sister she has? The only person who could put up with her dry personality for our two hundred and twenty-five years on this earth?" Zada's eyebrows arched.

Dru pinched the bridge of her nose and sighed again. Zada never let her forget their beginnings.

"Well, if it means anything, Dru didn't do much talking at all the last time we were together," Tomesha said quietly. Her gaze fell to floor. She reached up and tucked her hair behind her ear.

Dru cleared her throat and stepped forward. She didn't miss the small cough that hid Zada's laugh.

"Tomesha, may I present to you my sibling, master healer Zada Moldark. Zada, may I present to you Miss Tomesha Clay, my—" Dru paused. She didn't know how to introduce Tomesha. Her donor didn't sound right. Her lover? Her contracted prostitute? Dru bristled at the notion. They may have only been together once, but there was more between them than that.

"I'm her *sanguina* while she's here," Tomesha continued for Dru. She smiled and nodded at Zada.

"Well, either way, it's nice to meet you, Tomesha. You must be a special person if Dru is calling me to introduce you to me." Zada smiled warmly, and her blue-eyed gaze landed on Dru. "Is that all this call is for?"

"No. There was a reason for it." Dru cleared her throat again. Of course Zada would sense there was something else besides introductions. Dru hadn't introduced anyone to her family members because she'd been too busy with this war to think of finding a special someone or a mate. "It would appear that the last time I fed from Tomesha, I took too much and I was told that I almost bled her dry."

"And you thought to call me on hologram to assess her?" Zada folded her arms and cocked her head.

"Um, yes. You're the only one I would trust to ensure Tomesha was healthy enough to feed from again," Dru said.

"I told you, I'm fine. The healer gave me her approval to allow you to feed again," Tomesha said.

She turned to Dru, but Dru held Zada's gaze. They were at least a thousand miles away from each other, but Dru could still sense her. They could sense things through an unseen bond. Thoughts, feelings, emotions…pain. Which wasn't fair to Zada every time Dru had been injured in battle.

Zada gave Dru a nod. No words were needed. Zada sensed this unknown emotion swirling around inside Dru.

"How did they treat you?" Zada immediately fell into the role of healer.

Dru relaxed; Zada was the best at what she did.

She may not be here in physical form, but as a hologram was the next best thing.

"I was given ifalla tea to drink, they increased my kenaf weed dosage, and I've rested. I did sleep a lot and I just had my checkup this morning," Tomesha said.

Zada nodded. She asked a few more questions that Tomesha willingly answered.

"And how do you feel now?" Zada asked.

"I feel strong and back to my normal self." Tomesha glanced over at Dru.

Their eyes connected, and Dru's heart stuttered. It helped to know that the madam employed healers who looked after the humans, but she personally didn't trust a person she didn't know.

"Well, from the sound of it, the local healer was correct in her treatment. It would be the same I would offer the humans here if it happened to them. Her coloring looks good. I can't scent her—"

"Her scent is fine." Dru hadn't forgotten the basics of her training. She'd have noted if Tomesha's scent was off.

"My scent?" Tomesha turned to Zada with the question.

"Yes, we vampires can scent when a human is ill. Even if they aren't showing signs. As least ones who are trained to, and my sister had in-depth training as a healer. She just continued on a different life journey than me." Zada's words ended softly.

She'd been one of the first to support Dru when she'd announced she was going to pursue the life of a warrior.

"You were once a healer?" Tomesha asked.

"I was, but as Zada said, I had a different purpose in life awaiting me." Dru reached up and brushed Tomesha's hair from her face. "And I don't regret it. But yes, if I'd scented something different with you, I'd have said something immediately."

Tomesha nodded.

"Well, that's all I can do from here, sister. Is there anything else you need?" Zada asked.

Dru turned back to her and shook her head. She was sure Zada had plenty to do.

"I think we're all set here. I'm sure we'll be speaking again soon." Dru brought Tomesha to her side and smiled at Zada.

Zada's gaze flicked between Dru and Tomesha. "We most certainly will." That damn twinkle returned to her eyes.

Dru sighed but wouldn't expect anything less from her twin.

"Take care of yourself, Dru."

"I always do. Give my love to our parents," Dru said.

Zada nodded then spun on her heels. She walked away, and within seconds, her hologram disappeared.

"That was interesting," Tomesha murmured.

"I just wanted to ensure you're okay. I don't want to harm you again." Dru turned Tomesha to her. The sharp feeling lancing through her heart was unfamiliar to her. She stared down into Tomesha's eyes.

"It wasn't your fault. I'll take better care of myself—"

"It is not on the human to know when a vampire is sated in their feedings. Vampires should be able to control themselves," Dru snapped.

"And as a donor, I guess I should know my own body. I may be new at this but I'm learning. There are signals that I must have ignored, but now I know for the next vampire who feeds from me."

A deep snarl tore from Dru. A fiery ball of possessiveness claimed her. This was her human, and no other vampire's fangs would sink into Tomesha's soft flesh. She'd do bodily harm to anyone who came close. Dru didn't care that Tomesha worked for the madam.

She belonged to her.

Her fangs pushed through swiftly. Her hand shot out, and she gripped her human by the throat. Tomesha froze in place, her eyes wide, but she didn't try to bolt away. Dru inhaled sharply, greeted by a thick, tangy musk radiating from Tomesha. Her body softened, and she rested a hand on Dru's arm.

"No one else will feed from you," Dru growled. She pulled Tomesha to her and slammed her mouth on hers.

CHAPTER SEVENTEEN

Tomesha didn't know what had set Dru off, but something came over the vampire. The change was rapid. One minute Dru was apologizing for almost bleeding her dry, the next she was growling and getting all possessive of her.

Tomesha had to admit, it turned her on faster than she'd ever gotten aroused before.

She'd never had someone who wanted her like this. What did this mean? She didn't know, but she wasn't going to back away. Even with Dru's growls, her fangs descending, the hand on her throat,

Tomesha knew without a doubt this vampire would never hurt her.

It was apparent since she had called on her twin sister to assess Tomesha. Only someone who truly cared about her well-being would do that.

Tomesha leaned into Dru while the woman's tongue invaded her mouth. She sensed the urgent need from Dru and would provide whatever it was that she desired from her. Dru backed her up against the desk.

Dru reached up and tore her blouse from her body. The material fell to the floor in shreds. Tomesha gasped as Dru broke the kiss. The general didn't hesitate to push her skirt to the floor.

Dru bent down and lifted Tomesha by the backs of her knees and sat her on the desk. The fire in her eyes burned bright. There was an intensity in her stare that took Tomesha's breath away. Dru blew out a shaky breath. Her fingers burned a heated trail over Tomesha's chest and paused between her breasts. The hunger grew in her gaze when she took in Tomesha's two heavy mounds.

Her breasts ached; she needed Dru's hot mouth on them. She leaned back and offered them up to the vampire. Dru's gaze didn't move from them; she was captivated by Tomesha's body. That alone gave

Tomesha all the confidence she needed. This vampire was all that mattered.

"So damn beautiful," Dru bit out around her fangs.

Her fingers moved to one of Tomesha's mounds. She teased the beaded nipple, leaning down to capture it with her lips. Tomesha groaned the moment Dru suckled it into her mouth. There was hard tug as Dru worked her breast. Tomesha's moans filled the air. She spread her legs, the ache between them growing.

Here she was, sent to please the general, and it was the general giving her pleasure. Dru was a very generous lover, and Tomesha would get her opportunity to return the favor. She threaded her fingers through Dru's auburn hair. In the candlelight it was a bright red, and Tomesha loved the way her silky strands flowed through her fingers. She held on, and Dru continued to feast on her breasts.

"Dru," Tomesha groaned.

Dru's hand slipped up her thighs and pushed them farther apart. She dipped her finger into Tomesha's center, met with the evidence of Tomesha's desire. A growl rippled from Dru. She lifted her head and brought her fingers to her lips. She licked the creamy substance from them.

"Take more."

Tomesha leaned back on the desk. She didn't care that she disrupted the paperwork. They both ignored the papers falling onto the floor. She rested on her back and opened herself fully for Dru. Her body ached and burned for this woman.

"You cunt is so damn slick and ripe," Dru rasped. Her warm hand traveled up Tomesha's thighs to her center. She parted Tomesha's labia to expose her clit.

Tomesha inhaled sharply at the feeling of Dru drawing small circles on her sensitive nub.

"Look at all of this slickness coming out of you."

Her fingers teased Tomesha's opening, sinking into Tomesha. They stretched her and withdrew slightly, then thrust back inside her. She moaned, loving the feeling of Dru's capable fingers diving deep. Her intense gaze bored into Tomesha as she fucked her slowly at first. Tomesha couldn't look away from the woman if she tried. She felt a connection between them.

Her fingers felt heavenly. Being open and exposed for Dru sent a wave of need through her. She wanted to be everything this woman desired. The heat in her eyes stole Tomesha's breath away.

She watched with bated breath; Dru lowered her head between her thighs to join her hand. Her tongue connected with Tomesha's sensitive pearl. Tomesha's back arched off the desk, and Dru gave her the sweetest of tortures. She nipped and licked the swollen bundle of joy while thrusting those two fingers of hers into Tomesha.

The woman knew how to work Tomesha's body. She feasted. She consumed. This vampire was like a storm rushing in to destroy her.

She gave Tomesha everything she begged for. Tomesha's cries filled the air. Her body responded to Dru in ways she couldn't explain. She held on to Dru as if her life depended on it. The vampire's magical tongue and fingers brought her to the edge of ecstasy, only to pull her back. Tomesha's body shook from the electrical current racing through her veins. She'd only had a glimpse of heaven moments ago, and she was ready to die to reach her destination.

Dru latched on to her clit while her fingers continued to plunge into her. She twisted them around, seeking that one special place inside Tomesha that would send her to the stars. Tomesha's hips undulated, and she rode her vampire's tongue and face. Her eyes closed; she basked in the pleasure coursing through her. This vampire was dangerous.

Addicting.

What was Tomesha going to do when she left?

She'd never had these feeling before, and it scared her.

How would she survive without this vampire?

Tomesha pushed that thought aside, her breaths coming in pants. Her muscles tensed; Dru's fingers found their destination. A warming sensation pulsed through her core. She tried coasting through her orgasm, but the force of the climax was too much to bear. She threw her head back and screamed.

Her body shook uncontrollably, but Dru continued. She truly was here to ruin Tomesha. She was focused and determined in her mission of pleasuring. Her body tensed again. Another wave of her orgasm slammed into her. She couldn't breathe. She could do nothing else but feel what Dru was doing to her.

Tomesha gripped Dru's hair. Her hips continued to move of their own accord. She didn't know how, but her body appeared to be controlled by this vampire's fingers and tongue.

Dru's mouth disappeared from her center. She cried out at an intense pain striking her inner thigh.

Dru's fangs sank deep into her flesh. Tomesha's cries filled the air, another wave washing over her. The sensation of Dru drinking from her sent her well past the stars and the moon. She floated amongst the heavens. She basked in the warmth that flooded her. It was a feeling she'd never be able to explain. Pride filled her to know that it was she who was providing life-fulfilling nourishment for this strong vampire warrior.

Dru lifted her head from Tomesha's thigh. She dragged her tongue over the wound to seal it. Tomesha fell back on the hard wooden desk, unable to even move. Her heart slammed against her chest as if trying to pound its way out. Her breaths came in little gasps. She opened her eyes and met Dru's.

There was no doubt in Tomesha's mind that Dru was a vampire. From her bright-blue eyes, the large fangs peeking from underneath her lips, to the blood running down her lips and her chin. The sight of Dru like this should have scared Tomesha.

But it didn't.

This is what she was here for.

To provide pleasure and nourishment for Dru— her general.

Her vampire.

Tomesha didn't know if Dru felt what she did.

That was one thing she was afraid of bringing up. They hadn't known each other long, but how was it that Tomesha had such strong feelings for her? She'd hadn't had these with any of the other vampires she'd had sex with. There had been plenty since she'd started working for the madam, but none of them had done a number on her like Dru.

Tomesha reached out a steady hand and wiped away the blood from Dru's chin. It smeared a little, leaving proof that it had been there. Tomesha brought her finger to her lips and licked it away. The copper taste of blood greeted her. Dru's eyes darkened to almost black at the move. A growl rippled from her.

She snatched Tomesha from the desk as if she weighed nothing. Tomesha's legs automatically wrapped around her waist, and she was carried over to the bed. Dru placed her down as if she were the most precious thing on this earth. She stepped back from the bed, not taking her eyes from Tomesha. She stripped her clothing. Tomesha watched, not saying a word. She loved seeing Dru's naked body.

Her well-defined muscles. Her high breasts, narrowed waist, her small patch of red hair that covered her pussy. Once she was completely naked, she stood tall, and Tomesha took her in.

Tomesha brushed her hair from her face and scooted back to the center of the bed. She knew what Dru wanted.

What she needed.

And she was here to provide it all.

Her body still trembled from the orgasms that had been pulled from her. She should be exhausted from the force of them. She even had the feeling of completeness, but she desired more. Her body ached in ways that couldn't be explained.

She needed this vampire.

Only Dru.

She exposed her neck. A growl cut through the air. The bed dipped down, then Dru advanced on her. She slowly crawled until she was braced over Tomesha.

"You offer yourself in the sweetest ways, *miere*," Dru rasped, her voice thick and full of desire.

Tomesha turned back to her so she could meet her eyes.

"You need me," she whispered.

"That I do, but in more ways than you could understand," Dru said softly.

She reached up and brushed Tomesha's dark hair from her face. She trailed her fingers down the side of Tomesha's cheek in what would be considered a loving manner. Was Dru developing feelings for Tomesha? Or was Tomesha reading more into this than she should?

"Make me understand." Tomesha rested her hand on Dru's and brought it to her lips. She kissed her palm. She wanted to know all there was to this vampire. Where she was from. Who her family was. Why she'd made the decision to leave the life of a healer to one of a warrior.

Who was Dru Moldark?

Dru barely pushed her thighs open and arranged them to where her slick core brushed against Tomesha's. A sigh escaped from her as Dru slowly moved against her. Tomesha's hands came to rest on Dru's waist. She guided her in movement. She loved the feeling of their most intimate parts gliding over each other.

"You're unique," Dru proclaimed. She leaned down and pressed her lips to Tomesha's temple. Her warm breath slid over Tomesha's skin. She dropped another kiss to Tomesha's cheek. "Your body calls to me like no other. Why is that?"

"I don't know," Tomesha answered. She arched upward to meet Dru's thrust, biting her lip to keep from crying out. So she *wasn't* alone in this madness. Dru *was* feeling something for her.

Dru's motions quickened while she thrust harder. Her hand slipped down to Tomesha's neck again. Tomesha welcomed the strong hold on her and gazed up at Dru. The vampire's bright eyes darkened with lust. The fire in her eyes was all for Tomesha, and that gave her a sense of control, even though she was the one being pinned down.

Tomesha groaned and guided Dru's hips to her. The hand that had been on Dru's waist skated backward to cup Dru's bottom.

"Harder," Tomesha begged. She wanted to feel her vampire reach her climax.

Their clits abraded each other, sending a wave of desire through her. It was building inside her and would eventually erupt.

"Human, I shouldn't want you the way that I do," Dru bit out. Her hips jerked harder and faster against Tomesha. Her hand tightened slightly.

Again, Tomesha wasn't afraid of Dru.

She wanted to give this woman any and everything she needed from her. She whimpered and guided Dru down to where she could capture one of her nipples in her mouth. Tomesha parted her lips and suckled the mound as hard as she could. Dru's growl was the only answer. She licked and nipped the bud. Dru's skin was soft and pliable. She tasted of darkness and desire. Tomesha gripped the other one with her free hand while she feasted on Dru. She pinched and tugged on the other nipple which elicited another growl from the vampire.

"Fuck," Dru cried out.

She lifted her chest from Tomesha, drawing her breasts away from Tomesha's mouth. She brought Tomesha's leg up over her arm. Her thrusts were harder. Their pussies were slick and coated with their juices. Tomesha cried out from the new position. It opened her up so Dru's clit continually rubbed hers. Dru's hand returned to Tomesha's neck and held her down while she both took and gave pleasure.

Tomesha's cries filled the air once again. She couldn't care less who heard her. When she'd walked through the door of the inn, she was sure each warrior present knew what she was there for. She'd seen the interest in their eyes, but the moment they'd heard she was here for the general, they had cast their eyes away from her.

"Yes," Tomesha hissed.

She turned her pleasure over to Dru with a trust that downright scared her. She struggled to inhale deeply with the way Dru tightened her grip on her neck. Her air supply wasn't cut off, but she felt herself becoming lightheaded while her body was filled with pleasure. She gasped and tipped over into the sweet ecstasy at the same time Dru reached her peak.

Dru's growl ripped through the air. Her hips pressed downward, grinding her core to Tomesha's. She fell forward and continued to thrust. Tomesha breathed in deeply now she was free from Dru's hold. Their legs became entangled, their movements in sync with one another. Dru groaned again, and they slowed down.

Tomesha turned her head away and presented her artery. This was what her vampire needed. Immediately, Dru struck. Her fangs pierced Tomesha's delicate flesh. The pain was sharp but dissipated within seconds. Their hips ceased their movements while Dru fed from her. Tomesha held Dru's body to hers and took what she needed.

The tugging at her neck sent a tingle to her core. She relaxed, tightening her hold on Dru. Tomesha didn't want her to move from her spot on top of her. If she could, she'd stay here forever. Their naked bodies against each other, their slick cores kissing, and Dru's fangs in her throat. She floated among the clouds. She couldn't explain this feeling she got when Dru fed from her. She wondered briefly if this would happen when any vampire fed from her.

No one else will feed from you. Dru's words echoed in her head. Did she mean it? Would she be the only vampire to feed from her? Tomesha sighed. She wasn't going to worry about it at the moment. Right now, this was where she was supposed to be.

Dru slowly lifted her head, her fangs slipping from Tomesha's flesh. Tomesha whimpered, missing the feeling of those sharp teeth deep inside her flesh. Dru slowly bathed Tomesha's skin with her tongue. Tomesha's body tingled from the top of her head down to her feet. Her lips curved up in a smile as she drifted off into a blissful rest.

"Rest, *miere*," Dru murmured. Her body shifted off to the side.

Tomesha whimpered but felt herself be drawn into the warmth of Dru's arms. She snuggled in and allowed herself to be consumed by the awaiting darkness.

TOMESHA SIGHED AND ROLLED OVER. She froze for a second, then the night came rushing back to her.

Dru.

She smiled and opened her eyes. That curve in her lips slowly disappeared. Dru wasn't in bed with her. She felt the still-warm sheets. So, it hadn't been that long since the general had left. Tomesha lifted her head and took in the sealed windows. It was morning.

Where was Dru?

"Good morning." The object of her desire waltzed out of the bathroom fully dressed in her fighting leathers. Dru's hair was brushed up into a tight top bun, her blue eyes bright and sharp. She took Tomesha in.

"Morning. Where are you going?" Tomesha pushed up and dragged the covers over her to hide her nakedness. With it being daylight, where could Dru think she'd be going?

"I have a very important job to do while here in Butterbush. I'm being called to work," Dru replied with a smirk. She came over to the edge of the bed and reached out a hand toward Tomesha. She tipped Tomesha's chin up and pressed a soft kiss to her lips.

Tomesha's eyes fluttered closed for a brief moment. The kiss was over before she knew it. She pouted a little, wanting more.

"But it's daylight!" Tomesha exclaimed.

"That it is." Dru walked over to a closet and opened the door.

Tomesha's eyes widened at the sight of the amount of weapons held there. Dru casually pulled knives, a sword, and a gun out and placed them in strategic places on her body.

"But have no worries, *miere*, I shall be fine."

"But where do you need to go during the daylight that you couldn't go during nighttime?" Tomesha had a feeling this was none of her business, but she was so damn curious. Vampires were present during the daytime, that wasn't unusual, but it would be gloomy weather or days when clouds blocked the sun.

Dru glanced at her over her shoulder. "I'm going hunting."

Tomesha blinked. She didn't like the sound of it. What if she was injured?

Dru took out a double-edged axe and secured it in a sheath placed on her back. She swung around. Whoever or whatever Dru was hunting was in serious trouble. This vampire before her was fierce and on a mission. The deadly expression took Tomesha's breath away. This wasn't the same vampire who'd wrung hard orgasms from her just a few hours ago.

Dru came to stand at the edge of the bed. "You can stay for as long as you want. There will be a car waiting to take you home." Her expression lightened. She reached out a hand and caressed the side of Tomesha's face. Her finger lingered on Tomesha's bottom lip.

"Will you be needing me again?" Tomesha whispered.

Her heart's steady beat faltered. She held her breath and waited for the answer. She was drawn to this vampire. She adjusted herself to kneel on the mattress. It brought her to eye level with Dru. The vampire's gaze dropped to her lips.

"In order to feed or something else?" Tomesha said.

"I shouldn't feed from you again so soon. I'll need to be careful," Dru murmured. Her fangs peeked from underneath her lip. She leaned forward and pressed a kiss to Tomesha's lips. "Rest now, *miere*. I'll call on you later when I have concluded business."

Tomesha jerked her head. Dru spun on her heels and strode toward the door. A slight pain rippled in Tomesha's chest at the sight of the vampire leaving her. Dru opened the door and disappeared through it, closing it quietly. Tomesha fell back on the pillows and blew out a deep breath.

Not only had she caught feelings for this vampire, but she may be halfway in love with her.

That was going to be a problem.

Dru was her client. Tomesha was necessary for her to survive. She had something the vampire needed.

Tomesha rubbed her eyes, unsure what to do. She tugged the blankets up over her shoulder. This bed was certainly more comfortable than the one waiting for her at home. A yawn took over her. Maybe she'd take another nap then head home.

There she'd be able to think straight. All of this nonsense of falling for the vampire general was just craziness.

Or was it?

CHAPTER EIGHTEEN

Dru settled back in the vehicle as Orenda drove to their location. She ran her tongue over her fangs.

Will you be needing me again? Tomesha's words echoed in her head. She closed her eyes briefly at the memory of her big brown eyes and how she had watched Dru. It had taken everything Dru had to hold back from sinking her teeth back into Tomesha's vein. The taste of her blood was like nothing Dru had ever had, but she'd had to resist. She didn't want to cause any more harm to the small human. When leaving the inn, she'd ordered a cup of ifalla tea to be taken to Tomesha. She wasn't going to take any risk that her blood stores would be low.

Dru had been extremely careful.

She glanced out the window at the scenery flying by. Dru pushed all thoughts of the human and her delectable body from her mind. This wasn't the time to go down memory lane. Distractions like this during a mission could prove fatal.

"Our intel suggests there are plenty of traps on the property," Talbot announced from the passenger seat.

Dru blinked and came back to the present. She picked up her tablet and opened the device. They had been sent an updated map of Sol Winter's property. Some of the warriors had canvassed the area from a distance last night.

Today, they'd seek out the vampire.

"Then we'll enter quietly and swiftly. We wouldn't want to alert our target to our presence until we're ready." Dru studied the area. If she were a vampire staying off the grid, this would be the perfect place to live. She swiped the screen and took in pictures of the cabin. It didn't look modern, and she doubted it had running water. Which wouldn't be an issue for a vampire as old as Sol. He was from a time before all of the amenities that were taken for granted existed.

The quicker she could confirm this Sol Winters was Solomon Winterborne, the quicker she could conclude this mission. Her gut screamed that this was the same man. He was a traitor to the crown who'd murdered lycans and blamed it on the king.

But now he was possibly working *with* the lycans?

She narrowed her eyes on the document that had also been sent to her. It was information regarding the last lycan attack that had occurred in Butterbush. She quickly read through the file, paused at the end, and glanced back up.

"Did I just read this right? Sol confronted the lycans in the center of town and they just left?" she asked in disbelief. So one vampire faced a pack of lycans and they just turned and walked away from the vampire?

"That's how I read it." Orenda slowed the truck and made a turn at the corner.

The road opened to an empty highway. The landscape flew by in a blur. The other warriors who were accompanying them followed in two other SUVs. They'd drive to a certain point, then the rest of the trip would be done on foot. Luckily enough for them, the sun wasn't out. The sky was so thick with storm-born clouds that only a thin gray light filtered down. It painted the world in shades of steel and shadow. Dru inhaled deeply and scented the impeding storm. They'd need to move quickly to not get caught up in the rain.

But it's daylight! Again, Tomesha broke through Dru's thoughts. Her human had been worried about her. Dru couldn't remember when the last time someone had been concerned about her and her safety. It warmed her heart to think that Tomesha would be concerned about her out in daylight. The sun wouldn't instantly kill her. Sunburn could be severe. Vampires were deathly allergic to it, but a little sun wouldn't send her to the afterlife.

Dru sighed and struggled to keep Tomesha from evading her thoughts. She was on a mission and needed to focus.

"And no one suspected that one vampire could turn away a pack of lycans who'd been tearing through the town?" Dru arched an eyebrow.

Lycans who were on a mission of turning an entire town of humans would not stop. Their current life's mission was to get their numbers up by any means necessary. Why would they listen to a vampire? An enemy who'd hunted them down to the brink of extinction.

"The postmaster had proclaimed that it was the threat of more vampire warriors coming to help that scared the lycans off. There was still plenty of damage, deaths, and missing humans. The Butter-bush post was overwhelmed. Postmaster Alexander had put out a distress call to the surrounding posts who'd dispatched warriors to come," Talbot said.

Dru tapped on her screen and went through the reports the postmaster had submitted regarding the incident. She had read through them, but it had been before she'd looked at this newer file. Alarms were going off in her head. Was the postmaster that dense in the head to think a threat of more warriors coming would sway lycans on a rampage? Why hadn't he included that a vampire civilian had confronted the lycans? She made a mental note to address this with him. He was going to answer to her on why he'd left out such a vital piece of information.

Dru scowled. This was the doing of Solomon Winterborne. But if he'd orchestrated the death of the lycan king's family, who was he working for? If not King Niall's orders, then whose? What did he have to gain?

Or had that been his way to start the war?

Eliminate the Riskel family then take over the throne? Lethia and her sisters would have been young children when this occurred. It was no wonder none of them had known about the traitorous events of the right hand of the king. Eliminating King Niall, then Queen Mira, wouldn't have been easy. The royal couple were deadly warriors.

But starting a lycan-vampire war would have increased the odds.

And if he didn't have an issue murdering lycan children, he certainly wouldn't have had an issue killing Lethia and her sisters.

Dru bit back a snarl. She'd get to the bottom of this. The more she discovered about this vampire, the more the chances of his head being severed from his shoulders increased.

"We're coming up to the designated location where we'll need to leave the vehicles," Orenda said.

Dru turned off the device and slid it into the back pocket of the driver's seat. A deadly calmness came over her at the thought of this mission. She'd find this vampire and take him to the queen, and if he resisted, then she'd take his head.

Either way, he was going to be presented to the queen.

It mattered not to her if he wasn't *the* Solomon Winterborne. Whoever this vampire was had a hand in the attacks in Butterbush. She was certain of it.

The vehicle pulled off the highway onto rocky terrain. Orenda drove a few more minutes deeper into the woods. She tucked the vehicle off into a thick area of trees. The drivers in the other vehicles followed her lead. They didn't want to leave the vehicles out in the open where anyone would be able to see them and suspect anything.

She killed the engine.

"Let's hunt," Dru growled.

She opened the door and stepped out of the SUV. She slammed the door shut. They still had a few miles to cover, but with their vampire speed, they could reach their destination in minutes. The warriors stalked toward her. Each of them wore the same fierce expression. This wasn't a battle she was leading them into, but it was an important mission for the queen. Dru stood tall while her warriors gathered around her. She met each of their eyes before she began speaking.

"This is hostile territory we're entering. The

enemy doesn't know we're coming, but once we arrive, he'll know for certain who's at his damn door."

Chuckles went around. The air was tense as they listened to her. It was a simple mission. They'd capture the vampire and interrogate him. Simple, but as she'd said, dangerous. If he took the time to ensure the forest around him was riddled with traps, then this was no simple vampire.

"For the crown!" Dru thumped a fist on her chest.

Her warriors returned the same action. They turned and began their trek. They moved swiftly and silently. The forest pressed in on them, heavy with a thick mist and silence. The animals sensed the predators on the loose. Every step closer toward the cottage seemed to awaken the area. Dru's sharp senses detected everything from the distant crackle of leaves to the snap of a twig beneath a warrior's boot. They slowed as they made half the distance.

Dru led the charge and came to a halt. She raised her fist and ceased breathing. She drew her blade from her waist, having felt eyes on them. Someone knew they were there. She bit back a curse and glanced around. Talbot stood to her right, while Orenda was to her left.

Words were not needed.

They sensed it, too.

Dru used hand motions to signal for the warriors to spread out. They moved again, this time at a slower pace. The first trap soon revealed itself—a wire strung low to the ground, almost invisible to the untrained eye. Talbot pointed to it with the tip of his sword.

Dru's lips curled back in disgust. It was a simple trap, but there was no telling what was attached to the other end of the wire. They each carefully stepped over it.

"Keep your eyes open. There will be more," Dru cautioned in a low voice.

The nodding of heads confirmed they'd heard her. They continued on and soon came upon a crude pit disguised by a blanket of moss and large branches. They quickly bypassed it. There were more on their way to the cottage which gave away they were drawing closer to their destination.

Luckily enough, her men were the best at what they did, and no one fell victim to the crude traps. The hairs on the back of Dru's neck stood erect. For certain, this vampire did not want to be caught off guard with the amount of traps that had been set.

Her heart rate increased at the thought of the catch. There was something about the thrill of the chase that drove her on. Solomon would soon have to answer to Queen Mira.

The warriors fanned out more and continued on. The forest flew by as Dru used her vampiric speed to race through the forest.

The only sounds were that of the rasp of boots on damp soil. Finally the trees thinned out, revealing a small cottage half swallowed by ivy. They paused, remaining hidden in the thickness of the forest. Dru strode forward to the edge of woods and assessed the structure. The windows were dark, no smoke rose from the chimney, and the silence stretched long and far.

But what really stuck out to Dru was the lack of sound coming from the cottage.

She pulled her gun from her thigh sheath and replaced her blade. She didn't want to chance the vampire harboring lycans since the evidence pointed to him working with them. She gave a few hand signals before she stepped out of the woods. She strode to the front door while her warriors fanned out around the cottage, surrounding it as a hunting pack would on its prey.

Dru paused at the door and rested a palm on

the handle. With a quick flip of her thumb, the safety was now off her weapon. Talbot moved to a window near it and peered inside. He nodded to her. She backed away from the door and used her foot to kick it in. The door shattered beneath her kick. She aimed her gun true, met with a dark interior and silence. She didn't rush into the building. There was no telling what kinds of traps the traitor had set in his home.

The air was thick with the scent of an unknown male—Solomon's or Sol's. The cottage held an open floor plan, allowing Dru to see well into the kitchen, dining area, and living room. A bed was pushed up in the corner and looked as if someone had slept in it recently. She strode forward slowly, keeping her guard up.

The hearth was cold, but her attention went straight to the table where a chair sat overturned, as if someone had left in a rush. A cloak hung near the door on a ring, stiff and filthy. She flashed her fangs and snarled.

"He knew we were coming." Dru already knew who'd been watching them while they were in the forest. She moved back to the door. "He thinks he can outsmart us," she said, her voice cold and steady. She wanted each of her warriors to hear her.

"But he underestimates us. We will not stop until he's captured."

And if Solomon was watching and listening, she hoped he'd heard every word.

DRU LED her warriors back to the tree line. They had searched the cottage but found nothing, which left her in a foul mood. They entered the dense forest, but the air was thick with dampness and something else—an acrid musk that raised the hackles of the seasoned warrior. Dru slowed, her fist lifted in a silent command.

The warriors froze. Blades hissed, guns were drawn. The silence of the woods broke. Branches creaked overhead, and the crunch of the earth was loud slicing through the air. The familiar scent of a wolf entered Dru's nostrils.

"Lycans," she spat.

She took out her gun filled with argentite bullets. The ground rumbled as the enemy grew closer. Her warriors prepared themselves for the battle. She didn't need to tell them. They were ready for the beasts.

"For the crown!"

The first lycan burst forth from the underbrush in a blur of fur. He raced toward Dru, his teeth bared, hurling himself at her. Dru raised her gun and pulled the trigger. His head jerked backward; her aim true. A bullet pierced the middle of his forehead, sending his body flying backward. She strode forward swiftly, and when she arrived near his body, she fired again. His body jerked with each shot. She growled and focused.

Head.

Heart.

The argentite would spread through the beast's veins and guarantee its death. She swung around. Three more beasts broke through the trees. Her warriors engaged with the lycans in a heated battle. Talbot's sword pierced through one beast's chest, pinning it to a tree, while another one barreled into a warrior, sending them both crashing to the ground. More poured out of the woods, surrounding her and her men.

Dru didn't hesitate to rush into the fray. She fired her weapon until the magazine was empty. She ejected it and reached for a replacement on her waist belt. Then a force smacked into her from behind. She crashed to the ground and rolled over just as large claws slammed into the earth. Her gun fell to the ground, lost in the tussle. Dru snatched her axe out of the sheath on her back and whipped it around. She pushed up to her feet. The lycan stood almost seven feet tall, its fangs sharp and long. It was feral, one who was lost to the beast.

"Come on, motherfucker." She didn't know fear when it came to fighting these beasts.

Dru was a seasoned warrior, and a recently turned feral lycan was no match for her. She dove forward, slicing her axe, landing strikes. The lycan howled and snarled. It dodged her axe, the silver causing smoke to arise from its wounds. It dove at her, but gunfire filled the air. Its body spasmed multiple times before falling over.

Dru's head snapped in the direction of where the gun had been fired and found Orenda standing tall holding her weapon. Dru slipped her axe back into its sheath. She gave the warrior a nod, then turned to another beast flying toward her. It lunged at her, but she caught it by the jaw. She wrenched it to the side and ripped its skull open with her strength. These were all recently turned lycans.

Sacrificial beasts.

These were not pure-born lycans who'd match Dru's and her warrior's strengths. Even though Azura had been desperate to get her numbers up, she was also willing to sacrifice her people for the greater good of her kind. It would appear whoever was in charge now was using her methods. Dru spun around and took in the small battlefield. Her warriors held their own with the final lycans, but it wasn't the fighting that captured her attention.

A chill rippled through her spine.

A single figure at the far edge of the trees was visible through the haze. They stood cloaked and watching. Their eyes met for a heartbeat before he melted back into the shadows.

Rage boiled inside Dru. With a snarl, she took off after him and raced to where she'd seen him last, but there was no trace of him or where he'd disappeared to.

It had to be Solomon. This confirmed, without a doubt, the vampire had betrayed his people and sided with the lycans.

When the last lycan fell, quiet returned. Dru's warriors stood bloodied but unbroken. Their eyes burned with the same fire that consumed their general.

"Was that him?" Talbot strode forward through the warriors.

"I'm not one hundred percent sure, but I'd be willing to bet it was." Dru sniffed.

The forest stank of lycan blood and fur. The beasts lay broken in heaps, their howls snuffed out. Dru took in the footprints left in the damp earth near where she stood. This had been where the vampire watched them face the lycans.

The lycans he'd sent to attack them.

"We should go after him," Orenda murmured. The warrior bent down and wiped one of her blades on the fur of a dead lycan. She stood and sheathed her weapon.

Murmurs of agreement went around. As much as Dru wanted to follow behind him, it would be another trap.

"No," Dru snapped.

The word silenced the conversations. All eyes moved to her.

"He'd want us reckless and chasing after him. He knew we were coming. He waited until we didn't find anything at the cottage then sent his wolves after us." She paused and met each of their eyes. Oh, they would get the chance to go after the traitor, but now would not be the time. Solomon or Sol didn't understand who she was. She was cunning and highly intelligent. He was going to learn she was his worst nightmare. "We will not play into his hands."

The warriors nodded, the weight of her words settling on them. They trusted her. They bowed their heads and thumped their fists over their hearts.

Dru crouched, tracing a fresh set of lycan prints still pressed into the damp earth.

"This was definitely coordinated. Planned. He wanted us to find the cottage. He lured us out here in order to take us out. This is not the work of a traitor hiding from the crown. This is a traitor with allies."

Growls sliced through the air.

"Then what is our next move, General?" one of the warriors asked.

Dru rose to her full height. The cool air grew moist as a light sprinkle fell. They'd need to dispose of the bodies quickly.

"We burn the bodies, then we'll regroup at the inn. He knows we're after him. I want security tightened at the inn. I'll speak with the postmaster about this attack. The town may need to go on lockdown."

CHAPTER NINETEEN

Tomesha fingered the soft fabric of the dress that had been gifted to her. When she'd awoken from her nap, a light breakfast had been waiting for her along with a cup of ifalla tea. She'd scarfed down the food, working out that she'd last eaten an early dinner yesterday. She'd taken a shower, and when she'd returned to the bedroom had found an outfit waiting for her on Dru's bed.

A smile formed on her lips. Dru had thought of everything. Tomesha wondered where her vampire had gone and if she'd see her again.

But Dru had said she'd call for her, but

Tomesha just didn't know what that had meant. She'd at first thought about staying at the inn until Dru returned but knew she couldn't. Tarek would lose his mind if she didn't come home. She couldn't just lie around at the inn and wait for Dru. She had responsibilities at home she had to attend to.

But the moment Dru called on her, she'd go.

She glanced out the car window. She took in the passing scenery and realized they'd be at her home shortly. Her driver hadn't really said a word since escorting her to the car. She tried to study him from the back seat, but he kept his head forward and his lips sealed.

"Have you worked for the general long?" Tomesha asked in an attempt to break the silence. She was curious of everything about Dru. When she'd walked through the inn when it was time for her to leave, she'd noticed a good amount of the warriors were absent. They must have gone with Dru. That comforted Tomesha. Whatever Dru was hunting, at least she wasn't alone.

"I have," he said.

Welp, she guessed he wasn't going to elaborate. She fell back against seat and sighed. She'd hoped he'd share a little tidbit about working for Dru.

She'd have loved to have a sense of the person the vampire was.

He took a turn that put them on her street. She gathered her bag into her lap and waited for him to pull up to the curb in front of the home. A few moments later, he parked the car and exited the vehicle. She glanced at the gloomy sky as he made his way around to her door. Fat drops of rain splatted against the windows.

"Just great. Rain." She'd hoped it would have blown over, but by the looks of the sky, they were due for another storm. Normally she wouldn't mind. She liked cuddling on the couch near the front window and watching the clouds unload everything they had to offer. Lightning and thunder never scared her. She lived for a good storm. She always felt relaxed while Mother Nature handled her business. Even as a child, she'd have her face pressed to the windows so she could watch for the streaks of electricity across the sky.

She just hoped that Dru wouldn't change her mind about calling for her if the storm raged on.

Maybe she should have stayed at the inn. That way she could have waited. She could have sent a message to her brother and grandmother so they'd know she was working and safe.

"Thank you," she said.

The driver stood with the door open and a hand outstretched, waiting for her. She slipped hers into his and allowed him to assist her. She settled the strap of her bag on her shoulder and smiled at him.

"If the general calls for me again, will you be the one to come pick me up?"

"I'm unsure, ma'am." He stepped away from her and closed the door. He turned and folded his hands together, again dismissing her attempt at a conversation.

"Thanks again." She made her way to the house.

The front door swung open, and Tarek stepped out onto the small porch. It was early afternoon, and she was shocked to see him home so soon.

"What are you doing here?"

"Not much work today. They sent practically everyone home." Tarek eyed the vampire waiting by the vehicle. "Where are you coming from?"

"Work," she replied.

"You fed another one of them?"

"Not now, Tarek." She didn't want to start another argument with her brother.

He folded his arms and eyed the man who'd driven her home.

She paused at the bottom of the stairs. "And if you must know, it was the same one as the other day."

His gaze swung to her. He scowled then jogged down to the stairs. Questions lined his face, and she already knew what he was about to stay. She held up her hand.

"Not now, Tarek," she repeated. She didn't want the vampire listening and going back to report anything to Dru. She glanced back at him and nodded.

He bowed his head, walked around the car, and got in. The car pulled out of its spot and drove off.

"Who was that?" Tarek sniffed.

"Just the driver who brought me safely home." She rested a hand on his forearm.

His expression softened.

She smiled at him. "I'm okay. Where's Gran?"

"In the kitchen. She wanted to start supper a little early."

"Well, I guess I'll go help her." Tomesha laughed.

Her grandmother was a wonderful cook, and now that their pantry was always full, the woman was a cooking machine. Tomesha loved seeing her so happy while doing something she loved. Delonda always spoke fondly of her youth and spending time in the kitchen with her grandmother who'd taught her everything she knew.

The sound of heavy engines filled the air. She swung around and took in two large vehicles barreling down their street. They came to a halt in front of her home. Tomesha's heart raced at the sight of large armed men exiting the vehicles. Tarek pushed her behind him as the men strode forward.

"Tomesha Clay?" the first one barked out.

Tomesha peeked around her brother's form and eyed the men. These were definitely vampires and wore the royal crest on their uniforms. She doubted that Dru would send this amount of men after her to bring her back to the inn after she'd just left.

"Who wants to know?" Tarek demanded.

She tried to move from behind him, but he kept his body between her and the men. She rested a hand on his back while still trying to see around him.

"We're here by royal decree. Tomesha Clay has been identified as a human who will need to report for the draft," a deep voice snapped.

Tomesha's eyes widened. She'd been drafted? She shook her head. She couldn't believe that her name had come up. The vampire king's scientists had devised a simple blood test that allowed them to identify a vampire's fated mate. She'd been a kid when the draft rolled out. Tomesha didn't know how she felt about being matched with some random vampire.

There were plenty of humans who protested the draft and even some vampires who objected to it as well. Each of the vampire princesses had been enrolled and even mated as a result of it. All of them to a human. The media had been taken by storm when the heir to the throne had been matched and mated.

Dru's pale skin and bright-blue eyes came to mind. Was she registered as a vampire in the matching system? Was she in search of her mate? A twinge of pain lanced Tomesha's heart at the thought of Dru belonging to another. Or that her vampire would no longer desire her because her attention was on another—one who was meant to be with her.

"If that is Tomesha Clay, you mustn't stand in the way. It is a direct violation of penal code—"

"I'm Tomesha Clay!" She flew from behind Tarek and stood by his side. She already knew he'd try to stand in the way in order to try to protect her.

He scowled at her, but she shook her head. The last thing they needed was for him to be arrested.

She took a step forward. "Please forgive my brother. He's very protective of me, but I'm Tomesha Clay."

"Ma'am, the Sampson County Draft office has been unable to get a hold of you." The first warrior motioned for her to come forward. "You are to come with us."

"She's not going anywhere," Tarek snapped.

The warriors' hands dropped to their weapons on their waists in a very threatening manner. Tomesha spun toward her brother, wanting to squash a confrontation before it began. He'd be no match for the six tall, muscular warriors who had enough weapons on their body to take on a small army.

"Tarek. It's going to be okay," she said. There was no way for her to get out of the draft. There were repercussions for dodging it. She attempted to offer him a smile to get him to calm down, but it wasn't going to work.

His gaze was locked on the vampire warriors.

"Gran will need you, Tarek. I'm sure I won't be gone long."

Not that she knew every detail registering for

the draft entailed. She knew there was a blood sample that needed to be submitted. That was how the test was performed. She'd then be notified if she matched to a vampire.

"They can't do this," he rasped, his dark-eyed gaze falling to her.

"But they can. You know it's the law. It would be no different than if they were here for you. Please, don't cause an issue. Go back in the house. Hopefully I shall be home for dinner. Tell Gran I love her and I'll be home soon." Tomesha reached out and stroked his face.

His scowl deepened, but he jerked his head in a nod.

"Fine," he exhaled.

She patted him on the chest then took a step toward the warriors.

"She'd better come back unharmed."

Tomesha rolled her eyes at him but couldn't keep her lips from curling up into a smile. Only Tarek would be demanding of vampire warriors.

"No harm shall come to the human female while in our custody," the second warrior proclaimed.

That made her feel better. At least they'd get her safely to the government lab and then home.

She was escorted to the back of one of the SUVs and assisted in. The door slammed shut, and she glanced out the window. Tarek's dark expression remained as he stood watching. The warriors climbed into the vehicle with her, and soon they were off. She sent up a prayer that she hadn't lied to him.

Hopefully, she'd be home for supper.

TOMESHA WAS ESCORTED into an unmarked building about forty minutes from Butterbush. The aroma of antiseptic was overpowering. She made her way down a short hallway that opened up into a waiting area filled with people. Light music played softly through hidden speakers. It resembled any doctor's office. She relaxed and headed over to the check-in desk where a young man and woman worked quietly beside each other.

"Um, hello." She gripped her shoulder strap of her bag tight in one hand. Butterflies fluttered to life in her stomach as she stood waiting.

"Name," the woman asked, not looking up from the computer screen she was staring at. Her fingers flew across the keyboard. She paused then glanced over at Tomesha when she didn't respond immediately.

"Tomesha Clay." She spelled her name to ensure it would be correct in their system.

The woman nodded then reached for a clipboard with some papers attached to it. "I'll need you to fill out this form. Sign here. Initial next to these bullet points as you read them then return it to me when you're done."

Tomesha followed where the woman pointed on the paper. She handed a pen to Tomesha.

"Thank you." Tomesha took the pen and clipboard and moved off to the side. Her hands shook as she filled out the paperwork. It was a common form requesting her full name, date of birth, address, and her place of employment. She glanced up at the two behind the desk. They both looked vampire, but she wasn't one hundred percent sure.

She sighed. It was no use in lying on the form. They'd know everything about her, not that there was much to hide. It was a little strange that they needed to know clothing size, shoe size, and favorite colors. What did they do with that information?

She walked back over to the desk and handed the clipboard to the woman.

"Do you have proof of identification?" she asked.

"I do." Tomesha reached into her bag. She dug around until she found her wallet. She pulled out her identification card and handed it over.

The woman typed for a few moments without saying anything before she motioned for Tomesha to go behind the counter.

"I need to take your photograph." She slid Tomesha's ID card back to her.

Tomesha took it and slipped it back in her wallet. She walked around the desk and stood against a wall where the woman instructed her to. She took a few snapshots of Tomesha then pointed to the waiting area.

"Have a seat. Someone will call you when they're ready for you." She handed Tomesha a card with a number on it.

Two hundred and eight.

Tomesha found an available chair near the wall. She propped her bag on her lap while she took in the room. The door opened, and a man came in. He went over to the counter where he announced he'd been called down for the draft.

Tomesha closed her eyes briefly. What if she was matched with a vampire? Would she have to move far? Would she be able to stay in contact with her family? Would she even be appealing to the new vampire? Was it like the fairy tales? Love at first sight? Or would they develop feelings for one another over time? Tomesha just hoped it would be someone who was caring, gentle, and open to having a human mate. She shuddered to think that she'd be matched with a vampire who didn't want her.

But if they opposed humans, would they even register for the draft? For vampires, it wasn't mandatory. According to them, even though there were millions of them spread throughout the world, they needed their fated mates in order to procreate and keep their race alive.

That gave Tomesha a small sense of relief. Maybe luck would have it that she never matched with a vampire.

Numbers were called, and slowly the people trickled to the back. Tension laced the air. It didn't appear anyone was happy about being there, but at least it didn't take long for the donation. Maybe she'd be home for dinner. A few more people came into the facility and were registered then seated. Tomesha began to worry. Had they forgotten about her? She eyed the room and found that everyone who'd been waiting when she'd arrived were now gone.

Should she go and say something?

"Two-oh-eight!"

Tomesha glanced down at her card and saw it was her number. A tall woman with brown hair stood by the desk eyeing the room. Tomesha raised her hand and stood.

"That's me." Tomesha tossed her bag onto her shoulder and walked up to the woman.

"Miss Clay?" The woman took the card from Tomesha and walked down a sterile white hallway.

"Yes. Tomesha." She studied the woman in black scrubs. Her pale skin was flawless, and her brown hair was tied up in a high ponytail.

They took a few turns through a winding maze of halls.

"Will this take long?" Tomesha asked.

"Not at all. My name is Lou, and I'll be taking your sample. Here we are." She opened a door and motioned for Tomesha to enter.

Tomesha stepped inside and found herself in a standard medical exam room.

"Please have a seat."

Tomesha settled in the chair next to the desk. Lou settled in front of the computer. She typed in a few commands to awaken the monitor. Tomesha crossed her legs in an attempt to appear normal and not nervous. This was so sudden. She wished she'd have had a heads-up to be able to process what was happening.

"What do I have to do for the draft?" Tomesha was curious, and since she was here, she might as well ask. She hadn't really researched the process. Humans got drafted all the time, but in her town, it didn't happen that often.

"We'll obtain your blood sample and submit it. We'll run the sample and enter you into our database. If a match is found, then you'll be notified. Each evening you can watch the public broadcast where the positive matches are announced. If you're paired, an armed guard will escort you to your mate."

Tomesha's heart stuttered. Lou made it sound so simple, as if they weren't disrupting someone's entire life. What if her mate lived in Seattle or somewhere like that? That was a long distance away from her family.

Would her family be able to go with her?

Would her mate be willing to come live in Butterbush?

So many questions filled her mind. What if her

mate didn't want her family with her? That would be a deal breaker for Tomesha. Her brother and grandmother meant everything to her. She just couldn't see herself leaving her family behind.

"What are the chances of me being matched?" Tomesha asked. Now that she thought about it, maybe she didn't want to match with anyone.

"One in a million."

Tomesha blew out a deep breath. So maybe the odds were in her favor. Lou didn't take long drawing her blood sample. Three vials were obtained. Lou placed a bandage on the insertion sight and wrapped it up with soft tape.

"I don't scent any diseases that need to be addressed right away." Lou wrote on the labels she'd placed on the vials.

Tomesha blinked and stared at her. Apparently she was a vampire.

"Um, okay." Tomesha exhaled.

"We have to ensure that all of our humans entering the draft are as healthy as possible. If not, then we'll help get the medical care one would need. Vampires are very possessive of their mates and will want what's best for them." Lou stood and handed Tomesha a few papers. "Here is some general information about the draft and a number for you to call if you're interested in the other testing that's run on your blood work. Any questions?"

Tomesha paused and thought about it. She bit her lip, unsure if she should even ask, but she was dying to know.

"Would you be able to tell me if a certain vampire is registered?" Tomesha asked. She wanted to know if Dru was in the registry. That would give her a little hope. With the chemistry they shared, it would be hard to believe they weren't each other's match.

"I'm sorry. That is confidential information. Anything else I can answer for you?" Lou's head tilted to the side. There was a curious note in her expression, but she remained silent.

Of course it would be confidential about the general. Dru was a high-powered vampire. What was Tomesha thinking? She dug deep for a smile that she truly didn't feel.

"No, I think that is all. Thank you."

CHAPTER TWENTY

The door rattled on the SUV from the force of Dru's slam. She stalked toward the inn with anger still burning deep inside her. They had been so damn close to capturing Solomon. How the hell had he known they were on their way to his cottage? This was one failure she didn't want to report. They'd still go after him, but it would be on Dru's terms.

"General." Talbot's voice pulled her out of her thoughts.

She swung around to him with a growl.

His steps faltered before he continued to

advance to her. "Would you like the men to regroup behind the inn?"

"What I want is to know how the hell he knew we were coming," she snarled. She stalked over and stood toe to toe with him.

He didn't back away from her but kept his eyes forward. The others continued on to the building. She ignored them. Talbot had a hand in choosing the warriors who'd come to Butterbush with them. Had someone leaked their plans? She was never one who failed at anything, and this should have been a straightforward mission. This was unacceptable.

"I'm not sure, General," he replied. "But I'll find out."

"You do that. In the meanwhile, I want scouts out in the town and the woods. I want a man on the cottage." She didn't think Solomon would return there, but she didn't want to chance it. She wasn't going to let the traitor slip through her fingers again. He was going to answer for his crimes.

"Yes, General. I'll handle this right away."

She stepped back from him and motioned for him to leave. He moved past her. She blew out a deep breath to try to get herself under control. She was never one to lose her cool, but admitting failure didn't sit well with her. Talbot was a good warrior, and he'd better keep his promise or he'd be answering to her personally.

"General!" someone called out.

Dru glanced at the sky before turning. This day had started off so well and had quickly gone to shit. She'd better be getting some good news now.

"What?" Dru snapped.

Orenda jogged down the stairs of the inn and headed in Dru's direction, holding a cellular phone. "You have a call. It is the postmaster."

Dru snatched the phone from her. "This is General Moldark." She walked along the path that led to the back of the inn. This conversation she would take outside. There was no telling whose ears would be listening inside. She sensed Orenda following behind her at a distance.

"General. It is Postmaster Alexander. I have word that there was an issue today," he announced.

"Oh? And who shared that information with you?" Dru narrowed her eyes on the clouds. They'd already dropped a significant amount of rain since they'd finished burning the lycans. Word sure got around fast. She'd planned to call on the postmaster once she'd settled in.

"General, I'm insulted that you wouldn't

consider that I have men who patrol the town or the surrounding areas," he scoffed.

"Then why hasn't anyone reported lycans?" she demanded.

The line went silent. She paused and stared off at the multi-car garage that sat back away from the inn. The doors were open, revealing it to be empty. The landscaping of the grounds was immaculate. Had she been in a better mood, she'd maybe appreciate it. "Or did your men report to you the burning lycan bodies we left out in the woods?"

"Um..."

"So if that wasn't what you were calling about, then what?" Dru didn't like the hesitation in his voice.

"Well, yes, of course I was calling about the burning bodies. From the reports of my men, there were quiet a few bodies found," Alexander said. "The smoke could be seen for miles. They're working to bury the remains as we speak."

"What you're telling me is that you didn't know you had lycans residing so close by?" she demanded. She wasn't going to go into details about the lycans working with a vampire. Alexander didn't need to know that. "They openly attacked me and my men today, and believe me when I say they paid with their lives."

"I have been unaware of them. There hasn't been a lycan sighting since—"

"The lycan attack where you failed to report that a single non-military vampire stopped them from attacking the town?" Dru stood in place and rested a hand on her waist. She didn't like speaking over the phone to confront him about his reports and the information he held back.

"There were circumstances on why I decided to alter the report—"

"I definitely want to hear these circumstances. I don't want to speak on the phone about this. We'll meet tomorrow night." Certain conversations should be held face to face, and this was one of them. She wanted to be able to see his face as he explained to her why he'd left something as significant as a single vampire halting a dangerous lycan pack from destroying a town.

"Yes, General. I'll be waiting for you."

"In the meanwhile, I want warriors posted throughout the town. Those lycans were unprovoked, and we don't know if more are coming or if they'll converge on the town," Dru said.

"Yes, General. We'll secure the town. Have no worries."

"I won't." Dru disconnected the call. She spun on her heel and headed back to Orenda. She tossed the phone to her in passing. "The men can rest and feed for now. You, I, and Talbot will convene at twenty-two hundred hours."

"Yes, General."

Dru glanced down at herself and took in all of the lycan blood and entrails that covered her. She grimaced and decided before anything else she needed to get the scent of the mangy lycans off her.

One thing Dru knew, she wasn't going to allow Butterbush to come under another lycan attack. Not while she was here. The people didn't deserve it. Vampires and humans should be able to live in peace without the threat of lycans trying to overrun their small town.

Dru entered via the back door and headed up the stairs to her suite. Thoughts of Tomesha crept into her mind. Her gums burned at the thought of her human.

Will you be needing me again?

Dru opened the door to her suite and shut it. She leaned back against it and inhaled. She could still detect a hint of Tomesha's unique scent. Even though her human had been gone for hours, traces of her still lingered in the air.

She shouldn't feed from her, but that didn't mean Dru couldn't have other liberties with the female. There were two things that always helped Dru think with a clear head after battle.

Feeding and sex.

One could potentially cause Tomesha harm, while the other could no nothing but give her extreme pleasure.

Dru pushed off the door and stripped her filthy clothes off. She'd call on her human again. Just the thought of feeling her soft body against hers was already calming her anger.

The answer is yes, miere, Dru thought. *Yes, I'll be needing you again.*

DRU WALKED down the front stairwell to the lower level of the inn. She paused at the foot of the stairs and took in the casual conversations commencing in the main area. She nodded to the humans who worked the front desk, strode past them, and headed back to a bar area where she was sure more of her men would be seated.

The human inn owners kept prepared blood in stock as well as spirits. They had been very accommodating to her and her warriors since they'd arrived. She'd ensure they were tipped heavily for putting up with them. She entered the dining room where warriors were scattered around. Conversations ceased as all gazes landed on her.

"At ease." She folded her hands behind her and strolled over to the bar.

Talbot and a few warriors were seated. When she got there, a warrior stood and offered her his seat.

"Thank you."

"Can I get you anything, General?" a young human female server asked. She was dressed in the inn's standard uniform of white button-down shirt, black slacks, and an apron tied around her waist.

Dru shook her head. "I'm fine."

The woman smiled and moved down the counter. Dru wouldn't be staying here long. As soon as Tomesha arrived, she'd be escorting her human back to her quarters.

"Can I speak with you for a moment, General? In private?" Talbot gestured with his head toward the glass double doors that led to a patio.

"Sure." She followed him out the doors.

He shut the door and walked over to the railings.

She eyed the strong warrior and went to stand beside him. "What is on your mind?"

"I must apologize for my failings earlier," he began.

"We work as a unit. We all failed today," Dru replied. That was one thing she stressed to those training under her. Not one fighter went into battle alone. They either all won or they all lost together. "We did defeat the lycans. We worked together to eliminate that threat."

"I still feel as if this is somehow my fault." Frustration lined his face. He glanced over at her and shrugged. "I should have done more research. Maybe sent a scout closer to the cottage—"

"Then Solomon would have been alerted even earlier than he was." She rested a hand on his shoulder. While she'd been in the shower, even she'd run through every scenario that could have possibly happened. If it was anyone's fault, it was hers. She was the leader, and the responsibility of carrying out the mission was hers. "Things happen for a reason. We'll learn from this. We'll regroup and plan. I don't ever want to run into a situation unprepared. We'll sniff out the bastard."

"I put out a few feelers. I had a thought," he said.

She turned from him and took in the garden surrounding the patio. The soft fragrance of the flowers floated through the air. It was a pleasing scent that reminded her of Tomesha. She inhaled again and felt the twinge of pain from her fangs tapping on her gums. She blinked and tried to think of something else.

"And?" She arched an eyebrow at him. This was why she'd brought him with her. He was a highly intelligent warrior. She was sure he'd go far in his career.

"I began to focus on the missing humans who may have been turned during that last lycan attack and if their families are still here in Butterbush," he said.

"That's a good place to start. Put together a list and cross—"

"I've done that. Since we returned, I've done what you requested. I have scouts already posted through the town and two men on the cottage. If Solomon returns for anything, we'll know." He turned to face her and snapped his heels together.

She eyed him and slowly nodded.

"And this list; what have you found?"

"Some of them have stayed behind, while others have left due to fear of another attack," he said.

Dru could understand that. She was sure it was hard for families to feel safe in an area that had come under such an attack. That wasn't uncommon. Some opted to move to the bigger cities where there were more numbers and the chances of them being targeted by lycans lessened.

"I dug deeper into the ones who remained and found a few interesting things."

"And that is?"

"When we questioned how the traitor could have known we were coming, then the lycan attack, it got me to thinking. I know I can trust every single warrior who's here with us. There's no way any of them would betray you or the crown. I looked into the missing humans' families who remained and discovered two who are of interest."

"And who might they be?" She folded her arms. Talbot certainly held her attention. The warrior had been hard at work since they'd returned.

"One of the men who went missing had a son, and that son works here at the inn." He paused dramatically.

Dru froze in place. A deep, chilling notion

slipped through her body at the thought that Solomon had planted a spy amongst her men. It was a tale as old as time. Hold something over a human such as the possibility of their loved one remaining safe or returning. Humans—or anyone— would be desperate to save the ones they loved.

"Who is this male?" she asked.

"A groundskeeper. He didn't report to work today," Talbot said.

"Find where he lives and bring him to me," Dru snarled. She leaned against the railing and gripped it tight. The sky still held the memory of the light storm that had blown through town. She studied the clouds that hovered. The storm was far from over. Darkness had settled fully. A few stars pierced through the gaps, their light glowing brightly behind a veil of thinning clouds. "And the other person?"

"Another male who was deemed missing. His family remains and, General…" Talbot paused.

There was something in his voice that snatched her attention away from the restless yet quiet sky. The hairs on the back of her neck stood erect. Her stomach knotted as a sense of dread overtook her.

"What?"

"That male's daughter is your human donor."

Dru didn't blink. She didn't breathe. Tomesha wasn't a leak. She was too pure. Too innocent to be working with a traitor. Dru would have sense dishonesty in her when she'd drunk from her. She shook her head.

"Tomesha doesn't know anything." Dru ran a hand through her damp hair that she'd left down.

"And you're certain of this?"

"Are you questioning me about the female?" she asked.

"No, General. Not at all."

"I have tasted her blood. She knows nothing of what's been discussed here," Dru said.

Tomesha hadn't been amongst the warriors for long before being escorted up to Dru's quarters. She doubted the woman would have heard anything vital in the few moments she'd been downstairs.

Where are you going?

Her question had been innocent enough. The sight of her sitting up with her sleep-filled eyes, tousled hair, swollen lips, and naked figure had almost distracted Dru. But Dru hadn't revealed anything to Tomesha. The female knew Dru was here on business, and she hadn't alluded to anything else other than she was going hunting.

She glanced back up at the moon and frowned.

She'd called for Tomesha to be brought to her before she'd gotten in the shower. She should have been here by now.

The glass doors behind them slid open.

"General." A warrior, Leandro, stood waiting for her.

"What is it, Leandro?" Dru scanned the area behind him and didn't see traces of Tomesha. She stood straighter, already sensing something was wrong. "Where is my donor?"

The word sat sour in her mouth as she said it, but that was what Tomesha was for her. She'd paid a lot of money for her to be readily available for Dru and Dru only. The mistress had guaranteed it. She'd better not have gone back on her word. They had signed a contract.

"When I arrived at her home to notify her that she was needed, her brother shared with me that your female had been taken by royal guards. She's been drafted."

"What!" Dru roared. Her gums burned as her fangs broke through. She saw red at the thought that her human was now entered into the registry. She could be matched with another vampire. This was *her* human.

No other vampire should touch her.

Talbot and Leandro backed away from Dru. She clenched her fists, the urge to kill something coursing through her veins.

Dru didn't know how she knew, but she knew Tomesha was hers. She didn't give a damn what that test revealed. Dru would be willing to fight anyone who tried to take Tomesha from her.

"Where is she now?" Dru ignored Leandro's audible gulp.

"I reached out to the royal guards, and they're currently escorting Miss Clay home."

"Prepare a car. Now." Dru marched past him and entered the inn. She wasn't going to let the draft take her mate away from her. She stalked through the dining room.

Orenda was making her way into the room. "General. Are we still meeting?"

She skirted out the way of Dru who drew to a halt. Dru blew out a deep breath. She turned around and found the entire room watching her.

Fuck.

She had a duty. She was in Butterbush for a reason. Her gaze landed on Talbot who slowly reentered the building.

"Find the male. I want him here for questioning. I'm going after my female."

CHAPTER TWENTY-ONE

Dru drove like a bat out of hell. She tightened her hand on the steering wheel, and it took everything she had to not tear the damn thing off. She couldn't care less about the speeding laws. She dared a human officer to pull her over. The only thought on her mind was Tomesha.

The draft would be occurring tonight, as it did every night, and she'd be damned if another vampire matched with her human.

This was the one woman who Dru would do anything for—even defy vampire law.

She'd been loyal to the vampire crown her

entire life, but for once, she wanted to be selfish and take something for herself.

Tomesha.

The human had burrowed underneath her skin, and she didn't know or understand why. It wasn't like she'd never been with a human donor before. In her lifetime there had been countless of donors, but Tomesha was the only one who stood out.

The only one who made her cold heart beat.

Kept her distracted.

Was constantly on her mind.

But why?

Dru turned down the road where she was told Tomesha lived. It was working-class neighborhood. The people obviously didn't have much, but it was clear they took pride in the area. Dru found the house and parked in front of it. She exited the vehicle and slammed the door shut without cutting off the engine. They wouldn't be here long.

She'd take Tomesha away from here. She'd only be safe with her. There was no telling what vampire she'd match with or where they'd send her. Dru would cut down any vampire who tried to take her away.

Dru stalked toward the small house and jogged up the few stairs. She banged on the front door. She had half a mind to rip the damn thing off the hinges and go inside to collect her female.

Her heart pounded as she waited. She strained to listen and heard movement somewhere inside the home.

They weren't moving fast enough for Dru. She banged again, this time harder. The door rattled, almost caving in. Her heart hammered harder.

Was she too late?

Had the draft already happened? The royal guards were known to be swift with collecting the humans who were matched. There was a history of humans attempting to run to avoid being taken to the vampires. Would Tomesha run? Where would she run to? Dru sent up a swift prayer to every god she could think of that she wouldn't fall for a group like the Rebels if she had fled.

Even though the Rebels had been disbanded due to their connection with the lycans and abducting humans to give to them, there were still groups out there helping humans who wanted to escape the draft.

Dru's inhaled sharply, scenting a male on the other side of the door. She raised her fist to bang again, but the door opened.

"What the hell do you want?" a deep voice barked.

Dru eyed the male and recognized him as the one who'd been with Tomesha that day her vampires had intervened with the altercation. He stood holding a large knife. She bit back a smirk. This human male may be intimidating to some, but he'd be no match for her.

"Where is she?" Dru pushed into the house.

He tried to struggle with her, but her strength in this state of mind was too much for him. His feeble attempt to hold her back only ended with his body being thrown into the wall nearest them. He fell forward onto the floor, dazed, the knife skittering away. She stepped over him and continued into the house. She inhaled and picked up Tomesha's scent. It was strong. She was still in the home.

A door opened down the hallway just as Dru turned down it. Tomesha rushed out of the room tying the ends of her robe together.

"Tarek!" Tomesha cried out. She paused in the hallway and took Dru in. Her eyes widened at the sight of her. "What did you do to my brother?"

She raced forward and tried to go past Dru who caught Tomesha's smaller body and lifted her off her feet.

"He's unharmed," Dru growled.

"Put me down. Tarek!" Tomesha hollered.

She tried to wiggle free, but Dru had a strong hold on her. She walked back to the end of the hallway. The male pushed up from the floor and reached for his weapon.

"I wouldn't do that if I were you," Dru snapped. She lifted Tomesha higher in her arms. Another door opened behind her. She spun around and was hit in the face.

"Put her down!" an older woman screeched. She swung her weapon again.

Dru swatted at the object. Was she wielding a broom at her? The older female would come and attack a distinguished warrior? The older woman kept advancing on Dru, hitting her on the shoulder.

"Gran! Go back in your room!" Tomesha cried out. She finally broke free of Dru's hold and hit the floor. She moved quickly between the older woman and Dru. She held her hands up. "It's okay, Gran. I promise. Put the broom away."

"I may be old, but that woman is trying to kidnap you!" There was a fire in the old woman's eyes, and she appeared to be an older version of Tomesha. Her gaze was locked in on Dru. Her chest rose and fell, but her hold on the broomstick hadn't relaxed.

"I'm sure there's a good reason that Dru is here at this time of night." Tomesha glanced over her shoulder at Dru.

The look she gave had Dru feeling as if she were a wet-behind-the-ears warrior during their first sparring. Dru stood to her full height and glared at the older woman.

"This human is mine," Dru rasped. She reached for Tomesha and snagged her by the arm.

Tomesha tried to yank it away, but this time Dru wasn't going to let her go. This was who she'd come for and she wasn't leaving without her.

"My sister doesn't belong to anyone." The male hadn't listened to Dru and held the weapon in his hand with it pointed at her.

"Tarek! No. Put that away. Please!" Tomesha pleaded.

Dru growled and wrapped her arm firmly around Tomesha. The male was threatening her with her mate in front of her. Didn't he know that she'd be able to disarm him before he could blink?

This was her human, and she didn't care who stood in her way, she'd cut them down for trying to keep her from Tomesha. She whipped out her dagger from her waist and held it up with the tip aimed at the male.

"Don't come any closer," Dru threatened. She stood with her back to the edge of the hall where she could keep an eye on the old woman and the male. These were Tomesha's family members, and in the back of her mind she didn't want to hurt them. They were inexperienced in fighting a vampire—a general—and it would be an unfair fight.

But Tomesha belonged to her, and they weren't going to take her away from Dru.

"You expect me to allow you to barge into my home and just take my sister? Who the hell are you?" Tarek snapped.

"It's okay," Tomesha said. "This is Dru. The vampire I've been…um…assigned to." She tried to turn around in Dru's arms. She struggled but was able to force her way. She brought her hands up to Dru's face. "What has gotten into you? What's the matter?"

"You're coming with me." Dru didn't remove her eyes from the two who stood with their weapons aimed. The older female could be disarmed easily, but she'd certainly be injured. The male, he'd put up a fight, but he too would be injured.

"Why? I thought you'd call for me?" Tomesha said gently.

"I sent that vampire away. They came when you were gone," Tarek announced.

Tomesha's body stiffened. She frowned and glanced back up at Dru. "Is this why you're acting this way? You thought I wasn't available for you? Did you need to feed—"

"No." Did she have to feed? No. Did she have a burning desire to sink her fangs into Tomesha's soft flesh to mark her as hers forever?

Yes.

"Then why are you here?" Tomesha tried to keep Dru's attention to her, but it was easy for Dru to sense the other two in the room.

Dru finally broke the stare with Tomesha's brother and looked down at Tomesha. Concern lined her beautiful face. Her hair had been held back with a scarf that was half haphazardly on her head. Her soft body was pressed against Dru's, reminding her of what she desired most.

"Because." Dru paused. Common sense was reentering her brain as if a fog was lifting from her. She glanced around again and took in the damage she'd done. There was an indent on the wall where she'd tossed Tomesha's brother, other items were scattered on the floor, while Tomesha's elderly grandmother stood armed with a broom.

Had she not been so desperate to keep another vampire from her female, it would have been comical.

Dru swallowed, but she didn't relax her grip on the dagger. No matter what, Tomesha was coming with her.

"I was told you were drafted," Dru finally admitted.

Tomesha's features softened. "That's why you're here? Were we matched? You're here to collect me?" Hope shone in her eyes.

"What?" Dru blinked.

She tightened her hold on Tomesha who finally blessed her with a smile.

"I asked if we matched and you were here to collect me yourself? Is that why you come barging into our home late at night? We don't have a television, and I wasn't able to see the results. If that is the case then—"

"I am not registered for the draft," Dru admitted.

"Then I'm confused. If you're not here to claim me, then why are you here? Has someone else matched with me?" Tomesha's smile disappeared, replaced with a frown.

"I don't give a shit why she's here. You're not going anywhere with her." Tarek stood tall and glared at Dru.

"That's right. You're not taking my baby away from me," the older woman chimed in. She gripped that broomstick, prepared to swing again. She raised it and rested the wooden stick on her shoulder.

"Dru. You know as well as I do, that if I matched with a vampire and it's not you, you can't kidnap me," Tomesha said.

"No one is taking you from me," Dru growled. She didn't want to hear reasoning at the moment. She'd spent her entire life following rules, laws, enforcing them, putting her life on the line for her people.

Why was it that she couldn't have this one thing?

How was her human the voice of reason at a time like this? If anyone knew the laws of vampires, it was Dru.

And Tomesha was right.

She couldn't take her if she was to be claimed by another.

Dru's arm tightened around Tomesha even more.

"Dru. Please. Listen to me," Tomesha pleaded. Her hands came to Dru's face again, and this time she forced her to look at her.

Those big brown eyes of hers drew Dru in. Her heart stuttered at the look in Tomesha's eyes.

"We can't stop what's out of our control. If you're not registered for the draft, then you won't have any claim on me."

Dru glanced around the home. If Tomesha had been matched, the royal guards would have already been here.

There was still time. Dru knew what she had to do.

"I'll go and register," Dru murmured.

Once a human was entered into the draft, if there was no match, they weren't removed. They'd remain active in the registry forever until death. Even if it was a year or three years from the time a human had been selected, once their vampire was entered, the system would make the match and the notification was sent out.

"What?" Tomesha gasped.

"I said I'll go and submit for the registry." Dru glanced down at Tomesha. This was one risk she was willing to take. She didn't need science to tell her what apparently her body already knew.

Tomesha was her mate.

It just took Dru's mind a little while longer to recognize it. She reached down and laid a palm against Tomesha's cheek.

"You would do that? I thought you just wanted me for feeding and—" Tomesha's voice faltered. She glanced at her brother and grandmother, a nervous laugh escaping her.

Dru sensed a spike in her human's heart rate.

Tomesha leaned in closer and whispered, "—and, you know…"

"You're not leaving with her. I don't care what—"

"Tarek. I have to." Tomesha looked at him over her shoulder. "I'm under contract."

Tarek swiveled on his heel and walked a few steps while a multitude of curses fell from his lips. Tomesha cringed and turned back to Dru.

"You're serious. You want to see if you match with me?"

"I already know it's you."

As certain as Dru was that the life of a healer wasn't for her, she knew there was only one person for her, and that was Tomesha.

*** * ***

DRU ESCORTED Tomesha to her quarters. Having her near was calming down all of the manic feelings and thoughts racing through her head. She opened the door and allowed Tomesha to enter first. She closed the door behind her and flipped the lock.

"So I take it I'm staying here for a while." Tomesha spun around and paused.

Dru carried her bag over to the dresser and set it down. "Until I can make arrangements for you to go back to Crystal Cove with me."

"Wait, what? You want me to move with you to Maine?" Tomesha said.

Dru strode across the room and paused in front of Tomesha. She tugged Tomesha to her until there was no space between them.

"What don't you understand, *miere*? You belong to me. Where I am, you are," Dru replied.

"But you haven't even registered for the draft. How do you know I'm the one for you?"

"Because I do. Vampires have a sense about it. There's nothing that a blood test can tell me that I don't know already know. I feel it here." Dru slammed her palm over her heart. It was frustrating to think that her mate couldn't feel the pull. She didn't feel the bond that had been created between them.

The draft was created so that vampires could have a way to find their mates who they may not have otherwise found. It was a miracle discovery and it had helped so many vampires since its implementation.

"From the beginning of time, vampires have always been able to know from the moment they connected with their mates, who was meant for them."

"Then how come you haven't said anything before today? Why wait until now when you thought I'd been matched with someone else?" Tomesha's voice dropped low.

Dru stared at her. She didn't have any other answer but the truth.

"I just didn't realize what was in front of me. The signs were all there, but I just—" Dru looked away. She should be ashamed of herself. She couldn't bring herself to admit that she'd ignored what fate had been trying to tell her. "It doesn't matter now. All that matters is that we do belong together. I'm going to enter the draft just so I can prove it."

"I believe you," Tomesha said after a long

pause. She studied Dru then sighed. "But I can't just leave my family behind. We're all each other has."

"Then they'll come with us. We'll make arrangements for them," Dru said without hesitation. If her mate wanted her family with her, then so be it. She had plenty of funds to help set Tomesha's family up into a nice home in Crystal Cove.

"Really?" Tomesha eyes grew round as saucers. A smile played on her lips. She reached over and took Dru's hand in hers and entwined their fingers. "Why would you do that for me?"

"Because you're my mate and I would do anything to see you happy." Dru lifted their hands upward and brought Tomesha's to her lips. She pressed a soft kiss to the back of one. "Now if you're still tired, you can take a nap."

At that exact moment, a yawn overtook Tomesha.

"Oh boy. I don't know where that came from." Tomesha chuckled. She glanced over at the bed with a longing expression. "I guess I could rest for a little."

A knock sounded at the door. Dru bit back a growl. She'd given the order for her not to be disturbed. Tomesha stood on her tiptoes and pressed a kiss to Dru's cheek.

"This shouldn't take long," Dru said.

"It's fine. I'm sure you have general stuff to attend to." Tomesha yawned again. She giggled and grabbed her bag from the dresser and disappeared into the bathroom.

Dru stalked over to the door, prepared to gut whoever had decided to interrupt her after she'd given specific orders. She unlocked the door and gripped the handle. She snatched the door open.

"What?" Dru growled.

Orenda and another warrior stood on the other side. The tall warrior met Dru's glare.

"I know you said you were not to be disturbed, but you have an important phone call we were told you needed to take immediately," Orenda announced.

"From whom?"

"Princess Lethia."

Dru paused. If Lethia was calling again, then something must have happened. Dru stepped out of her suite and shut the door behind her. She pointed to the warrior.

"No one goes in here, and no one comes out. Is that clear?" Dru growled.

He nodded and stepped toward the door. He positioned himself in front of it.

Dru turned her attention to Orenda. "Where's the call?"

"We have a secured feed in the study," Orenda said.

Dru followed the warrior down to the first floor. They came to a room that had a guard outside the door. Orenda entered first with Dru behind her. The room was small but held a few tables taken over by computers and equipment. Two other warriors worked at their tables. At the sight of Dru, they bolted from their seats.

"General." They slammed their fists against their chest.

"You're dismissed." Dru went over to the fireplace in the corner.

The hologram device beeped a series of lights. Orenda followed the men out of the room and quietly shut the door, leaving Dru alone. She reached for the device and hit the incoming button. Within seconds, a hologram vision of Lethia stood in the center of the floor.

"It's about time. I thought you were trying to ignore me," Lethia murmured. The princess was dressed in pair of black leggings and a soft white tunic. Her hair was pulled back in a high ponytail with a few strands remaining loose.

By her appearance, Dru could see the princess wasn't waging war on anyone at the moment.

"I have been extremely busy, Your Highness," Dru replied with a hint of sarcasm thrown in there. She smirked and walked in a wide circle around Lethia. "By the looks of it, you're well rested."

"Can a vampire spend a few hours alone with her mate? Alima hates when I'm dressed for battle all the time," Lethia said.

"Please. We all know you love to play dress-up." Dru snorted. She stopped in front of Lethia's form and folded her arms. She eyed her princess. "So what's the nature of the call if not to tell me you've found the alpha and we're going to kill the bitch?"

"I wish I could say I was calling to tell you that, but unfortunately, the bitch is still eluding us all," Lethia said. Her small smile disappeared, and she suddenly turned serious.

This was no longer Dru's longtime friend, but Her Royal Highness. There was always a shift in Lethia when she was conducting royal business. It was ingrained in all of the sisters. Dru had seen all of them relaxed when amongst those they loved and cared about. The moment it became official royal business, they all changed.

"General Moldark, I am calling you with news."

"I had assumed you had, Your Highness." Dru bowed her head out of respect of the woman in front of her. "How may I be of service?"

"This has nothing to do with you serving me, but you serving our people." Lethia took a few steps toward Dru. Her bright-blue eyes didn't waver as she stared at Dru.

Had Dru not known they were speaking through the hologram device, she'd have sworn Lethia was physically in the room with her.

"There has been a royal decree handed down by my mother, the queen."

Dru paused. She studied Lethia. What had the queen announced that she hadn't already known about?

"And what is that, Your Highness?"

"You are to donate your blood and enter the draft. All members of the royal court have been ordered to enter." Lethia stared at Dru. "If you should defy the orders, there are warriors waiting outside the room—"

"Okay."

"What did you say?" Lethia blinked for a moment before relaxing a bit.

Dru smirked and shrugged.

"I said okay," Dru replied calmly. Now that she knew fate had been trying to get her attention all along when it came to Tomesha, this was just another sign that she needed to go and enter the registry.

"I thought there might be a little pushback or something."

"You said it was a direct order from the queen?" Dru asked.

"I did."

"And you do know that I am one of your most loyal vampires to the crown. Why would I defy a direct order from my queen?" Dru should feel insulted, but right now, seeing how shocked Lethia was at her reaction made everything better.

"I had hoped you wouldn't." Lethia took a few steps closer to her and inspected her. "Wait a minute. You've already found your mate, haven't you? That's why you're being nonchalant about this?"

"That is classified," Dru said with a straight face. She was going to make her princess sweat this out for a little bit. Dru wanted to be selfish and keep

Tomesha to herself for as long as she could. Once they arrived in Crystal Cove, it was going to be a whole new world for Tomesha. She'd be the mate to a high-ranking member of the royal court. Her life was going to change forever.

"Classified, my ass." Lethia rolled her eyes in the most un-princess-like manner. She blew out a deep breath. "Now I need to call Kane and notify him. I'm sure he's not going to respond as well as you did. You have until midday tomorrow to report to the lab. Failure to do so would be considered treason."

Dru gave a low bow to Lethia. If only she could see Kane's face when Lethia broke the news to him. He was a vampire who'd vowed to never take a mate, nor did he want a family.

"Understood, Your Highness." Dru turned on her heel and made her way back to the hearth where the hologram box awaited her.

"And Dru?"

"Yes, Your Highness?" She lifted the box and paused with her finger hovering above the discon-nect button.

Lethia stood in the middle of the room with her hands on her waist. "Congratulations. I can't wait to meet her."

CHAPTER TWENTY-TWO

Tomesha couldn't believe she'd slept as long as she had. By the looks of the shields covering the windows, it must be daytime. She slid her sandals on and made her way back to the bed. She didn't want to leave it in disarray before she left. She grabbed the edge of the thick comforter and made the bed. She didn't want the housekeepers to have to clean up after her. She was sure they had much to do with the amount of warriors staying at the inn.

After she'd woken up, she'd gotten dressed and made herself presentable. Her stomach let loose a rumble. She'd go in search of food. She was sure the inn's kitchen had some available. It was run by humans.

She moved over to the side where she assumed Dru had slept. When she'd first awakened, she'd thought Dru hadn't come to bed, but the sheets on her side had been faintly warm. Even though Dru was a vampire and a nocturnal being, had she'd taken a nap? Tomesha put the finishing touches on the bed and took a step back to admire her handiwork.

When they relocated to Crystal Cove, would they have a small home for just the two of them? Or was there plenty of room for Tarek and her grandmother? She bit her lip at the thought of the conversation she was going to have with her brother about them moving. Delonda would be easy to convince. Her brother, on the other hand, may give her some pushback.

Butterbush was the only town she'd ever known. This was her home, but in her heart, she knew that home was wherever her family was, and if Dru said they could come with her to Maine, then they'd create a new home together. This could be just what her family needed. She'd saved enough money that would hold them over until Tarek could find a new job, and maybe they could find something to help their grandmother stay busy. Even though Delonda's mind came and went, she still had hobbies she loved.

Maybe Tomesha could open a tailoring shop of her own? Or a dress shop. Everyone loved her creations that she made for the club.

She froze in place.

What was she going to tell Mistress?

That she'd fallen in love with her client and—

She reached out a hand to steady herself. She gripped the blanket on the bed and settled a hip onto the mattress.

Was she in love with Dru?

Everything had happened so fast, but she'd known she'd caught feelings for her, but was this love? Dru was always on her mind, she never wanted to part from her, and she now knew the chemistry she'd felt wasn't one-sided.

Dru had said she knew that Tomesha was her mate, but she hadn't mentioned the word love. Did vampires fall in love? Or did they just go batshit crazy wanting to claim someone as theirs? Tomesha frowned, unsure what all of this meant.

"Just take it a day at a time," Tomesha breathed. Her stomach rumbled again. She pushed off the bed and decided to go and find breakfast. She walked across the room and opened the door. "Oh."

Tomesha was met with the back of a warrior. He turned and eyed her.

"My lady. Good morning," he said.

"Um, good morning." She looked around the hall and didn't see anyone else. "Am I a prisoner or something?"

"No, my lady. The general has given orders to escort you down for your morning meal once you're awake," he said.

"Perfect, because I am starving." A nervous chuckle escaped her.

He moved to allow her to step into the hall.

She closed the door behind her. "Well, lead the way."

She wasn't sure why she'd need an escort to the dining area, but she wasn't going to argue. They walked down to the first level of the inn. There was a buzzing in the air. She could almost feel the excitement from the warriors.

"Is something happening today?" she asked.

A group of warriors stalked down the hall toward them and passed by without so much as a look at her.

"Nothing you should worry about, my lady," the warrior said.

She eyed him and wished he'd tell her more, but she was sure he had orders. That group of men appeared to be deadly, and she was happy to not be on the receiving end of their attention.

Tomesha's steps echoed softly against the polished hardwood floors as she followed the warrior through the grand interior. The building, once a private mansion, still retained its dignity of its former life. She folded her arms and took in how every surface gleamed with dark, polished wood. She'd never stayed anywhere so fancy before.

The club didn't count. It was an enticing facility, but it didn't hold the old-world charm this building had. She paused in front of one of the framed portraits of a man and woman. She wondered if they were the original owners. She turned and found the male watching her.

"I'm sorry. This place is so nice. Everything here is just beautiful," she murmured.

She took a few steps toward him to catch up to him. They passed beneath a chandelier and veered down a hallway lined with windows. Their shields were down. They arrived at a set of large doors with stained glass.

"You'll take your breakfast out here, my lady." The guard opened the door and waved for her to go first.

She brushed past him and stepped out onto a wide veranda where the house opened itself to the gloomy morning. The mid-morning air was cool, the grass in the yard covered in dew. She eyed the table that was set for one. "Will the general not be joining me?"

"The general is currently occupied with an important matter. I'm unsure if she'll be able to join you while you break your fast." He moved to the side and stood erect near the door.

She took her seat and inhaled.

The area near the veranda was beautiful. It would be the perfect backdrop for her and Dru to share a meal together.

Well, she at least would eat food. From what she'd learned, vampires did not consume it. Blood provided all of the minerals and nutrients they needed to survive.

There is no way I could be a vampire, she thought to herself. *No food?*

She immediately thought of her grandmother's cooking and knew she'd be unable to go without Delonda Clay's feasts. She smirked at the thought.

"Good morning, Miss Clay," a young woman said as she stepped out of the house and advanced. She had a warm smile on her lips and a tray balanced on her arm. "My name is Janet, and I shall be serving you."

"Thank you." Tomesha's gaze went to the tray. Her stomach grumbled.

Janet set a basket with warm biscuits in front of her along with fresh fruit, a plate with eggs, thick slices of bacon, and a bowl filled with grits. Tomesha eyed the entire spread, thrilled.

"Oh my. This all looks so wonderful."

"I'm happy you're pleased. Here is jam for the bread, and would you like coffee, tea, or juice?"

"Coffee, please. Can I have cream and sugar with it?" Tomesha sat up straight and tried to remember her manners. She didn't want to dive right into the food as if she had no home training.

"Of course. I'll be right back." Janet nodded and spun on her heel. She disappeared into the inn.

Tomesha didn't waste any time diving in. She buttered her first biscuit and slathered a healthy amount of jam on it. She bit back a groan at the taste exploding on her tongue. She doctored up her grits just the way she liked them then dove into them as well.

She almost didn't hear Janet return with her coffee. She set it down and left. Not needing anything else, Tomesha focused on her meal while the warrior remained at his post. The veranda was hushed but for the clink of silver against porcelain as Tomesha feasted. Everything was decadent, but something about the silence caused her to still.

There was no longer birdsong or the rustle of air. It was as if everything had stilled. The hairs on the back of her neck rose. Tomesha paused, her fork hovering midair. She was certain she was no longer alone with the guard. She glanced over at the warrior whose gaze remained straight ahead.

He wasn't watching her, so that couldn't be the creepy feeling she was getting.

She took the waiting bite of food and slowly chewed. She placed her fork down and reached for her coffee. She sipped and tried to appear normal. Her gaze swept the length of the veranda, then the area beyond the railings and out into the picture-perfect yard. Something beyond her sight, someone lingered out there.

Someone who was allowing her to notice them.

How she knew this, she was unsure. An unsettled feeling rested in the pit of her stomach.

"Um, guard," Tomesha whispered. She held on to her coffee mug to have something in her hands.

"Yes, my lady?" His deep voice broke the silence.

She glanced away from the yard and looked over at him. "Am I crazy? I feel as if we're not alone."

His attention moved to the yard, and he nodded. "We are, my lady."

She bit her lip and turned back to her feast. She suddenly no longer had an appetite. Someone had been out there. She was quite sure of it. Her focus lingered on an area near a small group of trees, and the feeling returned to her.

Someone was watching them.

Tomesha jumped at the sound of the doors opening. She spun in her chair and took in Dru stepping through the doors. Relief immediately filled her.

"How's your breakfast?" Dru asked. Her intense eyes watched Tomesha as she strode forward. They narrowed on her, and the smile that had been on her lips disappeared. "What is the matter, *miere*?"

Tomesha glanced down nervously. Maybe it had all been in her head. The guard certainly would have picked up on things before her had someone been out there watching her. He was a trained warrior, she was just a regular human with no fighting skills.

"The breakfast is fine. Everything is fine." She tried to offer a smile.

But Dru didn't relax. She continued to study Tomesha.

Tomesha waved a hand to the chair. "Please join me."

"What is the matter?" Dru asked again. This time her voice held a sharp edge to it.

Tomesha sighed, flicking her gaze back out to the yard. A determined glint flickered in Dru's eyes. She might as well tell her. If she said it was nothing, then it had to be all in Tomesha's head.

"I…um…this may sound silly, but I feel as if someone was watching me," Tomesha admitted. She placed her porcelain mug on the table.

"What?" Dru growled. She moved beside Tomesha and bent down to where they were eye level. She must have picked up on the sharpness of her tone as her facial features softened. "Tell me why you would think that, *miere*."

"I'm not quite sure, but I even feel silly for saying it. But as I was eating I kept getting this feeling that someone was watching me. I don't see anyone out there, but I swear there was. I told him —I'm sorry. I didn't catch your name?"

"His name is irrelevant at the moment." Dru's tone dropped low. She eyed the guard over her shoulder. "And what did my guard do when you shared this information with him?"

Tomesha had a sense that Dru wasn't speaking with her. The guard's color faded as he met his general's eyes.

"There is no one, General. I would have sensed them." He cleared his throat and stood taller.

"But did you check? Did you send anyone to patrol to ensure that my mate is secured when she's not feeling safe?" Dru slowly stood.

Tomesha's eyes widened at Dru's reaction. She was tempted to cut in, but something told her not to interfere when it came to Dru and her warriors.

"No, General. I did not," he replied after a momentary hesitation.

A growl rumbled from Dru that sent a flurry of worry through Tomesha. She felt bad for getting him in trouble. Maybe she shouldn't have said anything at all.

"It's fine. He assured me that—"

Dru's hand cut through the air, silencing Tomesha.

"I want the grounds searched. Now." Dru's voice was cold and hard.

"Yes, General." The warrior slammed a fist over his heart and bowed his head.

He reached up and placed a hand to his ear as he spoke softly into something unseen. He strode to the stairs of the veranda and jogged down them. He headed to the area where Tomesha could have sworn someone had been watching her. Seconds later, a few other warriors burst through the doors and took off in the same direction as the guard.

"I do apologize, *miere*." Dru returned to Tomesha's side. She pulled the other chair closer to Tomesha and took a seat. Her bright-blue eyes still held the dangerous glint in them.

Tomesha shivered at the look. Dru was a vampire who was powerful and dangerous—but yet so gentle with her.

"I don't want to get anyone in trouble. It was just a feeling I had. I didn't see anyone," Tomesha said softly.

"It matters not. You're very important to me, and if you felt unsafe, he should have acted on it." Dru took her hand and pressed a small kiss to the back of it.

Tomesha's core clenched at the heat that now appeared in Dru's eyes.

"If you ever get a sense of anything, you share it immediately. I get those same inclinations, and believe me when I say, it has saved my neck plenty of times."

"Okay." Tomesha reached out and held Dru's face. Her skin was soft and warm. This vampire who led warriors, was a high-ranking member of the royal vampires, felt she was important to her. "So I'm important to you?"

She offered a teasing smile to Dru. Her vampire arched an eyebrow at her.

"You have no idea, *miere*. No harm will ever come to you," Dru murmured. That dangerous glint appeared again. Her fangs appeared underneath her lips.

Tomesha's breath caught in her throat at the memory of feeling those sharp teeth sinking into her flesh. She shifted in her seat and tried to remain calm. Her heart rate spiked.

"Do you have the need to feed?" Tomesha asked. She hoped Dru did. She'd be only too willing to lead her vampire upstairs to their private quarters.

"Not at the moment," Dru replied.

Her gaze flicked over to the grounds where the warriors were returning toward the veranda. She released Tomesha's hand and settled back in her chair. The veil that fell over her face let Tomesha know she was now in her general role. Tomesha decided she'd remain quiet. This wasn't her place to interrupt. She wasn't sure who she needed to be protected from, but she'd listen to Dru.

She'd know best.

"Report." The one word dropped from Dru's lips as the warriors reached the bottom of the stairs.

They stood to attention. The one guard who'd been with Tomesha was front and center.

"There would appear to be footsteps near the tree line," he announced.

Dru sat forward and rested her elbows on her knees.

"I don't recognize the scent. Not human. Not lycan."

"Vampire," Dru growled. She moved lightning fast.

Tomesha blinked and found Dru gripping the large male by the neck, and she'd lifted him off the ground. He gripped Dru's hand while he struggled to drag air into his lungs.

"My mate detected someone watching her, and you failed to secure the area."

She slammed the vampire down on the ground. Tomesha gasped. So she hadn't been imagining things. Someone *had* been out there. She tore her gaze off the vampire who lay on the ground drawing in ragged breaths and focused on the area where she'd known someone had been watching her.

But were they watching her or the inn? Maybe she just happened to be eating while they were observing the building.

"There is no room for mistakes when it comes to the safety of my mate," Dru growled. She was in full warrior mode. This woman wasn't the same person who'd brought Tomesha to multiple orgasms on her tongue. This was the deadly vampire. A warrior. A killer.

And she was Tomesha's.

Tomesha blinked and exhaled a shaky breath. She clenched her legs together, signs of arousal between her legs. She'd never thought she'd be turned on by violent actions, but seeing this side of Dru did something to her.

It was all in her honor.

Again, she was unsure why she'd need to be

protected. She was just a regular human. A sex worker. Who would want to do harm to her?

"I want the grounds on lockdown." Dru snarled.

She glanced at the other warriors who snapped their heels. The one on the ground stood and got in line with the others.

Dru stood in front of him. "Will there be any other mistake, Leland?"

"No, General," he wheezed. He attempted to clear his throat. He turned his attention to Tomesha. "I must apologize, my lady. It will never happen again."

"You're dismissed," Dru barked.

The warriors immediately moved. Instead of entering via the door they'd exited, they walked around the yard and disappeared around the front. Tomesha pushed up from her seat and made her way to Dru who stared off in the direction of trees.

"Dru," Tomesha whispered. She arrived at Dru's side. She slipped her hand into Dru's and entwined their fingers together. She rested a hand on Dru's arm.

"I know you're confused," Dru began. She had yet to look at Tomesha. There was still a hardness to her. The muscles underneath Tomesha's hand were tense. "I've made plenty of enemies in my life-time. Any of them would want to retaliate at any time, and they'd go for the one thing they know would hurt me."

"What is that?" Tomesha whispered.

"You." Dru turned to Tomesha.

The raw emotions on her face almost had Tomesha stepping back. She'd never seen Dru look so vulnerable. She was a woman who was always intense, could be hard to read, calculating—who only showed emotions when she wanted to.

"Me?"

"Yes, you. There is nothing I won't do to keep you safe. Nothing." Dru reached up and brought Tomesha flush to her. Dru's hand gently rested on the base of Tomesha's neck. Her thumb drew small circles on Tomesha's skin, sending a shiver down her spine. "You belong to me and will be with me through all time."

"How? I'm human. Eventually I'll get old and die," Tomesha said. She'd cherish the times she'd have with Dru who'd already lived centuries and would continue to do so. A sadness spread through her that she wouldn't get to have a true forever with this vampire.

Dru brought her head down and rested her

forehead on Tomesha's. "Once I claim you officially, you'll walk through eternity at my side."

"What?" Tomesha's voice ended on a squeak. She studied Dru and saw she spoke the truth. "How?"

"I'll explain everything at the time, but I need to know if you'd be willing to spend forever with me?" Dru asked softly.

Tomesha nodded without hesitation. She'd fallen completely in love with this vampire in such a short time. She wasn't going to question this. It had to be fate. Vampires believed in it. Why couldn't she?

"You didn't even think about what I'm asking you." A smile appeared on Dru's lips. She sighed and rested a hand on Tomesha's hip.

Her touch was something that Tomesha had begun to crave. She liked having Dru's strong hands on her. She leaned into Dru, enjoying the feel of her firm body against hers.

"What is there to think about?"

"Forever means that your family and friends will grow old and die, while you will continue to age in calendar years but will forever look as you do now," Dru said gently.

Tomesha's heart skipped a beat. She couldn't

bear the thought of losing her grandmother or her brother. She bit her lip. She hadn't thought of that. How would she function without the woman who'd raised her? Or her elder brother who'd always been a protector for her?

Forever, forever?

She never would have had forever with her family. They would all eventually pass. It was a little morbid to think this way, but it was the honest truth. Humans did not live as long as vampires. It was a hard pill to swallow to think that one day her family would perish. She'd just have to cross that bridge when the time came.

"I'm not changing my mind. I want to be with you." Tomesha reached up and cupped Dru's face. She had a feeling this was even new for her vampire. If they were fated mates, then it meant Dru would have continued walking this earth alone without her had they not met or entered the draft. Sadness crept inside her at the thought of this woman never truly knowing love.

What if Tomesha had never applied for the job at the club? How would they have met? How would Dru have sensed what was ingrained inside her about Tomesha?

The draft. There was no changing that.

Tomesha would still have been called down to enlist in the registry. Would they match?

"Wait? Aren't you going to register?" Tomesha had almost forgotten Dru was doing that.

"That was what I was going tell you when I first came out here." Dru dropped a soft kiss on Dru's lips. "I am leaving now. Would you like to come with me?"

"Absolutely."

CHAPTER TWENTY-THREE

Dru settled back in the seat of the SUV as they drove to the lab. She was still angered by the thought of someone watching her mate while she broke her fast. The rage that had filled her almost had her killing Leland. She'd seen red the moment he'd confirmed someone had been watching Tomesha.

Had it been Solomon?

It wouldn't be hard to find out where she and her men were staying. She was sure everyone in Butterbush knew. She glanced over at Tomesha next to her with her face practically plastered to the window watching the scenery fly by. The vampire lab she'd report to was located in town. With the local post being in Butterbush, it made sense they'd have a facility here.

"We should be there shortly," Orenda announced from the driver's seat.

Another SUV followed behind them. With this recent threat, Dru wasn't taking any risks while traveling with her mate. They pulled up to a light and paused.

"There has been a message from Talbot."

"And that is?" Dru arched an eyebrow. She snagged Tomesha's hand and entwined their fingers.

Tomesha glanced over at her and smiled.

"He's found the human male."

Dru's head snapped around. She met the warrior's gaze in the rearview mirror.

"Is that so? Alive?" she asked.

"Yes. He has him at the inn," Orenda replied.

"Good." Dru would submit her blood sample and register, then she'd take her mate back home and interrogate the male. It wouldn't take her long to get the information she needed. "No one speaks with him until I return."

"I'll pass that on." Orenda sent a message on

her tablet while the stop light remained red. She slid her tablet back into her pocket just as the light changed to green.

"What human male?" Tomesha asked.

"He has some information I need." Dru kept the response short and sweet. She wasn't going to dive into details that Tomesha didn't need to know. She rephrased the answer at the worry that was in her gaze. "I'm looking for a vampire, and this male may have the location."

"The vampire you think was watching me?" Tomesha asked.

"Yes. He's very dangerous and is wanted by the queen," Dru admitted. It wouldn't hurt to share a little information with her.

Understanding dawned in Tomesha's eyes. "That's why you were really sent here? When you said you were going hunting, you were looking for this vampire?"

Dru nodded and lifted Tomesha's hand to her lips. She pressed a kiss to the soft skin. She should have taken her mate up on the offer she'd made earlier when she'd asked Dru if she had the need to feed.

The hunger burning in her belly had little to do with the actual need to consume blood but to taste her mate's sweet nectar and watch her reach her climax.

"Once you find him, then you'll return to Maine?"

"*We'll* return to Maine," Dru corrected her. When she left Butterbush, Tomesha would come with her. They'd never be separated. She'd ensure Tomesha and her family had everything they'd need to settle down in Crystal Cove.

"We're here." Orenda parked the SUV in front of an office building.

Across the street were a few stores. There was a general store, a clothing store, a shoe shop, and a bakery. Few pedestrians ambled down the sidewalk.

The cloud cover still held well to allow Dru and her warriors to be out during the day. She wouldn't have to worry about burning. The other SUV pulled in front of them. Her men immediately exited and began securing the area.

"Are you sure you want to come in with me? Would you like to visit those shops across the street? I could send a warrior with you?" Dru asked.

"I'm not allowed in there?" Disappointment lined her voice. Tomesha looked at the lab.

From the outside, it looked ordinary. A slab of gray concrete and mirrored glass nestled between two other offices. Its entrance was unmarked to the naked human eye. To any human passing by, it would seem like another faceless architecture in the small town.

This wasn't a place she'd want her mate to be exposed to.

But then as a mate to a high-ranking general, Tomesha would need to learn all there was to the life of a vampire. She was a strong female. Dru thought of the Riskel sisters' mates and how each human was a strong woman who handled life amongst vampires just fine.

Tomesha would be no different.

"Not sure what their protocols are, but you're welcome to come with me. If you're unable to, then I'll send Orenda with you to the shops." Dru wouldn't argue or throw her weight around if the lab had rules. If she had to send Tomesha away, she had the utmost confidence in her warrior.

Orenda exited the vehicle and opened Dru's door.

"I am interested in seeing if your process is the same as mine was," Tomesha said.

"Then let's go."

Dru stepped out of the SUV and strode to the other side. Her gaze swept the area. Her men had the area secured. The unknown visitor at the inn didn't sit well with her. She opened Tomesha's door and held out her hand.

"Come, *miere.*" Dru assisted Tomesha onto the sidewalk. She brought her close and pressed a kiss to her forehead.

Tomesha glanced up at her with a smile on her lips. Dru vowed at that moment to ensure her mate was always happy. This would be her life's purpose. It was ingrained in vampires.

Take, mate, and cherish.

It was a creed that most vampires lived by. Tomesha was an optimistic human. She'd been dealt a crappy hand at life and she'd taken what she had and prospered. There was a strength inside her that Dru respected. Not many humans were as accepting of the way of life after the war. Tomesha was worthy of being the mate of a general.

My mate.

She entwined their fingers and guided Tomesha to the building. The glass doors parted soundlessly at their approach. Inside, chilly air reached them. The empty lobby held a minimalistic modern look to it. Smooth white walls, a polished floor that gleamed brightly. A reception desk manned by a male speaking on the telephone in a perfectly controlled voice.

She strode up to the counter just as he hung up.

"Name?" the male asked without taking his attention from his screen. His fingers moved over the keyboard in a steady motion. He looked up and froze. His eyes widened at the sight of her.

"I am—"

"General Dru Moldark. Yes, we've been expecting you." He flew from his seat and stood. His face flushed as he took her in.

She eyed him wearily.

"I'm sorry. You're a legend. I've heard stories about you and Princess Lethia."

"You're a warrior?" Dru arched an eyebrow. He didn't look as if he could pick up a sword, much less wield one.

"No, ma'am. My father served under you when he was younger. He's since retired and works as a guard here in Butterbush," he stuttered. The skin on his face deepened in color. He reached for a tablet on his desk and swiped the screen.

"Who was your father?" she asked, now curious. That made more sense. This male would never make it through the basic training they put their new recruits through.

"Gattas Frey," he replied.

The name was familiar. Dru had fought with thousands of vampires in her years. It would be hard for her to remember every single one of them.

His gaze flickered to Tomesha. "The human lab is located elsewhere. If you need the address, I can provide that for you."

"We're only here for me." Dru tightened her grip on Tomesha's hand.

Her mate moved closer to her where her chest brushed against Dru's arm.

"Yes, we were notified that you were to come here today," he replied.

She glanced down at his name tag—Garth.

He tapped out a few commands on the tablet before glancing up again. "I just have a few questions to ask, then we'll get you back to the phlebotomist."

He rambled off his questions while she offered the required details.

"You're from Scotland?" Tomesha gasped.

Dru blinked and gazed down at her. It dawned on her that she and Tomesha had much to learn about each other.

"That I am," she replied.

"But you don't have a Scottish accent." Tomesha chuckled.

"That was a long time ago. I left there when I was much younger." Dru didn't want to remember why she and her family had to leave their home-land. The Grampian Mountains were beautiful. She was sure much had changed since the last time she'd been home. But it had been centuries since she'd last stepped foot in the town they had escaped from.

"Please follow me." Garth motioned for them to come around the desk. He led them to a closed door with the number five on it. He opened it and waved them in. "They'll be with you soon."

The examination room was colder than the hallway. Dru's body temperature ran lower than Tomesha's. She took in the shiver that passed through Tomesha. The air here was heavily laden with antiseptic and something stronger. A single reclining chair dominated the center while another chair sat next to a table and computer. The coun-ters and sleek instruments set out gleamed beneath the harsh fluorescent lights.

Tomesha took a seat in a chair while Dru remained standing. Garth nodded and shut the door. Dru didn't care to be enclosed in such a small room with no windows, no exit. It was the warrior in her. Now that she had her mate in her presence, her instincts were sharper, and the thought of a threat against her, or herself, weighed heavy. She had more than herself to think about.

Dru rested a hand on one of her daggers at her waist, comforted by the feel of the weapon.

"Are you just going to stand there?" Tomesha asked.

Dru glanced over at her and shrugged.

Tomesha rolled her eyes and sighed. "Well, I can say this is a little different than when I got processed."

"How so?"

"Well, one, they didn't ask you about clothing, or illnesses, or interests and stuff," Tomesha said.

"I'm sure that is so the vampire can prepare for the arrival of their mate. We wouldn't know anything about them. We may not have much time to prepare, but it gives the vampires a heads-up," Dru replied.

"Is that right? So you'd want to know what I'd be interested in?" Tomesha studied her.

"Why wouldn't I?" Dru frowned. The report she'd receive once it was confirmed they were a match would be basic. They were going to have a lifetime to get to know one another. Once Tomesha accepted her mating bite and blood, she'd walk this earth for centuries. They'd learn all there was to know about one another. "What is one thing you like to do?"

"I love to sew. I was a seamstress before I went to work for the madam," Tomesha said.

Dru had noticed at the club that Tomesha's outfit had been different than the other donors'.

"Your clothing at the club," she began.

"I made them. Mistress allowed me to create my own. I do love the creativity of designing my own clothing."

Dru tucked that bit of information in the back of her mind.

There was rap at the door before it opened suddenly. Dru clutched the handle of the dagger and tensed. A woman in black scrubs came in. Her gaze dropped to Dru's hand then darted back upward.

"I'm Phaedra. I'll be obtaining your blood sample. Please have a seat." She motioned to the recliner. "Please. This won't take long. I need you to pull your sleeve out of the way as well."

Dru walked over to the chair and sank down on it. The nurse gathered her supplies she needed. Dru remained still and kept a watchful eye on Phaedra. Dru barely felt the small prick of the needle. As a warrior, she was accustomed to pain. She'd been stabbed with much larger weapons in the past. Blood flowed into the vials. The rich and dark fluid would one day coat her mate's lips. She glanced over at Tomesha who watched the encounter with interest. Dru couldn't wait for the day she'd introduce her blood into her mate's mouth as part of the claiming. Her heartbeat quickened with the imagery that came to mind.

Her beautiful mate's lips coated with her blood.

She couldn't wait.

When it was over, Phaedra slipped a small bandage onto the tiny pinpoint wound. She stepped back and applied the labels to Dru's vials.

"Your registration will be deemed complete. You'll be notified if there is a match for you." Her gaze briefly flickered to Tomesha who she'd ignored from the moment she'd entered the room.

Dru grunted and pulled her sleeve back down. She stood and motioned for Tomesha who came to her side. Her mate slipped her hand into hers.

"I already know who my mate is," Dru murmured. She opened the door and led them out of the room. There was nothing this test could tell her that she didn't already know. She was relying on her basic vampire instinct.

She'd already had her mate.

Now she needed to claim her.

The corridor seemed longer on the way out. Each footstep echoed too loudly. Dru didn't like the sense that she was getting. The hairs on the back of her neck stood to attention. They passed the empty receptionist desk. She paused a few feet from the door so it wouldn't automatically open and listened.

"What is it?" Tomesha whispered. She moved closer to Dru who held up a hand.

Dru listened for a few moments more. This was one time she wished she'd worn a communicator. But if something was wrong, Orenda would have come inside to notify her.

"Something just feels off," Dru replied.

"That sense like I had?" Tomesha's eyes grew wide.

"Something like that." Dru took in the scenery outside the glass doors and didn't see anything out of the ordinary. She tightened her grip on Tomesha's hand. "You are to always to obey my orders."

Tomesha jerked her head in a nod. It made Dru feel good that her mate knew what she was speaking of. She strode forward to activate the doors. They slid open silently. They walked outside, and Dru scanned their surroundings. Her men were still visible, and the area seemed to still be secured. The street was nearly empty, though. She looked in the other direction, and the pit of her stomach gave way.

She sensed they were not alone. Someone was watching the street, and it wasn't human.

"Orenda!" Dru snapped.

Her warrior appeared from around the SUV that was still parked on the street.

Dru brought Tomesha to her side. "Put her in the truck *now*."

She handed her mate off to the warrior who promptly assisted Tomesha inside the vehicle. She strode forward and onto the street. Her warriors were now on alert. Dru felt the shift in the air. Her senses screamed that the enemy was present. She drew her dagger from its sheath and clutched it in her grasp, tight. She inhaled, and it was then she caught the scent of wolf.

Lycans.

CHAPTER TWENTY-FOUR

"Warriors," Dru said.

The sounds of growling pierced the air. She pulled out her other blade, prepared to meet the enemy. She wished she'd brought her axe with her, but she'd left it at the inn. Her warriors fanned out behind her and positioned themselves in preparation for the incoming lycans. The humans screamed and scrambled into the random storefronts.

Dru took a few steps forward at the sight of single male who appeared a short distance away. The lycans emerged from around the buildings, standing tall, snarling, their amber eyes burning bright. A few of the beasts surrounded him as if forming a protective wall around him.

Solomon.

"Solomon Winterborne." Dru's fangs had broken through her gums and slid into place. She pushed down the hint of worry about her mate hidden in the SUV. It was a military-grade vehicle and should hold up against an attack.

Keyword: *should*.

"There was a time I went by that name," the vampire sneered. He paced back and forth. This was the enemy. He should be dead, but here he was, living and breathing. He was a traitor to the crown, and by looks of it, his traitorous ways knew no bounds. "They have sent you to me. I'm sure they want my head."

"The queen sent me." She widened her stance, ready to honor the request of her queen.

"And you, the loyal soldier that you are, thought you'd be able to bring me to the queen? How is that bitch anyways?" He barked a sadistic laugh.

"You will show respect when you speak of Queen Mira Riskel." Dru itched to wipe the smirk from his face. "And I'm no ordinary warrior, traitor."

"Ah, that's right. You're a general, but that

doesn't scare me. I've faced many warriors like you in my past."

"But never me," she snapped.

"You're all the same. You pledge yourselves to the crown and you don't know that they'll soon enough send a sword through your heart than respect your loyalty," he shouted. He turned and faced her with his eyes feral and wild, his fangs on full display. He may be an older and strong vampire but he could be cut down just like any other foe.

"My loyalty is unwavering. Unlike you. You were the right hand of the king. You betrayed him—"

"He betrayed me first. Did they leave that out of their little stories? Did they not mention that?"

"It was you who ordered the killing of mere children." She took a step forward, already tired of this conversation. His head needed to roll. She'd do her queen a favor and take care of this traitor for her. There was nothing he could say that would sway her decision.

"We were at war. What were we to do? Allow them to grow up and then become the enemy? I did what that weak king could not," he said. "I was thinking of our people. I wanted peace, but I got painted as the villain. Even when I begged him for mercy for—"

He cut short and looked away. He paused his pacing and glanced at the sky. A growl was torn from him as he swung back to face Dru.

"I don't care that you begged for mercy. I have orders to carry out, and you're coming with me one way or another," Dru threatened.

"You don't know them like you think," Solomon barked. "They took everything from me. Even before I gave those orders. I begged them for one thing. One damn thing. But he took her from me. Killed everyone there, and he's worried about lycan children. I did him a damn favor."

Dru filed all of the information he was giving her in the back of her mind. Who was the *she* he was referring to? Who did the king have killed? Had what the king did lead to Solomon's actions as a retaliation? All of this wasn't making sense.

"It matters not. You're a traitor to the crown. Our people," Dru said.

"All of this loyalty. For what? To be able to settle down? You're coming from that damn lab that needs to be destroyed. Vampires don't need a damn system to find our mates. Niall is insane. He didn't want to consider my choice in a mate, but he's willing to have vampires mate with humans?"

"That will be between you and the king. You can have that conversation when I take you to him," Dru snarled.

"And that human in the truck? You think she'll accept a vampire like you?"

"That human is none of your concern." Dru didn't want the focus to be on the truck where Tomesha was safely tucked away. The mere mention of Tomesha had Dru ready to dismember him for even laying his eyes on her.

"Touchy subject, I see," he sneered.

"She means nothing. She's a whore and nothing else." Dru hated to even utter those words out loud. Tomesha was more than her profession. It didn't bother Dru at all that her mate had to make do with what she had in order to survive. "You, on the other hand, sold your soul to the lycans."

"I made an alliance with them. It's survival." He laughed, the sound dark and hollow.

Before she could reply, he lunged forward. He used his vampire speed to reach her in mere seconds. The clash was instant. Their blades met each other. Steel versus steel, strength against strength. The air grew thick as the battle ensued.

Vampires and lycans.

Behind them, her warriors and the lycans collided in a frenzy. The sounds of gunfire ripped through the air along with the angry growls and roars. Through all of the chaos, Dru focused on Solomon. The elder warrior was still quick and holding his own against her.

He moved like a shadow—fast and fluid. Every strike he threw at Dru carried fury and centuries' worth of rage. She countered, her own blows driven by a fierce need to protect her mate and to honor her queen's request. This vampire wasn't going to win. Dru would prevail. There wasn't going to be any other outcome.

"A general, huh?" he said.

They broke apart and circled each other. He was slightly out of breath. Dru took in every detail about him. She'd adjust her strategy. It was what she taught her soldiers who trained under her. He was already underestimating her. He may use his strength and brawn, but Dru was a calculating warrior.

"General Moldark." She flashed her fangs at him, not in the least bit intimidated by him.

"I'll make sure to remember that when I send

the queen your body parts cut up in small pieces." He stalked toward her.

They clashed again. He tried to use his weight against her, but as he'd mentioned, she was a general, not a wet-behind-the-ears warrior. She threw herself into the fight, ignoring the brawling going on around them. She was certain her warriors would be able to handle the lycans.

Then she heard it—the shattering of glass and the unmistakable crunch of metal. Dru's heart skipped a beat at the scream that followed.

Tomesha.

Her head whipped around toward the SUV. Two lycans circled the vehicle. One lunged on top of the hood. The windshield shattered, glass spreading around the street. The other lycan dragged its claws along the frame. They were in an enhanced frenzy at the scent of Tomesha's fear.

"I thought she was just a whore who didn't mean anything," Solomon taunted.

Rage flooded Dru so hot that her vision blurred. She drove him back away from her with brutal strikes of her dual daggers. She forced him to the curb. He staggered but caught himself. The harsh laughter that spilled from him sent Dru over the edge. She spun around at the sound of another of

Tomesha's screams piercing the air. One lycan tried to fit inside the shattered windshield while the other worked on the door.

For a split second, Dru froze. Duty screamed at her to finish Solomon while at the same time she was being driven to go and save her mate. If she didn't capture or kill Solomon now—if he slipped away from her—she'd have failed in her mission.

"General!" Orenda's voice sliced through the air.

Dru spun around just in time to meet the traitor's blade. She twisted around using his momentum against him and slammed her dagger up beneath his ribs. His expression faltered as shock and disbelief appeared on his face. She drove him backward until this time he tripped over the curb and fell to the ground. She followed him down.

"She's not for you to worry about," Dru spat. She twisted the weapon around and pushed it in deeper. Her hands became covered in his warm blood as it escaped around the wound. She withdrew the blade and stood.

Solomon's head fell back onto the ground. Blood slipped from his lips, and he fought to breathe. The sounds of gurgling met her ears. She turned away from him and took in the scene around her.

She didn't know where her other dagger had fallen, but it didn't matter. She locked in on the lycans attacking the vehicle in a frenzy. She flew forward using her speed and vaulted into the air. She landed on the back of the lycan on the hood. The lycan howled and tried to throw her off him. She wrapped an arm around him and yanked him backward. The air escaped her when she hit the ground on her back with the beast still in her grasp. She tightened her hold on the lycan. It tried to break free. She whipped her blade forward and sent it directly into its neck. She slashed completely across the width of it, severing the arteries, veins, and tendons to the point where she almost decapitated it.

She winced at the amount of blood that sprayed. She tossed the animal to the side and rolled to her feet. She ignored the amount of blood that covered her. Orenda had arrived to the second lycan and sent her sword through it's back. The lycan's howl pierced the air but grew weak, the life draining from it. The body fell to the ground, lying still. Behind her, the last of the lycans fell.

Dru raced over to the door and yanked it open

with all of her strength. An urgent need to get to her mate filled her. She glanced inside and saw Tomesha huddled on the floor.

"Dru!" Tomesha cried out.

Dru reached in and dragged her mate into her arms. Relief crashed over her.

Tomesha wrapped her arms around her, trembling. "Are you okay?"

"I'm fine. Are you okay?" Dru murmured. She pulled back and hated the fact that she'd gotten the lycan's and traitor's blood on her mate. She'd take her back and personally wash all of it off, but for now she was grateful Tomesha was unharmed.

"Wasn't that man a vampire?" Tomesha scanned Dru's body as if she were looking for wounds.

"He's the traitor to the crown," Dru explained. She didn't have time to go into too many details about Solomon. She was satisfied at the moment that he'd got a taste of her blade. His head would make the perfect gift for her queen. It would be unfortunate that he wouldn't be able to answer for his sins against their people, but his head would suffice as payment.

"There were so many lycans. Where did they come from?" Tomesha's bottom lip trembled.

Dru held her tight. The citizens of the town were still hidden away. Dru was glad that none of them had ventured out during the battle. This was another attack on them out in the open, and this time, the damn beasts didn't care that they had been in the middle of town. She bit back a growl at the thought of them growing so bold while there was a vampire warrior post located here.

"The traitor. He's in league with the lycans. But don't worry, *miere*. We'll take care of everything." Dru didn't like the fear that emanated from her mate. If she could kill those lycans who'd dared attack the vehicle again, she would. Their death should have been long, drawn-out, and painful.

"We have a problem, General," Orenda murmured.

Dru's gaze flew to where she'd left Solomon's body.

He was gone.

The only evidence that he'd been there was the pool of blood that remained on the concrete sidewalk.

A curse escaped Dru's lips. He couldn't have gone far. Her attention was snatched away by the arrival of large military vehicles. Soldiers poured out of them. Postmaster Alexander was amongst them. Dru tugged Tomesha behind her and stalked toward the male.

"General. We came as soon as we heard," he announced.

He and his warriors were dressed for battle. She released Tomesha's hand just as she arrived in front of him. She flew forward, slamming him against the armored truck. Silence fell around them. She didn't care who watched. The postmaster was in charge of the local base, and it was his responsibility to be the first line of defense for the townspeople.

"This is the second time me and my men have been attacked by lycans," she growled.

His eyes were wide, panic-stricken, and they met hers. Those damn lycans had been after Tomesha. She tightened her hold on him, his feet lifting from the ground.

"How would I have known?" he wheezed.

"It's your job to know. It's your job to protect this town. It's your job to ensure we have top-notch warriors who'd have detected the lycans before they even made it to town," Dru roared. She shoved him away before she did something she'd later regret. She took a few steps away from him and turned back to glare at him. "This town is to be on lockdown. No one in. No one out unless they're vampire military."

"Yes, General." He righted himself and stood to his full height.

Dru despised incompetence, and right now, this post was revealing its weakness. The base was designed to be a command center for all of the vampire military operations to put in security measures to not only protect but to deter their potential enemies.

"Your ineptitude at ensuring this town and the surrounding areas are protected will be reported to the princess." Dru strode over and stood toe to toe with him. She flashed her fangs. "Maybe it's time we choose someone else who'd be more effective in this role than you."

His audible swallow was the only response. She flicked a gaze at Tomesha who silently stood by watching the interaction. She had to get her out of here, but she couldn't leave. This wasn't a safe area for her. Dru turned back to the postmaster.

"My mate came under attack. I want her secured at the base. Are you able to do that?" Dru asked.

"Of course, General. I assure you that she will

be secure on the base. No lycans or enemies will infiltrate the facility," he vowed.

"If any harm comes to her, it will be your head." This was a promise that she'd fulfill. She motioned for Tomesha to come to her side. She turned to her and rested her hands on her shoulders. "You're going to the base where they'll keep you safe."

"What about you? Are you going to go after that vampire?" Tomesha asked

"My mission is not complete. Go to the base. I'll come collect you when I return." Dru pressed a kiss to her forehead. Once she returned, she'd claim her. Nothing would keep her from Tomesha's side.

"Please be careful. You have to come back to me." Large tears teetered on Tomesha's eyelids.

Dru's heart swelled with emotion at the sight of them. This was new for her, and at that moment she knew that she'd do everything in her power to not let her down. Dru caressed Tomesha's soft skin on her cheek. She'd already memorized every facet of this woman's face. This was the person she was to spend her entire life with, and she couldn't wait for their forever to start.

But first, she had a vampire to kill.

"Believe me when I say that nothing will keep me from you. Now go, so I can concentrate."

* * *

ALEXANDER'S MEN had succeeded in locking the town down swiftly. Not a soul could be found on the streets. Dru and her warriors were on the hunt for the wounded traitor. Dru followed the small trail of blood until it disappeared.

His body was starting to heal.

She separated from her men to allow them to cover more ground. She wouldn't need anyone with her. She'd grabbed a communicator where she could stay in touch with Orenda and the others. The quicker they found the traitor, the sooner she could return to Tomesha. Having her guarded in the most secure place in the town allowed her to focus on the mission at hand.

With the town on lockdown, it was too quiet. Eerily so, but it allowed Dru to hear everything with her enhanced senses. The sky darkened as another set of thunderous clouds rolled in. The scent of rain reached her. Soon those angry clouds would open up and unleash the impending storm.

Dru moved through the silence like smoke—

swift and soundless. She was a deadly vampire on the hunt. The former right hand of the king continued to underestimate her, but she'd prove that he was no longer the regarded warrior he once was. He'd feel the edge of her blade again.

The scent of Solomon's blood led her forward. She took in the last drop and cursed. She turned down the slim alleyway between two buildings where the blood trail had led her. It was a long area, a trash receptacle placed near the middle. She stepped into the alley and inhaled. She immediately wished she hadn't. The strong aroma of waste hit her. She scowled and crept forward slowly.

A broken window caught her attention, its jagged edges stained dark. She stepped closer and narrowed her gaze on it. A growl rumbled low in her chest. He was attempting to hide like the coward he'd become. She had to catch him before he escaped and vanished once again.

The wind shifted, and she picked up the scent of his blood. He was close by. A door had been left ajar. She slipped her serrated blade from her waist sheath and silently stalked to the door. She wouldn't attempt to go through the window. She'd bust the damn door in if she had to in order to search for him. The moment she rested her hand on the handle, it flew open.

Solomon lunged toward her with his fangs bared. The once highly decorated warrior was gone, and what faced her now was a cornered beast. The force of his body slamming into hers carried them across the alley and into the wall of the neighboring brick building. The air escaped her lungs, but she ignored it. She drew in a ragged breath and forced him off her.

"You should have died," she snapped.

He brought up his blade, but she deflected it with her own.

Steel clashed in the tight area as they fought. In his current state he was no match for Dru. There was desperation in his eyes, but Dru ignored it. He slashed at her but missed. She landed a hard kick to his abdomen, sending him flying into the building behind him. He crashed into it and fell to his knees. His weapon clattered to the ground a short distance away.

"You think killing me will stop the lycans?" he bit out around his fangs. "You think the king and queen won't turn on you?"

"Your path was chosen the day you betrayed our king," Dru sneered. She was different than him. She was loyal to her king and queen—to their kind.

"He's no king of mine. He had my mate and her family killed," Solomon spat. Blood dripped from his mouth. The wound of his abdomen must have reopened from their fight. There was now a large pool accumulating on the ground underneath his knee. "Because she was a lycan!"

"So you're a traitor not once, but twice." Dru stalked toward him with her blade gripped in her hand. It mattered not what he tried to tell her. She couldn't—wouldn't—trust a word he said. He'd betrayed them all and he must pay.

"Her name was Darda. She was beautiful and kind. Wouldn't hurt a fly. She was killed just because she was a lycan who loved me." He knelt on both knees before her, weakened, but he held his head up high and met her gaze.

For a brief moment she almost pitied him—the high-ranking warrior he once was; the respect he'd once earned was now gone. But pity had no place here.

His loyalty had shifted. He'd betrayed their kind. He sent those lycans to the town to attack her and her men.

He'd almost had her mate killed.

She struck.

Her blade slid through his neck with a clean, decisive sound, ending the argument in silence. He fell back against the wall, his eyes dimming as the light left them. Blood flowed in twin rivers from the wound. She'd ensured she'd severed both major arteries on each side of his neck for a quick death. He'd bleed out in minutes.

She stood over him, waiting until the final beat of his heart ceased. Dru reached up and tapped on her communicator in her ear.

"I have the traitor," she announced quietly.

"I'm headed your way now," Orenda replied.

Dru's hand fell away from the piece, and she eyed the dying male before her. His pallor became pale. What was left of his blood trickled from him. Fat raindrops hit the pavement around them as the clouds opened. It was fitting that the gods would see fit to wash away the atrocity of the vampire who lay dying. The rain picked up into a heavy pour.

"May the gods decide your fate, Solomon Winterborne," she whispered.

The last agonal breath escaped him, and his heart pounded no more.

CHAPTER TWENTY-FIVE

Tomesha clutched her hands together. The vehicle that carried her from the attack site moved fast. The warriors with her remained silent as they drove. She didn't mind the silence. She actually welcomed it after what had just happened. The sight of the lycans showing up, the fighting, all of the blood, and then there was Dru.

She'd faced down that larger man—a vampire. Tomesha wasn't sure how she knew he was a vampire, but all she knew was that he hadn't shifted into the form of a lycan beast. He'd been strong and hadn't hesitated in facing Dru. Her vampire was certainly a bad-ass warrior. She hadn't backed down from the man who'd wanted to do her bodily harm.

She hadn't wanted to leave Dru, but she knew she had to. At that moment it wasn't safe, and she understood Dru had to hunt down that man. When he'd gotten up and disappeared, Tomesha didn't know where. She hadn't heard anything, and apparently, Dru hadn't either.

She bit her trembling lip to try to help rein in her feelings. She'd never been so scared in her life. The growls of those lycans still echoed in her head. The screeching sound of metal being clawed at by the beasts and the shattering of the windshield had Tomesha praying to every god she could think of. She wasn't ready to die and certainly not at the hands of a lycan.

It brought back so many memories of her past that she didn't want to think of.

The night her father went missing was the same night the lycans had attacked their town two years ago. He'd gone out to purchase another bottle of his favorite whiskey. Tomesha had tried to talk him out of leaving. He'd been drinking heavily, more than his usual. But nothing she, Tarek, nor her grandmother said would change his mind.

He'd gone out a little before supper. An hour later, the town had come under attack. The sirens blared, signaling for all to take cover and hide. Tarek had hesitated to secure the house in hopes that Maynard would be arriving home in time.

But he never did.

Tears rolled down Tomesha's cheeks at the memory of her brother's face when he'd come down to the cellar where they'd hid. That haunted look in his eyes had stayed with Tomesha all of these years.

She reached up and wiped the wetness from her cheeks. Had her father suffered? Did he have a quick, painless death? She hoped for the latter. Even though he'd been a shell of the man he once was, he was still her father and she'd loved him.

The truck rocked as they turned onto a dirt road. This was a part of town she didn't recognize. They flew down the bumpy road. She held on to the door handle tight. Soon a large building came into view. She'd heard of the vampire post but had never had reason to come this way before. She stared at it with wide eyes. She wasn't sure what to expect from a vampire military base, but this certainly wasn't it. The driver parked in front of the building. It loomed above her like a fortress carved from shadow and stone. The large doors burst open, and a few warriors rushed down to stand on the stairway.

The vampires escorting her exited the truck with one of them coming to her door. It opened, and a hand was held out for her.

"My lady. Allow me to assist you," the warrior said.

She nodded and slipped her hand into his. He helped her down and guided her to the stairs where the greeting party waited. These warriors were intimidating with the amount of weapons on their bodies. She tried to remain calm. Dru wouldn't have sent her here if she didn't think she'd be safe.

The air carried the faint scent of rain, metal, and something darker. The guards watching barely moved as she was escorted toward the entrance, their uniforms black as midnight with blue insignias printed above their hearts. Eyes watched her, assessing, and though none of them spoke, the air pulsed.

"Miss Clay, please come with me. We'll get you settled." A young woman dressed in a soft, pale-pink blouse and a black skirt stepped from behind those gathered on the stairs.

This was no warrior. Tomesha relaxed at the sight of her. She came down to stand in front of

Tomesha and stuck her hand out. Her welcoming smile revealed her fangs.

"My name is Silvanna Webb. I'm the postmaster's aide."

"Please. Call me Tomesha." She took Silvanna's hand in a firm shake before releasing it. She nervously glanced around at the men standing to attention.

"I received a message from the postmaster regarding the attack. Please come. You'll be safe here," Silvanna said.

"Thank you." Tomesha smiled. She had to pull it from the depths of her belly. At the moment, worry filled her. She followed Silvanna and entered the building.

"This post has been here for centuries. No lycans have ever penetrated these walls," Silvanna shared.

Tomesha walked alongside her and nodded. She blew out a shaky breath and glanced around. The interior was elegant with its black stone floors polished to a mirror shine, walls lined with brushed steel and the occasional gold banner that bore the insignia of the royal house. Her footsteps echoed off the stone floors as she was taken deeper into the stronghold.

"So you have known about the lycans longer than we have?" Tomesha asked.

The quick look given to her by Silvanna had her wishing she'd held her question. Of course they'd have known. Humans had only known about vampires since the beginning of the millennia.

"Vampires and lycans have been mortal enemies since the beginning." Silvanna guided Tomesha to a small corridor, where the lighting was softer. Candles burned in sconces lining the walls. It was apparent that this was an area of living quarters. She stopped in front of a heavy door of dark oak reinforced with steel bands. "Your quarters. We also have orders to ensure you get cleaned up and rest until the general arrives."

"But what about my family? My brother? My grandmother? I need to know they're safe," Tomesha said.

"I can have warriors go and check on them," Silvanna offered.

Tomesha shook her head. There was no way her brother would answer to vampires. He'd see them and immediately worry. "I need to go home—"

"We have direct orders to keep you here. You will not be allowed to leave until the general arrives, my lady." Silvanna reached out and opened the door to Tomesha's room. "I can assure you that the warriors will be respectful and can provide protection to them if need be."

Tomesha bit her lip. If they wouldn't let her to leave, then she'd have to allow them to send someone to check in on her family. Something was better than nothing.

"I'll send a note. Tarek will worry otherwise if I don't at least communicate somehow with them." It reminded her that now they were in a better financial state that maybe they should get a telephone as a way to communicate. Before it had been one extra expense they couldn't afford.

"Of course. I'll retrieve some paper for you, my lady." Silvanna nodded.

A tall figure ambled down the hallway dressed in the warrior uniform, a sword on his hip and a gun strapped to his thigh. Silvanna motioned to the warrior who stopped next to her.

"This is Kristoph. He'll guard the door for you. Everything you need has been provided, including clean clothing, but if there's something else you need, please don't hesitate to pick up the phone by the bed."

"Thank you." Tomesha hesitated for a moment

inside the doorway. She glanced at the two and blew out a deep breath. She just hoped Dru wouldn't be long. She stepped inside the room and found it small but thoughtfully arranged. A narrow bed dressed in dark linens. A dresser. A low table with a single lamp that gave off a warm, golden glow. To one side was a door which led to a private washroom. Steam already fogged the mirror above a basin carved from stone. Someone had anticipated her arrival. Clean clothing waited folded on the bench at the foot of the bed.

Tomesha exhaled slowly and allowed the tension in her shoulders to ease. The door sealed quietly behind her, leaving her alone. She could almost pretend she was away on a vacation, somewhere she could relax and enjoy.

Almost.

The stench of the blood that marred her clothing was a blaring reminder of what had occurred not too long ago. She just hoped that all of the blood that had been on Dru wasn't hers. She made her way into the washroom. The clawfoot tub that had been out of sight before came into view. Steam lingered above it. The light scent of roses floated through the air.

Tomesha removed her dirty clothing and

walked over to the tub. She stood next to it, trailing her fingers through the warm water. The quietness in her quarters allowed her to get lost in her thoughts. She caught sight of her partially obscured reflection in the fogged mirror. Her hair clung to her skin while her eyes were shadowed with worry. She quickly reached up and braided her loose hair to keep it from getting soaked while she washed.

She slipped into the warm water and settled down. The aches she hadn't known she'd carried were immediately loosened. A deep breath escaped her as she rested back. She reached for the cloth that rested on the edge and dipped it in the water. She ran it down her neck and across her shoulders. The warmth of the water soothed her, but her mind refused to rest.

How would she get used to the fact that her mate would always be in danger?

Once I claim you officially, you'll walk through eternity at my side. Dru's words echoed in Tomesha's mind.

All eternity? How? The thought of forever with Dru both thrilled and frightened her. Would she need to be changed into a vampire? How else would "eternity" be obtained for two individuals who were separated by mortality itself?

A shiver ran down her spine. Could she become

a vampire? Bite someone? Drink blood? If that was what it meant in order to be with Dru—then so be it.

Thunder rumbled faintly in the distance. Was Dru safe? Lycans were powerful and had attacked their town before. If anything happened to Dru…

Her throat tightened. She pressed the cloth to her face and breathed in deep to calm her racing heart.

Dru was a powerful warrior. The fact that she was a general had to mean something. She'd be fine. Tomesha straightened in the water and exhaled. She couldn't be a woman who lived in fear. Dru would want her to be strong.

"Come back to me," she whispered. She cleared her throat as if Dru could hear her. "Come back to me whole and unharmed."

* * *

TOMESHA CURLED up on the bed. A yawn escaped her. She'd finished her bath and had dressed in the clothing provided for her. Silvanna had returned as promised and allowed her to write out a note for the warriors to take to Tarek. She only hoped it would be enough to assure her brother that she was protected and fine.

While waiting, Tomesha had drifted off to sleep. She wasn't sure how long she'd slept. She was surprised that it had been restful. No nightmares or dreams that she remembered. She shifted higher up in the bed and leaned back against the pillows. She glanced over at the windows. The shutters were lifted, hinting that it was now nightfall. The steady beat of the rain comforted her. She always did like a good rainstorm. She only hoped that it didn't impede Dru's mission.

Her stomach rumbled, announcing her hunger. It had been a while since she'd eaten. She wondered if there was food here. Being that it was a vampire post, would they even have food for a human? She rolled over and reached for the telephone on the nightstand. She lifted the receiver and placed it to her ear.

"Yes, Miss Clay. How may I be of service?" a warm male voice asked.

"Hi. I was wondering if I could get something to eat." She reached up and brushed the few strands of hair that escaped her braids away from her face.

"Certainly. I'll send someone right up with the meal. Will there be anything else?"

"Has there been any word on the general?" It wasn't like she could call Dru and check in on her. She wouldn't want to anyway for fear of causing a fatal distraction.

"No. There hasn't been. I'm so sorry."

She warmed at the niceness he displayed on the phone. She exhaled and didn't need anything else but for Dru to return to her.

"That's all then." She placed the receiver back on the cradle. She slid from underneath the blanket and went into the bathroom to answer nature's call. She finished her business and stopped over at the sink and washed her hands. She stared at her reflection in the mirror and was happy to see that the dark marks underneath her eyes were gone. Maybe rest was truly what she'd needed.

She made her way back into the room. She glanced around and wished there was something she could do to occupy her time until Dru came for her. There was no television for her to catch the news to see what was going on.

A knock sounded on the door.

"Well, that was fast," she muttered. She padded over to the door and turned the handle. She pried it open and gazed through the opening. Silvanna awaited her on the other side. She opened it completely. "Silvanna."

"Miss Clay, I'm so sorry to bother you."

The vampire's solemn expression didn't sit well with Tomesha. The bottom of her stomach gave way. Something was wrong.

"What is it? Where is Dru?" Tomesha took a step out into the hallway.

She paused at the sight of the large men standing behind Silvanna. They were dressed differently than Kristoph and the other warriors of the post. They were intimidating, large, and looked as if they were made of stone.

"We do not have word on the general as of yet. But there is a slight problem." Silvanna sighed. The woman seemed drained, and she glanced over her shoulder at the males before turning back to Tomesha. "It would appear that when we sent the warriors to check on your family—"

"Is everyone okay? My grandmother? Has something happened to her?" Tomesha felt panicked. She had to get home. She didn't care that she was in danger. She had to see to her family. She'd never forgive herself if something happened to them.

"Your brother and grandmother are both fine. The note you wrote to your brother was received," Silvanna assured her.

Tomesha took a step back, confused. "Then what is it?"

"Miss Clay. It would appear that when our warriors went to your home, they were intercepted by the royal guard. They're the draft guardsmen." Silvanna motioned to the two men behind her.

Their expressions were blank. They studied her, not saying a word.

"Okay. What does that have to do with me?" Tomesha asked.

Why would the draft guards be looking for her? She glanced at the men again. The blond-haired male stepped forward and bowed his head.

"Tomesha Clay. You have been drafted. We're here to escort you to your mate," his deep baritone voice rumbled.

Her stomach dropped. She couldn't have heard him right. She'd been drafted?

"I'm sorry. You're mistaken. I have a mate. Silvanna, tell them that I am with my mate." Tomesha had to force her voice to remain steady. She shook her head. She couldn't believe it. Dru wouldn't lie to her. Dru said that they were fated mates, that she felt it as she would, being a vampire. Had Dru made a mistake? "You have the wrong person."

"You're going to have to come with us," the blond vampire said.

"You're not listening to me. I have a mate already. She's just not here. She'll return soon. Please. Wait until she gets back," Tomesha cried out. She backed away and moved to slam the door shut, but a boot blocked it.

"You can work this out later." The vampire pushed the door open and strode into the room.

Tomesha backed away again quickly. She blinked back the tears that threatened to fall. She had nowhere to run, and by the looks of the two royal guards, they could overpower her with their little fingers.

"All I'm asking is for you to wait." She sniffed. The first tear fell, and soon the others trailed after it.

Why wouldn't they listen to her? Dru would return and order them to leave her. She was Dru's mate. That test must have been wrong. She felt it in her heart that she was meant to be with Dru and no one else.

"We don't have that luxury. You must come now."

Her breath hitched. The room suddenly felt even smaller, the air too thin. Her heart pounded so hard she could feel the pulse in her throat. Every instinct screamed at her to run—but to where? There were two of them standing before her, and even if she somehow evaded them, the entire post was vampire military. She'd be captured.

"Please," she whispered as one last plea.

The guard with the dark hair motioned for her to come forward.

"Don't make this difficult," he warned.

Tomesha's shoulders slumped. She jerked her head in a nod. There was no use in fighting them. No matter where she ended up, she'd find a way back to Dru. She wasn't going to allow some other vampire to put their claim on her. She knew who she belonged to. There was no doubt in her mind, and one thing she knew about her vampire—Dru would come for Tomesha.

CHAPTER TWENTY-SIX

"The arrangements are complete. We're set leave for Savadeen tonight. The queen will be expecting us," Orenda murmured.

Dru nodded. Now that she'd completed her mission, she'd need to report to the queen and present her gift. The royal couple lived deep beyond the Canadian border. This trip was one that Dru would not mind taking. The queen's words echoed in Dru's mind.

Then you have my permission to bring me his head.

And his head she would present.

She held on to the leather bag that held the

queen's gift as they strode to a new SUV that had been given to them. The postmaster would be in charge of ensuring the town was returned to order. Warriors worked diligently to remove the bodies of the dead lycans. She arrived at the vehicle and opened the back door. She placed the heavy bag on the floor and slammed the door shut.

She inhaled sharply. A sense of unease settled in the pit of her stomach. She glanced around and didn't see anything out of the ordinary. Men and women in uniform worked together to clear the carnage, while others checked on the humans hiding in the storefronts. Darkness had fallen while the clouds had opened up and poured down a heavy rain. It had finally slowed to a light drizzle.

Dru tried to make sense of what she was feeling. The sensation increased. Her heart rate skyrocketed. She glanced around and didn't see anything she considered a threat.

"General. Is everything okay?" Orenda paused near the hood, her gaze locked on Dru.

"I believe so." Dru exhaled and reached for the handle of the passenger door.

Orenda studied her for a moment longer before heading over to the driver's side.

Maybe it was the effects of coming down off her adrenaline rush from the battle.

Or was it not her own emotions and feelings she was picking up? Dru froze. Was this Tomesha she was sensing? Was her mate afraid? It had to be. There was no other explanation for this. A smile appeared on her lips. This just proved that they were meant to be together. She didn't need science to prove what she already felt deep down to her soul.

Her smile disappeared. If these were Tomesha's emotions, then why the fuck was she scared or uneasy?

"We need to get to my mate. Something is wrong," Dru snapped.

"Yes, General." Orenda jumped into the driver's seat.

Dru followed suit and got into the truck. A warrior flagged her down. She held up a hand to halt Orenda from driving off.

"General. There is a call for you." The warrior rushed over to the truck.

Dru opened the door and stepped out. "From whom?" She glared at him and snatched the phone from him. Who the hell would be trying to reach her now?

"It's the postmaster," he stuttered. He took a step back away from her but not before she caught the hint of fear.

"This is General Moldark," she growled into the phone. This had better be important. The postmaster was keeping her from going to collect her mate. She had a short time to help Tomesha get ready for the long trip they needed to take. They needed to make plans for Tomesha and her family to move to Crystal Cove. Once she'd presented the queen with her gift, Dru would be free to assist her mate in relocating her family.

But for her to leave for Savadeen, her mate was going with her.

"General," the postmaster said.

Dru scowled at the sound of hesitation in his voice. She remained quiet. She had no time for games or another failure.

"It would seem that we have another problem," he said.

"And that is?" She glanced back to the truck and met Orenda's curious stare.

Her warrior had the truck on and ready to roll. Dru reached up and rubbed her chest. That sensation returned. She wasn't sure what the hell was going on with her, but she certainly didn't like it.

She paused and tried to weed through the emotions swelling in her chest. Sadness. Fear. Uncertainty.

This wasn't her.

It had to be Tomesha.

"What is it?" she barked.

"It would be your mate, General. She's gone."

The phone crumpled inside Dru's fist. She roared her anger and tossed the remains of the phone down. She ignored the stares of the warriors in the area. She flew into the truck and slammed the door.

"Drive. We need to get to the post *now*!" Dru growled.

Orenda didn't question. She put the vehicle into drive and sped off.

Who the fuck had taken her mate?

How did they get her?

She should have been safe and secure inside the walls of the vampire post. Dru's hands balled into tight fists at the thought of someone snatching her away.

The engine roared. Orenda drove quickly. Dru seethed in her seat. The incompetence of the postmaster riled her. She'd given direct orders that her mate was to remain at the post. Even royal guards should have been turned away. Orenda blew past the gates that blocked the road to the post.

The moment she brought the SUV to a stop, Dru was out. She was a blur of fury. Warriors froze where they stood around in the courtyard in front of the large building. The air seemed to thrum with her rage. She pounded up the stairs just as the postmaster exited the building with warriors behind him.

"Where is she?" Dru's words were low and lethal.

The postmaster did not answer fast enough. Dru's usual calm and calculating nature was gone. She crept up the final stair until she stood in front of the postmaster to stare him down.

"My mate. Where. Is. She?"

"It would appear that two draft guards arrived earlier. They said that Ms. Clay had been drafted and—"

"You let them take her?" Dru moved a step closer to the postmaster, her ire barely contained.

"It is the law, General. No one is to interfere with the draft. You know the rules."

"Did anyone verify their claims? Verify they were true royal guards from the draft?" Dru demanded. There was no way Tomesha had been matched with another when Dru was certain beyond a doubt that Tomesha was hers. She went off the age-old knowing that all vampires were born with. Tomesha was hers. No one else's.

"My assistant stated that they were dressed in the royal uniforms—"

"So, no, you did not," Dru growled.

Behind him, the warriors took a step back. The air tightened around them. Dru could no longer retain the anger and rage at the lack of competence the postmaster showed. She threw him down the stairs, hard enough the stone cracked beneath him. He lay there, his breaths coming out in a tight wheeze. His eyes were wide as he watched her walk down the stairs.

Her chest throbbed. It had to be the bond. The connection between her and her mate. There was no other reason. The draft was wrong. Dru was always a loyal vampire to the crown, but it would appear this time, the king's scientist had got this wrong.

Tomesha was hers, and she'd find her.

"I want to know where they took her," Dru snapped.

Alexander pushed up from the ground, the stench of fear sharp and tangible. She glanced around at all of the warriors. They were useless. None of them had tried to interfere in stopping the supposed guards from taking her woman.

"General. You know they will not tell us—" His words died off the moment her gaze cut to him. He jerked his head in a nod. "I'll reach out and tell them that you want to know where the human went."

Tomesha's fear clung to her. Wherever her mate was, she shouldn't be scared. The farther apart they were, the stronger the pulse of her mate's emotions became. It was enough to make Dru see red.

She needed to get her back.

"General." Orenda's voice broke through her haze.

Dru snapped her head around to face her warrior.

"We have to go. The queen is expecting us. The jet is fueled and ready."

Dru wanted to hit something. Break something. Kill someone. She had a duty to the crown, and at that moment, she wanted to ignore that. Never in all her years had she ever questioned anything she'd done for the crown, for her people. That had been her purpose since becoming a warrior.

Now, she wanted to only do what was right for her.

And that was go after her mate.

But Orenda was right. The queen would be expecting her. She couldn't risk being labeled as a traitor for abandoning her mission. The moment she handed over Solomon's head, she'd leave.

Whoever had taken Tomesha had better hope they were not there when Dru arrived. Their heads would roll. And whoever the vampire was who'd supposedly matched with Tomesha would turn her back over to Dru.

Or they'd die.

"Find where they sent her," Dru ordered.

The postmaster pounded a fist over his heart. She stalked to the vehicle and snatched open the door. She slid in and slammed it shut. Her body shook with the uncontrolled rage and fury that burned deep within her.

"Don't worry, General. We'll find her," Orenda murmured. She put the truck in gear and drove off.

Dru settled back and thought of Tomesha's expression when she'd sent her off to be protected at the vampire post. Her mate had trusted her.

Dru would get her back, and when she did, she'd never let her go ever again.

* * *

"WHAT DID YOU JUST SAY?" Dru stared at the second pilot who came from the cockpit.

He visibly shuddered at her glare. "I said that there is going to be a delay with landing, General." He reached up and tugged on the collar of his shirt. He swallowed hard before continuing. "There is a herd of caribou blocking the runway."

Dru blinked and glanced over at Orenda and Talbot who'd joined them. Seven hours of flying had Dru's skin crawling. This was time that was being lost from her searching for her mate. She ran a hand along her face.

Caribou was blocking the runway?

"Why can't you just plow through them?" Dru grunted. How was this even possible? She stood from her chair on the private jet.

The pilot took a step back. The scent of fear filled the air. She shook her head and moved over to where her thick coat lay on a couch. The party traveling with her was small. She didn't need a full battalion to accompany her to the king and queen.

Savadeen would be extremely cold this time of year. Even though she was a vampire and her body could acclimate fine to the weather, this type of cold was something else. She lifted her leather coat and put it on. It was a thick and lined with fur and would be perfect to shield off the chill.

"Our plane would take significant damage. The ground crew is working on clearing the caribou. We should only be delayed fifteen or twenty minutes," the pilot said.

"You have ten minutes to get this plane on the ground." Dru returned to her chair and took her seat. She wasn't going to settle for more delays. The quicker she could make her delivery to the queen, the quicker she could begin her next mission—finding Tomesha.

In the seven hours since she'd left Butterbush, the postmaster had not found Tomesha's whereabouts. Dru made a mental note to remove him from his command. She did not accept failure in anything, and he'd be replaced. She had a few prospects in mind who would be perfect for that position. There were trustworthy vampires who wouldn't let her down.

"Yes, General." The pilot bowed his head before retreating to the cockpit.

"There will be transport awaiting us," Orenda said.

"Good. We're going to make this quick." Dru

turned to Talbot who was working on his tablet. She'd put him on the search for her mate. Someone knew where she was. The draft kept extensive documentation on the human-vampire matching. They kept up on the matches and even released statistical information each year to prove the success of the unions. Someone had to know something. "Have you discovered anything about Tomesha?"

"Not yet, General. There's so much red tape to get through. This is not the norm," he murmured.

Dru scowled. This wasn't what she wanted to hear. How was it that she was a general and no one would give her the information she demanded? Her position should mean something.

Talbot glanced up at her. "But I'll continue on."

She stared out the window and took in the winter wonderland that awaited them below. Orenda, Talbot, and the few warriors accompanying her prepared for the descent into the cold, remote area. It had been a long while since she'd visited the royal castle which was located in the Northwest Territory of Canada.

The pilot's voice came overhead, announcing they were preparing to land. Dru felt some satisfaction that it hadn't taken as long as they'd suspected. They safely landed without incident. Once the doors opened, Dru stood and reached for the heavy leather bag that held the traitor's head. She strode to the door and breathed in the frosty air. She peered around and took in the barren land that surrounded the small airport. A log cabin positioned off in distance acted as the terminal.

Out on the tarmac were several vehicles with the royal insignia on them. Dru jogged down the stairs of the plane behind Talbot and stalked toward their arranged transportation. It shouldn't take them long to arrive at the castle—Dorston Keep.

Dru was escorted into one of the waiting vehicles. The trip to the keep did not take long, for which Dru was thankful. Her skin crawled at the thought of her mate and wherever she was. Dru couldn't get Tomesha off her mind. Worry filled her again. Was she safe? Was the vampire who had her treating her with respect? Had they laid a finger on her?

Dru bit back a growl. If one single strand of hair was out of place on her mate when she arrived, Dru would burn down the world.

Savadeen was carved from ice and silence during this time of year. The sky stretched out dark and endless with the faint shimmer of aurora. They arrived, and the vehicles parked. Dru's door opened. She clutched the handle of the bag and stepped from the ride. The faint snow that drifted in the air hit her like shards of glass. She scowled at how damn cold it was here. Great Bear Lake lay beneath the darkened sky, a mirror of black glass, its frozen surface reflecting the jagged peaks and the iron silhouette of Dorston Keep.

The castle rose from the edge of the lake, a beast in the snow. The ancient stone walls were covered in frost, its steeples hovering against the dark morning sky like shadows. Gold banners marked with the royal crest snapped in the cutting wind, their edges frozen in ice.

Dru adjusted her coat, the thick leather helping to shield her from the cold. It creaked as she moved. The traitor's head weighed down the satchel at her side. It was a gruesome token of victory that should have had her feeling proud at her accomplishment. This moment was dimmed by the fact that her mate was missing.

The weight of Tomesha's absence was heavy. Her mate should be by her side at this time. Dru would have been honored for the king and queen to meet her. To have a union blessed by the royal couple was an honor that she'd live for, but she wouldn't be robbed of this opportunity. Once she'd obtained her mate, she'd be sure to introduce Tomesha to the Riskels.

The bond between them was a dull ache behind her rib cage. Every moment they were apart scraped at Dru's nerves. She promised herself that her mate would not be absent from her side for long.

Dru's warriors flanked her side as the massive doors of the keep opened. They stalked through them, Dru intent on meeting with the queen who expected them. Royal guards in their armor were posted at the entrance. They bowed their heads in respect as Dru walked past them.

"General. Welcome to Dorston Keep." A guard stepped forward.

Dru and her warriors stopped.

The warrior, tall and wide, came to stand in front of them. He was a high-ranking guard by the looks of the insignia embedded in his uniform. "The queen awaits you. Please allow me to escort you. She's in the throne room."

"Thank you," Dru murmured.

The guard spun on his heel and led them inside the keep. More of the royal guards trailed behind their small party. It was much warmer inside, which

Dru appreciated. The sconces on the walls burned bright with fire, while portraits of past dignitaries lined the way. Their footsteps echoed on the marble floor. Every step felt as if she were getting farther away from her mate. She held back the restrained violence that wanted to be released.

Get this over with, she instructed herself. *Deliver the head. Bow down to the queen and king. Then burn the world to find your mate.*

At this moment, she couldn't care less about how she'd be rewarded for completing the quest from the queen. She hadn't taken this mission for recognition. It had been the right thing to do. But it was now done. She had the traitor's head, and the king and queen could have closure that a part of the past could be buried.

As she moved deeper into Dorston Keep, the cold seemed to follow her. Not the chill of Savadeen, but the kind that came from within, a fury held too tight. Beneath the weight of her anger and rage, one thought pulsed steady and sharp.

Hold on, miere. *I'm coming.*

They arrived at a set of massive twin doors engraved with the royal crest. They groaned as the guard pushed them open. He stepped in and moved to the side to allow her to enter. Dru and her warriors followed him. The throne room was a cathedral of shadows and power. Lights from crystal chandeliers throughout shimmered across the obsidian pillars carved from stone. At the far end of the chamber, beneath a ceiling so tall it vanished into darkness, stood the twin thrones sitting upon a dais of black marble veined with gold.

King Niall lounged in his with his assessing stare, watching them approach. Every inch of him spoke of a predator, a warrior—a king. Beside him sat the very elegant Queen Mira, her blue eyes unreadable as she leaned against her throne's armrest.

Dru walked with precision straight to the dais. Her long coat swayed against her legs. She tightened her grip on the satchel which held the stains of blood from the severed arteries. It had been brutal yet satisfying to cut Solomon's head from his body. She smirked at the memory. The rest of him had been burned along with the bodies of the lycans he'd sided with. It was an all-too-fitting end for the traitorous vampire.

"General Dru Moldark." The guard's voice echoed through the room.

Dru stopped at the base of the dais and went

down on one knee and bowed her head. Her warriors did the same behind her. The powerful couple before them was due respect. She kept her gaze on the floor and inhaled.

"Your Majesties," she murmured.

"Rise," the king said, his voice smooth but carrying the hint of an edge and authority.

Dru stood, her jaw tight. The scent of blood drifted up from the bag. It was the stench of the traitor, and it turned her stomach. Dru met the steady gaze of both king and queen. Mira's lips curled up in the corner as her gaze dropped down to satchel Dru held.

"My mate tells me that she chose you for a mission," the king said.

"That is correct, Your Majesty," Dru replied.

"And by the looks of it, I would say I chose the perfect person for the job." Queen Mira reached out a hand and rested it on Niall's arm. She graced her mate with a beautiful smile. Her blonde hair was in a sophisticated updo, while she was dressed in the finest gown that money could buy.

Even though the woman was dressed formally, Dru knew the queen. She'd have plenty of weapons on her person somewhere in order to defend herself.

Once a warrior, always a warrior.

"So tell me, General Dru Moldark. What have you in the bag?" King Niall asked.

"I was given two options, Your Majesty. It would seem the traitor decided on his own which I would be presenting to you," Dru said. She unlatched the satchel and withdrew her grisly prize by the hair. She held the head of the traitor for all to see. His dead eyes stared sightlessly ahead.

The royal couple stood from their thrones. The room was deathly silent as everyone waited for their reactions. They walked down the stairs and stopped a few feet from Dru. Niall's gaze was locked on the face of the traitor.

"This would be the second time I have looked upon this face in death," King Niall said. An unreadable expression crossed his face. He turned to his mate and nodded. It would seem that the success of her mission was giving the king something he'd needed.

"I assure you this time, Your Majesty, he's dead," Dru replied. "Even all of these years, he continued to betray our kind. He was in league with the lycans."

"He was once a great man. Someone who was

close to me." The king stood to his full height as a scowl appeared on his face.

"His betrayal cost us plenty." Dru slipped the head back in her satchel. If what she suspected was true, this vampire had even cost Tomesha her father who'd disappeared during the lycan attacks. This male deserved his death ten times over.

The king snapped his fingers. A royal guard appeared their side. She handed the satchel over to the guard who turned and walked off with the bloody bag.

"You appear to be unsettled, General. I thought you would be pleased that you were able to present such a gift to me and my mate. Is there something else disturbing you?" the queen asked.

It was no surprise that she'd picked up that something else was on Dru's mind.

Dru's breath caught in her throat. She was unsure if she should burden the royal couple with her personal issues. She glanced up before deciding it wouldn't hurt. The queen had asked a question, therefore, she should answer her.

"It's my mate. She was taken from the Butter-bush post." It hurt her to even admit those words aloud. It showcased her failure to keep Tomesha safe.

"Taken? By whom?" The queen arched a perfectly sculpted eyebrow.

"I'm told the royal draft guards," Dru snarled.

The king and queen grew still. They exchanged a quick glance before the queen stepped forward.

"If she was your mate, then how did she match with someone else? Are you certain you were fated? Did you enter the draft?" the queen asked.

"I did, Your Majesty."

"The science is never wrong," the king said.

"With all due respect, Your Majesty, this time it was wrong. I know what I felt, and my heart belongs to Tomesha Clay," Dru gritted out through clenched fangs. Her body was coiled tight. She glanced at the both of them. "I'll find her and will right this wrong. She needs to be with me and not someone else."

"And you're certain," the queen asked again.

Dru jerked her head in a fierce nod. She straightened to her full height.

"The draft has never been wrong," the queen said, "and I hope this will be the only time. I'll send a message to the draft for confirmation. Please stay the day. Rest. We'll have answers by nightfall."

"I must respectfully decline. I need to seek out my mate. I will not rest until she's back with me.

Permission to leave." Dru snapped to attention. She kept her eyes forward as she waited to be dismissed. If they didn't, then she would defy orders for the first time.

Without hesitation.

The longer she waited, the longer it would be until Tomesha was back in her arms. The king studied her for a moment longer before he nodded.

"Granted. May the hunt end in your favor," King Niall said.

Dru bowed again then turned on her heel. She strode through her warriors who parted for her. They followed behind her as they made their way back through the throne room. The queen's voice followed behind, a soft whisper to the king.

"She'll tear the world apart for that human, Niall. I pity whoever has her."

The queen had no idea. Dru was ready to unleash hell upon anyone who stood in the way of her getting Tomesha back.

CHAPTER TWENTY-SEVEN

Dru stared out the window of the plane. The scenery wasn't that of the Butterbush airport where they'd taken off one day ago. She stood and stalked to the front. The door opened with a member of the ground crew on the familiar tarmac.

"What is the meaning of this?" Dru roared.

They were to supposed have flown back to Butterbush where she could begin her search for Tomesha. She stood in the doorway and glared at the male who stood on the staircase that led down to the ground. He flew down the stairs and out of her way.

"The pilots had orders to fly you here," Kane announced. The cocky son of a bitch had the audacity to grin. He strode forward and motioned for her to join him on the ground.

Dru bit back a curse. She hadn't seen Kane and the warrior behind him. She'd only focused on the poor soul who'd opened the plane door. This wasn't the time for her to have to report for another mission. Whatever it was needed to wait. Dru had something else pressing that needed her attention.

Seeking out her mate.

"I am needed back in Butterbush," Dru bit out around her fangs.

She walked down the stairs with her warriors following close behind her. She was going to have to speak with Lethia. If there was something that was needed of her, Lethia could have Kane handle whatever it was. He may be a little deranged in the head, but he was a fine captain.

"You'll need to take that up with the commander. She's requesting your presence." Kane's smile disappeared.

It was then she realized that Lethia had sent Kane on purpose. If she chose to defy orders, he was one of the vampires who could handle her in a fight. She swore under her breath.

"Fine," she snapped.

He nodded and waved her on past him. She eyed the vehicles waiting for her. He walked alongside her to the SUV where a warrior held the door open. She slid into the back seat and scowled. The weather here was warm and fall like. The cold back in Savadeen was bitter and had chilled her down to the bones.

The drive to the castle was done in complete silence which allowed Dru to think. The general in her was a calculating bitch. She would find her mate. It was only a matter of time. Once she found out what Lethia wanted with her, she'd be on her way.

Once at the castle, Dru strode through the main doors. She ignored Kane's chuckle that floated through the air behind her.

"Where is she?" Dru barked over her shoulder.

Servants scattered out of the way and pressed back against the wall as she passed, their eyes adverted. She growled at the simple fact that she'd been brought back to Crystal Cove. She was being treated like an unruly child and not the general she was promoted to be.

"Princess Lethia is waiting for your arrival out in the gardens," Sterling announced, stepping out of the formal receiving room. The older vampire bowed his head.

She continued on past him, not slowing. She turned down the corridor that led to the formal gardens. She was alone, glad of this because she was going to get some things off her chest with Lethia that she wouldn't be able to do with an audience. She burst through the doors and inhaled sharply. The floral scent accosted her. Any other day she'd appreciate the beauty of the landscape around her, but now, she couldn't care less.

She followed the stone path deeper into the gardens. Lethia waited by the fountain, her stance poised and steady. Her blonde hair bound tightly at her nape, her fighting leathers molded to her body. She was draped in plenty of weapons, and here was a gleam in her eye that Dru couldn't read.

"General," Lethia said. "Welcome home."

"I won't be long, Your Highness," Dru said.

Lethia's brow arched. "Oh, is that so? I distinctly remembered ordering you and the warriors home."

"I have some important matters back in Butterbush, Your Highness." Dru rested her hands on her waist. "Anything you need of me, Kane can do until I return."

"General."

"I will not be gone long. I need to leave imme-diately—"

"General." Lethia's voice whipped through the air.

Dru froze, startled by the sharpness of her old friend's voice. It was cold—an order. "You're not to leave the castle."

"You dare—"

"I dare," Lethia interjected. "Because you're needed here."

Dru's chest rose and fell with restrained violence. She had to make Lethia see why she had to leave. She could not be grounded at a time like this, and if it had something to do with the lycans, she'd find her mate then join the rest in the fight against their enemy.

"Lethia. It's my mate. She was taken. I have to—"

"She wasn't taken."

Dru froze. She blinked hard. Was her friend not understanding her?

"Why would you say that? You don't know what happened back in Butterbush," Dru began but ceased her plea at the raise of Lethia's hand.

"You have been matched, Dru." Lethia's face softened.

"Now is not the time to bring up the damn draft. That test is wrong. I know who my mate is, and she was taken!" Dru shouted. Her hands trembled with her restrained anger and rage. She took a step back, and for once in her career, she'd go against everything she held dear to her.

"Listen to me, Dru." Lethia must have recognized the change in Dru. She held up both of her hands as if trying to calm down an animal about to charge. "Your mate—the human—is here. In Crystal Cove."

For a heartbeat, Dru couldn't move. She couldn't breathe. It was as if the world had paused.

"What?" Dru stared at Lethia for a moment. She struggled to understand what the princess was saying to her. Was Lethia speaking of Tomesha or another human?

"Her name is Tomesha, right? She's here. She was brought here by the royal draft guards. It was confirmed she was your mate," Lethia said.

"No," Dru whispered. She shook her head and tried to swallow the lump that appeared in her throat. "But I felt her fear and anxiety."

"I'm sure she was scared when the guards

showed up and removed her from the military post. She didn't know what was happening, but have no worries, she's been safe here. Alima helped get her settled in while she waited for you to return home."

For the first time since she'd discovered her mate had been taken, she faltered. Her pulse pounded in her ears. All of the rage that had been inside her dissipated, and in its place was a raw ache and need.

"My Tomesha? She's here?" Dru whispered.

"She's waiting for you in your quarters—"

Dru didn't wait for permission to leave. She was already moving. She had to get to her mate. She had to see for herself that Tomesha was here and unharmed. She tore open the door and raced through the corridors.

Every instinct, every ounce of control she'd once had, dissolved into something primal.

She was going to take her mate, claim her, and keep her by her side forever.

THE FIRE CRACKLED SOFTLY. The air in the castle was quite chilly. It may be fall here in Crystal Cove, but it was much cooler than what she was used to during this time of year. The shutters on the windows had been raised not too long ago, allowing Tomesha to view the landscape that surrounded the castle.

But for now, she waited.

She sat on the edge of the bed, her fingers twisting the edge of the blanket she hadn't realized she'd been clutching. The last day and a half had been a whirlwind of emotions. When the registry guards had taken her from the vampire military post, she'd thought she'd never see Dru again. Imagine her surprise when she'd learned that her destination was Dru's home.

Tomesha chuckled. Of course her vampire had been right. They'd been matched in the draft. The only reason they'd taken Tomesha to Crystal Cove was because Dru's home address was here. They hadn't known she was already with her mate.

Her smile slowly faded. She hadn't heard much word about Dru. The only thing she'd been informed of was that she was completing her mission. Tomesha wasn't sure what was going on, but she'd been experiencing emotions she was sure weren't hers. The amount of pain, anger, and rage that had filled her, she knew it wasn't her.

It had to be Dru.

When she'd arrived at the castle, she'd met with Princess Lethia's mate, Alima. Tomesha had only ever seen the woman on television. She was just as beautiful in person as she was on the small screen. Alima had helped make sure Tomesha was comfortable and settled in while they waited for Dru to arrive. She'd shared with Tomesha that she and Lethia were able to sense each other, too.

Now she was worried. She hadn't felt anything from Dru in a while. She'd been assured that Dru was alive and well. Every sound, every echo of footsteps, every howl of the wind sent her pulse racing.

Dru was alive.

She kept reminding herself of that, but until she saw her, until she got to hold her in her arms, would she finally believe it?

Then suddenly, a pulse in her chest. A hot electric thrum that made her heart rate skyrocket. Was that Dru? Was she okay?

"Dru?" she whispered. Would her vampire hear her?

The door slammed open with such force that Tomesha whipped around at the commotion.

Dru stood staring at her with hunger and need in her eyes. Her auburn hair was pulled back away from her face, her bright-blue eyes wide as they took her in. For a moment, neither of them moved. Tomesha could barely breathe. She was completely elated and relieved that Dru was there.

"Dru," Tomesha repeated, only this time louder.

In the blink of an eye, Dru was across the room. Tomesha barely had time to rise before she was swept up into Dru's strong arms. Her feet left the floor as Dru held her close. She wrapped her arms around Dru's neck. The scent of the outdoors and an aroma that was Dru filled her nostrils. She breathed in deep, memorizing the smell of her vampire.

"I thought I'd lost you," Dru rasped. She set Tomesha down and buried her face in the curve of Tomesha's neck.

Tomesha pulled back and rested her hands on Dru's face in order for her to stare her in the eye.

"I knew without a doubt wherever they'd have taken me, you would have come for me," Tomesha said softly. Tears blurred her vision, and she took in the tortured look that radiated from Dru's eyes. "I felt you. Somehow I felt all of your emotions. When I thought I wouldn't see you again, I felt you here." Tomesha touched the area above her heart.

Dru's eyes softened, and she gazed down where Tomesha's hand rested.

"It really is the bond between mates. I could feel you, too. I sensed when you were afraid—"

"And I sensed all the anger and rage you held," Tomesha whispered. She cupped Dru's face and studied her. All of which she felt from Dru wasn't normal. No one should have that much built up in them. Even Tomesha had felt as if she wanted to do bodily harm to someone.

"It was because I thought they were taking you from me," Dru replied. She reached up and took Tomesha's hands in hers. "When I heard you'd been taken due to the matching system, I almost lost it."

"Almost?" Tomesha arched an eyebrow. With all of the dark emotions she'd experienced, she was surprised Dru hadn't already left a trail of bodies somewhere.

"You're mine, and soon you'll carry my mark." Dru reached up and placed her fingers on Tomesha's neck. Her fangs peeked out from underneath her top lip. She exhaled a shaky breath before lifting her gaze to meet Tomesha's. "You'll always be safe. No one will ever take you from me again."

Tomesha's breath caught in her throat. She

wanted that. She wanted to belong to this woman forever. He heart raced at the thought of being able to be with Dru for all time. Just thinking of how this woman was tortured with not knowing if she'd ever see her again triggered something deep in Tomesha.

"Will you do it tonight? Claim me?" Tomesha whispered. She didn't want to wait another moment.

"Are you sure, *miere*?" Dru asked.

Her eyes held a bit of concern, but Tomesha wasn't worried. She trusted Dru and knew her vampire would never do anything that would cause her harm.

"The bond is forever," Dru said.

"I don't ever want to be apart from you again."

Dru lifted Tomesha into her arms and deposited her on the bed. She lowered her head and took Tomesha's lips in the softest of kisses. Tomesha leaned forward and wrapped her arms around her vampire's neck. The love she had for this woman took her breath away. She hadn't lied.

She wanted forever.

Dru's hands quickly worked to remove Tomesha's clothing. The cool air caressed her naked skin. Tomesha fumbled as she tried to remove Dru's clothing, but her uniform was a little tricky to get off.

"Allow me, *miere*," Dru murmured.

She stepped back away from the bed and stripped her clothes from her body. Soon she stood naked where Tomesha could see all of her. From her firm, high breasts with her rosy areolas, to her well-defined abdominal muscles and her bare mons —all of which belonged to Tomesha. If she were to be claimed by her vampire, then she'd do some claiming of her own.

"Come to me," Tomesha whispered.

She motioned with her single finger for her vampire to return to her. She inhaled sharply at the sensation of her core, preparing itself. Moisture seeped from her slit at the sight of Dru moving back to her. She scooted back onto the massive bed until she was in the center. Dru knelt on the bed and crawled over her, forcing her down on to her back.

Tomesha smiled and reached for Dru to bring her closer. She wanted to feel Dru's body against hers.

"Fate has willed the two of us together," Dru whispered.

She lowered herself to where their bodies were entwined. Tomesha parted her thighs to allow Dru's to rest between them. Their breasts were pressed to each other, and Tomesha loved the feeling of Dru's muscular frame on top of her. Dru rested on her forearms as she took Tomesha in.

"It has," Tomesha agreed.

She slid her hands along Dru's shoulders and down to her arms. Her hips undulated upward to Dru, allowing her center to brush Dru's firm thigh. A growl rippled from Dru's chest. Her fangs were noticeable underneath her lip. Tomesha's core clenched at the sight of them.

She wanted—no, needed—to feel those sharp fangs pierce her flesh.

Dru brought her wrist to her lips and nicked it. Blood flowed from the small wound. She pressed her wrist to Tomesha's forehead.

"We shall thank the fates for the bond that has formed between us," Dru said.

Tomesha's heart raced. She felt deep down that this claiming was an ancient ritual amongst vampires. She'd accept it as part of her vampire whom she loved with all of her heart. A warm trail of blood slipped down her skin. She couldn't look away from Dru.

Dru swiped the blood from her wrist and placed it on Tomesha's lips. She had to fight the urge to lick it off. Her lips parted, and Dru placed more of it on her mouth.

"We shall forever be joined together. Through our bond, you shall live throughout time standing by my side," Dru said.

Those powerful words opened Tomesha's heart even more for this vampire. Dru truly wanted her. It wasn't just fate, it was this vampire who wanted her—forever.

Dru moved her arm down to the center of Tomesha's chest to allow her blood to flow onto her. The warm river of blood dripped, painting her brown skin with Dru's dark-crimson lifeline. Tomesha's breaths came in pants. Her heart pounded, and she watched the blood coat her. Tomesha reached up and rubbed the warm fluid into her skin. A moan slipped from her.

Dru growled as she watched. Her eyes grew to an iridescent color. They followed Tomesha's hands. Tomesha brought her blood-coated fingers to her lips and licked the metallic-tasting liquid. Dru's firm hand reached out and tilted Tomesha's head to the side in order to present her neck for her. Tomesha's breath caught in her throat.

This was it.

The moment she'd become Dru's mate.

"I vow to protect you, to honor you, and to please you. Forever," Dru whispered.

She lowered her head to the crook of Tomesha's neck. Her warm tongue ran up the column of her throat, eliciting a shiver through Tomesha. Dru's fangs sank deep into her neck. Tomesha gasped, her body going taut. Dru drank from her, the tugging at her neck sending an electric current down to her pussy. Her core became flooded, her honey escaping her. Tomesha's hips moved, and she rode Dru's thigh. Her swollen clit brushed over Dru and sent a wave of pleasure through Tomesha.

This feeding was somehow different than the other times Dru had drunk from her. This somehow had meaning to it. Tomesha's pulse settled down into a steady, even beat. It was as if she and Dru had become one.

Dru lifted her head, nicked her wrist again, and presented it to Tomesha.

"Drink, *miere,*" Dru encouraged.

Tomesha reached for her wrist and brought it to her lips. She didn't hesitate to cover the wound with her mouth, nor did she hesitate in suckling it to bring more of Dru's blood into her. Dru's low growl cut through the air, and her gaze locked on Tomesha. She held Dru's gaze as she swallowed every drop of her blood that graced her tongue.

"Enough."

Dru's voice was husky and laced with passion. She took her wrist from Tomesha's lips. She slammed her mouth down onto Tomesha's. She parted her lips immediately and welcomed Dru's tongue. Their kiss was heated and deep. Tomesha wrapped her arms around Dru and held on. Dru broke the kiss and blazed a hot trail of open-mouth kisses down to Tomesha's chest. She captured one of her nipples in her mouth and sucked hard.

Tomesha's back arched off the mattress. She entwined her fingers in Dru's hair, displacing the bun that had contained her fiery hair. She cried out, her body growing warmer. Her eyes clenched closed tight, and she shook and trembled. Dru's hot mouth drifted to her other breast and captured that one. Her fangs brushed the beaded bud and elicited a cry to spill from Tomesha's lips. Her hips bucked and gyrated against Dru's leg.

Dru's hand forced her way between Tomesha's legs. Her fingers connected with Tomesha's clit and strummed the sensitive bud.

"Yes," Tomesha hissed. She threw her head back; her body needed a release.

Dru slipped two of her fingers into Tomesha's slick core.

Tomesha's fingers tightened on her vampire's hair as she fucked her slow and hard. "Please. I need more."

Dru lifted her head and brought her mouth back down on Tomesha's. Their kiss was frantic and hard. Dru withdrew her fingers and inserted three this time. Tomesha cried out and moved in rhythm with Dru's fingers. She spread her legs far apart to allow Dru to have full access to her. Dru's talented fingers slipped in and out easily with the amount of wetness that seeped out of Tomesha.

"My mate," Dru whispered.

"My love," Tomesha replied automatically.

She dropped hard kisses on Dru's face then switched to her neck. She buried her face in the crook and cried out; Dru rotated her fingers. Her pace quickened, and she slammed her finger over and over into Tomesha.

Tomesha's body felt so hot. Sweat beaded her forehead, and her skin became slick with moisture. She cried out when Dru's thumb worked her clit. The sensations were overwhelming and sent her skyrocketing to the heavens. A cry erupted from her. She bit down on Dru's skin, reaching her climax.

Dru's groan filled her ears, and she rode the orgasm that washed over her.

"Yes, *miere*. Bite me harder," Dru gasped.

Through her passion-filled haze, Tomesha bit her again. She didn't know what was coming over her. The shakes and tremors were coming even harder. She released Dru and fell back onto the bed.

"Dru," Tomesha sobbed. She writhed. The heat took over her body; her skin felt as if it were on fire.

Dru shifted to the side and gathered her into her arms.

"What's wrong with me?" Tomesha asked.

"It's the change, *miere*. Here, drink more," Dru encouraged.

She placed her bleeding wrist back to Tomesha's mouth. She latched on to it again and drank.

Dru softly brushed Tomesha's hair away from her face. "You will not become a vampire, *miere*. You'll remain a human, but you'll no longer age as a human, but as a vampire."

Tomesha opened her eyes and met Dru's. There was nothing but love shining from Dru's blue eyes. Tomesha gave a nod of understanding. Her tremors continued but weren't as violent. Tomesha finally released Dru's wrist. The blood spilled from her lips and ran down the side of her face. Dru chuckled and bent down to lick the trail of blood from Tomesha's skin before pressing a soft kiss to her lips.

"My mate," Dru whispered again.

"My mate," Tomesha echoed. Her eyes grew heavy, and she felt the pull of darkness. She wasn't ready for sleep and tried to fight it. She blinked and tried to focus on Dru.

"Yes, *miere*. We now belong to each other. Don't fight the slumber. Your body is going through a change, and you will need to rest. When you wake up, I'll be here." Dru adjusted them on the bed so they rested against the pillows.

The warmth of the comforters covered Tomesha and allowed her to snuggle into Dru's arms. This was where she wanted to be forever.

She sighed and allowed the darkness to drag her under.

CHAPTER TWENTY-EIGHT

The club pulsed with a low, thrumming bass vibrating through floor. Tomesha hesitated at the threshold, the memories of working there flooding her. She was thankful for everything this place had provided her, but it was time to move on. This had been her world, but no more. It had been a little over two weeks since she'd left Butterbush. Now she was back to sew up some loose ends so she could start her forever with her mate. She glanced over at Dru who stood by her side and smiled.

"It's okay, *miere*." Dru gripped her hand and entwined their fingers. "We won't be here long."

The moment they stepped inside, the atmosphere shifted. All eyes turned to them. Tomesha moved closer to Dru and tightened her hold on her hand. Dru's presence commanded attention. She was an imposing figure with her weapons on her waist. The woman never went anywhere without them. She was dressed in all black with her fiery hair flowing around her shoulders. Anyone who met her gaze immediately looked way.

Tomesha walked a half step behind Dru as she led her farther inside the establishment.

"General, it is good to have you return." Callidora stepped in front of them.

Dru halted her stride and brought Tomesha to her side.

Callidora's gaze widened when she saw Tomesha. "Tomesha. Welcome back."

"Callidora." Tomesha nodded. She wasn't sure if word had reached Butterbush about her mating. They were here to inform the mistress that she'd no longer be employed by Madam.

"I want to see Mistress," Dru announced.

"Mistress Beatrix was not expecting you," Callidora murmured.

"She will see me," Dru said. Her tone left no

room for debate. The muscle in her jaw tightened, showcasing her agitation.

In the short time Tomesha had known Dru, she'd begun to learn more about her vampire; she'd discovered that Dru had little to no patience when it came to certain things.

With her, Dru had all the patience in the world.

"Of course. Please follow me." Callidora bowed her head and gestured for them to follow her.

They continued on. The air was heavy with heat, the sounds of pleasure, and the coppery scent from the open feedings. Tomesha held on to Dru. She glanced around and took in a few familiar faces.

Conner currently entertained a client. He glanced over in her direction. He nodded to her. She smiled softly and waved. Ava worked the bar as usual with Viessa placing goblets on her tray in preparation for serving them to patrons. There were no signs of Starla. She must be with a client, or it could be her day off.

This had been Tomesha's life.

She moved closer to Dru who glanced down at her.

"What is it, *miere*?" Dru asked.

"Nothing." Tomesha shook her head. She

exhaled, and deep down, she knew this life wasn't meant for her. At least, not in the long run. Life as a Madam employee had helped her get her and her family on their feet and in a better financial situation, but it wouldn't have been something she'd have wanted to do forever. Eventually, she'd have lost her appeal to the vampires. No one would want an old donor or an aging woman for sexual release.

They exited the main floor and began the descent down to where Mistress's office was located. It had seemed as if it were forever ago when she'd been summoned by the mistress.

They arrived at the massive, glossy, black-lacquer double doors etched with golden thorns. Callidora rapped on one of them.

"Mistress," Callidora called out. "General Moldark is requesting an audience."

A muffle response was returned. Callidora opened the door and waved for them to enter. Dru stepped in first, bringing Tomesha behind her. The door shut behind them with a soft click. They walked across the room and stopped before the massive desk. Tomesha came to stand next to Dru and took in the mistress.

The overseer of the feeding club was regal and as beautiful as ever. She sat behind her desk and met Dru's intense stare without a word. When her gaze shifted and landed on Tomesha, something flickered in her eyes. Her lips curved up in a smirk.

"I would ask to what do I owe the pleasure, but I can see already why you're here." Romana settled back and tucked her dark hair behind her ear. She reached for her crystal goblet filled with crimson liquid and took a sip. She licked her ruby-red lips and casually held the goblet between her hands.

"Mistress, I was drafted and matched with the general," Tomesha said softly.

Romana's gaze darted back to Dru who met her stare without flinching. Dru appeared to be carved out of ice as she stared down the mistress.

"She's mine," Dru announced.

"Well, it's a shame. Tomesha was one of my best humans." Romana shrugged. She crossed her legs and grinned widely. She tilted her goblet in Tomesha's direction. "I, for one, would never get in the way of fate. I honestly knew it before you probably did, General."

"Is that so?" Dru arched an eyebrow.

"I've been doing this a long time. Even before we decided to place this establishment here. I've seen many vampires fall for their donors, be it love or fate. You, I knew instantly the moment you came to me.

It was the possessiveness for a human you'd only been around once. The expression in your eyes when you negotiated for her. I could have asked from you a much higher price and you would have paid it."

Tomesha's eyes widened. She didn't know how much exactly Dru had spent to have her as a private donor, but she was sure it was astronomical. She only knew what was given to her by Mistress.

"I do want to thank you for everything," Tomesha said. Even though she was leaving her employment, she didn't want Mistress thinking she was ungrateful. It was because of her that Tomesha had been given a chance. She thought of all the money she'd earned and saved and how it had helped her family. She'd never forget this place and what it had done for her family.

Mistress waved and snorted a very unladylike snort. "What did I do for you? Offer you a way to sell your body? Help you get out of poverty? You would have figured that out on your own." Her smile disappeared, and she became serious again. "Not many humans who cross these doors are as lucky as you are. Thank the fates that they've destined you to be with someone like the general."

"I do. I am thankful for every moment we have

together." Tomesha glanced up at Dru who'd been watching her.

Dru lowered her head and placed a chaste kiss to her lips.

"Your contract with Madam's is now null and void. You're no longer a Madam employee, Tomesha. Go. Live your life."

Those words held more meaning than Mistress would know. A door was closing on Tomesha's past while the one that led to her future stood wide open. Tomesha was so happy in this moment she felt as if she'd burst.

"I will." She backed away and turned on her heel with Dru beside her as they walked back to the doors.

"Will you be wanting any of your belongings from your room?" Mistress called out.

Tomesha paused and glanced over her shoulder. There was nothing there that she'd want to take with her. She had everything she'd ever need.

"No. I won't need any of it."

Dru opened the door, and they stepped out of Mistress's office. A weight had been lifted from Tomesha's shoulders. She'd thought Romana would have put up a fight in letting her go, but it would appear that beneath the brothel mistress's hard demeanor, she was a romantic at heart.

* * *

"ARE YOU OKAY?"

Dru sidled up to stand beside Tomesha who stared at the home she'd grown up in. This had been the only home she'd ever known. It held so many memories for her that she was a little sad to be leaving. Memories of her father sitting on this very porch. Her mother and grandmother cooking in the kitchen when she was younger. She and her brother playing out in the yard as children. This had been a center point for her family.

It had taken much effort to convince Tarek to move to Crystal Cove. Tomesha didn't want to leave him or her grandmother behind. Dru was able to arrange for housing for them and even a few job opportunities for Tarek to choose from. As for Delonda, she'd receive the best medical care money could buy.

"Yeah, I'm good. It's just bittersweet, you know."

Dru wrapped an arm around her shoulders and placed a kiss on the top of her head. She leaned into her and sighed. Dru had arranged for a company to help pack up their belongings they'd be taking with them. Everything they owned was now packed away in a moving truck parked out on the street.

Tarek and Delonda stepped out of the house. Her brother helped their grandmother down the stairs. Tomesha stepped forward and took Delonda's hands in hers.

"Are you ready, Gran?" Tomesha asked softly.

Delonda turned her bright eyes to Tomesha and smiled.

"This has been a long time in the making. We've needed a fresh start. Both of you," Delonda said. She reached for Tarek and pulled him close to her and Tomesha. "And, boy, stop the scowling. Everything will be fine."

"I know, Gran." He tugged them into his arms and squeezed them tight.

Tomesha's heart swelled with love for her brother. He hadn't wanted to leave, but he was doing what was best for them. There was truly nothing left in Butterbush for them. They were the only family each other had. "You know, moving isn't a bad idea."

"Oh, it isn't?" Tomesha chuckled.

The argument he'd put up a week ago would beg to differ, but he'd finally caved in and agreed. She leaned back and took in the teasing glint in his eyes. She loved when he was in his playful moods. They'd all been stressed about surviving for too long.

"I just wish Mom and Dad was here to go with us," he said.

Their smiles died off at the mention of Maynard and Maggie. Tomesha inhaled. Neither of their parents had any reason being dead and gone. Life was unfair, but she was sure the two of them were reconnected in the afterlife.

"Your parents will always be with you. Right in your hearts." Delonda released the two of them and stepped back, her big brown eyes bright and loving. "Now right those faces and let's go. We can't keep these people waiting long."

Delonda turned and ambled over to the waiting car. One of the drivers opened the door for her and helped her inside. Tomesha faced her brother.

"Are you ready?" she asked.

He stared at their childhood home and sighed. He wrapped an arm around her shoulders and squeezed. "I'm actually looking forward to this. It'll be good for us."

Tomesha sensed a presence on the other side of her. She glanced over and found Dru standing next to her.

He looked over at Dru and nodded to her. "Thank you. For everything."

"There's no need to thank me. You're my mate's family, therefore, you're my family." Dru motioned to the house. "There will be cleaners who'll come and make sure the house is in good shape once we're gone."

"Well, my grandmother will have my hide if I don't give my thanks," Tarek said. He pressed a kiss to Tomesha's forehead. He jerked his chin toward the car where their grandmother was. "I'd better go get in with Gran before she talks their ears off."

Tomesha chuckled and took in their grand-mother just chatting away with the vampire guard who stood outside of the vehicle. Tarek jogged over to the car and slipped in beside her. Tomesha spun back to Dru who took her hand in hers. She entwined their fingers and squeezed.

"Thank you," Tomesha murmured.

Dru shook her head and brought Tomesha's hand up to her lips. She kissed the back of it and gave a rare fangy smile.

"You don't need to thank me for anything," Dru

said. "I wish I had answers about your father's disappearance."

"We have accepted that he is lost to us. I just pray that if he died, his death was swift. I wouldn't want to imagine that he is one of those beasts." Tomesha shuddered. She truly did miss her father and prayed every day that he was in Heaven with her mother. This was not the time to become sad. She glanced back at their home one last time. "But seriously, thank you."

"Again, no need for gratitude."

"You heard my brother. Our grandmother will have our hides if we don't thank you, and believe me, you don't want to get her upset," Tomesha teased. Their grandmother had always been a firm believer in ensuring her grandchildren grew up respectful and with manners. She stepped closer to Dru and wrapped her arms around her waist. "I love everything about you and how you're willing to step in to help my family."

"And I love you," Dru said softly.

Tomesha froze. She hadn't thought she'd ever hear those words. She knew that they were mated, and it was fate and Dru was following her vampiric instincts when it came to discovering the one person she was supposed to be with forever, but nowhere had Tomesha assumed Dru loved her.

"You love me?" Tomesha whispered. She reached up and placed her hands either side of Dru's face. She studied her vampire and saw the truth in her eyes. How could she not know that Dru loved her? Everything this woman did was love.

"If you have to question my love for you, then I need to work much harder where you can sense it," Dru replied.

Tomesha brought her head down and covered her lips with hers. The kiss was soft, sweet, and short. Dru rested her forehead against Tomesha's.

"I love you, too," Tomesha said. She grinned and couldn't help but tease her intense vampire general. "Work harder? You've done so much already. What more could you do to show me you love me?"

"*Miere*, this is only just the beginning. I have forever to prove how much I love you."

EPILOGUE

The streets of Crystal Cove were covered in mounting snow. The town appeared to be a winter wonderland. The bite of the air was crisp, and even Dru felt the chill. Tomesha's gloved hand rested in hers as they strolled down the sidewalk of the market district. The streetlights glowed bright, piercing the gloomy evening sky.

Most of the shops were closed except for a few cafés where warm light spilled from their frosted windows along with the scents of bread and seasoned meats. As a vampire, Dru had always been curious about the food humans consumed. It always did smell wonderful. She glanced around, and a calmness overcame her. There was much still going on in the world around them, but right now, at this moment, she was focused on the woman walking beside her.

Tomesha glanced up at her and smiled shyly.

"You've been awful quiet as of late," Tomesha said. She studied Dru for a moment. "Almost as if you were planning something."

"I'm a general on the brink of war, I'm always planning." Dru smirked. She squeezed Tomesha's hand.

They arrived at the corner. She guided Tomesha down a sidewalk where the snow was untouched. The streetlights were bright, casting away any shadows. Dru had no problem seeing in the dark, but she knew her human mate might. At the end of the lane was a small shop, its front newly restored, the door painted a deep navy with silver trim, making it stand out against the pale snowdrifts. Above the shop's window hung a blank wooden sign, waiting for a name. They slowed to a stop.

"What is this place?" Tomesha stepped forward and glanced at the window. She wiped away the frost and peered inside.

Dru froze for a brief moment. It was rare that she was rendered speechless. She'd practiced what she'd say on this day countless times. Now, seeing Tomesha's beautiful face in the evening light, all of the words she'd memorized were gone.

"It's yours," Dru said.

"Mine?" Tomesha's head whipped around. She stared at Dru and walked back to her. "What do you mean, mine?"

Dru reached inside her winter coat and brought out a silver key. The metal gleamed as she pressed it into Tomesha's hand.

"You once told me that you loved the creativity of creating your own clothing. Well, I purchased this shop for you. It's yours to do with as you please."

The world went silent. Small snowflakes fell, landing on Tomesha's dark curls and melting on her eyelashes.

"Dru you didn't have—"

"I did." Dru stepped forward and brushed a lock of hair from Tomesha's cheek. Her mate's eyes shone bright, full of unshed tears.

There was a tremor in Tomesha's hand as she raised the key and stared at it.

"I can't believe this." Tomesha sniffled.

"Believe it. Now open the door," Dru encouraged.

Tomesha squealed and spun around on her heels. She inserted the key into the lock and pushed it open. They stepped inside with Dru shutting the door behind them.

The shop smelled of pine and fresh paint. The floor gleamed, and the front windows caught the reflection of the streetlight positioned out front. Tomesha spun around in a circle, her gaze sweeping the area.

Dru stepped forward and watched her mate move around and explore. Seeing Tomesha's expression had her heart pounding. It had been the right thing to do. Her mate had spoken of her love of sewing, her old job, and how much she loved creating beautiful pieces of clothing. It led Dru to having an idea of helping her follow a dream and doing something she loved.

"There is so much to do," Tomesha exclaimed.

Her smile was wide, and the happiness on her face took Dru's breath away.

"So much material I'll need to order, supplies, equipment!"

"It can wait until tomorrow." Dru chuckled.

"You think I'll be able wait until tomorrow? I'll

have to start making a list of everything I'll need, start looking for vendors—"

"Don't worry. I know someone who has plenty of connections," Dru said. She'd run her idea of purchasing the shop by Lethia who'd already volunteered to share her resources to help get Tomesha established. She snagged Tomesha's hand and drew her close.

"Is that so?" Tomesha arched an eyebrow at her. She leaned into Dru's embrace and offered a beautiful smile. "I love you so much."

"And I love you." Dru captured Tomesha's lips in a slow, passionate kiss. Through this kiss, Dru ensured her mate knew how much she loved her, the promises she'd forever keep, and a future that they'd share with each other.

They parted, out of breath. Dru rested her forehead on Tomesha's.

"You've made me so happy. Never in a million years would I have thought that my future would have turned out the way it has," Tomesha murmured. She brushed off an invisible piece of lint from Dru's coat.

"There's nothing I won't do for you, *miere*. You're the reason my heart beats. Anything you desire shall be yours." This woman's happiness would be the sole purpose of Dru's existence. She'd never known how much having a mate would change her. With the impending war, she now understood what love was and what she was truly fighting for. No longer was it just her, she had a mate to consider. A mate who loved her.

A mate she'd burn the entire world down for.

"Now come, *miere*. Let's go home so you can start working on your shop, but there's one thing you must do first." Dru took Tomesha's hand and led her out of the shop.

Tomesha slipped the key in and locked it.

"And what is that?" Tomesha asked.

Dru pulled her into her arms so her back was pressed against Dru's front. Dru pointed to the blank sign.

"You must now name your business."

FROM THE AUTHOR

Dear Reader,

Thank you from the bottom of my heart for joining me on this journey through the Immortal Reign world. It has taken me a while to get Wicked Allure out, but I hope you love it just as much as you loved the other books in the series.

Your passion for these characters, your messages, reviews, and excitement have meant more than I can ever express. Every page I write is fueled by your love for this series, and knowing you've chosen to spend your time in this world with me is the greatest gift.

I'm endlessly grateful for you—and I can't wait to share what comes next. (Yes, we are getting more books in this world!)

Happy reading,

Ariel Marie

P.S. Don't forget to leave a review of this book on the platform you purchased it. All reviews matter! That's how I know if you want me to keep this series going!

The Nightstar Shifters

No wolf can resist the call to mate.

Strong female wolves are in search of their mate. The desire is strong for these women who long to find the one person meant for them.

They are fierce and determined, putting their trust in fate.

If you love lesbian wolf shifter romance filled with action and adventure, then you will love the Nightstar Shifters series.

Ready to start the Nightstar Shifters? Download this series today!

ALSO BY ARIEL MARIE

<u>The Immortal Reign series</u>

Deadly Kiss

Iced Heart

Royal Bite

Wicked Allure

<u>The Lunaterra Chronicles</u>

The Iron Oath

<u>The Montana Grizzlies</u>

Hot For Her Bear

Claimed by Her Bear

Bound to Her Bear

<u>The Nightstar Shifters</u>

Sailing With Her Wolf

Protecting Her Wolf

Sealed With A Bite

Hers to Claim

Wanted by the Wolf

Taming Her Mate

<u>Blackclaw Alphas (Reverse Harem Series)</u>

Fate of Four

Bearing Her Fate (TBD)

<u>The Midnight Coven Brand</u>

Forever Desired

Wicked Shadows

<u>Paranormal Erotic Box Sets</u>

Vampire Destiny (An Erotic Vampire Box Set)

Moon Valley Shifters Box Set (F/F Shifters)

The Dragon Curse Series (Ménage MFF Erotic Series)

<u>The Dark Shadows Series</u>

Princess

Toma

Phaelyn

Teague

Adrian

Nicu

<u>Stand Alone Books</u>

Dani's Return

A Faery's Kiss

Tiger Haven

Searching For His Mate

A Tiger's Gift

Stone Heart (The Gargoyle Protectors)

Saving Penny

A Beary Christmas

Howl for Me

Birthright

Return to Darkness

Red and the Alpha

WARNING

Due to the explicit language and graphic sexual scenes, this book is intended for mature (18 years +) readers only. If things of this nature offend you, this book would not be for you. If you like a good action story with hot steamy scenes with lesbian vampires and their human mates, then you have chosen wisely…